MARTIAL LAWLESS

CALM ACT BOOK 3

GINGER BOOTH

Join my reader group at

gingerbooth.com/freebooks

to receive free prequels, bonus content, news, etc.

CANADA

QUEBEC

Montreal

ONTARIO

Ottawa

VERMONT

MAINE
(Canada)

Lake Huron

Link

Toronto

Lake Ontario

UPSTATE

NEW
HAMPSHIRE

NEW
ENGLAND

Buffalo

Cullen

Boston

Detroit

Lake Erie

HUDSON

MASS.

Erie

Meadville

Taibbi

Scranton

CONN.

NARRAGANSETT

Totoket

Cleveland

PENNSYLVANIA

Schwabacher

Pittsburgh

State College

Newark

Apple

LONG ISLAND

Harrisburg

Columbus

Trenton

Philadelphia

Atlantic Ocean

OHIO

Morgantown

MARYLAND

JERSEY

WEST
VIRGINIA

Washington D.C.

DEL.

KEN-
TENN

O'Hara

VIRGINIA

Evolving Borders

State / Province
State - defunct line
Canada
Military Governor
Population Control

1

Interesting fact: February 2016 was the month the northern hemisphere first exceeded the 2 degree Celsius temperature rise that climate change scientists warned we must not exceed. Beyond that, there was great danger of planetary climate systems becoming chaotic, or even runaway temperature rise warming the planet beyond the ability to maintain liquid water. The UN's previous goal was to limit temperature rise to 2 degrees C by the year 2100. We crossed that line abruptly, and 84 years early. Of course, a planet is a very complex system indeed. They couldn't know whether the fateful number wasn't 1.5° C or 2.5° C.

"Emmett, you need to see this," I warned. I beamed a video clip onto the big display in our shared office in our Brooklyn brownstone. *Mob Murders Resco* was the lurid headline on the accompanying breaking news report.

Lt. Colonel Emmett MacLaren, martial law resource coordinator for rebuilding the Big Apple – my partner and lover – kept his eyes on his own computer displays. "Kinda busy, Dee," he murmured. "Video conference with General Cullen in half an hour."

"I know that, Emmett," I said. "And you need to see this first."

He finally looked up and took in the headline. "Oh, hell," he said.

We're a lot alike, Emmett and me. Unlike about 95% of the viewing audience, he digested the whole article before playing the video, just like I had. Our friend Major Cameron once quipped that the two of us really bonded over data analysis. I suspect Cam's point was that our relationship was peculiar to us, and I should stop asking his opinion. Point taken.

On the news story, what we knew so far wasn't much. A putative militia member in Pittsburgh had posted the video clip to Amenac, my social web empire, on a public forum. He'd taken the video with his phone, answered a couple questions on Amenac, then went offline. The Resco of Pittsburgh – Resource Coordinator, same position as Emmett and Cam held – had been addressing some kind of rally. The crowd surged forward and back. Cut to a closeup of the Resco where he lay beaten to death on the gravel. And the video ended. We didn't even know his name.

"Major Dane Beaufort," Emmett supplied, after replaying the video a couple times, trying unsuccessfully to hear what the Resco said before his death. "I can confirm that much. Yeah, he's Resco of Pittsburgh."

"Did you know him? I'm sorry," I said.

"Yeah. You going to release this on PR?" Emmett asked.

Emmett looked rattled, but I couldn't tell whether from grief or very real concern for the consequences.

I sent the item back to the Project Reunion news team with those points confirmed, and signed off on publication. PR was mine, too. The Project Reunion website was powered by Amenac, our social web empire. PR News published official news with high production values, as vetted and sanctioned by us, rather than a social babble of peers on forums. Not unbiased news –

created to support the humanitarian relief of New York City, PR was staunchly pro-Resco, and supported the martial law governments.

"Have to publish," I replied to Emmett. "That video's gone viral on Amenac, and rumors are flying. PR has to say something. You can bet Indie will."

IndieNewsWeb was PR's burgeoning new competition in supplying news to the Northeast. Naturally, since PR was pro-Resco, Indie's greatest growth niche was anti-Resco, attacking PR as a pawn of the martial law governors. Indie gave voice to another point of view, and not a rare one. In fact, some of Amenac's staff still probably wished they could change sides. I tried not to take it personally, and often failed. IndieNews' personal attacks on me and Emmett were hard to stay philosophical about. But on the bright side, Emmett and I were heroes of Project Reunion. Attacking us left Indie shooting itself in the foot, popularity-wise. That could change, though. Indie's editors were growing smarter. PR's leadership, including me, needed to get smarter, too. Competition was good for us. And annoying as hell.

"Send me the links," Emmett requested. "PR's treatment, and the source posts on Amenac. I bet Homeland Security can figure out what Dane was saying."

I sent him the sources promptly, and muttered under my breath, "Why does HomeSec still exist..."

Emmett forwarded my links off within a second of receiving them. And sighed, "That meeting with General Cullen..."

"Yeah, yeah," I conceded. "Can I stay for it?"

This was pushing my luck. I often stayed in the office while Emmett consulted with his Resco peers, but Cullen wasn't a peer. He was martial law governor of all New York–New Jersey. But drat it, my future was on the line, too. The end of September was drawing near, and with it the end of our appointed time in Brooklyn. I had my heart set on Long Island next, to live near Cam and his husband Dwayne, back on the rocky marshy shores of the Sound again, just across the water from home. This call with Cullen could decide our future.

"No," Emmett replied categorically.

I gave up wheedling, and we got back to work. I was deep into the still unfolding story of one Dane Beaufort, deceased, when Emmett's video call came in, a few minutes early. I dutifully picked up my work to move to the dining room, stood, and hung arrested at the sight of the screen before me.

General Sean Cullen, head of New York–New Jersey. General Ivan Link, ruler of New England. Air Force General Seth Taibbi of Pennsylvania – the others, like Emmett, were Army. And General Charles Schwabacher of Ohio–West Virginia. *Wow.* No, this wasn't about whether Dee Baker's boyfriend got reassigned to Long Island like she wanted.

Emmett swallowed, and asked the generals to wait a moment. He escorted me by the elbow to the French doors at the end of the library. He locked me out in the garden, and drew the curtains.

Now, that was pretty heavy-handed. I was tempted to defy him, and sneak back in to eavesdrop. There were two other doors into the garden, leading to the kitchen and the housekeeper's lair downstairs. Or if those were locked, I could hop the garden wall into the militia barracks brownstone next door, and back around to the front door.

What stopped me was the begging, haunted look in Emmett's eyes as he closed the door, and mouthed, "Please."

EMMETT SLIPPED OUT TO THE GARDEN 20 MINUTES LATER, AND kissed my forehead. "Thank you, darlin'. Sorry."

He perched on the teak lounge chair next to mine, in the

dappled shade of a stressed-out maple, already turning scarlet despite the Indian summer warmth. Most of this sad and ravaged city I wouldn't miss. But I loved our back garden, safely walled in the interior of the block.

"How rude," I commented to Emmett, but then let it go. "Can you tell me anything about the big brass meeting?"

He shook his head slightly. "Not done yet," he said. "They're conferring. Probably call me back in a few minutes with new orders. I need to go back in. Could you stay out here? Please, darlin'. Conflict of interest with PR."

My eyebrows rose. "I guess they saw the article. Are we in trouble?"

"PR's not in trouble," Emmett said. "Murdering a Resco is a big honking deal, though. Please, darlin'?"

"Your career. PR vs. IndieNewsWeb," I said. "No contest. Besides, via you, we might get a scoop. The lip-reading of Dane Beaufort's final words."

"'We know what God demands of us,'" said Emmett. "Was the last thing Dane said." He gazed at our lap pool thoughtfully.

"Can I use that?" I asked.

"Don't see why not," Emmett replied. "Lots of people can lip read."

"And, um, what does God demand of us?" I inquired.

Emmett sighed, and said, "Quite a lot, really. I don't know what Dane meant." Emmett went back inside to await word of his fate from on high, if not quite that high. Far above us, anyway.

I typed, erased, and retyped several emails to the PR news team back home in Connecticut. I almost called our military censor Lt. Colonel Carlos Mora for advice. But in the end, I gave up and chose to tell them nothing.

My problem wasn't the lip-reading, but rather not saying that the rulers of the Northeast were conferring about the death of a Resco, and that somehow Emmett was caught in the middle of it.

And as Emmett pointed out, plenty of people could lip-read. So I could let that part come from someone else. I put work aside, and jumped into the pool in my shorts and tank top, to swim my laps before the afternoon cooled.

Emmett's feet dangled into the pool to greet me at the end of about the fiftieth length, and I popped up out of the water for a breather, with a smile. Swimmer's high is a lot like runner's high. The water was beautiful, the sky almost blue, our lonely maple flaming red, and everything was wonderful. "Coming in?" I invited.

He smiled briefly in return, and shook his head. "Maybe after I'm packed. Got a train to catch. Pittsburgh. Wanna come?"

I stared at him. "They made you the new Resco of Pittsburgh?" I asked, alarmed. I couldn't imagine New York–New Jersey giving away the savior of New York City.

"No. Dee, I leave in three hours," Emmett returned. "Plenty of time to talk on the train. By phone, if you're not coming with me."

I nodded slowly. "Sure. I'm with you. Are we coming back?"

He gazed around the garden, eyes pausing on his chickens at the far end. Emmett loved fresh eggs for breakfast. He'd raised chickens most of his life. He shook his head. "Don't know."

"Emmett, we can't pack up the house in three hours!"

He chuckled wryly. "Army created the problem, Army can solve it. No, Dee, we just pack up ourselves and go. Gladys will take care of everything here, for now."

We could trust our housekeeper Gladys. Most of our urban farm here was hers, anyway. I claimed the giant brick planters at the back of the garden, but Gladys farmed the roofs.

Emmett rose and held down a hand to me. "Glad you're coming with me, darlin'," he murmured.

"As a PR reporter?" I asked, toweling off beside him. He'd brought me the towel.

"...Partner," he said slowly. "We'll see about the rest. Dee, this is explosive."

"I think I got that, when four military governors showed up for your career review with General Cullen," I said. "What kind of explosive?"

"What happens when a cop is killed?" Emmett asked.

"The other cops go nuts?" I hazarded. "Leave no stone unturned? Somebody has to pay for it." I recalled an incident last year when I was visiting Major Cameron on Long Island. A rape gang had tried to harass me and my camera-woman Kyla. Cam had the lot of them executed on the spot. Attempted rape aside, he mentioned that interfering with a Resco was a capital offense, and that included his house-guests.

"Murdering a martial law governor?" Emmett confirmed my suspicions. "Much worse than that." He stroked my upper arm. "You can take notes, darlin'. But every word has to go through censors before you send it to PR. Not up to me. This isn't my show."

"Why are they sending you, then?"

He shrugged. "Specialist. My job is to tell them whether Dane Beaufort was a good Resco. And make recommendations. Whether Pittsburgh should get another Resco. Stuff like that."

I stared at him. "That would be a death sentence on a whole city, to leave them without a Resco."

"Maybe," Emmett allowed. "But they killed the Resco they got. And there aren't enough Rescos to go around. Default is Pittsburgh doesn't get a second chance."

"That's too much, Emmett," I argued. "For what? To make an example of them? Do you have any idea what the public backlash would be? Punish a whole city for the actions of a few? That's beyond the pale! It would destroy public support for martial law."

"Would it?" Emmett countered. "It's a passive aggressive move, Dee. You don't like us, Pittsburgh? Fine. We'll leave you alone. The train won't stop here anymore."

If it were only the train, that might not be so bad. But without a Resco, Pittsburgh's power, communications, fuel, food, supplies, defense, and everything else would stop too. They'd be on their own.

2

Interesting fact: Pennsylvania has two major cities – Philadelphia and Pittsburgh – widely separated by rural areas. The cosmopolitan port of Philadelphia was the 5th largest city in America, second only to New York City on the East Coast. Pittsburgh, to the west, ranked down around 60th.

"Lieutenant Colonel MacLaren, Ms. Baker, thank you for meeting with us in our car. I'm Special Agent Aidas Kalnietis, IBIS," the man said. "My partner, Donna Gianetti."

Kalnietis was tall and fit, with short brown hair, maybe in his early 50's. Gianetti was only a few years older than us, maybe 40, lean and angular, luxurious dark brown hair pulled back into a tidy ponytail. They both shared that special blandness of expression and well-fitted grey business suit, a signature of the FBI. When the Federal Department of Justice had refused to lend the FBI to the task of domestic spying and enforcement of the Calm Act, Congress axed the FBI's budget in favor of Homeland Security. Most FBI agents had the choice of a transfer to HomeSec, or finding another line of work. With no Federal government left, the scattered remains of the FBI now went by IBIS, for Interstate Bureau of Investigative Services. I'd never run into an IBIS agent before personally.

"Your rail car is much nicer than ours," I assured them with a weary smile. Emmett and I took our proffered seats at the booth. Their dining car had latched onto our train at the Pennsylvania border just after dawn, across the river from Trenton New Jersey. We'd already been traveling all night to cover barely 70 miles. Restoring the New Jersey rails was still a work in progress. Our latest train car was a rather down-at-heel standard commuter model, with a couple dozen soldiers for company. Here in the new dining car we had some privacy to talk.

"So will you be leading the investigation, sir?" Emmett asked.

"We hoped that you'd be the public spokesman, Colonel, if you don't mind," Kalnietis replied, with a self-effacing air. "The two of you are well-known and respected. We'd prefer a quieter profile. But yes, we'll handle the investigation into Major Beaufort's death."

"Is there someone else leading the whole expedition?" Emmett clarified.

"You're welcome to take that role, too," Kalnietis encouraged. "In fact, I have a document here from General Taibbi. I believe this is an honorary commission to full Colonel of the Commonwealth Army of Pennsylvania. Congratulations."

Emmett read the document once, carefully, then folded it and stuffed it into his field camouflage pocket. "Lot of red tape," he muttered.

"I understand completely," Kalnietis returned. "Agent Gianetti and I spent the last two years in the Virginia militia. We reactivated in IBIS just last month."

Ah, so these two had not unbent enough to work for Home-Sec. Interesting. And they were from Virginia–Delaware–Maryland. Yet another northeastern super-state was in on this affair.

"I understand you knew Major Beaufort, Colonel?" Kalnietis asked lightly.

"Yes."

"Tell us about that," Kalnietis urged.

"Beaufort was logistics officer for my brigade combat team, my last deployment in the Middle East," Emmett supplied. "I was a field officer. Both 101st Airborne. So, first worked together six years ago? When we rotated back to the States, we both studied at Fort Leavenworth, the ILE program. Intermediate Level Education."

"Not the SAMS program?" Kalnietis asked sharply. "He didn't work to vet the Calm Act?"

Emmett's eyes narrowed, surprised that Kalnietis was so well informed about this secret. "No. Beaufort wasn't SAMS material."

"What do you mean by that, Colonel?"

"ILE is required education for a middle-grade officer," Emmett explained. "There's also a master's degree level of the program. Requires writing a thesis. Dane didn't bother with that. SAMS is farther still, after that. Highly analytic, planning complex inter-service operations like joint Army–Navy–Air Force."

"Out of Dane's league?" Kalnietis suggested.

I noticed that Kalnietis was tracking Emmett's switch to Beaufort's first name, but I doubt Emmett did. It's harder to catch mind games when you're the target.

Emmett rocked his head in polite disagreement. "There are a lot of career tracks in the Army. SAMS wasn't his."

"Did you spend much time together at Leavenworth, outside of class?"

"We didn't spend time together in class at Leavenworth," Emmett qualified. "Same program, different classes. No, I mostly saw him at social functions. Softball games. Cafeteria. Church."

"You attended the same church?" Kalnietis probed.

"Yeah. We're both born-again Christian," Emmett said, subdued. "Were."

I sighed slightly, and caught Gianetti's eyes drinking in my reaction. She smiled at me vaguely. That was unnerving. No, I'd never really come to grips with Emmett's religion, and Gianetti easily picked up on that. Emmett didn't press his views on me. We didn't discuss Christianity much. In New England, it's just rude to spew evangelical comments like 'Jesus loves you.' The dominant creed is Catholic. He attended rowdy born-again church services in New Haven, with an elderly black lady gospel singer named Liddy. But he mostly kept quiet about God otherwise. He allowed me my denial, I suppose.

"What was your first reaction, Colonel," Kalnietis asked, "when you learned of Dane Beaufort's final words? What were they exactly…"

"'We know what God demands of us,'" Emmett supplied. "I don't know what he meant by it."

"I understand," Kalnietis assured him. "But what was your first thought?"

Emmett struggled with that a moment. I reached over and squeezed his hand for moral support. "I thought it was a mistake," Emmett finally said. "To play the religion card. That was a bad idea."

"So the two of you share the same religious beliefs –"

"No," Emmett cut Kalnietis off. "Well, partly. We were friendly, but not friends. Because of our religious beliefs. Dane was more…mainstream…for an evangelical. Intolerant, homophobic, blame the victim. Right-wing reactionary politics. I believe Jesus Christ is my savior, and He asked us to judge not, lest we be judged. Dane and I crossed swords a few times over politics. I was too liberal for his taste."

"So you'd call yourself a liberal evangelical Christian?"

Emmett replied crossly, "I call myself Emmett MacLaren.

Labels are just a lazy way to judge people. But my convictions are on the left side of the born again bell curve, yeah."

"Was this a strong hostility between the two of you?"

"No," Emmett said. "Friendly, but not friends. No hostility."

Kalnietis moved on. "So, you last saw each other at Resco training?"

"No," Emmett differed again. "I trained at south-central muster in Memphis. Trainer, actually. I transferred to New England the following month." Emmett looked thoughtful. Kalnietis waited for him. "Just a random thought."

"Please share," Kalnietis invited.

"There was a flame war on Amenac. On the Resco forums," Emmett explained. "Between the northeast and the south-central Rescos. I was thinking the last time I talked to Dane was during my SAMS year at Leavenworth. But no, it was during that flame war, in the spring. Just a few months ago."

"Explain this flame war?"

"Oh, it was...no, it wasn't stupid," Emmett waffled. "During muster in Memphis, Sunday after church, we got together for a sort of panel discussion on using religion. As a Resco. It was an important talk, I thought. Anyway, it came up on the Resco boards. The northeast muster hadn't covered religion. Not surprised. People up here take separation of church and public life for granted. In the Bible Belt, or even in the Midwest, it's just not that way. Religion is always a part of life. People talk about it. It was hard for me to learn, at West Point, then coming back a couple years ago. Have to censor myself. Don't mention Jesus Christ."

"The flame war?"

"Oh, I got in trouble by saying yeah, we need to enlist religious leaders, but maintain Resco authority above them. The more I explained, the more I got flamed by the northerners. The southerners already understood, and backed me up. And Dane

Beaufort emailed me. Said he wished he'd been to my muster instead of stuck with the damn-Yankees. Some other things."

"Such as?"

Emmett shrugged. "Dane was ticked off that I had a gay room-mate my second year at Leavenworth."

"Major Cameron?" Kalnietis confirmed. This IBIS agent knew a surprising amount about the SAMS who vetted the Calm Act. Emmett and his classmates worked hard to keep their past secret, especially Cam. Officially, Cam was in ILE that year, not SAMS. Even the other SAMS weren't aware of his role.

"Yeah. Anyway, Dane's email brought that up again." Emmett had his phone out, to search his vast collection of emails and texts. Apparently he found the exchange with Beaufort, and reviewed it. "Dane was concerned that Dee wasn't a good Christian woman. Probably meant sex out of wedlock. I asked him how it was going, with communications restored outside Penn." He paused and re-read Beaufort's reply, and worried his lip with his teeth. "He said the public still didn't have access. But it was an eye-opener for him."

"In what way?" I asked. Kalnietis frowned faintly, but probably would have asked the same.

"Didn't say." Emmett handed the phone over to Kalnietis, so he and Gianetti could read the originals.

"What do you make of the Bible quotes at the bottom of his emails?" Kalnietis inquired.

Emmett shrugged. "Nothing. You can hook a random Bible quote generator to your email."

"Is that professional, for a Resco?" Kalnietis suggested.

"I wouldn't do it," Emmett allowed. "But those were personal emails, to another born-again Christian. Nothing inappropriate."

"Isn't it odd, that most people still didn't have Internet access?" Gianetti inserted.

Emmett nodded gratefully. "Yeah. I didn't think anything of it at the time. In the Apple Zone, most people only have meshnet."

The Apple Zone was the region we'd just left, encompassing North Jersey, New York City, the northern suburbs, and Long Island – inside the epidemic control borders. The region the Calm Act walled in to die before Project Reunion.

Emmett continued, "Seems strange for Pittsburgh. But Tolliver interdicted Internet for the whole state, before the war. I thought they kept internal comms, though."

"Was Pittsburgh in particularly bad shape?" Kalnietis asked.

Emmett shrugged. "I was focused on the Apple."

"Would you have expected Pittsburgh to be in bad shape? It was a large city."

"Not that large," Emmett countered. He took his phone back and brought up the stats. "Only 300k in the city. Big metro region, couple million people. But that's stretching into West Virginia and Ohio. Plenty of agriculture. Hell, they even have fuel. Lots of fuel." He sighed. "New York, New England – we could wish for this resource profile."

"I understand Rescos, like yourself, use a 10-point scale to describe the 'level' of an area," said Kalnietis. "With this profile, what level would you expect, under a 'good' Resco?"

"Level 6 to 9," Emmett replied. "Sky's the limit, really. But Schwabacher said Pittsburgh was fishy."

"The governor-general of Ohio?" Kalnietis confirmed. "'Fishy'? What do you think he meant by that?"

"Don't know," replied Emmett. "But he was the one pushing for me to come out here. Taibbi – Penn's governor – didn't argue." Emmett looked pained. "Taibbi didn't seem to know much about Pittsburgh. Anyhow, Ohio and Penn have a re-industrialization plan, centered on Pittsburgh. One of the main planks of Schwabacher's 5-year plan for the Ohio valley. But Pittsburgh was already 'fishy', and now this."

"But you report to General Cullen, in New York–New Jersey," Kalnietis probed. "Or do you revert to New England, after Project Rebuild in the Apple Core?"

Emmett sighed. "I work for the Army. Somebody's Army. I was due for reassignment. So they figured I was available. They asked me to do this first."

Gianetti stepped in again. "Why would the hero of Project Reunion be reassigned out of New York City?"

"I was expecting Long Island or North Jersey," Emmett allowed. "Cullen wants to spread out his senior Rescos. He wasn't happy having two of us in one city. It's Ash Margolis' home town, and he's senior to me. So we agreed I'd stay to get the Apple Rebuild off to a good start. Then leave the Apple Core to Ash and move on."

"You're not offended by this?" Gianetti pressed.

"Relieved," Emmett replied. "Not my kind of town. Just felt obligated. I care about the apples – the survivors there. Been through hell. Admire them, you know? Couldn't leave in good conscience until they were set on a good road." Emmett still had mixed feelings about leaving them, his heroes, and it showed on his face. "But Ash is solid. They're in good hands."

"So what do you see as your assignment in Pittsburgh, Colonel MacLaren?" Kalnietis redirected. "And how can we help?"

"Well, I hope IBIS can tell us why Dane Beaufort is dead," Emmett replied. "The mechanics of it. Who killed him. They want me to figure out whether he was a good Resco, what he did right and wrong. Assess Pittsburgh. And recommend whether Pittsburgh should get a new Resco. Default is no."

"No?" Gianetti asked sharply.

"No," Emmett confirmed. "A Resco is a privilege, not a right. The default is that they're on their own. Sink or swim."

"But they're in good shape to survive that," suggested Gianetti, "based on their resource profile?"

"That's the crux of what I have to answer," said Emmett, "in my recommendations."

"What law governs that decision?" Kalnietis asked.

"None that I know of," Emmett replied. "Resco is a military posting. General Taibbi can assign a Resco wherever he sees fit. The murderers will be executed, though. Under martial law."

"What would happen if General Taibbi were at fault?" Kalnietis asked delicately.

"War," Emmett replied. "That's what happened to his predecessor, General Tolliver. Until Taibbi's forces killed him. Depends on how bad Taibbi was, of course. Cullen and Schwabacher wouldn't bother to fight him, unless he was a problem for them."

"So if he were just a Pennsylvania problem..."

"Pennsylvania would have a problem," Emmett confirmed. "That's the theory. At any rate, I'm not here to judge Governor-General Taibbi. Just offer suggestions."

"I see," Kalnietis said neutrally. "And you, Ms. Baker? I understand you're Colonel MacLaren's partner?"

"Yes," I said sunnily. "Just keeping my sweetie company."

"Uh-huh," said Emmett wryly. "That's not fair, darlin'. Agents Kalnietis and Gianetti are on our team here. Agents, you already caught the part where Dee is one of the principals behind the Amenac and Project Reunion web empires? Set up meshnet communications for the whole Apple? Among other tricks."

This seemed to catch the IBIS agents off guard. I was a bit miffed and unimpressed that they hadn't looked into me as closely as Emmett. Perhaps they thought they already knew who I was. As what, a Project Reunion reporter and love interest for MacLaren the hero?

"That's about it for tricks," I soft-pedaled. Looking inoffensive and unimportant was my usual strategy. It's easier to be devious when people aren't watching you carefully.

"Co-author of Project Reunion itself," Emmett added.

"What do you mean, co-author of Project Reunion?" Kalnietis asked.

"She co-authored the plan with me," Emmett clarified. "It was her idea in the first place, to use Tom Aoyama's quarantine scheme to save New York. We were partners on it all along. The governor-generals asked me to bring Dee to Pittsburgh. Civilian perspective. Dee knows more Rescos and Cocos – community coordinators – than just about anybody."

"Does that mean I get paid for this trip?" I inquired sweetly.

Emmett tapped the letter in his pocket, appointing him a temporary Colonel of the Commonwealth of Pennsylvania. "Got 90 meal tickets. Want some?"

"Meal tickets?" Kalnietis asked.

"One year's food for one adult male," Emmett clarified. He shrugged apologetically. "That's what Rescos get paid. Our own food too, of course, but Dee and I grow our own. The meal tickets are to invest as we see fit. As a light colonel, I get 75 meal tickets in New York–New Jersey. Only 1800 calories a day there. Penn pays 2500 calories a day on a full meal ticket, darlin'."

"Sweet!" I said. "Huh. Then I wonder if a meal ticket is worth much here."

"Didn't he just say it was worth more?" Kalnietis asked, puzzled.

I smiled at Kalnietis ruefully. "If Penn can afford 2500 calories a day, people can't be very hungry."

3

Interesting fact: Pennsylvania was home to tens of thousands of Amish and Mennonite farmers, expert in low-tech sustainable agriculture, quite a prize at this time. They concentrated closer to Philadelphia.

For most of the ride through Pennsylvania, Emmett was glued to the window, taking notes on his phone and taking photos. I found the view rather repetitive myself, after Philadelphia. Lots of trees and fields. Increasingly hilly. Occasional towns. Aside from the picturesque Amish now and then, Pennsylvania looked an awful lot like New York and New England. Eight hours of it was more than sufficient, and I dozed off half the time. We both grew more alert as we passed into the urbanized landscape of Pittsburgh.

Suddenly we stopped. We were in a rail plaza of some kind, but with no passenger platform. It appeared to be an industrial district, possibly rail heads for coal and ore trains into the old steel mills. But those giant dinosaurs lay quiet, the smokestacks out of business.

Emmett waited a couple minutes patiently, then raised his voice to prompt, "Report."

Captain Johnson, in charge of our train car of soldiers, replied, "Conductor isn't sure why, but track signals told him to stop here, Colonel. He's inquiring. No answer at Pittsburgh. Send out scouts?"

"Not yet, Captain," Emmett replied. He took out his phone and tried our local contact, but got no answer. "Stay here, darlin'," he advised, and clambered over me to confer with the IBIS dining car.

I studied Pittsburgh through the windows. Like the rolling Pennsylvania landscape, it wasn't greatly different from a familiar New England mill town. Steep hills rose to either side beyond the industrial district, covered with deciduous trees and wood-frame houses. But where our train sat was the basic, standard-issue concrete, brick buildings, and gravel rail bed of Rust Belt industry, from a time gone by before I was born. Deserted.

Someone in Army camouflage, with a rifle, scampered between two buildings. "Captain Johnson?" I called. When I had his attention, I pointed out where I'd spotted an armed someone.

"Alright. Stay down, Ms. Baker. Look alive, guys. Shooter spotted."

From what I overheard, apparently the train conductor was leery of going forward against the signals without some kind of explanation. That was how rail collisions happened, and a number of lines converged in Pittsburgh. For all we knew, we were honestly giving another train right-of-way. And although our train carried passengers and a few container cars of produce, that wasn't the norm. Most trains passing through Pittsburgh these days carried coal and fuel. A collision would be a disaster.

That explanation didn't seem to gibe with armed militia sneaking around behind the buildings, though. Not a single civilian was in sight, not even driving by on the bridge. I'd never seen a city this devoid of people. Barely one person in ten remained in Brooklyn, and it was downright lively compared to this.

I jerked upright to the sound of gunfire, from down the train in the produce department. The door between cars shushed open and Emmett's voice came up the aisle behind me, complaining over the phone. "Now got active shooters... Are you in charge of this militia or not?... We're at..." I held up my phone showing our location on the map, and Emmett conveyed this information. "Could call in an air strike if I wanted. Seems overkill."

Emmett sank into the seat across the aisle from me, and gestured for me to scoot toward him, away from the window. "No, councilman. That was not a joke... Enough. Call me with an all-clear into Union Station." Emmett cut the call. "Captain Johnson? Looters attacking the food. Help the transit guards kill them, please. Try to wing a couple for questioning."

"Sir, yes sir," Johnson replied promptly. There was some typical grousing among the soldiers about how protecting the food shipment wasn't their job. Johnson shut them up and got them moving down the train toward the gunshots. Emmett gazed at me ruefully.

"Never a second chance to make a first impression," I quipped, with my best attempt at a cheerful smile.

"Uh-huh," said Emmett. "Joker on the phone seemed to think I was their new Resco. Commanding these people attacking the train was my job. Why does everyone want to make their fucking problems my problem today? Pardon my language, darlin'. This is just irritating."

"Emmett? You just ordered our guards to kill people," I said. "Kill people in uniform. That's not 'just irritating.'"

"Uh-huh." I continued to stare at him, concerned, until he conceded, "It's not ideal. Dee, I shouldn't have brought you here."

"I'll be careful," I promised. Not because I was thrilled to be there. I felt as useful as galoshes on a fish. But there wasn't any way to go except forward, and Emmett had enough to deal with at the moment. "Let me know if I can help."

He reached over and squeezed my hand. The level of gunfire increased markedly, with some yelling, maybe five cars back. Emmett asked me, "How far are we from Union Station? That's where we're going."

I swallowed and looked it up, trying to focus on the task and not cringe at each barking shot. "Only two miles. We could walk," I reported wanly.

"Uh-huh. I don't trust the weather today," Emmett quipped. The gunfire gradually died. His walkie-talkie pinged him with a report of mission complete. One non-serious injury, two prisoners in hand, and a green light from the conductor to continue. Of the attackers, a good dozen were bleeding or dead on the ground, the rest fled. "Good work, Johnson. Tell the conductor to proceed when you're aboard."

"So this councilman at Union Station?" I inquired. "Did he arrange our hotel reservations?"

"Uh-huh," Emmett agreed. "Can't wait to meet him."

CAPTAIN JOHNSON SENT OUT OUR BRACE OF PRISONERS FIRST UNDER guard, to kneel on the platform, fingers laced behind their heads. I was relieved to see that they weren't bloody. Our reception committee stood uncomfortably before them while our troops fanned out to check security at the train station. When they gave the all-clear, I finally exited the train car with Emmett and the IBIS team, and a few soldiers reserved as our bodyguards.

"Colonel MacLaren!" a middle aged businessman greeted him. He swallowed nervously. "I'm Alex Wiehl. We spoke on the phone. Some porters to handle your luggage. Party of thirty, I understood?"

"Thirty-two at present," Emmett replied, pointing to the prisoners. He narrowed his eyes. "Councilman Wiehl? You are Major Beaufort's second in command?"

"Oh, no!" replied Wiehl. "I run the hotel?"

"I see. And where is Major Beaufort's second in command?"

"I don't know who that is," admitted Wiehl.

"But you're on the Pittsburgh city council?" Emmett pressed.

"Yes... We don't meet very often," said Wiehl.

Emmett was clearly growing exasperated with this game of twenty questions. Though he wasn't physically in the train fight, his adrenaline was still too pumped up to play nice.

I stepped in, with a friendly smile, and offered my hand to shake. "Dee Baker, Colonel MacLaren's partner. Nice to meet you, Councilman Wiehl. We're all very tired from the trip. You have transportation for us, to your hotel? I don't think we need help with the luggage, do we, Emmett?" Indeed, our soldiers had already commandeered the luggage trolleys from the porters.

Wiehl was clearly relieved to be allowed back onto his familiar script. He gratefully led the way to a couple shuttle buses waiting for us on the street. That street was Liberty Avenue, one of the main drags of downtown Pittsburgh. I would have expected limited parking right in front of the train station. But the hotel shuttles were the only vehicles in sight. Our party were the only people in sight.

"Is it always this empty downtown, Mr. Wiehl?" I asked.

"Oh, no one lives in the triangle anymore, Ms. Baker," he agreed.

I admitted to never having had the pleasure of visiting Pittsburgh before, except the airport, and egged Wiehl on to play tour guide. As a hotel manager, naturally he was happy and competent to oblige. My traveling companions, all still adrenaline-poisoned, quietly eavesdropped while we prattled away. Apparently the Golden Triangle, downtown Pittsburgh, was where the broad Allegheny and Monongahela Rivers, flowing west, met in a V to give birth to the mighty Ohio.

Our shuttle turned a corner onto utter devastation. "Torna-do," Wiehl explained. "We had over two hundred touchdowns in the city last year. More in the suburbs, of course. Only twenty-something touchdowns this year, so far. But don't worry, Ms. Baker – the foundation of my hotel is an excellent tornado shel-ter. One of the sirens is on our roof."

Shocked, Emmett asked, "All from a single storm front?"

"Oh, no," replied Wiehl. "Spread over six months or so. Started getting bad about this time two years ago, with the Alberta Clippers. They just wouldn't quit."

"Did you have many Alberta Clippers?" I only remembered a few of those storms in Connecticut that fall. The thunderstorm fronts barreled across the continent out of a blue sky, traveling over 75 miles per hour.

"Oh, yes. Maybe a dozen," Wiehl supplied. "Ah, here we're back on Liberty. This is the only undamaged bridge left across the Monongahela." He pointed downriver, toward a double rail track up a steep hillside. A pile of reddish rubble lay at its base. "Over there is the famous Monongahela Incline. The immigrants who worked in the steel mills built a funicular, so they could live on Mount Washington without having to climb up there after work. The incline isn't operating anymore. But the Duquesne Incline is still running. The inclines are very popular with tourists. Breath-taking view from the top."

I smiled at the 'popular with tourists' part. Alex Wiehl was an optimistic man. I was probably his first tourist in years. And I was only playing at it in order to ease the social tension. A brief tour couldn't hurt.

Past the bridge, we turned left along the river and soon pulled up to an ordinary middle-class chain hotel, a long five-story block of brick with a valet zone driveway and portico. The outdoor national brand name signs had been replaced with 'Mononga-hela Inn', so professionally that I wouldn't have noticed the name change, except that the door mat still bore the original branding.

"Did you work for the company long before the borders closed, Mr. Wiehl?" I asked.

"Yes, fifteen years," he replied. "I'd only just transferred to Pittsburgh, though. I was in Johnson City before that. Tennessee."

"And you were elected right away to city council?" I asked, surprised.

"Oh, no, I was just appointed to the council a few months ago," he demurred. "I joined the Chamber of Commerce right away. Great way to make friends in a new city. Ah – should I just hand out keys and let you people sort out room assignments?" he offered hopefully. "The entire hotel is at your disposal."

"Johnson," Emmett ordered. Captain Johnson further delegated, and a sergeant accompanied Mr. Wiehl to the registration desk.

"Our only contact is useless," Emmett commented to the IBIS team.

I poked him. "Emmett, I think he's one of the movers behind the Penn–Ohio joint venture. Don't write him off just because he isn't who you thought he was. Schwabacher and Taibbi's re-industrialization plan is important."

"Uh-huh," Emmett said sadly.

We both brightened immeasurably when we stepped into the hotel lobby. This provided tastefully bland lounge seating areas, a closed bar, and an open buffet, brimming over with delicious wafts of dinner. Our prisoners were already being escorted to a ground-floor conference room for questioning. The troops stared at the buffet, but apparently hadn't been given leave to devour it yet.

I didn't have that problem. I dumped my gear in a booth near the lobby and started filling my plate. Emmett and the IBIS pair followed my lead.

After nearly 24 hours travel from our home in the hungry devastation of New York City, that buffet was just about the most beautiful thing I'd ever seen and smelled. We had roast beef. Pork loin. Pot roast. Fried chicken. Macaroni and cheese. A choice of five cooked vegetables. Fresh tossed salad with all the trimmings and choice of four salad dressings. Potatoes three ways. Fresh chicken and dumpling soup. Warm fresh bread. Unlimited butter.

In New England and New York–New Jersey, we didn't have enough wheat flour to make bread, let alone enough oil to waste on deep-frying. A single plate from this amazing buffet held more treats than any of us in the Apple had eaten in the past six months combined. And that was just the dinner buffet. I carried my mounded plate beyond to stare at the dessert spread. Peach and blueberry and apple pies, blueberry cobbler, yellow cake with frosting, pastries, fresh apples and grapes and a selection of cheeses and crackers. My mouth hung open at the beauty of the colors, the riches arrayed here before us. Apparently sugar wasn't in short supply here, either.

"You can't eat your first plate, piglet," Emmett commented beside me. But he stared at the color-drenched desserts just as raptly as I did. And his dinner plate was mounded even higher than mine, with three different rolls perched precariously on top.

Captain Johnson called out to the troops, "As soon as the Colonel is seated, we will proceed by rank to the buffet. With decorum, ladies and gentlemen."

We slipped into our booth with alacrity, to let loose the ravening horde.

"You may be right, Ms. Baker," Kalnietis offered from across our shared table. "Penn has plenty of food."

I nodded, eyes smiling, teeth sinking into warm fresh bread dripping with real butter, like everyone else at our table. Judging from their plates, our new IBIS friends from greater Virginia were just as starved for wheat and meat and deep fried things as we were.

It seemed briefly that there might be war at the hot buffet, as rolls ran out before the lower-ranked soldiers got any. But a smiling overweight middle-aged woman emerged to save the day with another vast platter of dinner rolls and Texas toast. She was trailed by a possible daughter, around age 20, wheeling out replacement hot trays of more roast beef and fried chicken.

"I like Alex Wiehl," I proclaimed, when my mouth was temporarily empty. "I like Penn. The war, completely forgiven." My dinner companions nodded emphatically, their mouths full.

We could have happily gorged the evening away. But before we had a chance to sample the dessert buffet, the interrogators emerged to report what they'd learned from the prisoners. Wisely, Captain Johnson and his top sergeant had sent in plates for them.

The lead interrogator was Sergeant Tibbs.

4

Interesting fact: Strictly speaking, the American 'Bible Belt' refers to the southeastern and south-central states, stretching from the Carolinas and Florida in the east, to Texas, Oklahoma, and Missouri to the west, where evangelical Protestants rule in religion and politics, and over 60% of adults consider themselves 'highly religious.' But there is also a religious gradient between the Northeast, where religion is nearly taboo in public discourse, and the Midwest, with more evangelicals and Bible Belt sensibilities. This religious shift takes place somewhere between Philadelphia and Pittsburgh.

To my delight, New England – or its top-ranking resource coordinator, at any rate – had sent along my old pal Marine Sergeant Tibbs to aid our investigation. We had an odd relationship, Tibbs and I. He was my jailer once on a Navy ark, when HomeSec arrested me for founding Amenac. In that role, I'd say he helped launch the ideas that led to Project Reunion. Last year, he'd worked security at the conference that officially launched Project Reunion. Tibbs was a quiet lad, methodical and bland, who looked like a dull teenage linebacker. I liked him.

A table was moved to the end of our booth for the two prisoner interrogators and Captain Johnson and his second, Sergeant Becque, to join us. The rest of Johnson's men and women had naturally chosen seats as far away from the celestial Colonel as the dimensions of the dining room allowed, giving us a modicum of privacy.

Tibbs dove in. "They were after you, Colonel, not the food. They attacked the produce cars because they had visible armed guards. Had to take them out first." The food train guards rode between and on top of the food container cars. "Unfortunately, these two don't know much."

Sergeant Becque offered, "They were easy to catch. Hanging back and avoiding action. Figured they were running the raid."

"Sorry, no," said Tibbs. "Just disobeying orders."

Tibbs summarized what little our captives knew. Their militia leader, Sergeant Lohan, was indeed hanging back from the fray to supervise, and escaped clean. Lohan had told the attacking squad that there were investigators on the train from New York, and they were to prevent the party from reaching Union Station and the city council. Their goal was to take us to another militia leader, Sergeant Bremen.

Beyond that, our sources were of murky understanding. All they really knew about Bremen was that he was Lohan's boss, and older, maybe 35. They weren't clear on whether we were to be taken hostage, or if this was just an unfortunate attempt to talk to us. The prisoners weren't normally in Lohan's troop, and had refused to attack the train, because that would be looting.

"My advice," continued Tibbs, "is to set them loose with a message: we want to talk to Lohan and Bremen. I'm not sure they'll deliver the message. But these guys are no use to us."

Puzzled, Emmett asked, "Can't they just give us Lohan's phone number?"

Tibbs frowned. "Apparently the locals don't use phones. There are only a few surviving cell towers. We're sitting under one of them, and the railroad has comms. But no land lines. Tornados played hell with their long-distance cables. The lines are broken everywhere."

Emmett looked to me. "Sure," I said. "I can set up a Pittsburgh meshnet after dinner." That was the messaging network I'd commissioned for the Apple Zone in New York, near-field communications passing phone to phone. The mesh was only good for text messages and low-resolution images, not voice. But it didn't require any infrastructure. Our mesh software also tracked people and resources on a map. "Could take weeks for people to adopt the system, though, Emmett."

"No," said Emmett, "it spreads fast once people know it's possible. Provided they can charge their phones. But we have power."

"They don't," Tibbs clarified. "Most people don't have power. They don't eat like this, either." He tilted his head to the buffet. "The prisoners were drooling at us while we ate. Furious that the city council was pretending things were all hunky-dory here. Apparently the area around this hotel is an island of the old normal. The citizenry doesn't have much."

Tibbs looked thoughtful and tilted his head. "Colonel, I don't think there are many people left in the city. If we're going to wait to give them phones and the meshnet, anyway... Maybe I'll bring them some plates of food. Get chummy. Let them talk about life here."

Emmett nodded. "Do that. Once you've got the gist, I'd like you with me to have another chat with Wiehl later. Thank you, Tibbs."

Tibbs and his assigned sidekick moved on to the buffet, to select seconds and desserts for themselves, plus a generous feed for the prisoners.

"Is that wise, Colonel?" Kalnietis asked. "To give people communications at this point?"

Emmett shrugged. "Makes it easier to talk to them. And Dee and I can monitor what they say."

"Spy on them?" Gianetti blurted.

Emmett nodded, and held her eye. "That's how the meshnet works. Amenac too. And the PR News website, since it's built on Amenac's infrastructure. Nothing private about it. All tracked."

Gianetti didn't like it. She and Kalnietis really were old-school FBI, out of the loop, if invasion of privacy made them rigid. To me, that was old news. The Calm Act relieved us of any right to privacy, and the martial law governments weren't rushing to give it back.

I left them to take out my computer in the lobby and set up a meshnet, wondering what kind of Pandora's box I was about to unleash. If most of Pittsburgh had been offline for two years, since the borders went up, its people had some rude awakenings in store.

I figured the far end of Long Island had more in common with isolated Pittsburgh than our community mesh in New York City did. So I lifted Major Cameron's configuration files as a starting point. He had a very thin feed of news from outside going to a bulletin board post, along with basic help files, local government orientation, and announcements.

Weather reports and warnings needed to go front and center, of course. I tweaked the parameters for weather and the news feed for Pittsburgh relevance. I dithered a little about whether I should be more even-handed, and provide IndieNews as well as Amenac's meshnet feed for news. But Indie stories made it to the top 10 on Amenac's new feed often enough. I couldn't say anything about the local government, so replaced that with 'to be completed.' For now, I introduced our investigation, with links to bios on Project Reunion, Emmett's and mine, if anyone was curious.

I added a single announcement:

IMPORTANT: Investigating death of Major Dane Beaufort. Witnesses contact @IBISAKalnietis#Beaufort. Pittsburgh community coordinators, contact @RescoEMacLaren#Pitt-Coco. Also wish to speak to Sergeants Lohan and Bremen at @RescoEMacLaren#PittTrain.

With any luck, that should start generating leads for Emmett and Special Agent Kalnietis, neatly sorted into message buckets. For our troops from New York, meshnet propagation was a simple tap on a button. We were already on our neighborhood Brooklyn meshnet, and several others. Everyone else in the hotel with a functioning phone also got a prompt, as the viral software insinuated itself into the neighborhood. I hoped I wouldn't need to wander through the hotel, person to person, and explain. Nope. Kalnietis, Gianetti, Tibbs, and Wiehl popped onto the net quickly. Kalnietis even took the hint and set his mesh handle correctly to 'IBISAKalnietis.'

Two more problems to solve. One, I had no intention of donating my equipment to Pittsburgh. I wanted another computer to run the meshnet. Two, I needed more phones to hand out, and recharging centers, to spread the net wider and faster. The sun had already set, and Pittsburgh hadn't looked open for business even in daytime. So I thought those challenges would have to wait on tomorrow.

But a brief consultation with hotel manager Wiehl worked wonders. The hotel kept lost-and-found bins of abandoned items. This provided my choice of three laptops, over fifty phones, and all manner of charging cords. And just off the lobby, the hotel featured a high speed Internet cafe room, where guests could plug in when the WiFi was clogged. The Internet room charging stations in plenty. All I had to do was warn our door guards, and advertise the charging station on the meshnet resource map.

I'd barely managed to plug in the discarded laptops to start charging before the first locals arrived. By the time I finished sorting out the rejects from my spare phone collection, the room was filling up nicely. I'd explained what was going on to enough locals that they mostly educated each other now.

A rather intent pair of guys in militia camouflage even helped me plug in my spare phones. At a guess, they'd been posted outside to observe the hotel. I popped off a quick note to Tibbs and Emmett about them, but limited myself to being friendly to everyone. Soon Tibbs' side-kick, Nguyen, wandered in to recharge his phone and lazily kibitz with them.

Mission accomplished in the recharging station. I took my pick of the three free laptops back out to the lobby with me, plugged it back in, and cloned the meshnet master terminal software onto it. Within a few minutes, I was able to let it take over the meshnet traffic load.

Less than two hours from start to finish, and our new meshnet already had over a thousand users. Two more charging centers even advertised themselves on the map. Ours had a waiting line of 40 people the guards kept outside, the limit they'd allow in before we closed for the night at 11:00. Visitors were allowed to charge up to five phones at a time, provided there were enough cables. This kept the parking lot social scene lively, as those turned away bargained with people in line to charge a phone for them. Nguyen and his new pals left their phones plugged in, and wandered outside to continue socializing while they helped insure good behavior.

BACK IN THE DINING ROOM, I DELIVERED A KISS ON THE CROWN OF Emmett's head. "You left me some dessert!" I said with a smile. I'd snagged blueberry pie and a pastry on the way in.

"Uh-huh," Emmett agreed. He pulled me down to his seated level and returned my kiss and grin. "You do good work, darlin'."

I settled into the booth beside him. Our IBIS agent friends stared at me in fresh consternation. I smiled sunnily at them. "Any leads?"

They nodded slowly. Kalnietis murmured, "You're scarier than he is," with a nod to Emmett.

"Good!" I assured him, and dug into my pie. I'd hoped we could let the meshnet spread and collect up leads, while we headed for bed. I should have known better. Emmett and the agents were glued to their phone screens.

"Darlin', what do you think of these churches?" Emmett asked.

I shrugged. Churches and I coexist amicably in the world. I didn't plan to visit one tonight. They seemed to be popping up all over the meshnet map. I was happy for them, to the limited extent that I cared. Anyone on the mesh could add markers to note places of interest – eateries, charging stations, warnings, churches, whatever.

But Emmett tapped a church marker open to show me. Normally, a church would add a bit more detail to their marker on the map, like on the curbside sign outside a church. Denomination. Pastor's name. Hours for religious services. A brief thought for the day, like 'Jesus loves you', or 'Happy Easter.'

This church had all that. But then the pastor launched into a diatribe against Emmett, or at least some fictional straw man labeled Resco MacLaren. This MacLaren was a godless New Yorker. He shamelessly brought his harlot Baker in tow. That would be me. The tirade reminded the congregation that phones and Internet were the devil's tools, and they'd seen God's fearsome punishment. 'Consort not with the godless, and carry no tales! Testify only for the Lord!' was his strong close.

"What about it?" I asked Emmett. "Doomsday loons are a dime a dozen. It's been Doomsday for a couple years now."

"Uh-huh," Emmett said unhappily. "Think I should reply that I'm born again?"

"No," I stated categorically. "Weren't you just saying that this morning? None of their business. And their religion is none of your business, Emmett."

"They're all like this," Emmett complained. "Fast as their pudgy little fingers can tap. They're all posting sermons."

"It's a public service," I suggested, as an alternate perspective. "Come to our church if you agree with us. Sample sermon provided." He looked deeply disturbed, though. "Emmett? Why is this getting to you?"

"Don't underestimate religion here, Dee," he murmured. "Bible Belt, or close enough. My home turf. Hacks me off that they call you a harlot."

I narrowed my eyes at him. "Do you think I'm a harlot?" I looked to Gianetti for backup. "That's so assymmetric. Why is it that women are always painted the whore? Why isn't he a whore?" Gianetti smiled back.

Emmett canted his head and glared at me. "Uh-huh."

"New top story on the news," Kalnietis interrupted softly. He read the headline, "Reunion Lovers to Judge Pittsburgh."

The rest of us switched to the news feed to read the story. IndieNews, of course, at their muckraking best. The story included a portrait of Emmett with his arms around me at last year's Thanksgiving feed of Manhattan's starving. Brandy O'Keefe had the by-line, my personal nemesis. She told me privately – and I believed her – that her sleazy innuendos about Emmett and me were nothing personal. We were wildly popular public figures. Attacking us made her stories sky-rocket in the rankings. The text of tonight's article was fairly accurate. When Emmett left New York, he told people his assignment was to 'evaluate' the situation in Pittsburgh. And I went with him.

O'Keefe didn't have any more facts, so she posed provocative questions. Will MacLaren take over as Resco of Pittsburgh? What heads will roll? Why send a New York Resco, instead of Pennsylvania's own? Was Pittsburgh in revolt against martial law? Why would MacLaren bring his pretty paramour?

Yeah, because our private life was the important part of all this.

"Sex sells," I murmured. "Should I cut the news feed?"

Emmett looked unsure. Kalnietis offered, "The second story is from Project Reunion News. States the same facts more calmly. Cautions against wild speculation. Does the news feed do us any harm? I think it shows the eyes of the Northeast are on Pittsburgh. That this investigation is important. Might help us."

"Uh-huh," Emmett breathed. He added sourly, "Also keeps their eyes on me and Dee instead of you."

"That too," Kalnietis agreed.

When we broke for bed, the waiting line for the recharging station had moved indoors, due to a sudden thunderstorm. The IBIS agents continued on ahead to the stairs while I paused with Emmett to check on the meshnet propagation. It didn't take the locals long to recognize us as the 'Reunion Lovers' from the news photo and start pointing. Judging from his pursed lips and dangerous gaze on them, Emmett's sense of humor was fraying.

So I called out to the line on the way to the stairs. "Good photo of us, huh?" I grinned cheerfully. "You should know, I work for the competing news service, PR News. IndieNews takes a cheap shot at me every chance they get," I confided rufully. "But we're not all bad. Gave you the meshnet. Good night! Hope you enjoy the meshnet!"

I waved jauntily. Emmett turned his back on them.

"Harlot?" I asked, as Emmett slid into bed beside me. The hotel room and bath were bland and restful, draped in pastel peach and olive green. Heroic measures had been taken to clean and freshen, but I suspect this hotel room had lain unused for years. Nothing could quite mask the underlying miasma of mildew and dust wafting from the mattress.

"Really tired, Dee," Emmett growled. But he pulled me over onto his shoulder and lay facing the ceiling, our usual posture for talking things over in bed. So I waited him out. He eventually sighed, and continued, "I'd rather be married, yeah. Kinda stings."

"As a marriage proposal, that kinda sucked, Emmett," I informed him.

"Chill," he said. "I understand what we're doing. We're in a monogamous committed relationship. I intend to marry you. When we're ready. I think you feel the same way." He paused. "Don't you?"

"I'm not going to hurry up and marry you because some preacher called me a whore," I replied. I figured that was good for a chuckle, but he didn't deliver. "Yes, Emmett. I intend to marry you. I think we still have a lot to work out."

"Do we?" Dammit, he was going analytical on me. "What do we need to work out, Dee?"

I scowled. "Is it too much to ask that we be lovers even six months? Long distance doesn't count."

Emmett remained analytical. "Five months now, in person? Long distance ought to count for at least one more month. Talked to each other every day. Worked together. Known each other a year and a half."

"Would it make you feel better to call us engaged?" I countered.

"No," he whispered. "I want you to answer the question. What do we need to work out?"

My claustrophobia? My fear of choosing wrong? Our current deal was that I wanted to wait until I couldn't imagine not being with him anymore. Then we'd call ourselves engaged for another couple years. I could mock up a lot of wedding dresses in two years. I could escape. I could refuse to admit I was getting married. I could give him time to run away from me.

"You're not sure you want to be with me," Emmett murmured. "And that hurts." He extracted himself from me and rolled away.

I put a hand on his back. "That's not true, Emmett. I love you. I'm just really claustrophobic. Marriage scares me."

"Go to sleep, Dee," he said huskily.

I tried a little harder to re-engage him. He threatened to find another room if I didn't leave him be. It's so hard to sleep when we know we're both lying awake thinking unhappily of each other.

5

Interesting fact: Pittsburgh has 700 outdoor public stairways carved through its hills, with more than 45,000 steps, and 446 bridges, 3 more than Venice. Despite the hills, it is also touted as bicycle-friendly.

The last thing I needed was the first thing to greet me when I came down to breakfast in the morning.

"Hi, Dee!" called Brandy O'Keefe of IndieNews, grinning and waving manically. But not too manically – she wouldn't want to obstruct her camera man. Whose lens was pointed straight at me, of course. Naturally, she also stood right next to the line of locals waiting for the recharging station. Who were indoors again, due to a soaking rain.

"Brandy, you bitch!" I greeted her. "Fancy meeting you here!" I beseeched the guards, "Get them out of here."

"Oh, Dee, don't be like that!" Brandy said, still grinning. Alas, the woman was my match that way. Gorgeous straight auburn hair, outdoorsy plaid flannel over jeans, clean fresh makeup, and she could wield a smile as both offense and defense. Though I wore Army cammies today. To be inconspicuous. Yeah, that wasn't going well.

The senior soldier on guard duty, Penny, scratched her head sheepishly. "I'm not sure what grounds I have to exclude them, Dee. We're letting the public in."

"Brandy's not public," I argued. "She's press." Penny screwed her face up at that. "I'm not here as press. I'm assisting an investigation." Drat, I didn't want to say that in front of Brandy.

"Oh, no, Dee!" Brandy cried. "I'm a hotel guest too! There is no other hotel in Pittsburgh."

"You'll just sleep in the gutter, then, Brandy," I returned. "You're used to it."

"Dee gets so so cranky when her face grabs the headlines," Brandy shared with the onlookers. "Maybe a little makeup?"

"You want a scoop?" I returned. "Reunion Lovers Split By Paparazzi?"

Brandy cooed delight at my slip. "Ooh! Bad night, huh, Dee?"

Penny wisely called in a higher pay grade to deal with the cat fight. Captain Johnson emerged from the breakfast buffet. "What's all this, ladies?" he interrupted with a hopeful smile.

"I don't think IndieNews should be in our local HQ," I said.

"But there is no other hotel," said Brandy. "So we're staying here. Besides which, you have PR News here. Dee Baker."

"Too early for check-in time," Johnson evaded.

"We're *exhausted*," Brandy assured him. "Drove all night to get here. Someone wouldn't let us on the train you took. I wonder who. But we'll happily pay for last night's lodging." She batted eyelashes at him, and looked tired and vulnerable. "Oh, there's the colonel!" she cried.

Emmett and his usual daybreak guards pushed into the hotel, clearly just back from their morning run. Brandy and her camera man pivoted to push microphone and lens at him. Two guards blocked them with rifles. Brandy ignored them and called out, "Colonel MacLaren! Have you found the murderers yet?"

"Get them out of here," Emmett ordered Johnson. To their cries of this being the only hotel in Pittsburgh, my beloved replied, "They can sleep in the van." The stairway door closed behind him, as he headed upstairs to change out of his running shorts. He'd never stopped walking across the lobby.

"I'll be back for press conferences," Brandy pledged. Penny caught her elbow and started leading her to the door. Brandy kept talking over her shoulder. "Dee! You have to call me, and get me into press conferences!"

"Yeah, yeah," I said.

The lobby grew very quiet as the door closed behind our press intruders. I realized I was standing next to the locals line. I caught an older woman's eye on me.

"Brandy and I work for competing news outlets," I explained wanly. "But mostly I partner with Colonel MacLaren. Doing tech stuff. Like the meshnet. Are you enjoying the meshnet?" They broke out in nods and a weak round of applause. "Thank you. Yeah, I set up the meshnet. Excuse me. I should eat before I say something stupid." *Too late,* was only implied.

I was long done with breakfast and studying my meshnet propagation in the lobby when Emmett re-emerged, flanked by Tibbs and Nguyen and a pair of our usual guards from New York. "Emmett! Where are we going?" I called out to him.

Emmett glanced at the line of locals, who were watching rapt, and prudently walked over to me to talk quietly. "You can stay here. Finally got Beaufort's address. Need to pay my respects to Marilou Beaufort and the kids. Find out where they want to go."

I glanced over his formal uniform. He clutched a book in his hand. "Is that a Bible?" I asked in surprise.

"Dee?" he bit out. "Yes, it's a Bible. This is not my first bereaved widow, or fallen comrade."

No, I imagine he'd done that before. With his Army division based in Kentucky, he'd likely prayed with them, too. I swallowed, and whispered, "Let me come with you, Emmett."

"Not now. Come with IBIS later."

'Later' turned out to be less than half an hour. I had time to visit our room to change into a somber navy dress, flexible enough to cover business meetings or funerals. Emmett had left a note on my pillow.

Need to cool off. E.

At least he hadn't moved out of the room like he'd threatened last night. I was sitting on the bed, unhappily contemplating the note, when my phone chimed with a mesh text from him.

Everything missing. Bring IBIS.

MAJOR BEAUFORT'S PLACE WAS A MODEST WOOD-FRAME HOUSE ON Mt. Washington, not far from the hotel. The ever-popular 'level lot' was accomplished by a postage-stamp front yard at one level, stairs down to a back yard a full story lower, and practically a cliff off to the right. Fortunately we drove there. The house had quite a view from the cliff side, down over the Monongahela River and the skyscrapers of the downtown triangle, over the tops of the trees below.

We stepped into a nicely furnished living room, with wood floors and a fireplace. Someone had opened up the living room to the next room, leaving partial load-bearing walls at the edges. Beaufort had selected that middle room for his office. Emmett, Tibbs, and Nguyen were rifling it. Beyond lay the kitchen, completing the street-level ground floor.

Emmett emerged and flopped onto the couch, gesturing us to take seats. "No sign of Marilou Beaufort and the kids," he reported. "Computer and phone are here, both wiped. Tibbs might be able to get something off them anyway. Can you help with that?" he asked the IBIS partners.

Gianetti left us for the office to see.

Kalnietis asked, "Found Beaufort's second in command yet?"

"Nope," Emmett breathed. His phone chirped, and he took it out immediately for some reading.

At Kalnietis raised eyebrow, I showed him how to set meshnet ring tones for preferred contacts. Emmett used a chirp to indicate a fellow Resco, and his mother and me set to chimes. "Different chimes," I hastened to clarify. Kalnietis smiled wryly.

Emmett was done reading his chirp. He stared off into space, looking grim. "Something wrong?" I asked.

Emmett roused. "It can wait," he said. He brought up his lead buckets of messages, responses to my meshnet announcement. "They don't know what a Coco is. When we get back to the hotel, maybe I should just talk to locals. Need to understand the social structures around here."

A Coco was a community coordinator, a civilian leader reporting to a Resco, usually a militia leader. At least, we called them Cocos in New England and New York–New Jersey. I thought that was standard everywhere.

"What would you like me to do?" I asked. The other four seemed more capable investigators than I was, and they were searching the house.

"Don't know," Emmett replied coolly. "You think differently. Look around?"

Well, that was vague, but not entirely pointless. I understood the big picture of what Emmett needed to accomplish in Pittsburgh. And I had questions. For instance, why communications were so limited in this city.

I wandered back to the kitchen. There was a washing-machine sized footprint on the vinyl floor, a faintly rusty outline surrounding a square where the vinyl pattern was less faded. Something stood there for years. It was heavy enough for its wheels or legs to leave dents in the floor. The missing object's position relative to the room yielded no clues. That box wouldn't have fit anywhere else.

I tried the gas stove. It worked fine. Hot water in the tap. The house had power, too. A quick thermostat test generated heat as well, but no air conditioning. The fridge was nearly empty, and the cupboards. Yet there were clean dishes in the dishwasher, and a soaking casserole dish in the sink, maybe meat and pasta. The only remnants in the fridge were bowls of leftovers covered in plastic wrap. Canned chili with egg. Broccoli with cheese sauce. Beaufort cooked and ate here. Whoever wiped his computer also stole his food, anything they could pack and carry. That probably wasn't all they took. The kitchen trash was empty, with a fresh trash bag. He still used plastic wrap and trash bags. A trash can somewhere might bear clues.

I found the trash bag and plastic wrap boxes. The plastics were biodegradable, made from crop residue right here in Pittsburgh. I tucked the boxes into my purse to discuss with Emmett later. We sorely needed these products back home.

I wandered back into the office. Based on what I overheard, Gianetti and Tibbs labored to read data off the computer's wiped SSD drive. It didn't sound like they'd succeed. Solid state drives can be erased pretty thoroughly. I admired the view from the generous window on the cliff side of the room. The rain had paused. Low-scudding clouds and the darkness of the sky suggested this was temporary.

Why would Beaufort have his office here with no communications? Emmett lived on his phone.

I took my security sniffer out of my purse. My founding partners on Amenac, the Ameni hacker team, were wizards in the cyber security arena. They developed these gizmos for surveillance protection during the heyday of HomeSec enforcing the Calm Act. Our lives depended on it. We'd made our peace with HomeSec now, but I still carried my comms sniffer wherever

I went – handy for finding a better phone signal. And after repeated exposure to mortal threats, the paranoia is slow to wear off.

The living room had only the familiar meshnet chatter. The desk in the office likewise. But yes, there was a WiFi signal by the office window. A bookcase stood beside the window, maybe 7 feet tall. I retrieved a three-step stool I'd seen in the kitchen to stand on. Yes, atop the bookcase was the usual accumulation of dust – who dusts above eye level? – with a scuffed blank spot. I held my sniffer there. Yeah. Right about there was a good enough WiFi signal to use a repeater.

To test my theory, I replaced the sniffer with my phone. Yes, my voice-over-WiFi app would work there. But the WiFi was password-protected. On a lark, I tried 'Marilou', but that wasn't it.

"Dee, what are you doing?" Emmett asked, causing me to jump in surprise. He'd stepped into the office behind me to watch.

"Investigating the house," I said. "I think Beaufort had Internet and voice-over-IP. Someone took it, but I think he had a repeater right here to boost WiFi through the house. Probably a string of repeaters up the mountain from the hotel. Good system for giving a few people true Internet. Bit slow. You wouldn't want many people sharing, though. Too little bandwidth. Say, Emmett, what were the kids' names? Beaufort's kids."

I tried Colin, Reba, and Beau as WiFi passwords to no avail. The name of their pet beagle. Then Beaufort's 10-digit phone number in Pennsylvania, then from Leavenworth, which Emmett still had on his phone. That one did the trick.

"Well, cool," I said. "I don't know what good it does us."

"Plenty," Tibbs assured me. He rattled off the winning password from memory and wrote it down. "Dee, I'll follow this up. See what else you can find."

Emmett didn't even give me an atta-girl. He just walked back to the living room with his phone, still trying to make some sense out of his leads. I sighed and looked around the office, sitting perched atop my step stool. Where would he keep his backup drive? It's possible the intruders hadn't found it. Your average American, from before the Calm Act, might trustingly use backups to the cloud, or skip backups altogether. Beaufort wasn't an average American. He was an Army Resco, like Emmett.

Beaufort was also fairly tall, over 6 feet. Why keep a step stool in his kitchen? I relocated my step stool to mid-kitchen, then stood on its top step to gaze around. I wouldn't put an electronic backup near anything electronic, the microwave, the fridge. My eyes fixed on the cabinets. They were just boxes affixed to the walls, with no crown molding. There was over a foot of gap between cabinet top and ceiling. I climbed down and moved the step stool to the cabinets farthest from the fridge, and climbed up. I was still shorter than Beaufort, and couldn't see or reach the back of the cabinets, so I stepped up on the counter.

"Got it!" I said, astonished it was that easy. I held up my prize to show Tibbs. "Backup drive."

Tibbs accepted my prize and gave me a slow smile. "Thank you. Do it again."

"Slave driver," I muttered. I looked around, still standing on the counter. While I was up there, I might as well look at the top shelves of the cabinets. I found a corroded key, unlabeled. It was so old that I doubted it was Dane's. He was a fastidious type of guy, like Emmett. But the key might open some part of the house. I climbed down from the counter and studied the kitchen drawers again more carefully.

In the cutlery drawer organizer tray, I found a man's gold wedding band, simple and heavy. The engraving said, 'God For Me Provided Thee.' I brought it to Emmett in the living room. "Could this be Dane's?" I asked him, and told him where I found it.

Emmett swallowed as he read the engraving. His voice had a

catch in it. "Yeah. I heard Marilou say that to Dane. Joking around. Sounded nice."

I needed to keep in mind that Emmett knew these people. They'd fallen out over politics, but they cared for each other once. I lay my hand on his in sympathy, over the ring. He was still mad at me, so my touch was tentative. His wasn't. He grasped my hand between his two, and squeezed.

"We'll get through this, Dee," Emmett said huskily. No one else was in the room with us. "If you want to."

"Of course I want to," I murmured. "I love you, Emmett."

He nodded brusquely. "Not here. Not now." He gave my hand another squeeze and let me go. "Look upstairs?" he suggested.

I wandered up and looked around. There were three bedrooms. Sadly, I was already fairly sure that no one named Marilou, Colin, Reba, or Beau had ever lived here, nor even their beagle. A man would stow his wedding band in the silverware drawer to keep it, not misplace it, but never use it again. Dane had lived and died here alone. The furnishings and belongings upstairs confirmed that.

A framed photo of Dane and his family sat atop the dresser. Judging from his uniform, the Army plane, and a sea of milling military families, a friend probably took the picture before his last deployment. From what Emmett told us, he was on deployment in the Middle East when the U.S. unilaterally pulled the Army out of all of our foreign engagements in a rout. For a logistics officer, that must have been a betrayal and a nightmare.

Dane and Marilou were both smiling blonds, as were the two younger kids. The third, eldest boy was biracial, but had his mother's smile. Dane hugged him close. At the time of this picture, Colin looked to be about 14. Dane must have married his mother when Colin was a pre-schooler.

Drat. I was starting to like one Dane Beaufort, deceased.

His bedside table held a Bible, unsurprisingly. I picked up the heavy softcover to find a little memo pad stowed beneath. Dane apparently kept it to jot down thoughts while in bed. I didn't read it. Emmett was better equipped to make sense of these things. He was a tidy man, Dane Beaufort. The Bible wasn't betrayed by any sex toys or pornography in the room, just a bland officer's wardrobe, neatly put away. Under the socks I found an old family album, photos from before digital took over.

I brought my lean collection back to Emmett, and suggested he look over Dane's uniforms for spares for himself. He shook his head. "How much longer are we here?" I asked. The four investigators seemed to be studying our found artifacts in the office, and Emmett wasn't looking at the house at all.

"If I said an hour, what would you do next?" Emmett asked.

I frowned at him. "Check the lower level, I guess."

He frowned back. "Concrete slab."

"No, just a concrete front porch," I returned. "The house is on a slope. The back yard is down one story."

Kalnietis overheard this, and traipsed along with me outdoors, down the side stairs and to the back yard. Yeah, no children had played here. The youngest Beaufort boy would be maybe 8 years old by now. There would be signs of that – bikes, balls, a basketball hoop. This compact urban back yard held a bit of grass and a vegetable garden, with a rusty old lonely lounge chair. With no other back yard at the same level, it could have felt intimate. But instead a giant brick apartment building, upslope, partly walled one side. Apartment windows overlooked the yard to the great downtown view.

The house wasn't just stilts in the back, to compensate for the slope. The lower level was walled in. It probably held the mechanicals, since I hadn't found the furnace and hot water heater yet. I was too short, but Kalnietis peered in the single window and confirmed this. We found a door around the opposite side from the outdoor staircase. Kalnietis started to pick the lock, but I handed him the corroded key to try first. It worked.

Stepping into the gloom, the half-floor looked like a typical basement to me. The laundry was in here, a trash can, lots of boxes. There was an old indoor staircase that once led up to the kitchen, but now dead-ended at the ceiling. Some decade or another, someone wanted a bigger kitchen more than they wanted indoor access to the laundry, an architectural choice I personally disagreed with. Especially in Pittsburgh, which received a lot of snow. The residual staircase now served as shelves, of a sort. There were a few spare WiFi routers, in their original boxes, of the sort one could use as a repeater. I nabbed one, then had to brush more dust off my only sober dress.

Kalnietis poked in the boxes. "This is an armory!" he exclaimed. "Dee, could you get Emmett?"

I shot Emmett and Tibbs a meshnet text, without comment. "Sorry," Kalnietis mumbled. "I could have done that."

I didn't feel drawn to poking around in the dust of an 'armory.' The undisturbed arrangement of munitions might mean something to Emmett. Not me. So I rolled the trash can out into the yard as a gift for Tibbs. Tibbs wore dirt-defying camouflage and latex gloves. I placed the WiFi router like a cherry on top. I wandered back to the garden, trying not to get my low pumps too muddy.

The apartments blocked the southeast exposure, but the garden plot got some southwestern light. Judging from the vines, not quite enough sun for tomatoes, but plenty for everything else. He'd tended his garden well, Dane Beaufort. Most of the summer vegetables had been replaced by cool weather crops. Broccoli, cabbage, and lettuce were ready to pick, and some lingering tomatoes. I didn't disturb the potatoes to check those.

And yes, that handmade structure in the back corner was a chicken hutch. No chickens, however. Unless... I peered over the back fence, another half story down, into a neighbor's sloping back yard. A boy, maybe 6 years old, was playing with a few chickens.

"Well, hello!" I called with a smile. "My name's Dee. What's your name?"

"Michael," he admitted. "You shouldn't be there. That's Major Beaufort's house."

"It's OK," I assured him. "We're friends, trying to figure out what happened to Major Beaufort. Are those his chickens?" The boy nodded. "Did you know Major Beaufort, Michael?"

"My parents work for him," Michael said. "I'll go get them."

I waited for him. My eyes fell on the chicken coop. This could have been Emmett. All of Dane Beaufort's home, except for the missing family. Before I met him, Emmett's life in New Haven probably looked a lot like this. I wondered if he'd been lonely. Easy enough to think that no one would have wanted to kill him. Except, the weather changes and impending end of the world made people awfully crazy.

6

Interesting fact: Before the Calm Act, Pittsburgh was not especially devout for an American city. About 32% were Catholic, 25% Mainline Protestant, 15% Evangelical, 4% non-Christian, and 18% non-religious. However 85% believed in God, similar to Dallas Texas or St. Louis Missouri; 76% considered religion important in their lives, and 77% prayed regularly. Rural areas surrounding Pittsburgh were more religious, and more Protestant.

Paddy Bollai, Michael's cammie-clad father, stared at the bookcase in Beaufort's office with open mouth and furrowed brow. He seemed an ordinary blue-collar guy, maybe 30 years old. "So you already took stuff?" he asked, puzzled.

"No," I said. "Someone went through the place. Wiped the computer, the phone. Stole the food. I think it was at night."

"The *food?* Hell!" said Paddy. "Just brought in a whole butchered hog and steer, too. Took most of it to the hotel. But still." He ducked into the kitchen and scowled. "Whole freezer of meat. Gone." So that's what the washing machine shaped footprint was on the kitchen floor.

Paddy turned back and pointed around the office. "That bookcase was a whole bank of electronic stuff. Big-screen TV over there. Couple monitors. Another computer. Missing filing cabinet."

"What makes you think it was at night, Dee?" Kalnietis asked.

"Took the food, but didn't touch the garden or the chickens," I said. And they hadn't rifled the armory. Just to be safe, Emmett had closed up downstairs before Paddy arrived. We weren't mentioning the munitions unless he did. "I don't think they were familiar with the place."

"Oh, it was last night, all right," Paddy confirmed. "I came by around ten to drop off Dane's phone for you, and everything was fine."

"Do you have the WiFi password?" Tibbs asked softly.

Paddy provided one, different from the one we had. Tibbs made a note of it. "Oh, and there's another password. But I don't know that one. Password on the computer was Colin, capital C. Draw a Z for Zorro to unlock the phone. How'd you get in?"

"Spare key under the doormat," Emmett murmured.

Paddy Bollai snorted and shook his head.

"Say, Paddy, do you know where Marilou and the kids are?" Emmett asked. "Dane's wife and children." He led us all back into the living room to sit and talk.

"Dane moved here alone," Paddy replied. "Never mentioned a family. Didn't say much about his past, really. He was Army Airborne, based in Kentucky. Served in the Middle East."

That seemed a pretty skimpy biography. During the introductions on our way upstairs from the back yard, Paddy told us he ran errands for Dane, as well as serving in the militia. His wife Alice was Dane's housekeeper. Dane had lived in this house, with the Bollai family as personal helpers, for two years. It seemed strange that Paddy didn't know about a missing wife and kids. But on second thought, I had a neighbor for several years with a teen-aged boy. I never learned where they came from, or who the boy's father was, until after she died and Alex became my fosterling. If it's painful, sometimes you don't mention your past.

Emmett moved on. "Alright. One of my top priorities is to contact Dane's second in command. Where is he? *Who* is he?"

"Davison?" Paddy asked, looking grim. "Yeah, you probably want Dwight Davison. We couldn't reach him, so I dealt with the body."

Special Agent Kalnietis pounced. "You've seen the body? Where is it now?"

"Took it to the coroner's office," Paddy replied. Good heavens, Pittsburgh had a coroner's office? If we still had such things in Connecticut or New York, I hadn't heard of them.

Paddy showed Kalnietis how to get there on a local map. Pre-border maps weren't very reliable, as tornado damage wasn't reflected. And there weren't any new maps. Paddy used the old maps with the streets overlaid on the satellite photo view, which showed tornado gashes fairly well. The old coroner's office, police headquarters, and city hall were all tornado casualties, but the coroner herself survived. The new morgue was in a shopping district downtown.

"Did you witness the murder?" Kalnietis followed up.

"Murder?" Paddy asked. "Sorry. Dane was beat up real bad. I don't know anything about murder." As an afterthought, he answered the question. "No. I wasn't there."

"But you saw the video? On the Internet?" Emmett prompted.

Paddy shook his head. "Haven't had video in a couple years. Except right here. With Dane."

"Dee, could you find us the video?" Emmett requested. "I never saw the original post."

We hadn't set up the replacement WiFi repeater, so I went back to the office window to hunt for the oldest post on Amenac, and downloaded the video. Kalnietis continued grilling Paddy about details of his involvement. Apparently there was a rally that afternoon in a suburb, which Paddy didn't attend. Someone called him over the WiFi voice network hunting for Davison, because Dane was seriously injured in an attack. When Davison couldn't be found, the same person, a stranger named Paul, called back a couple hours later and asked Paddy where to deliver the body.

Paddy hadn't realized Dane was that badly hurt from the previous phone call. He was furious that the body had been moved before anyone investigated. But by then, Dane's remains were in a flatbed truck heading into Pittsburgh. Paddy directed Paul to his house, and took over the body from there. He brought everything to the coroner.

Hotel manager Wiehl called Paddy yesterday afternoon during the train attack. It was news to Paddy that we were coming to investigate the death. When he'd delivered the meat to the hotel the day before, Wiehl was expecting a delegation to talk about the industrial joint venture with Ohio. After Wiehl's call yesterday, Paddy retrieved Dane's cell phone from the coroner, and left it here in the house for us.

I returned with the video to show Paddy, and texted a link to my co-investigators for later. I supplied Dane's apparent last words, 'We know what God demands of us.'

Paddy looked alarmed at that. He shook his head while he watched the soundless clip, slightly puzzled at first, building to flat-out denial. "No... No, that's not right..." he murmured.

When the clip ended, Paddy asked if he could see it on a bigger screen. Tibbs started to ask what the issue was, but the IBIS agents discouraged questions at that point. So we re-played the video on Tibb's portable, the largest display we had with us. Gianetti and Kalnietis flanked Paddy's seat in the office, where they could watch the screen and him at the same time.

Paddy didn't shake his head and mutter denials this time. He was glued to the screen, looking for something in particular. He replayed the video a couple more times, then sloughed back in his seat. He didn't look happy. "I'm not sure, but this guy," Paddy advanced the video, then pointed at the screen with a pen. "That might be Paul. The guy who brought me Dane's body."

Tibbs stepped in, zoomed in on the possible Paul, and ran the video through again. Paddy shrugged. The video wasn't high enough resolution for the zoom to help much. Paul wore militia camouflage. Maybe a third of the crowd did.

"Is anything else strange here?" Kalnietis asked neutrally.

"Everything," Paddy complained. "That's a crazy thing to say in front of *that* crowd. This guy Paul told me Dane was attacked in Green Tree. But that's Station Square, down by the river. Not a half a mile from here."

Yet the text of the post said 'Dane Beaufort killed by crowd in Green Tree PA.' It was posted by someone with the unhelpful handle 'Matt1034.'

"That crowd?" Emmett prompted first. "What do you mean by that?"

"That's an Apocalyptic rally," Paddy supplied. "Green Tree is Shaker territory."

"Shaker territory," Emmett repeated. "Apocalyptic? I don't understand."

Paddy sighed. "You know the Apocalyptics, right? These are the end of days. Want to help God wipe out the Earth faster so they can hurry on to Judgment Day. Nut jobs. Shakers are sort of like dancing Quakers, only celibate. Pacifists. Died out a century ago. These are some kind of revival movement." He shrugged and shook his head. "I'm Catholic myself."

"How do you know it was an Apocalyptic rally?"

"The ones flanking Dane. They're the Apocalyptic leaders here on Mount Washington," Paddy replied. He looked up at a ruckus outside, as a couple trucks of our soldiers arrived. "What's all that?"

"It's fine," Emmett assured him. "My people. Taking some supplies Dane had in the basement."

"You're taking the armory?" Paddy accused. "You can't!"

Emmett frowned. "Army munitions, issued to a Resco. Dane's gone. They're mine now." He held out a placating hand. "And I may issue them, once I understand what's going on. For now, I have more questions. Do you know a militia leader named Lohan? Or Bremen?"

Paddy pursed his lips, still fixated on the troops confiscating the armory. Emmett pushed harder. "Paddy, a militia group under Lohan attacked my train. Men died. If another Resco dies here in Pittsburgh, you're in for a world of hurt."

Paddy Bollai shook his head unhappily. "You don't know what you're doing here. This new meshnet will help everyone coordinate attacks. Disarming my militia. It'll be a bloodbath tonight. We worked out truces. You'll unbalance everything."

"Maybe," Emmett said, narrowing his eyes. "But I think you've got ammo to last the night." Paddy dropped his eyes, conceding the point. Emmett continued, "Lohan and Bremen. Who are they? Where are they?"

Paddy gave in with a sigh. "Never heard of Lohan. Reverend Bremen runs the Baptist forces around Carnegie-Mellon and Schenley Park. East of downtown. Father Uccello might know how to contact him. Or Dane's phone." He provided Father Uccello's contact information.

Emmett looked unhappier by the minute. "You said Bremen 'runs the Baptist forces.' Does Uccello 'run' the Catholic forces? They lead the militia?"

"Well, sort of," Paddy said. "Uccello leads the Catholic community on Mount Washington, see. Bremen does the same around Schenley Park, with the Baptists."

"How could the city get divided up by religion?" Emmett asked, in increasing frustration. Kalnietis was staring at him, as though wondering why Emmett was so hung up on the religious landscape. Or at least, that was why I was staring at him.

"Well, it isn't exactly," Paddy allowed. "It's just, after the tornados, the local churches lead the cleanup. Help the survivors.

Hand out food and clothes, provide shelter. Then people need to find somewhere else to live. It just keeps getting more sorted. You know? People double up. Or if the homeless don't want to join one of the religious communities, they leave for the countryside. This hill, Mount Washington, is controlled by Catholics and Apocalyptics. The militia, anyway."

"So what's your command chain?" Emmett asked. "From you, up to Dane?"

"Well, I worked for Dane directly, too," Bollai said. "But in the militia, I report to Captain Baumgartner. He answers to Father Uccello. Um…"

"Father Uccello reports to a bishop somewhere," Emmett suggested.

"Yeah, Pittsburgh has our own bishop," Paddy said, nodding. "Ah, I'm sure he'd help if Dane asked. Usually."

"Uh-huh," Emmett breathed. No, Emmett definitely did not like what he was hearing. "Dwight Davison, Dane's second. What can you tell me about him?"

"He's north of the Allegheny," Paddy replied. He gave Emmett Davison's phone number on their voice-over-Internet system. He didn't know where Davison lived, and hadn't been able to contact him for days. "I think he's Mainline. Uh, you know, the normal Protestant churches. The liberal ones. What are you?"

"I," Emmett replied, "am a Colonel in the Penn Army at the moment. No, I know what you meant. But my religious beliefs are strictly off-duty."

"That makes a lot of sense," Paddy agreed. "Look, the family's expecting me back. Can I go now? Feel free to call and all, but…"

"I can't let you go until the armory is safely back at the hotel," Emmett replied regretfully. Paddy looked annoyed, but seemed to understand the necessity. On second thought Emmett added, "Are my troops in danger out there?"

"Probably not," Paddy said. "This block's my turf. I'll get a call if anything's going down."

Kalnietis asked softly, "What religion was Dane Beaufort, Paddy?"

"Evangelist," Paddy replied. "Didn't hold it against him. Dane was alright."

I didn't realize Emmett was holding his breath for the answer, until he blew it out in relief. I gathered Emmett was afraid that Dane had converted to one of the new doomsday faiths.

Kalnietis took over the conversation, walking Paddy back through the details of the day Dane died. I wandered out to the living room after Emmett, and took a seat while he labored away with his phone. "Can I help?" I asked.

"Just asking around after Marilou and the kids," said Emmett. "Resco boards. Fort Campbell." Fort Campbell was the home of the 101st Airborne Division, the outfit Emmett and Dane both served before their common schooling in Leavenworth.

"Matthew," I suggested. "Maybe we could ask around this 'Apocalyptic' community for Matt1034? The guy who posted the video."

Emmett looked up at me thoughtfully. "If that's his name. Or..." He plied the phone again. He got much better WiFi in here than I did, courtesy of a military-grade phone, no doubt. "Could be Matthew 10:34," he concluded, and read, "'Do not suppose that I have come to bring peace to the earth. I did not come to bring peace, but a sword.'"

7

Interesting fact: Pittsburgh began manufacturing steel in 1875, and by 1911, produced half the steel in the U.S. After 1970, foreign competition led to the collapse of the Pennsylvania steel industry.

I suppose it makes sense that in a murder investigation, job one is to nail down the facts. For instance, we still weren't entirely sure that 'murder' was the right word. Emmett desperately wanted to lay hands on one Dwight Davison, Dane's second in command, who should have been acting Resco for Pittsburgh, and figure out why he wasn't on the job. But there wasn't much more we could do about that, after adding another leads-wanted item to the meshnet announcement. And dearly as Emmett wished to dive into Dane's computer and phone records, the data needed reconstruction first. Hanging over Tibbs' shoulder wouldn't speed that up.

So we dropped off Tibbs and the armory at the hotel, grabbed a late lunch, and set off with the IBIS agents again, plus a fresh quartet of armed guards. At a guess, the IBIS agents and Emmett were significantly more deadly than our soldiers. But Pittsburgh wasn't feeling too friendly so far.

First stop was Station Square, a few blocks down the Monongahela River from our hotel, at the base of Mount Washington. The famous incline was just across the street. One of the adorable twin rail cars, wedge-shaped and multi-leveled for people to sit upright despite the steep slope, was latched to the station at the top of the rail. The other car, presumably, was mixed into the pile of kindling and wreckage at the base of the hill. The rails themselves were pulled apart and tangled with splintered trees for the lower quarter of their track. The road running perpendicular to the incline base had a couple lanes cleared for two-way traffic. The building across the road was broken open by the tornado as well.

I studied this mournful wreckage from several directions, several times, as Gianetti drove us in circles hunting for where the video was taken. Finally my reluctance to be a back-seat driver broke down. I claimed Emmett's phone with its superior Internet connection, and surfed Google maps and streetview until I found a likely spot. I directed Gianetti in.

"But it says bridge out!" she objected. So that's why we hadn't driven this way yet.

"We're not crossing the bridge," I assured her. "Just turn left, now left into there...and left again." Yes, that was far from obvious. "See the Hard Rock Cafe? Stop just before there."

Hidden in a sea of low brick buildings, a pair of walkways opened up to the right, leading into an open-air plaza. Since no one else was moving, I handed Emmett back his phone, and climbed out of the car. The guards in the trailing car hastily exited as well.

Not that there were any threats in evidence. The place was empty of the pedestrians and window-shoppers it once held, a grown-up playground where no one came to play anymore. Someone had spray-painted 'Dec 10!' and 'Remember 12-10!' in red across several abandoned storefronts. At a guess, that was the day Pennsylvania closed its borders, and left the world behind. I can't say that I noticed at the time, that the state had gone missing. No one in Connecticut looked beyond their own problems and the Ebola outbreak in New York City around then.

What a strange thing, to have the entire world disappear. In New England, our borders closed. But we still had Internet, censored as it was. We had television news, of steadily decreasing credibility. On rare occasions, we could even punch through the borders with a personal phone call. Amenac was up and running and bypassing the censorship within a month or so of the border lockdown. The view was a blurry one, sure. Our worlds got much smaller. But we'd never been cut off completely. Not like Pennsylvania. Their own martial law governor, General Tolliver, had severed Internet and phone connections at the Penn borders. For 15 months, Penn stood alone, an island adrift. The war with New York, that blasted open Penn's communications again, began 10 months ago, at Thanksgiving. Yet contact with the outside world strangely still hadn't reached here, for normal people.

Those events seemed so very far from Pittsburgh. I walked into the plaza, idly wondering what that isolation did to a people's psyche. I pointed out the low rectangular fountain across the far side of the space, turned off, but full of rainwater. In the video, Dane had stood a couple heads taller than the crowd. The fountain's edge looked like his likely pulpit.

The IBIS agents pounced on that, to find the exact spot where Dane was swallowed by the crowd. Given that the space was surrounded by recognizable objects, it didn't take them long. I left them to it, and drifted past the fountain.

The plaza's far edge was a sort of non-railway platform. It had the styling of a railway platform, riveted steel supporting an open-air roof for shelter. There was even a railroad running past. But between the platform and the tracks was an iron picket fence. The train didn't stop here. An easy stone's throw across the rail bed were docks on the river, with a few boats. A pedestrian bridge rose to my left, and crossed the rails, providing safe access across the tracks. The non-platform was more of a covered walkway, a lovely riverside promenade stretching in both directions from where I stood, with a great view of the downtown high-rises. Off to the right, I could clearly see what was wrong with the bridge, too. Its last expanse, on the downtown side, had fallen into the river. At least one building over there was crushed, as well.

Decorating the promenade space, the designers had placed a giant pig-iron blast furnace by the rail-side. Steel city, after all. I dutifully read the tourist sign providing an explanation, and walked around the immense furnace, about four times my height. As my eyes dropped to the ground, I thought it was a shame about the rust on this side. The rust that appeared only on the concrete under the pig furnace. The humongous egg-shaped machine itself was painted a quarter inch thick. It was completely rust-free.

I looked over my shoulder. My back faced the IBIS agents and Emmett, right across the long rectangular fountain. If Beaufort was standing on the edge of the fountain, and the crowd rushed him, he might have been pulled forward into the crowd. But more likely, he would have stepped backward, into the fountain basin. And sloshed across, trying to escape. It rained hard last night, and maybe more than once in the past – three days? But the walkway roof and the bulk of the pig iron furnace would have kept the rain off underneath. The concrete was slightly higher there, preventing puddles.

"Darlin'?" Emmett asked, seeing my sad look. "Find something?"

I nodded and explained my theory. They traipsed around the fountain toward me, and Gianetti soon confirmed that the rust was indeed blood. She easily found more traces now that she had a path to follow.

Emmett and I sat out of the way on the fountain's edge while she and Kalnietis developed their model of events. Assuming that the blood was Beaufort's. That would be easy to check, if we had a body and a coroner.

Dane made it clean away to the furnace, where the bleeding began. He would have run slow, a big man in sodden heavy clothing from splashing through the fountain water. But after the furnace, he broke free again, and ran for the river. More blood under the black picket fence. A light trail across the gravel of the railroad bed. He'd almost made it to the docks, where boats held tantalizing promise of escape. Maybe he could have hid under the docks, or swum out into the current. But he didn't make it. A whole lot of blood happened in the gravel just past the rails, and none beyond. Dane didn't make it any farther.

Fascinated by the proceedings to my left, it took me a while to notice that Emmett was far too quiet on my right. He sat hunched forward, elbows on his knees, hands clasped, staring. That brought me back to earth. This wasn't just a mystery for Emmett. Dane Beaufort was a friend. More than that, the friend held the same job as Emmett, serving a community as a resource coordinator, the personal representative of the martial law government. And that community had killed him, right here, run him down and murdered him, in a way that was becoming all too vivid. In a flash, I pictured not Dane, but Emmett running that gauntlet, and losing.

I leaned forward to match Emmett's posture, and placed a hand on his thigh. "I'm sorry about your friend, Emmett," I murmured.

He grasped my hand, squeezed his eyes. A tear squeezed out. I've always loved that about Emmett, that he wasn't too tough to cry when it hurt. "Dane was perfect for this job," he said, voice cracking a little. "Desk chair warrior. Detail-oriented paperwork prick. Self-righteous in theory. Not in practice."

"What do you mean?" I asked.

He sighed and shrugged. "He'd disapprove of women dressing like sluts. But Marilou didn't just dress like a slut. She was one. Drugs, drinking, whoring around. Not even sure who Colin's dad was. But she didn't want to be that person anymore. He adored her for it. Dane was like that. Talked all prissy and judgmental. But he didn't act it. He cared for people."

I didn't care for his example. "You want to argue about the harlot thing again? Now?"

His answer was slow coming. "No," he eventually replied. "Are you? A harlot? Slutty, whoring around? I don't think so."

"You go analytical at the weirdest damned times, Emmett," I complained.

"Uh-huh," he breathed. "Off-balance." He stared at the pig-iron furnace, the gravel rail bed beyond, and swallowed.

I squeezed his hand. "You know, it doesn't matter, Emmett," I said softly. "What Dane did to deserve this. Nobody deserved to die like this."

He let out an explosive breath. "Uh-huh," he said. He took me in his arms, laid his chin on the crown of my head. "People do shitty things, in a mob."

"Can't judge a whole city," I suggested, "for what a mob did."

After a long pause, he said, "No. I don't want to judge anybody at all."

"Do you have to?" I asked, gently extricating myself from his arms. He didn't need a teddy bear. He needed to break out of his funk and move, was how I read it. I stood and twisted back and forth, to release my spine.

"Probably," he said, following my lead to rise and stretch his back. "Yeah. The guilty have to die. The city, that's a different problem."

One he didn't need to stew on right now. He didn't have enough information to make stewing useful, so his thoughts would keep turning to the violent death of a friend, right here. Distraction, that was the ticket. "I think that's a ThingSpace over there," I said, pointing to a passage out of the plaza.

"A what?"

"The Internet of Things," I elaborated, and started walking that way. "They had a great ThingSpace in Stamford. Very, um, glittery. Sort of a live demo to market all the things you could control by voice, movement, phone."

The corridor was mostly a pedestrian passage back to the street. They wouldn't have left it running all the time, for the ThingSpace to prey on passersby. There would have been...yes. A giant green button, twice the width of my fist, like the one that activated a water park by a town beach back home. Just for grins, I mashed the button. I didn't expect the ThingSpace to turn on. I didn't expect there to be power anymore to this abandoned mall. But there was.

A bank of LED fairy lights rippled down and back 10 feet up, to right and left, showing us the active portion of passageway before us to interact with. I stepped forward, to a *ta-dump!* from hidden speakers. I stepped back and forth, and waved my hands to verify where the *ta-dump* sensor fired – around shin level.

"Darlin', this is silly," Emmett complained.

If he was calling me 'darlin'' again, I definitely disagreed. I'd contributed a lot, and he'd been chilly to me all day. 'Darlin'' was a distinct improvement. "Play with me, Emmett," I said in challenge, shooting him a grin over my shoulder. "You know you have to."

He scowled, but stepped in to sound *ta-dump*.

"ThingSpace, play dance music!" I attempted. No response. "Alexa, play music!"

"What music would you like?" replied the ThingSpace, in a woman's sultry alto voice.

"It wants to dance with us!" I said in delight.

"Alexa?" Emmett demanded. "How'd you know that?"

I shrugged. "It's like Siri. Just a name."

"My partner is a machine whisperer," Emmett groused.

"I love cool tech," I agreed. "I really do. Alexa, play music. *Walk on By,* by Dionne Warwick." I don't know why I picked that song. Pathos, perhaps. Sure enough, the song started to play.

> If you see me walking down the street
> And I start to cry each time we meet
> Walk on by, walk on by

I took Emmett's hand and sashayed him down the corridor, one step facing half-together, next step facing half-away. This was nearly guaranteed to make him dance – Emmett was far too dominant to let me lead. He was a good dancer, too, especially swing. His mother had tended bar at a country-western club in Branson Missouri when he was a kid. After a few reluctant steps, Emmett took over, and spun me around. Step together, step apart, turn in place with me stepping backward to him stepping forward, then tossed away in a spin again, and pulled back into his arms. Half of me enjoyed his touch, and the accelerations as he pulled me around, and the sway of my own hips, to the slow sultry beat.

> Foolish pride
> Is all that I have left
> So let me hide
> The tears and the sadness you gave me
> When you said goodbye

The other half of me tracked the sensors in the walls. A glissando, a bass, a chime, all tuned to complement and exaggerate the music at that exact moment. I told the music to replay twice, as we got the hang of what effects were available. I broke from him to stomp on a double foot-print painted on the sidewalk. That gave a deep drumbeat and a lasing light, gold and magenta. I found a spot that yielded cymbals with a right hip-jut, and a drum to the left. I danced with the man and the machines, hung between Emmett and the ThingSpace, grinning from ear to ear.

As the song ended for the last time, I doubled over laughing out loud. Emmett gathered me up in his arms and kissed me. I resumed chuckling as he rested his forehead on mine.

"You're kinda crazy," he observed.

"It's the end of the world as we know it, Emmett," I countered. "Live a little. That's a song, isn't it? Perfect! Alexa, play music, *It's the End of the World as We Know It!*"

Too rowdy a song for country swing steps, we bopped all over the corridor, playing with the ThingSpace and playing off each other. The squares around the painted footprints played a great sequence when I jumped hopscotch on them.

> Uh-oh, overflow, population, common group
> But it'll do, save yourself, serve yourself
> World serves its own needs, listen to your heart
>   bleed
> Tell me with the Rapture and the reverent in the
>   right, right
> You vitriolic, patriotic, slam fight, bright light
> Feeling pretty psyched
> It's the end of the world as we know it, and I
>   feel fine!

This time, at the end, Emmett doubled over laughing along with me, eyes watering in mirth. I stood up straight first, and laid an arm around his waist. As my eyes rose, I spotted a passerby out on the street. He stood frozen, grey plaid wool jacket over grey pants, grey hair, hunched forward, bent by the weight of the world. All that stood out from his greyness was threads of red in the plaid, and murderous hatred in his eyes.

"Emmett," I murmured. "On the street."

"Guards!" Emmett called out. He pointed. "I need to talk to him!" The guy took off in a running shamble. Our fit young guards had no trouble catching him at all.

8

Interesting fact: When the U.S.A. was officially abolished in March, during a Project Reunion news broadcast, Major Cam Cameron suggested that each super-state adopt a simple constitution to declare itself a nation. His military governor, Sean Cullen of New York–New Jersey, dragged his feet, hoping another super-state would go first. None did.

The IBIS agents, Kalnietis and Gianetti, along with all the guards, gathered around as Emmett attempted to chat with our grey visitor.

"*When ye therefore shall see the abomination of desolation, stand in the holy place!*" he admonished us. "*Flee into the mountains!*"

I wondered if a nut-case homeless man would be any use to us at all. But Emmett apparently recognized the gibberish. "Whole lot of Matthew today," he commented. "Sir, did you happen to see the abomination here, three days ago? A rally?"

"She is the whore of Babylon!" the grey man accused, pointing at me.

"What does that even mean?" I asked Emmett sourly. He touched my elbow and gestured for me to go stand with the IBIS agents and stay out of this. Kalnietis swapped places with me, placing his body between the man and us women.

"Sir, do not insult my wife again," Emmett rebuked the man sternly. I didn't object to the promotion to wife. Clearly we weren't communicating well enough for fine distinctions. Emmett introduced himself and our group, and managed to pry out a name in return: Brian Altmann. In between superfluous creepy Bible quotes, sadly it became evident that Altmann attended the rally here three days ago, that led to Dane Beaufort's death. Emmett and Kalnietis were too polite to say so, or at least wanted to wring more information out of him first. But Brian Altmann was likely a dead man, as a member of that mob.

They made a good team. Kalnietis gently tugged at any threads of sense. Emmett knew more Bible than I ever suspected, and turned Altmann's quotes back on him. Being understood, sort of, helped Altmann be more forthcoming. But progress was slow and half-nonsensical, and the clouds were darkening again.

I wandered off with Gianetti to help pick up her blood samples. I offered her a trash bag from the locally produced package I picked up in Beaufort's kitchen. I was gratified that she, from Maryland, appreciated my prize as much as I did. Trash wasn't so bad out in the suburbs, where homes these days tended to have compost heaps nearby. In New York City, the 'Apple Core' as we called it, life without trash bags was a real misery. I wanted these bags back in the Core.

The rain started spitting again, and the afternoon was growing late. We deposited Altmann at the hotel for further questioning, and continued on to the coroner's office. We hoped that Emmett could definitively identify the body as Dane's. I only went along to hold him afterward.

Yes, it was Dane. And as of today, the coroner had another body. Dwight Davison, Dane's second in command, had washed up on the bank of the Ohio River, just a couple miles downstream. She believed that the two men died within hours of each other.

Both men were badly beaten. The coroner concluded that the eventual cause of death for Dane was brain swelling from his head injuries. Gianetti showed her the crime scene photos on her phone. The coroner agreed that the fatal weapon was likely the archaic blast furnace beyond the fountain in Station Square. Someone bashed the back of Dane's head into it.

If Dane hadn't been a Resco, the homicide might be involuntary manslaughter, a much lesser offense. The perpetrators hadn't even killed him – he died later of his wounds. Because of Dane's position, this distinction was irrelevant.

The coroner theorized that Davison tried to swim for safety, lost too much blood in the water, passed out, and drowned. That is, assuming Dwight Davison was a victim at the same rally. But she didn't have any conclusive evidence of that. The blood loss in his case was dominated by several knife injuries, and internal bleeding, probably from kicks to his ribs and kidney.

She promised to get back to us the next day with the blood DNA match tests, which might place Davison at the same scene.

But at this point, it was pretty clear we knew how, where, and when Dane Beaufort had died. And possibly his missing second in command as well.

"Don't," I said to Emmett, tugging his hand. When we arrived back at the hotel, he automatically headed for the prisoner interrogation. "Let Tibbs deal with Altmann, Emmett. You need a break."

Emmett looked indecisive, but Kalnietis surprised us. "Yes, let's regroup." He led us into the dining room to 'our' booth. It's funny how territorial people are. We'd claimed that table, the soldiers held the side of the dining room behind the buffet from us, and that was that. The kitchen staff was setting up for dinner, but our troops weren't eating yet. Apparently supper was set for 6:00, and we had some time yet. We nabbed fruit off the dessert buffet to tide us over, and a waiter served us water glasses and a pitcher.

I finally got to deliver my prize trash bags to Emmett. He and Kalnietis made appreciative noises. Emmett promised to get to the bottom of this, how we could make or import these for the Apple Core.

"You were fantastic today, Dee," Gianetti praised me. "Ever consider a career in law enforcement?"

I smiled, and said, "I play for the other team."

"Uh-huh," Emmett said wryly. "Be good, Dee. She's on my team," he added to the IBIS agents. Fortunately, they elected to leave this be.

"So," said Kalnietis, getting back to business. "At this point, we want to identify who was at the rally. And why they killed Dane Beaufort?"

"Uh-huh," said Emmett. "Who, anyway. Mobs...might not find a 'why.'" Kalnietis prompted him to expand on this. "A mob is just angry. Why it's angry isn't why it kills. A mob kills because it's angry and out of control."

"A mob mentality?" Gianetti asked doubtfully.

"That's practically why martial law exists," said Emmett. "When people are out of control, job one is to get them back under control. Dissolve the mob. Turn them back into people, with a conscience. A mob doesn't have a conscience, doesn't reason, doesn't behave. Just lashes out."

"So you're not concerned with why?" Kalnietis asked.

"Oh, I'm concerned plenty," Emmett insisted. He tapped the box of plastic trash bags. "I need to recommend what to do with Pittsburgh." He frowned. "Seems like a pretty nice place."

"This mob was different," I suggested. "Looter mobs in

Connecticut, mobs in the Apple Zone, they were scared and hungry."

"We've had religious mobs too," Emmett said softly. "We censor them out of the news."

"You can't censor them out of Amenac," I objected. How could he manage that?

"Uh-huh," Emmett replied. "My priority now is the community leaders of Pittsburgh."

"Not to prosecute the mob murderers?" Kalnietis pressed.

"I'd appreciate it if you identify them for me," Emmett said. "Bet I'll find them before you do, though."

Sergeant Tibbs approached Emmett deferentially, a computer under his arm. He delivered this, and said, "Sir. Beaufort's computer reconstruction. I need to ask if you authorize enhanced interrogation. For the prisoner, Altmann. He is not cooperative."

Emmett stared at him, and answered slowly. "No, Sergeant." Tibbs nodded and turned to leave. Emmett continued, "Sergeant? Torture is a war crime. It's also ineffective."

"Sir," Tibbs acknowledged stiffly.

Emmett contemplated him unhappily. "You're a good man, Tibbs. Stay that way. Thank you for the computer. Dismissed." Emmett made a to-do note on his phone. *Niedermeyer – torture.* Tibbs had come to us from Coast Guard Captain John Niedermeyer, the highest ranking Resco in New England.

"I'm relieved," Kalnietis said guardedly.

"Don't be too relieved," Emmett murmured. "Everyone you identify in that mob is going to die. They just won't be tortured first." A brief flash of outrage managed to escape Kalnietis' control. Emmett pursed his lips. "And anyone outside the mob who incited mob violence. We don't have another solution, Special Agent."

"A better life," I suggested.

Emmett looked pointedly at the buffet. "Already got a better life than the whole Apple Zone." That was true. The Apple Zone

– New York City, its New York and New Jersey suburbs, Long Island, the whole area once cordoned off by the epidemic borders – was still destitute, eating meagerly off charity.

Emmett continued, frowning in puzzlement. "No reason they don't have Internet and power, so far as I can see. Have them here in the hotel. Cables are easy to fix. So why didn't Dane fix them?" He shook his head, clearing that thought. "No, they don't need a better life. Someone's firing them up to be angry instead of grateful. Lash out instead of pull together. We need to find out who, and stop them. Instill gratitude if we can. I don't get that, either. Pittsburgh wasn't a pissy kind of town. Newark, Baltimore, you expect this kind of crap. Not here."

Kalnietis and Gianetti exchanged glances. "You'll excuse us, Colonel," Kalnietis said stiffly. "IBIS is only a few months old now. This is new to us. Our business was law enforcement."

"Uh-huh." Emmett smiled back at him crookedly. "Think you'll find there aren't many laws these days, Agent Kalnietis. Oh, speaking of which, we need to catch a broadcast tonight, darlin'. Cam's presenting his new constitution for New York–New Jersey. Hudson," he corrected himself. "Seven o'clock. You're welcome to join us," he invited the IBIS agents.

"Oh, wow!" I cried, and pounced on my phone. "So they must have published it by now."

Emmett had seen the drafts, of course, but they were classified. He refused to discuss it with me, the rat. No one was allowed to see the new constitution until the big presentation via Project Reunion News over the Internet. PR News planned to post the text a couple hours early, for people to read and think about before the broadcast if they wanted. This was the major news event of the month in the Northeast. Hudson would be the first official new nation to emerge from the ashes of the United States. I eagerly pulled up the document to read it at last.

Kalnietis and Gianetti quickly followed my lead, to read on their own devices. The scuttlebutt was that the other northeastern super-states planned to let New York–New Jersey – Hudson – go first, to watch and learn from our mistakes. The IBIS agents' own Greater Virginia Constitution could well be based on ours soon. Or Virginia–Del–Mar, or whatever they ended up calling it.

Emmett dug into Beaufort's computer instead. Tibbs left him a crib sheet of the contents, where Beaufort had stored what.

On the Constitution, my eyes immediately jumped to the number one question in my mind. "You're on the succession!" I breathed. "Emmett?" I gazed at him stunned.

"Uh-huh."

"You could have told me *that!*"

"Wasn't final until today," Emmett said, subdued. "Sean was still playing with the order."

Naturally, the Hudson line of succession wasn't the top concern of our IBIS agents from Virginia–Del–Mar. "This Bill of Rights is bizarre," Kalnietis commented.

We settled in to read the shiny new Constitution from the top.

CONSTITUTION OF HUDSON

We the People of Hudson, in order to form a more perfect Union, establish Justice, insure domestic Order, provide for the common Defense, promote the general Welfare, and secure the Blessings of Liberty to ourselves and our Posterity, do ordain and establish this Constitution for our State.

(1) Hudson is a nation-state. We claim the right and responsibility to establish a currency, defend our borders, and enter into binding treaties as a sovereign nation. Hudson is coterminous with the previous States of New York and New Jersey, and supersedes them.

(2) Our form of government is martial law. We deem this necessary due to extreme natural threats and domestic chaos resulting from the actions of a prior government. Our head of state is Governor-General Sean Patrick Cullen. The military and all civilian governments in Hudson are ultimately answerable to this Commander-in-Chief.

(3) Our line of succession is determined by the Governor-General, and shall consist of 4 names, in order, to assure orderly transfer of power. At this writing, those individuals are:

1. Asher Vered Margolis

2. Chandy Anthony (Tony) Nasser
3. Peter Michael Hoffman
4. Emmett Christopher MacLaren

(4) Our rate of taxation shall be 25% of all agricultural production, paid to Hudson, to support national defense personnel, infrastructure objectives, and as resources permit, contribute to the livelihood of those not employed in agriculture. This tax rate does not include local taxation, which cannot exceed an additional 25% of agricultural production. All levels of Hudson government are required to publish the budget, that being the tax rates, gross proceeds, spoilage rate, and dispensation of these taxes, in aggregate form, on an annual basis.

(5) Our currency is the hudson dollar, a digital currency. Hudson dollars represent food, and expire two years after creation. When a citizen dies, his dollar balance transfers to his spouse if any, or dependents if any, or to his local government. All hudson dollars revert to the national treasury upon expiration.

(6) Hudson hereby grants certain Rights and Privileges, within limits, to its citizens.

(a) All current human inhabitants of Hudson, and their descendants born in Hudson, are hereby granted citizenship. Emigration and immigration between Hudson and other states is a matter of national agreements, not a right of citizens.

(b) Citizens aged 16 or over, including the incarcerated, may apply for the right to vote. Voters must pass a literacy and numeracy test, and prove fluency in English.

(c) Citizens enjoy private freedom of religion, private sexual conduct, and marriage and dissolution of marriage between any two citizens. To preach or promulgate a religion in public requires successful completion of a regulatory training program, and a license.

(d) Free access to the Internet and Meshnets is a public good, to permit constructive discourse and dissemination of information between citizens. Availability may be limited by local conditions. There is no right to privacy on these free public nets.

(e) Speech, including on the public Internet and Meshnets, may be limited or channeled to promote public order. Interference with the clear communications of the government or the military is a crime.

(f) Citizens have the right to bear small arms for the purposes of hunting, sport, and self-defense. Small arms are arms that can easily be carried, cannot seriously interfere with vehicles including aircraft, nor able to injure more than 8 persons before reloading. Weapons that exceed these limits are permitted to the military, police, or militia sanctioned by local governments, but not to private citizens.

(g) Citizens have the right not to work, and the right to die. If employed by another, they must be paid and free to exit their employment within one year. This also applies to military service. Hudson will not tolerate slavery.

(h) Voters have the right to petition the Governor-General to make changes. The text of a valid petition shall not exceed 150 words. Its scope shall be a single subject of national interest. A minimum of 10,000 signatures is required before a petition will be reviewed.

(7) The Governor-General shall, on an annual basis in November, report publicly on the budget, progress on previously announced objectives, the state of the nation, and any amendments or clarifications deemed necessary to this Constitution. The annual address shall also respond to the 10 petitions with the most signatures.

(8) This Constitution does not require ratification, and shall stand until a new Constitution is established.

9

Interesting fact: Nearly 1700 tornados struck the U.S. in 2011, the most ever recorded up to then. This super-outbreak was followed by a 3-year lull. America experiences more tornados than anywhere else in the world, especially in the 'Tornado Alley' region of the Great Plains.

For our first attempt to watch the Constitutional Big Reveal, we settled into the conference room next to the public phone-charging room. Hotel amenities included a 60" wall display, Internet jack, and computer hookup. Tibbs, his sidekick Nguyen, Captain Johnson and his second Sergeant Becque, and the hotel manager Alex Wiehl and his wife, claimed seats at the table with us. Four other soldiers claimed to be our guards for the night, and stood at the back. We equipped ourselves with three pitchers of beer, two of ice water, and a mountain of fruit and cookies.

The wait screen for Project Reunion News featured a revolving cast of characters with helpful explanatory subtitles. Governor-General Sean Cullen, Hudson's new head of state, looking fit and dapper in a civilian suit. Army General Terrance Houston, new head of the armed services, the only black in the lineup. The numbered four successors listed in the Constitution. Lt. Colonel Ash Margolis, Resco of Manhattan and the Bronx, the heir apparent. Lt. Colonel Tony Nasser, top Resco for upstate New York, doomed to merciless teasing on the unveiling of his legal name Chandy. Colonel Pete Hoffman, top Resco for New Jersey in particular and ranking Resco overall – Emmett's boss. And last but not least, Lt. Colonel Emmett MacLaren, Resco of Brooklyn and Queens. I knew them all, except for Houston.

I nibbled a cookie thoughtfully. Back home in Brooklyn, I would have been tempted to take the train back to Totoket and Project Reunion News HQ, to be in on the big show. This was PR's biggest broadcast since the end of the United States in March, really. I'd even been on screen, albeit unplanned, for that one. I was on the broadcast with Major Cameron when he proposed this simple constitution, including the four-name succession scheme. But this time, I hadn't been involved at all. It felt very strange to be a simple spectator on this big night, out of the loop, for the news network I founded.

My partner and confidant Emmett was oblivious to my discontent, head stuck in Beaufort's reconstructed data again. At two minutes to broadcast, I poked him irritably. He scowled, then paused as he took in my expression. He closed the computer and said, "Look, Ma, the baby done grown up. PR News goes on without us."

"I wasn't ready for the baby to grow up," I groused.

"Uh-huh."

"Hello, hello! Amiri Baz here on behalf of Project Reunion News, speaking to you from my home in Poughkeepsie, New York. Excuse me! Hudson," he corrected himself, with a grin.

Amiri was PR's Pulitzer-prize winning top journalist, once a war correspondent, our most popular announcer. "Speaking with me tonight by video, is the man with the plan! Lieutenant Colonel Cam Cameron, Resco of Long Island, from *his* home in Riverhead. Author of the first new Constitution in the ex–United States."

("Cam got promoted?" I asked Emmett. "Effective today. Shh," Emmett replied.)

"Not the author!" Cam objected, with his signature boyish smile. Definitely better looking than the four Rescos on the new Hudson succession, Cam was tall blond and handsome, and a few years younger than Emmett. "Instigator maybe. Sean Cullen wrote the Constitution. I was in charge of vetting it, incorporating feedback, and so on."

"You're being too modest, Cam," Amiri chided. "On my show six months ago, on the end of the Calm Act, this was the Constitution you described."

"Parts of it," Cam conceded. "But on that show in March, you'll remember you had a voting widget. Asking people, do you support a simple constitution for your super-state? The choices were *Yes*, *Not Now*, and *Not That Simple*. In Hudson, the results were fairly evenly split between the three choices. And that was true for other super-states, too – New England, Ohio, and so forth. Now, there are several different ways you can interpret that. For instance, you could say that the winning sentiment was *Not*. But Governor Cullen decided that *Yes* plus *Not that Simple*, equaled majority support for a new Constitution. That wasn't quite so simple."

"Mm, yes," Amiri nodded. "This is definitely not that simple. Where to even begin? Oh! Before we get into that – last we spoke, I believe you were a Major, Colonel! Congratulations on your promotion!"

"Thank you, thank you," said Cam, beaming. "My husband was promoted as well, now Captain Dwayne Perard. He'll take over as Resco here in eastern Long Island, while I move west to organize the middle of the island."

("Wasn't that where we were going?" I pestered Emmett. "Shh," he repeated.)

"Wow!" said Amiri. "But you've split like this before in your marriage, yes?"

"Yes, we're not worried," agreed Cam. "It's pretty much the same way we worked in Connecticut. Just up one level in rank." He smiled. "But on to the new constitution! There's some radical stuff in there." He grinned impishly. "But, we've play-tested it here on Long Island in a number of communities. It's interesting. In a good way." They both laughed.

"Now when you say play-tested –" Amiri began.

I punched the pause button, as sirens split the air. Yes, in a city that received 200 tornados in a single year, tornado warning sirens were a top priority.

WIEHL AND HIS WIFE ROSE FIRST. "TEN MINUTES OUT. IF WE'RE lucky," he informed us with a practiced smile. Clearly he'd captained this ship through this kind of storm before. "Plenty of room in the basements for everyone." His wife was already out the door at a trot.

"Soldiers last into the basement," Emmett directed Captain Johnson. "Police the halls quickly. Let's bring this downstairs with us." He waved vaguely at our electronics. The IBIS agents set to that task. Tibbs jerked his head to indicate the room where we held the prisoner, and left to bring him downstairs. "Mr. Wiehl, do we have cameras and lights on the outside of the building?"

"Yes, security cams," Wiehl confirmed. "And designated tornado shelters turn on floodlights. My wife's taking care of that. Please understand, we take in all comers during a siren."

"As it should be," Emmett agreed. He looked to Captain Johnson, who nodded.

"Shall I handle the phone queue?" I volunteered. It was my

fault we had random civilians on-site. "And Indie," I added reluctantly. Brandy's news team might be camping in the parking lot.

"Please," Emmett agreed.

And we scrambled.

In the Internet cafe we offered for public phone charging, half the crowd had already split, apparently trying to reach home before the storm. Or before the tornados, rather – a thunderstorm was already lashing rain outside, winds strong. Likewise, about a third of the waiting queue was gone. I freed the remainder to plug in their devices pronto, then get below. Faces were grim, and prone to nervous ticks, especially when lightning flashed, or thunder grumbled. Like me, some froze at the flash, counting out seconds to the thunder. But no one panicked.

Mrs. Wiehl and the kitchen staff busily set out large A-frame easel 'Tornado Shelter' signs, with arrows, at the lobby entrance and blocking the elevators, directing traffic to the stairs instead. Orange cones marked the path, clear and easy to comprehend even at a dead run in a panic, and spaced to channel four people abreast.

Yes, the IndieNews van was still in the parking lot. And no, the idiots hadn't come to the door. I called Brandy's phone and told her to get her butt inside. Yes, snacks and the constitution broadcast would be provided. She was inclined to chat when she made it inside, hair plastered to her head sideways by dashing through the thunderstorm. I firmly shoved her down the orange cone road. "Talk to you downstairs!" I called over my shoulder.

Time was up for the Internet cafe, I decided. "You've plugged in enough – get downstairs! Now, *now,* people! Hustle!" I turned off the lights and shut the door, and yelled, "Phone banks clear!" to the lobby guards. Two of them moved to check that wing one final time, the other two remained at the hotel entrance. The hotel was getting a trickle of random passersby, looking much like drowned rats, apparently with no other haven close by.

I joined Emmett beside the shut-down elevators, where he

was plying his phone. A brace of guards flanked him. He finished writing off a text message, then looked up to smile at me, then glance around the lobby appraisingly. "Uh-huh," he said in approval. He set a hand on my back to direct us to the end of the short queue for the stairs that had bunched up momentarily.

"I love thunderstorms," I murmured, staring back out the lobby windows. The storm was coming on hard now, thunder only two alligators past the flash. Sheeting rain turned to a flowing pond across the floodlit parking lot, trees tossing from the waist. The hair on my arms stood up from the electricity, my whole body wired with adrenaline and excitement, both from the ions in the air and from my little bit of first-responder action. Emmett nodded agreement and kissed my temple.

The warning siren took on a different warble just as we reached the steps. Mrs. Wiehl stood station there, flanked by orange cones forbidding access to the upward stairs. I paused and directed a puzzled frown at her, pointing up to indicate the siren.

"Tornado spotted," she confirmed softly. "There's one more level, for touchdown."

"Nearby?" Emmett asked in shorthand.

Mrs. Wiehl shook her head slightly. "Sirens don't say that. Please, downstairs." Indeed, a late trio had already dodged around us and pelted down. We nodded thanks and stepped down briskly.

The main room downstairs provided neatly arrayed hard plastic chairs for several hundred, with plenty of aisles. Mr. Wiehl directed down here, insisting that guests not rearrange the chairs for now, and fielding other questions. The room already boasted a huge display in front of the seats, showing webcam feeds of the storm from above the front doors and behind the building. The IBIS agents were setting up to resume Cam's Hudson Constitution special. Further well-planned signage directed guests to lavatories, bedding supplies, and the remains of the dinner buffet.

Clearly the Wiehls had found a true vocation in hospitality and emergency management.

The front row of seats was reserved for our group, transplanted from the original conference table upstairs. Brandy, bless her pointy head, had managed to not only claim a block of the second row for Indie News, but picked her seat right behind mine and Emmett's.

"Oh, goody!" I said to her with a grin, taking a seat sideways in my chair. "Sorry, couldn't chat upstairs, Brandy. I was clearing the phone bank." Emmett snorted and took the seat beside me, hunched forward and plying his phone again.

"We got an extension cord to the van," Brandy told me sourly. "We were watching the constitution special on PR. Dee, had you read that before?"

I shook my head. "Just read it over dinner. The agreement was that PR got it three hours before the show, then posted it two hours before. The other governors and the Rescos got it earlier in the day, I think. As a courtesy." Emmett nodded beside me.

I turned to the camera man beside Brandy, and bestowed him an especial nose-wrinkling impish smile. "Blake! So good to see you again! Have you filmed all the arrangements down here? Interviewed Pittsburgh natives about the tornados? There's a buffet! Blankets! I would so love to mirror your footage on PR! So get your effing camera out of my face. I'm sitting in a chair. You mind?"

Brandy petulantly jerked her head sideways to send Blake Sondheim and another reporter off to do my bidding. Brandy wasn't budging. Nor did I expect her to. "What's he doing?" she asked, pointing to Emmett.

I held up a wait-a-minute finger, and draped myself over Emmett's shoulder, to kiss his ear and read his phone. At the moment, it showed satellite storm-tracking. He zoomed out for me to show that this mother storm front stretched from Lake Erie to our north, down to around Jackson Mississippi, with bands of thunderstorms and supercells a hundred miles wide. He zoomed back in to the immediate neighborhood.

"Two twisters sighted so far in greater Pittsburgh," Emmett told me quietly. His back was firmly planted against Brandy, and likely to stay that way until after the web special. "Serious punishments around here for false reports. Forecast is for thunderstorms to keep re-spawning here through midnight. Orange dots are supercells."

"Supercells?"

"Like a twister incubator," he clarified. "Strong bit of thunderstorm, spinning. I was reading up. Seems tornado alley has moved east. Sent texts from us to congratulate Cam and Dwayne. Said we were watching, with interruptions. Copied sundry." I took this to mean he'd let his peers back in Hudson know that he was running behind for the big show.

I gave him another kiss and turned back to Brandy. "He's studying up on tornados. Get comfy. We'll be here all evening. You heard about the two hundred tornado touchdowns in Pittsburgh last year, right? Forty so far this year?"

Brandy stared at me, stricken. "No. We hadn't heard that." I nodded pleasantly and looked around the room, drinking in the expressions of the natives. We'd collected maybe 75 new friends. Brandy took the hint, and looked around, too. "My God," she said thoughtfully.

"That's the big story here so far, I think," I suggested. "Check out the satellite view maps of this place. Scars all over the place. Big ones."

"Dee," Emmett warned me. I touched his arm to acknowledge his desire that I change the subject.

"What news on Beaufort?" Brandy asked, noting the by-play. "I hear you were investigating his death all day."

I frowned. "You know we can't discuss the investigation, Brandy. Give it up. If it makes you feel any better, I'm censored out, too."

Apparently that did brighten her evening. "Then let's talk constitution!" she suggested.

"Let's not," I sighed.

"C'mon, Dee!" Brandy said cheerfully. "That's some radical stuff in there!"

"Oops! Announcements," I whispered, in a triumphant stage whisper, as Wiehl stepped to the front of the room. Grateful, I firmly turned my back on Brandy, too.

"Welcome, everyone!" Andy Wiehl boomed out. "I think we're all in now, so let me do some introductions." He made Emmett and the IBIS agents stand and say hi, then Brandy and me. "For a treat tonight, we'll be watching a special on PR News – Ms. Baker's network. Today our neighbor New York–New Jersey, where these guests are from, has declared itself the new nation-state of Hudson!"

Wiehl paused for applause. There was none. He pressed on. "Hudson has a new constitution. This is a first for the ex-U.S., I guess they're calling it now. So we'll rewind the program and watch it from the top, yes?"

Emmett nodded. He also spun a finger to suggest Wiehl speed this up.

Four very wet new guests stepped in, wearing militia camou-flage. Wiehl froze ever so briefly. I trusted the front door guards had relieved them of their weapons. "Uh, perhaps I should repeat the introductions for our newcomers –"

"No need," Emmett directed wryly, clear as a bell. The militi-amen were probably detailed to keep an eye on the hotel, after all. Emmett crooked a finger to beckon one of our guards, and whispered instructions to her. She bore his message to the newcomers.

Wiehl tried to ignore all this, and continued, pointing, "Bath-rooms, a buffet of free food, blankets and towels. If your clothes are wet, please take a blanket. And then we'll settle in quietly to watch the show. I hope to get started in five minutes. And remember – a tornado shelter is a conflict-free zone. Anyone breaking truce, goes outside."

Drat, on the delay. To escape conversation, I switched seats to the audio-visual table the IBIS agents had set up, and rearranged the big display. I showed the new constitution to the left, stacked the webcam feeds to the right, and gave two thirds of the screen to the main event. Then advanced the constitution another paragraph. Gianetti already had the special queued up to run from the beginning. I found the introductions loop to run first. And settled back to advancing the text a few lines at a time, for people to read.

I glanced back at the audience to gauge reading speed. A sea of intent frowns, not least from our own Hudson army members. Most of them hadn't read this yet. I found a soldier who raised her hand in unconscious protest each time I scrolled too soon, and took my pace from her.

"Why's Colonel MacLaren last on that list?" was the first upset outburst. One of ours. That had been my first reaction, too, but I was biased. On the other hand, Emmett was by far the most famous name on the succession. That was probably a common reaction.

"Hold questions to the end," Emmett sang out. He was hunched over his phone catching up on email.

I filched a notebook from Gianetti and made a note of the question. I noticed that Brandy took my lead, and was taking far more notes. I wondered how long it had been since most of the Pittsburgh folk had watched anything on TV besides stormcams. It took more than five minutes to read through the constitution and view the intro sequence. Wiehl had to quiet a general angry murmur a couple times. But eventually we got through it.

"Dim the lights please?" I requested. "And now tonight's feature presentation." I froze as the third version of the siren started. Apparently tornado touch-down was signaled by a kind of strobing tone through the prior undulation and warble. I swallowed and glanced nervously at the webcams. I imagine everyone behind me did the same. No tornado visible to front or back of the hotel. But it wouldn't be visible, in the dark.

"You'd hear it, darlin'," Emmett murmured behind me, a hand reassuringly on my back. "Not just the siren."

"You've heard a tornado before?" I asked.

"Uh-huh." Of course. Emmett was born in Tornado Alley, as well as the Bible Belt.

I re-started the PR constitution special from the top.

10

Interesting fact: Meteorologists theorize that it was the New Dust Bowl that pushed Tornado Alley eastward. A pattern that used to span the entire Midwest compacted into half its previous width, from Mississippi to Georgia in the south, Chicago to Pittsburgh in the north. Warm Gulf moisture no longer visited the high plains, instead concentrating heavier rains and instability eastward. The supply of cool dry air off the Rockies and Canadian Shield remained reliable. The two air masses – wet and warm below, cool and dry aloft – move in perpendicular directions, providing the wind shear that set the updrafts and downdrafts within a thunderstorm to turning, to generate supercells and tornados.

"—We unleashed the constitution in a few communities on Long Island," Cam replied to Amiri, when we reached the point in the broadcast where we were interrupted upstairs. "We only have meshnet there. So we could keep the project under wraps, and really test it. In fact, we play-tested the new currency that way, too, back in May. That went well, so Hudson went ahead with the hudson dollar in June, in advance of the rest of the constitution. I have some video clips."

"Yes! We're looking forward to those," Amiri said. "But since the currency came up first. I've been using the hudson dollar – we all have – for a few months now. And we'd never suspected its depths!"

Cam laughed. "Like, 'we're naming the country Hudson.' Surprising how few people caught on to that one."

"Why Hudson?" Amiri took the bait.

"We wanted a name that included our totality," Cam replied. "Jersey, upstate, Long Island, the city. And considering the climate crisis that birthed our nation, we wanted to celebrate our natural landscape. We are blessed. I know, it's easy to feel hard done by. Especially in the Apple Zone. We've been through a lot. But in all the ex-U.S., Hudson is one of the jackpot winners for real estate. We tried a lot of names. Woods, Adirondacks, shores. But the Hudson River and its watershed touches all four of our regions. And no other resource is as crucial as fresh pure water."

"Pretty," Amiri agreed, nodding admiringly. "And a beautiful river."

"It is," Cam agreed. "We held our wedding on the Palisades," he offered lightly. "The cliffs overlooking Manhattan, across the river," he clarified for the non–New Yorkers in the audience.

"You went to college on the Hudson, too, didn't you?"

"I did!" Cam agreed. "Didn't choose West Point for the scenery. But it was a nice bonus. And didn't expire after two years, like our new currency does."

Cam's boyish charm was working wonders. I shook my head in admiration yet again at the man's grace under fire, and ability to make light going of hard topics.

Amiri laughed. "Nice segue. So Colonel. About that."

Cam grinned. "Our currency is for food book-keeping. We Rescos have been doing this ever since the borders closed. The full meal ticket. How do you trade milk for apples fairly. Taxing food production to support the military. Taxes for local projects. Paying for power, and Internet, trains and road repair. Project Reunion made the book-keeping even more complicated. Soup kitchens versus take-home handouts. And most of it depended on Cocos and Rescos. The systems didn't match, and the book-keeping was a nightmare.

"Now you get paid in hudson dollars. Eat where you want. No one is required to accept hudson dollars for anything but food. But, they do."

"But your money expires," Amiri prompted.

Cam nodded. "Food is perishable. The money reverts to the government, for liquidation. In the Apple Zone, most people are paid laborers, in hudson dollars about to expire. And the real food that the hudson dollars represent, is stored food nearing expiration. And that's distributed. Fed to the troops. And made available for paid laborers to buy."

"And they're taxed on this money?" Amiri asked.

Cam shook his head. "No, you can only pay taxes with food. When food is sold into the government food distribution system, or someone pays taxes, a hudson dollar is born."

"So someone who receives wages, pays no taxes?" Amiri confirmed.

"That's right," Cam said. "No income taxes. No sales taxes or property taxes. Just food production. The hudson dollar is book-keeping on our food supply. One of the most interesting things about this, to me, is that there is no amassing of wealth, with hudson dollars. I mean, what good does it do you, to have ten times, or a thousand times as much food as you can eat? And it's all going to expire and revert to the government. The *only* thing extra hudson dollars are good for, is to exchange with someone else.

"You know what? The highest paid people in all of Hudson? Are the Rescos. As a major – most Rescos hold the rank of major – I got paid fifty full meal tickets a year. Now, I could use that to pay servants, of course, or buy things. But the real purpose is seed money. That's a base Resco budget for starting companies, or paying for skills, or odd-ball projects. For example, Project Reunion. That really started with Emmett MacLaren using his own salary to set up the quarantine on Long Island, and fund Amenac. He pays your salary, too, Amiri, or used to. Our power grid started from Tony Nasser hiring a bunch of engineers upstate. I bootstrapped the University of Connecticut back to life."

Amiri asked, "So people apply to Rescos for money?"

Cam laughed. "No. Usually, the way it works is that I have a private wish list. Problems I want to solve, but haven't figured out how yet. Might not even be my problem. Maybe Pete Hoffman or Ash Margolis has a problem. Then someone wanders along with an idea that might work. And I ask her what she needs. Give her a little. If she does well with that, give her some more. Angel investing, basically."

"But with no profit motive," Amiri pointed out. "There's no profit anywhere with hudson dollars, is there?"

Cam shrugged. "Social profit. Social entrepreneurship. I mean, I'm trying to accomplish something, right? I need to keep me and mine fed, sure. But beyond that, there are changes I want to see in the world. Problems I want to solve. Things I enjoy doing. I honestly don't need to spend any of my salary on me. My needs are met. But I have a job to do, which is to raise the standard of living of the communities entrusted to me. The only way that can happen is a balance of public investment on infrastructure, and private industry. My salary is for kick-starting those."

"But this isn't *money* in any sense we've seen it before," said Amiri.

"Nope," Cam agreed. "And later, there may be a place for that. Probably is already. I'm sure plenty of people hoard gold. If you want to join the gold-bartering club, go right ahead. But everyone needs to eat. And for now, that's what the Hudson government needs from money. A tool in our food distribution system."

Amiri shook his head. "And that's only the first radical thing in this constitution."

"In practice, testing this out?" Cam offered. "Hudson dollars were an instant win. The most controversial part of the constitution is the voting and citizenship. In any democracy, you've got to answer the question of who gets to vote. At the dawn of the United States, it was basically only white property owners. Then it slowly expanded. In this constitution, we have a very different kind of democracy than the ex-U.S. Usually direct democracy, at the local level. No representatives. May or may not have locally elected officials – that's up to the communities. Most local leaders in Hudson, at this time, are not elected."

"They're not?" Amiri honestly looked surprised.

"No," Cam confirmed. "Most are Cocos – community coordinators. Chosen by a Resco to safeguard an area." He waved his hand. "This isn't new, Amiri. What's new is a national standard for what qualifies people to vote in local affairs. We've basically said, hey, you're here, and you can't go anywhere else. So you're a Hudson citizen. Right? Doesn't matter where you were born. But, it does matter, in a direct democracy, that you can communicate. In English. We have a huge immigrant population in Hudson, especially in the Apple Zone. New York City was around forty percent immigrant."

"That high!" said Amiri. "Of course, I'm an immigrant."

Cam laughed. "So am I. I was born in New England. Though I did graduate college in Hudson."

"And got married," Amiri said with a smile.

"Yes. My husband is a native Hudson, from Hoboken," Cam played back. "Anyway, to have a direct democracy, you need to understand each other. In English. And have rational discussions. If you're voting on taxes to fund public projects, you've got to be numerate enough to understand the math. Can we watch a clip now? Of the voter testing."

"Alright," Amiri agreed. "These are actual Hudson citizens, on Long Island, performing a voter qualification test."

A BLACK YOUTH SAT DOWN AT A SHADED PICNIC TABLE, ACROSS FROM a middle-aged black man, the test-giver judging by the accoutrements before him – paperwork, pencils, calculator, tablet and phone. They were on a summer beach, a volleyball game in progress beyond the picnic pavilion. The tester wore T-shirt and loose shorts. The prospective voter was huddled in a hoodie. Both were still lean from the starving year, but seemed healthy now.

"Aren't you hot in there?" the tester said. "You need to show your face. I'm Terry Grimes. You're Dewar Booker?"

Reluctantly, the younger man emerged from his hood. "Yeah. Book." He swallowed. "I never finished high school or nothing. Got jail time."

"That's fine," Terry assured him. "You can read and write, though, can't you?"

"Yeah, I guess," Book replied. "Kinda stupid. Everybody says so."

"Enjoying the beach today?"

"Yeah, me and my guys have the day off. I work on the railroad."

"Perfect," Terry said, and made a notation on his sheet. "Congratulations, Book, that's a perfect ten out of ten on the first segment of the test." He smiled encouragingly. "You speak English fine, and you're polite. You need 80 points out of 100 on this test to pass. So far you're doing great."

"Oh, yeah?" Book said, surprised. Clearly he was unaccustomed to perfect scores.

"Next, I need you to read this," Terry said, and handed him a laminated sheet. "Sections 6 a and b. Out loud, please."

Terry haltingly read the part of the constitution that defined a citizen and how a citizen became a voter. "Huh!" he said at the end. "What's em-migration and im-migration mean? Or am I supposed to know that?"

Terry shook his head. "Ask anything you want. Emigration means leaving the country, immigration means coming in. Any other questions?" Book shook his head. Terry referred to his tablet to read the test. "OK, imagine someone has a history of armed robbery, served time for drug dealing. He was born in Somalia and entered the U.S. illegally five years ago. Now serving time in Ronkonkoma. Is he a citizen of Hudson?"

"Uh, yeah," said Book, eyebrows raised. After a moment's reflection, he added, "If he's over sixteen."

"Another perfect score," Terry encouraged him, with a smile. "Now read section 6h. You don't have to read it aloud." After Book finished, looking bemused, Terry handed him paper and a pencil. "You have to write a petition to the Hudson government. I can give you a suggestion if you want, but the prompts are kinda weird. Like that last question. It's better if you use your own idea."

"Uh... With the schools closed, how are kids gonna learn to pass the test?" Book asked. Terry nodded and pointed to the paper. Laboriously, Book wrote out his idea. He pushed his paper across to Terry and turtled down into his neck again.

Hudson shud make all kids get skool so they can pass the test and vote.

Terry read it, and circled the misspellings. "That's one point off for spelling. When you write a petition, I recommend you get a few people to read it over and make suggestions. But this is less than 150 words, deals with one topic, makes sense, and it's clearly of national interest. Congratulations, Book, you've aced the

English and literacy sections of the test. Now we move on to numeracy."

"That means math, right?" Book asked with grave misgivings.

"That's right. First question. You grow 100 cabbages. The tax rate is 25% to Hudson, and 11% to local taxes. How many cabbages do you owe in taxes?" Terry pushed the paper and pencil back to him.

Fearful of math, Book asked Terry to repeat the question a couple times, and took notes with great trepidation. He accepted the calculator. Then he sat up and said, "Oh! Thirty-six."

"Thirty-six what," Terry prompted mechanically.

"I pay thirty-six cabbages in taxes?" Book asked.

"Perfect 20 out of 20 points," Terry told him. "Now, the last question is much harder. Take your time. Say we have an opportunity to build chicken coops to produce eggs. We have two proposals. Proposal A costs 6% additional taxes for one year, pays 4 months wages for building chicken coops, and then gives jobs for 8 people. The chicken coops produce 1500 eggs a day for the community."

"That's a good deal!" Book exclaimed.

Terry nodded. "Proposal B provides the same number of chickens and jobs, but costs 2% additional taxes over two years. We'd get half the chickens each year, and half the jobs each year."

"So the second proposal costs less," Book said slowly. "Don't matter. We need the jobs, and get more eggs for a year. I vote for proposal A."

"Me, too," Terry agreed. "You understood the question, the costs and benefits to both proposals, and gave a good argument for your choice. Perfect score." He stood and held out his hand to shake. "Congratulations, Book, you're now a voter." Book rose and bashfully shook hands, with a slow grin.

"And Book," Terry added, "you got 99 out of 100 points on this test. And that last question was confusing as hell. Don't let anybody tell you you're stupid. Hope to see you Tuesday!"

"Tuesday?"

"Town green, six o'clock, the democratic town meeting."

Dewar Booker left the picnic table pavilion and caught up with his friends, three other young men huddled in hoodies against the fine summer day and ocean breeze, looking furtive. "Passed the test," he told them, showing off the 'I'm a Voter!' sticker on his sweatshirt.

"You? Yeah, right, you're a fucking idiot," one replied.

"I'm not stupid," Book denied. "Aced the test. Gonna go vote Tuesday. Town meeting."

"What do you want to do that for?" another demanded.

"Make the town better, fool," Book said. "We live here too. What, you got something better to do Tuesday?" He scuffed away in the sand.

"THAT'S A TOUGH TEST!" AMIRI EXCLAIMED. "I'M IMPRESSED WITH that kid. Dewar Booker?"

"Yeah," Cam said, eyes alight, nodding. "I attended his first town meeting that Tuesday, back in July. Lot of voters were impressed with him. It was a great meeting. Everyone was polite. You could understand what they said. Had great discussions, made good decisions. I asked them at the end, whether they thought the testing was worth it. Over ninety percent agreed, using the voter test to pick good voters made the meeting much better. Again, like with the currency, I offered to reverse it. No way. They wouldn't go back.

"And Book? You could see, this is not a guy who was used to being treated with respect. But at the meeting, he just wouldn't give up on that chicken coop idea. My husband Dwayne worked with him and a few others. It's been a few months. They've got their coop now." Cam laughed. "Only 200 chickens so far. But it matters."

"It matters a lot," Amiri agreed. "Especially on Long Island. Now, these are all public service spots, right? Viewers can see them all on HudsonVoter.gov." The web address scrolled across the bottom of the display. "Seemed like one for every color!"

Cam shrugged. "Yeah. We felt it was important, for everyone to see *themselves* as a voter, you know? Or someone who just speaks to you. My favorite was this young Pakistani woman in hajib. Her family's gone through hell, you know? Her husband worked as a translator for the army. Our lives depended on guys like him, during my tours in the sandbox. They had to immigrate to save their lives. Modest, shy, devout Muslim woman, three little kids. Fits the stereotype to a T. Shunned by her neighbors – you know how Islamophobic Americans can be.

"But she gets to the town meeting, a newly qualified voter. Speaks flawless English, British accent. And she asks her neighbors for help with day care. Because she wants to pursue her career. Turns out she's a trained nurse-midwife. Specialty in women's reproductive health and family medicine. Yeah, who needs that, right? Only *half of Long Island*. But no one knew. No one talked to her. Until she was vetted as a Hudson voter. Now she's out of the house, and women have health care again in the town. For her, for Dewar Booker – their voter qualification was like an entry visa into the Hudson mainstream."

"That's great," Amiri agreed. "Now, how many people pass this test?"

Cam admitted, "Only about forty percent. Sad, right? Governor Cullen and I went back and forth on this. Should we make the test easier? Should we require a review class first? But he's adamant that we set the bar high. That this is the minimum necessary level of skills to make good decisions. People may have to work for it. And then being a Hudson voter can really mean something. And it does. In our test communities, that's something you can say on a job interview. I'm a qualified voter, not just another day laborer. Employers even demand it, for a supervisory position. Voters land jobs through their contacts from the town meeting, too."

"And people can try again, if they fail the test?" Amiri asked.

"Absolutely," Cam agreed, subdued. "But most don't. The testers work with them, show them what they got wrong, offer classes, encourage them." Cam shrugged. "You have to want it."

"And most Americans didn't vote before," Amiri led.

"No," Cam agreed. "Mid-term elections, you'd rarely see more than forty percent of eligible voters vote. More for a presidential election. Less for local elections."

"Fascinating. This will be a very interesting experiment in democracy," Amiri said. "And I'd like to point out to our viewers, there are already petitions up on the HudsonVoter.gov website. Lots of variations on schooling, so kids can pass the test!"

Cam nodded affably. Back in Connecticut, he was the only Resco who kept the primary schools open through the worst of the first year. But he let it pass for now.

"But in the interest of time, we need to move on," Amiri continued. "Instead of freedom of religion, we have licensed religion! What does that mean?"

The room behind us growled in anger.

"*SHUT UP!*" Sergeant Becque yelled helpfully.

11

Interesting fact: Before the Calm Act, 76% of the U.S. considered themselves Christian, about 1.2% Jewish (religious or not), and 0.9% Muslim, with most of the rest non-affiliated. Protestants made up 47%, and Catholics 25%. The hundreds of evangelical denominations, white and black, combined to 33% of Americans.

I had to rewind and restart Cam's explanation of licensed religion several times. Five Pittsburgh locals needed to be removed to the buffet room and forbidden to return. Sergeant Becque spent most of this segment of the show standing, the better to glare at our visitors. Emmett and Captain Johnson did that officer thing, where they look away blandly while the sergeant does the swearing. I still found that very odd to watch. The continued throbbing, warbling ululation of the tornado sirens tipped the scene well into the surreal. I could feel that siren thrumming in my bones.

Meanwhile, Cam explained that apocalyptic religions and blamers and haters were behind much of the unrest the martial law government had to put down the past two years. These new religions, and new twists on old religions, were understandably popular. People were scared, stressed, hurting, unemployed, grieving. Their worlds were turned upside down. Unfortunately, it was also easy to whip such people into a mob mentality. Good people were being led to do bad things.

At the same time, religious leaders and their congregations were stepping up everywhere to provide public services that didn't otherwise exist anymore. Soup kitchens. Day care. Schooling. Counseling. Even hospice care and first aid. Our communities depended on them. They were granted an extraordinary level of trust. And most of them deserved it.

The Hudson folk in the audience were in the same boat I was. We saw both of these faces of religion every day in the broken shards of New York City. Hellfire and brimstone street corner hawkers accosted us to tell us we would burn for all eternity. I had armed guards to shove them off. But every so often, we'd turn a street corner to find a clump of the loonies with a poor woman or teenager backed into a wall, terrorizing a innocent passerby. My soldiers left the guilty bloody on the sidewalk. But the militia couldn't keep up with them. Street-corner proselytizers infested the city like cockroaches.

Yet nine out of ten apples – our slang for the survivors in the 'Apple Core', New York City – probably ate a meal every day at a church or synagogue or mosque. Most apples had serious emotional scars from their starving year, from the survivor guilt of watching 9 out of 10 of their neighbors die. Of the 50 official communities of the new Apple, 6 even had a religious rather than secular leader. Most of the others had serious religious backing.

Religion mattered in our new world order. It mattered a lot.

"So seeking converts is forbidden?" Amiri prompted.

"Absolutely forbidden," Cam confirmed. "For example, a soup kitchen in a church. You can have religious posters on the walls. You can have a sign inviting people to come back on Sunday. Or

Friday, or Saturday. But you cannot – absolutely *cannot* – disrupt people's breakfast by preaching at them. You may attract, by being a good example. You can tell people *who ask* about your church. You can even wear a button saying, 'Ask me about God!' But you cannot accost people. You cannot hold rallies to seek converts. You cannot try to persuade people to your faith except during regularly scheduled services. They have to come because they want to. You're not even allowed to hand out flyers."

"I see," said Amiri. "You and I have spent a lot of time in the Apple Zone, of course. And I understand this completely. I mean, we see the abuses every day there. I wonder if the people outside the Apple are as familiar with the problem. If they won't be more offended at the idea of licensing and... Well, repressing freedom of speech regarding religion, really."

Cam nodded. "Maybe. But, please understand. If you're lucky enough to live in a community where these abuses aren't happening? You aren't negatively affected by the law. On Long Island, I expected a lot of push back. What I found instead was that the religious leaders were delighted. Ah, I can't really vouch for the public. I'm a pretty heavy-handed Resco that way."

Amiri laughed. "You never allowed proselytizing in the first place."

"No," Cam said categorically. "Forbade it immediately. Forced a few pushy new religions underground. Where they stayed. And shrank. Because they're not allowed to seek converts." Cam didn't pretend to apologize.

Cam went on to explain that the licensing roll-out would take time. Clergy could continue their duties until after the December holidays, but by January needed to complete the licensing requirements.

The requirements were pretty steep. They needed 20 character witnesses, vouching for 4 different skill sets. Full disclosure of the tenets of their creed. And they needed to attend a multiday interfaith training seminar, and be sanctioned by their instructors. Continuing education required them to attend shorter seminars annually.

The ban on proselytizing, however, was effective immediately. Street-corner preachers and soup kitchen evangelists were simply a public nuisance, like peeing on a wall or failing to pick up after your dog.

THE TORNADO SIRENS CEASED EARLIER THAN EXPECTED, AND I paused the program. We stood and stretched. Amazing how a noise like that seeps into your neck muscles. I'd been bracing myself against its onslaught for hours, pushing back at sound.

Most of the local audience remained seated. "Can we stay and watch the rest?" a woman called out.

"And ask questions after?" one of the late-arriving militia added.

"Is PA getting a constitution, too?" asked a third. Alas, this unleashed the questioning reflex, and lots of hands went up.

Brandy of IndieNews didn't raise her hand. "Colonel MacLaren! Why aren't you at the top of the list of successors?"

"*SHUT UP!*" yelled Sergeant Becque, at a slight glance from Emmett.

Emmett waited until every last whispering voice fell silent. "Mr. Wiehl?" he asked mildly.

"I'd like to see the end," Wiehl confessed. "I think the hotel staff would appreciate it, too." Our soldiers nodded their heads emphatically. They could watch it on their phones, but that wasn't nearly as good as the big screen. And most of them were dying to hear Emmett answer Brandy's question. He's got ardent supporters, the Hero of Project Reunion.

"Alright," Emmett relented. "I need a 10-minute break, then

we'll resume." He wanted to make sure our walk-in militia guests stayed to talk with him later.

In the meantime, he handed me his phone, which had been chirping mercilessly. The entire senior Resco list of Hudson was on the message queue, but nothing red-flagged. I didn't read the messages, just wrote back to all of them.

> Watching Cam with 50+ Pitts in tornado shelter. Running late. Deeb.

> PS Thought center LI was ours. Thief! Deeb.

That second text was intended only for Cam. I realized a moment too late that I'd copied all of them again – including Governor Cullen. The same list I'd used for the first text. Drat.

> PPS Oops. PS was joke to Cam. Haha. Congrats C&D! Deeb shuts up now.

I handed the phone back to Emmett when he returned, and showed him the interchange. "Sorry..." He blew out an unhappy sigh, but didn't say anything.

The rest of the constitution special went fairly quickly. They didn't have details yet on two sticky bits – how weapons would be collected, and how troops would be released to resign from the military. Up to 10% were free to resign effective immediately, provided they had a community ready to accept them. The hangup was that the border garrisons belonged to no community except the army. So where would they go? And what would they walk away with? Their contracts promised major veteran's benefits. But the government which made those promises was defunct.

("PR could do another adoption database for retiring military," I suggested to Emmett. He nodded, seemingly with reservations.)

Apparently our Governor Sean Cullen and Cam both felt strongly about the anti-slavery clause. At the outset of the Calm Act, all then-serving U.S. forces lost the right to resign. A number of conscientious objectors, who refused to police the borders against fellow Americans, were still serving time in military prisons. Localities and employers had also started offering indenture and sharecropper deals, such as contracts for farmland in exchange for 7 years service, or job training in exchange for long terms. New England had proposed a price for a degree at UConn, that students be required to serve New England for 6 years. This trend reminded Sean and Cam of the migrant slave laborers they'd seen in the Middle East, bereft of their passports and stuck for years in dire working conditions and labor camps, trying to pay off the cost of their airfare. They wanted to set a standard where citizens might not have much, but at least they had the freedom to walk away from a bad deal.

Cam's original proposal back in March, when the U.S. was disbanded, had been a simple constitution that declared us a country, enough to be getting on with. It skipped any bill of rights, which was the major objection to it. As Amiri pointed out, this new constitution went far beyond the original concept, and granted us a rather quirky set of liberties. As Cam pointed out, quirky was better than none, and we had the means to petition for more.

"This constitution doesn't require ratification," Amiri prompted, reaching the end of the document.

Cam shrugged cordially. "We considered weasel wordings. But the truth is, we are under martial law. We sought direct citizen input, by testing the new rules in sample communities. We decided on this document, and the rules by which this document can evolve. And in the end, it really doesn't require ratification."

Governor Cullen joined the broadcast briefly to say some encouraging words, and thank Cam for all his hard work. Yes,

Cullen had shared the constitution earlier in the day with the other ex-U.S. military governors. They said nice things for public consumption. Sean Cullen didn't divulge any hints as to their private concerns. He received congratulations from far afield, including super-states we didn't often hear from, including Florida, Arkansas–Louisiana–Mississippi, and Wisconsin–Illinois.

Canada had already formally recognized Hudson as a nation, our most powerful surviving nation neighbor left in North America. Also chiming in were Bermuda, Puerto Rico, Cuba, and – surprise! – the Naval Republic of Hawaii. Apparently Hawaii had voted itself a nation a couple weeks ago, but was still drafting the announcements and constitution. Owned lock, stock, and barrel by the ex-U.S. Navy, I wasn't sure who voted in Hawaii. Cullen didn't elaborate. He didn't mention Mexico, either.

Amiri asked when the governor foresaw Hudson getting the right to vote at the national level. Cullen said it really depended on the weather. But for at least the next five years, he anticipated Hudson would need to focus on its primary goal of uplifting all communities to level 5 and above. And communities already above that level should seek to improve locally.

"The first annual address will be this November," Cullen said. "I encourage Hudsons to earn the right to vote as soon as possible, and make your voice heard via petitions. This constitution is intended to be an evolving document."

He signed off, and Amiri and Cam discussed how that was possible, to implement widespread voter qualification so quickly. Cam explained that Long Island, with several months' experience in voter vetting, was offering testers and tester trainers as a work for hire, at reasonable rates. Also do-it-yourself packages for less complex communities, and how-to-test seminars in cities across Hudson. The Apple Core had already contracted for 100 Long Island voter registration trainers.

(I raised an eyebrow at Emmett. He nodded.)

Long Island's clergy were also happily leading the first religious licensing seminar, already waiting-list-only, to be held in Port Chester. The HudsonVoter.gov website provided details of all this and more. Yada yada. Special ends.

Emmett blew out a slow breath beside me. Reluctantly, he stood up and faced the crowd, as I set the big screen to show the website.

∽

"HI, GUYS," EMMETT SAID HOPEFULLY TO OUR SMALL CROWD. "Let's have just a few questions, OK? It's past my bedtime. And I have a whole lot of email to answer tonight before I sleep."

Indeed. Emmett's phone had gone berserk with the chirping ever since my faux pas. I suspected his Resco peers and coworkers in Hudson were annoyed, to say the least.

The room erupted in babble. *"SHUT THE FUCK UP!"* Sergeant Becque reminded them.

Emmett waited for pin-drop level silence, then invited mildly, "Raise hands, please, and I will call on you. Yes, Ma'am?"

This was one of the random Pittsburgh passersby who took tornado shelter with us, a thin but athletic twenty-something in bluejeans. Emmett was likely as curious about her as she was of him. She said, "Your name was on the list. On that constitution. Who are you, please? And why are you here?"

Emmett blinked. "That's a large question." With considerable back-and-forth, it became evident that most of the Pittsburghers had never heard of Project Reunion and the relief of New York City. Never heard of Emmett MacLaren. Were a bit hazy on what a Resco was. They'd heard of Dane Beaufort, but most seemed shocked to hear that he was dead.

The militia men standing in back were not surprised, however. They looked grim, and intently studied their boot toes.

"My IBIS associates are here to investigate the death,"

Emmett wrapped up. "And I've been asked to make recommendations about where we go from here."

One of the militia stepped forward and raised his hand aggressively. Emmett pointed at him to go ahead. "What are the possibilities? About what happens next?"

"I'm not sure," Emmett replied guardedly. "General Taibbi has not given me parameters yet."

"Who?"

Emmett stared at him, discouraged. "Air Force General Seth Taibbi? The military governor of Pennsylvania?"

"What happened to Tolliver?" the militia man returned, equally puzzled.

"Wow," Emmett returned. "General Tolliver was executed during a military coup in January. Eight months ago? That ended the war between Penn and New York–New Jersey. Now Hudson. Were you people aware that Pennsylvania attacked New York last Thanksgiving? That we were at war? Until the January coup."

Apparently not.

"Outstanding," Emmett breathed. "OK, it's late. Let's stick to current events. Sergeant?"

If he was trying to avoid this question by not calling on Brandy, it didn't work. Sergeant Becque asked what was foremost on all our guards' minds. "Why aren't you first on that succession list, Colonel?"

Emmett nodded. "I appreciate your loyalty, gang. Really. It means a lot to me. But please understand – I think I belong at the bottom of that list. Obviously, that list is the senior Rescos of Hudson. That makes sense. We're the intermediaries between the national and local levels. We're the face of the martial law government. I am the youngest, newest, least experienced, lowest ranked of those lead Rescos. They're native Hudsons. I'm a hillbilly from the Ozarks. When I grow up, I want to be like those guys. OK? Please don't be offended for me. Because I'm not offended. I'd be honored to serve under any of them. And – I already do. Next?" He sighed, and said, "Brandy."

"Colonel, what have you learned so far about Beaufort's death?"

"Our topic tonight is the constitution broadcast," Emmett replied. "I will not discuss the investigation. Yes, Mrs. Wiehl?"

"Could we have that here? Free universal Internet access? Voter testing and licensed religion?" A hiss like a swarm of wasps arose from the Pittsburghers. Sergeant Becque advanced menacingly and they shut up.

"I'm new here," Emmett replied hesitantly. "I don't know enough about Pittsburgh yet to form an opinion. Yes, Penny?" It was our guards' turn again.

"How do I resign from the army?" she asked. "I don't want to leave you, sir. But my tour was up two years ago." Becque advanced on his own troops this time, as the room erupted in 'me, too!'

Emmett shrugged. "We'll look into it when we get back to Brooklyn. Unless, are any of you from western Penn?" Apparently not. "Well, I can't release you here, then. If you want to head west from here, talk to Captain Johnson. Hi, Brandy." Brandy's hand only lowered while she was speaking.

"Are you in favor of this constitution, Colonel?" she asked. "Specifically, do you support limiting freedom of speech and religion? And how can you, when you're one of the principals behind Amenac and PR News?"

Emmett smiled crookedly. "Hudson's governor and constitution have my complete support. Next?"

"But sir!" Brandy demanded.

"Asked and answered, Brandy," Emmett said firmly. "People who ask the same question twice get to leave the building. Yes, sir?" He selected an elderly Pittsburgher in the back.

"Can we keep the meshnet?" he asked. "When you go?"

Emmett looked to me. I nodded. "Yes. That can be arranged," Emmett replied. He pointed to another Pittsburgher.

"Are you and that woman living in sin?" the man asked. "Like the preachers say?"

Emmett's mouth hung open briefly. He closed it, scowling. "Sir, my private life is not your concern. However – as all of Hudson knows – Ms. Baker and I are partners in a committed relationship. Eventually, I expect we'll get married." Then he looked like he was kicking himself internally for reacting to that one. He could have let it go with 'none of your business.' "Alright, gang, now I'm tired and cranky. Last two questions. Yes, Brandy."

"Why is PR News being allowed access to your investigation, and not IndieNews?" she demanded.

"Ms. Baker is helping with my investigation. At the request of the military governors," Emmett replied. "Both of us are management with PR News. That's true. But that's not what we're here for."

"But you'll share announcements?" Brandy followed up.

Emmett wobbled his head so-so. "We'll share military censors, that's for sure. Last question! Sir. In the back."

"Any chance you'll stay on as our new Resco, Colonel?" another militia member asked. His buddies pursed their lips at him. "You've given us better communications than we've had in two years. Tornado touchdowns are already marked on the meshnet map. You've only been here one day."

"Currently, I intend to return to Hudson," Emmett replied. "That could change. But I'm glad you like the meshnet. Ms. Baker set that up. My partner does great work." He smiled at me tiredly, and gestured for me to rise. I stood briefly, smiled and waved.

"Good night, everyone," Emmett said. "Thank you for sharing your beautiful tornado shelter with us. Beats heck out of my momma's basement. Her spiders bite." He smiled and waved to the crowd in general, then pointed at the militia men in back and the buffet room. He headed off to rendezvous and talk to them, Tibbs and the IBIS agents trailing.

Emmett left me his phone again. I contemplated it sadly. Lots more texts, still no red flags. I wrote again to the rulers of the shiny new nation of Hudson, trying not to feel totally out of my league.

Q&A just ended. Six tornados and done. EM meeting random militia. Deeb.

12

Interesting fact: Before the Calm Act, the least religious part of America was New England, where as few as 33% of adults considered themselves 'highly religious.' In contrast, West Virginia, which wrapped Pittsburgh to south and west, was 69% highly religious. Alabama and Mississippi tied for most religious, at 77%.

"Dee, did you know about this religious crackdown in New York?" Dave demanded shrilly over the phone.

Dave wasn't really the head of the Ameni hacker group that powered Amenac and PR News. But he gave a fair impression of it, and ran our headquarters in Connecticut. Ameni refused to tell anyone who their real head was. Dave was certainly their public spokesman.

I blearily noted that I must have fallen asleep before Emmett made it back to our room last night, and he was already gone again. Dave's call woke me at 7 a.m. Emmett's a morning person. I'm not.

"Hudson," I corrected Dave vaguely. "New nation of Hudson." And as an afterthought, I answered his question. "Saw new constitution first time last night. After you, probably."

"They're rounding people up in the streets in the Apple Core and throwing them in jail!"

"You woke me up, Dave," I mumbled. "Who's doing what now?"

"The militia in the Apple Core is rounding up street corner preachers, and soup kitchen preachers, and throwing them in jail!" Dave continued, clearly incensed. And that was saying something, as I groggily realized. Dave was the mild-mannered unflappable Amenoid. "They're saying a second offense gets 7 days in jail at half rations. Third is 30 days in a work camp! Dee, these are pogroms!"

"I think you have to kill people to qualify as a 'pogrom,'" I disagreed. "'Persecution' maybe." I yawned hugely and forced myself to climb out of the warm covers and face the day.

"Your *censor* Mora won't let us publish!" Dave complained.

That made me stop and blink. Lt. Colonel Carlos Mora was the military censor for Project Reunion News. This normally paid us huge dividends. If Mora OK'd something, we skated past every other censor in the ex-U.S. In my experience, if Mora forbade something, he had an awfully good reason. It still felt like an oxymoron – probably always would – but Carlos Mora was a *good* military censor. And I firmly believed he was on our side.

"What do you want me to do, Dave?" I asked. "I'm in Pittsburgh on Resco business."

"Just call Mora for me, alright?" Dave requested.

"OK."

"I bet Emmett knows what's going on," Dave grumbled.

"Emmett hasn't told me anything," I insisted. "He wouldn't. You know that. Look, I'll call you back after I talk to Carlos."

I washed my face and got dressed before tackling Carlos, dawdling a bit due to deep misgivings. Dave was right. I couldn't imagine they carried out this big preacher roundup on the streets of the city without Emmett knowing it was coming. But Emmett had every right to not tell me about plans for a martial law operation.

"Hi, Carlos," I greeted him. "Sorry to call you so early. But the Amenoids are in an uproar. So, why can't PR News report on the religious loon roundup in the Apple?"

"It's all over Amenac," Carlos said. "They're not completely gagged. But Governor Cullen asked for a 7 day grace period on PR and IndieNews. Whichever fails to honor his request first, loses the right to publish in Hudson. Just on the religion crackdown. Though he'll probably ask for another moment of silence when they crack down on civilian weapons. That's gonna get ugly, too. Uglier."

"And you're OK with this?" I asked.

"Yeah. Look, Dee, sometimes martial law is gonna look like martial law," Carlos reasoned. "Probably won't make you feel any better, but I inquired with General Link." Ivan Link was Hudson Governor Sean Cullen's counterpart in New England, and the top of Carlos' food chain. "Link told me absolutely, positively, to honor Cullen's request. And for what it's worth, I agree with what Hudson's trying to do."

"You do?" I asked. "Does Emmett?"

"You have a problem with Emmett, take it up with Emmett," Carlos replied primly. "But yeah. Cam explained it last night. Churches are being entrusted with government functions, providing social services and food distribution. They need to be trustworthy. New rules. So we give Hudson 7 days for the dust to settle, and then talk about it."

"I can see both sides," I said.

"Me too," Carlos agreed.

"But we don't have much choice," I concluded.

"Nope," Carlos agreed. "Dee, I suspect something happened that Hudson will never allow to go public. Could be that something was in Pittsburgh. More likely, a bad pattern, with something big in upstate New York – west Hudson, whatever. But we'll never know. Hudson's Rescos still need to do their job, though. If religious movements are out of control, they need to wrest control back. That's that."

"I'm guessing you already told Dave this?"

"He didn't like it," Carlos confirmed.

Experimentally, I said, "I wonder if it's an accident that they rushed to air the big constitution reveal special report when Emmett was out of town."

"Emmett and you," Carlos suggested. "No. Not with Dane Beaufort's death, either. No coincidence."

I sighed. "OK. Thanks for being so forthcoming, Carlos."

"I didn't say anything," Carlos denied. "Be careful out there, Dee."

I called Dave back. And no. He didn't like it. I argued that PR News supporting the martial law governments was our brand, our niche. At that, he hung up on me, which was probably just as well. I needed to have a chat with my own conscience, not Dave's.

The thing is, I detested the street-corner prophets. Life was hard enough in the Apple Core these days without hellfire and brimstone over cornflakes. There were ghastly hate-mongers, blaming loose women and shameless homosexuals for climate change. And people were listening. Defenseless women and gay youths were beaten, even stoned to death in the streets, because some holier-than-thou fanatic blamed climate change and the Calm Act on them.

But PR News didn't report that, either, to any great extent. Nor the mass killings, when some loon went on a rampage with an automatic rifle. We kept those events quiet at the Rescos' and martial law governors' request. They argued that this sort of hysteria was contagious. The militia needed to know about it, and act, and they did. But the knowledge would not help ordinary citizens, just make them anxious, which helped disorder spread, made it harder to stamp out. I knew about these violent disorders, not from Emmett or Amenac or the news, but from the meshnet. I lived in the Apple. People marked these events on the map, and the militia scrambled to respond. Our enclave in Brooklyn wasn't bad, though there were some hate crimes and vagrant preachers even there. Some parts of Manhattan and the Bronx were a nightmare.

The Hudson government's discretion put them in a bind, at the moment. With this new constitution they took extreme steps. But they'd never admitted the threat was extreme enough to justify those steps.

And here I was, knowing all of this. Ever since the Calm Act went into effect, I'd known more than the general public did about what was really going on. For myself, I chose to know the facts. For Amenac, I'd risked my life to publish a subset of the truth. Weather forecasts and safe market travel routes. And here I was again, visiting someplace where even that pittance of truth was hard to come by for ordinary people.

"Hey, darlin'," Emmett said, returning from his run. "Good morning." He froze in concern at the look on my face. "What?"

I pursed my lips. "Sean Cullen put a gag order on PR News for 7 days while they start enforcing this new not-freedom of religion. I was just thinking that through."

Emmett blew out a long breath and perched on the edge of the bed. "Uh-huh."

I shrugged. "Talked to Dave. Carlos. Dave again. Now I'm trying to decide what I think. I think...Sean's making a mistake."

"Uh-huh," Emmett said. He didn't meet my eye. He started to say something else, but didn't.

"It's not just that I believe in freedom of speech, though I do," I elaborated. "Or that I believe in freedom of religion, though I do. And I'd happily cure the religious loons if I could. I want violent lunatics controlled and off the streets. But we all have a different idea of what constitutes lunacy."

"Uh-huh." Emmett untied his sneakers. For him, that was

almost rude. Usually he paid careful attention to me while strewing these 'uh-huhs' about.

A light dawned. "You weren't behind this licensed religion move, either," I accused.

It took some wheedling, but he finally admitted, "Look, I consider it a collection of behavior problems, not a religion problem. I don't care what people believe. None of my business. I care what they do. Public nuisance, put them in jail. Hate crimes, execute them. If there's a pattern of bad actors from one religious congregation, lean on the preacher to shape up. Send militia to their services. Close down their soup kitchen. Whatever. Escalate until the problem is resolved. Cam and I both. The other top Rescos, and Governor Cullen, thought religion was off-limits, so they didn't."

"Ash didn't follow your lead?" Ash Margolis was the other Resco in the city, in charge of Manhattan and the Bronx directly, and supervising the Resco of Jersey-borough as well, the Jersey side of the Hudson River, just as Emmett had oversight on Staten Island in addition to direct responsibility for Brooklyn and Queens.

Emmett looked rueful. "Ash is my senior, not my subordinate, darlin'. Cam and I only talked to each other about it. We never asked permission. Didn't think we needed it. Our prerogative. Mine, really, since I was Cam's boss until yesterday. I'm not sure what Tony's policy was upstate. He was awfully quiet in that discussion. But Ash, Pete, Sean – they felt we were out of line."

"Your way would have worked better," I said softly. "Wouldn't raise so many hackles. Not so 'un-American.'"

"It did work better," Emmett agreed. "But Dee, Pete Hoffman is my commanding officer. Sean Cullen is our commander in chief. Sean felt that the way Cam and I went about it was dishonest. He wanted to be upfront about what we were doing and why. And he felt licensing religion gave us more control."

"You lost the argument."

"Uh-huh," Emmett confirmed. "Darlin', I need to be a team player on this. Yeah, I think Sean made the wrong call. Not morally wrong. Just, my tactics worked better. But it was his call to make. My job is to make the new constitution work. He's the boss."

"I thought maybe they hurried up and aired the constitution special report because we were out of town," I prodded.

"Uh-huh. I want breakfast," he said decisively, and fled into the bathroom.

EMMETT DECLARED A DAY 'IN' AFTER BREAKFAST. HE WAS FED UP with talking to people without sufficient background briefing. Tibbs had given him a reconstituted laptop, and Emmett intended to study Dane Beaufort's computer records until he could wring no more meaning out of them without...talking to people again.

Apparently his interview the night before, with the four militia who waited out the thunderstorms with us, had been another frustrating conversation. Yes, they were Apocalyptics, and so was their captain. Mount Washington, where Dane lived, was largely split between Catholic and Apocalyptic militia units. Yes, other people lived there, too. Yes, there was an Apocalyptic rally at Station Square that morning, though none of them attended. The sect was using the abandoned pretty plaza as an open-air church. Yes, their captain asked them to keep tabs on what our expedition from New York – Hudson – was up to.

No, they didn't have anything against Dane, and they didn't think their church did, either. As for 'what God demands of us', their theories were split four ways between the Ten Commandments, the Sermon on the Mount, the New Testament as a whole, and the idea that God only gives you a cross that you're strong enough to bear. The four agreed that none of those guesses were specifically Apocalyptic. Trying out Matthew 10:34 on them unearthed the fact that two were originally Evangelist, like Emmett, and spoke fluent Bible. But that problematic Bible quote wasn't any clearer to them than to him. 'Do not suppose that I have come to bring peace to the earth. I did not come to bring peace, but a sword.' All four – five counting Emmett – felt that verse contradicted the bulk of Christ's teachings elsewhere in the New Testament.

The foursome honestly didn't seem to know anything about Dane's death. And that was peculiar. The version they'd heard matched Paddy Bollai's – Dane's neighbor and handyman – that Dane died of a beating in Green Tree. Nothing to do with the Apocalyptics.

Emmett showed them the video of the rally, of the crowd surging against Dane. The militia men correctly pointed out that the video didn't show violence, just a surging crowd. Then later, a dead Resco. And that the video showed Station Square, not Green Tree. They supplied names for about a dozen people, including Apocalyptic leaders at the front of the crowd, and Paul Dukakis, the one who brought Dane's body to Paddy Bollai, Dane's handyman. They claimed Paul was a member of Judgment, though, not Apocalyptic. The named collection of Apocalyptics included their pastor and their militia captain, standing right by Dane in the video.

No one had ever spotted Dwight Davison, Dane's second, in that video.

Basically, the militia men seemed perfectly forthcoming, and the Apocalyptic worldview not nearly as rabid as Paddy had led us to believe. They also didn't believe the video showed anything amiss. Kalnietis vetoed telling them that our evidence seemed to confirm that Dane died at Station Square. He wanted to speak to the pastor and captain first.

For today, the IBIS agents set out to interview all these people. I kept Emmett company in a conference room downstairs, intending to tweak the meshnet and start looking for a local administrator to hand it off to.

"No," Emmett vetoed my plan. "Controlling the meshnet gives too much power. We don't know who to trust yet. We need to control it ourselves for now. Do something else for me, darlin'? I'd like a number, what percentage of land was affected by the tornados. If you can automate it, I'd like numbers for the surrounding Resco districts too."

"OK," I said. "Why?"

Slowly, Emmett replied, "I think people here are spooked. By the storms. But even a few hundred twisters probably wouldn't affect more than 5% of the land. Less. People here just aren't used to it. Like back in Connecticut, you know how freaked people got by the ball lightning. But winter hurricanes and snow cyclones? Nah. Those spooked *me*. Twisters, I'm used to. Pittsburgh needs to chill out about the tornados. Our troops, too."

"You're not spooked by tornados?" I said in surprise. "Really?" I'd never seen a tornado. With a little warning, I rather enjoyed hurricanes and blizzards. I suspected he might have a point. Tornado hysteria might be fueling the unrest in Pittsburgh.

"No," he said. And I believed him. "It's just what you're used to, darlin'. Numbers help. Make it more objective. Yeah, a tornado is powerful. But it's small. Not like a hurricane. Those are huge. Terrifying." He mock-shuddered and grinned at me.

So I enlisted my GIS – graphical information systems – specialist back in Connecticut again. Reza was eager for the commission, as usual. We tried and failed to characterize 'a tornado trail' for pattern recognition. But that we could work around, by doing a landscape comparison between satellite surveys from different years, provided we had the old data. Leland, my Amenac sponsor from Canadian intelligence, was happy to supply us with intelligence-grade surveys again, and seemed honestly intrigued by the project. Tornado weather didn't stop at the Canadian border, after all.

I was studying a landscape change test run on the big screen, with before and after years side-by-side. August's summer growth. Unchanged land with a magenta tint. Possible tornado scars marked out with yellow boxes by our latest recognition pattern.

Apparently Emmett was watching me. "Hey, darlin'? Could you keep all the landscape changes? Just sift them onto different layers? Tornados. New buildings. Agriculture. Unknown. Whatever."

"Sure," I agreed. "That's a lot of data, though, Emmett. Anything in particular you're looking for?"

He shook his head thoughtfully. "Just making it objective. This is the land. This is how the land changed. Yeah, this a lot more helpful than just the tornado coverage. Thank you."

I wondered what he saw that I was missing. But he wasn't telling.

"I WONDER IF THE APOCALYPTICS WERE FRAMED," IBIS AGENT Kalnietis concluded over lunch. He and Gianetti were filling us in on their progress of the morning. "And the Shakers, too, with the original misdirection into Green Tree. For local consumption."

They'd succeeded in meeting with the Apocalyptic leaders Reverend Hollywell and Captain Sykes. The two confirmed what the militia had told them, and said that the rally ended peaceably. There had been a ruckus in the back that caused the forward surge of the crowd, and Dane fell backward into the fountain. Captain Sykes simply offered Dane a hand back up onto the fountain's edge after the end of the video clip. Reverend Hollywell ordered the people causing the upset removed. After that, Dane finished his point, and Hollywell gave a sermon. Dane lingered to socialize after the service, but the captain and pastor left. They hadn't heard anything of further events.

Reverend Hollywell dismissed Dane's purported mystery last words as part of a straw man. Dane's full statement was something like, "There are some sects – perhaps even some of you – who claim that we know what God demands of us." As Dane's handyman Paddy Bollai had implied, these were fighting words to some, and incited the scuffle that knocked Dane into the fountain.

In contrast, the pastor awarded Beaufort points for style. Dane successfully incited an emotional reaction from the crowd. Good public speaking technique, in the preacher's view.

Both Apocalyptics reported that Dane was there trying to rally support behind his re-industrialization initiative with Ohio, to get the steel mills up and running again. A fair number in the Apocalyptic community – including the pastor – considered this pointless at the end of days. But their leadership, Hollywell and Sykes chief among them, 'treasured' their standing with the Resco, and 'galvanized' their followers to support him.

I got the impression that Agent Kalnietis detested them, especially the pastor. Though not as badly as Gianetti did. Hollywell kept pointing a finger at her and talking about 'whoring ways.' Preacher Hollywell seemed incapable of sticking to the topic at hand when there was a 'whore' in front of him to 'reproach.' Gianetti gave up and waited in the car for the end of that interview.

But, obnoxious as the IBIS agents found the Apocalyptics, they believed them. The agents found a couple other people on the list of names supplied by the militia the night before, and the stories remained consistent.

Dane Beaufort used a florid phrase while asking for support at a religious rally. In return, he fell into a fountain and got wet. No big deal. And still no leads on how to find Paul Dukakis, the man who delivered the body. Reverend Hollywell and Captain Sykes confirmed that Paul Dukakis wasn't one of theirs. Dukakis also obviously wasn't Matt1034. Or at least he wasn't the person who held the phone that recorded the video, since he appeared in front of the camera.

And if Paul Dukakis was involved in Dane's death, it was clear as mud why he would take pains to deliver the body, and try to frame the people of Green Tree. Why didn't he just toss the body into the Monongahela River?

Emmett asked doubtfully, "So now your angle is who framed the Apocalyptics?"

"No." Agent Kalnietis sighed. "Now I have a verified crime scene, and persons of interest I can't seem to find. The frame is just a theory. Two frames, counting Green Tree. Your turn. Was your morning interesting?"

"Uh-huh," Emmett said. "Dane was a liar and a mutineer. And with a few tweaks, Pittsburgh should be a level 9 community." He sighed.

"Level 9?" Kalnietis inquired. "That's the best there is, isn't it? Isn't that good? Beaufort was a good Resco?"

"Uh-huh," Emmett allowed. He smiled wanly. "Mostly."

13

Interesting fact: Military governor-general of a super-state was a three-star posting. The U.S. system for ranking generals was peculiar. Three-star was not a permanent rank, but rather conferred by the job. That said, Sean Cullen, Charles Schwabacher, and Seth Taibbi were three-star generals in their prior posts. Ivan Link was a one-star general before assignment to lead New England.

"I don't understand, Colonel," Seth Taibbi complained, military general of Pennsylvania. We were holding a video conference with Taibbi and Governor Sean Cullen of Hudson on the big screen. "Pittsburgh was level 5 on the Resco scale."

"Yes," Emmett agreed. "Technically, it could qualify as level 5 due to lack of power and communications. But there is power capacity. They're just not distributing it. Likewise communications, likewise suppressed. Major Beaufort was...misreporting his situation."

"Emmett?" Sean Cullen interjected. "Out with it."

"Sir. Major Beaufort chose to go dark last Thanksgiving in

response to General Tolliver's plan to invade New York. They couldn't do anything to stop Tolliver. So they cut themselves off."

"They," Cullen repeated. "Other Rescos nearby went along with this?"

"Beaufort may have been the instigator," Emmett said. "I haven't spoken to the neighboring Rescos yet."

Taibbi objected, "But I ousted Tolliver in January, eight months ago."

"Yes, sir," Emmett agreed.

I wasn't clear on why Emmett was being so cagey. IBIS agents Kalnietis and Gianetti, professional bureaucrats native to the D.C. region, sat bland and sphinx-like in their unreadability.

Cullen glowered. "Seth, who's lead Resco out there? Beaufort's commanding officer."

"All the Rescos report to Colonel Schneider in Harrisburg," Taibbi replied. "I believe they always have."

"Oh," Cullen said sadly. "Emmett, do you know this Schneider?"

"Yes, sir."

Cullen growled, "Don't make me play twenty questions, Emmett."

"The local Rescos mutinied for cause, sir," Emmett replied. "I request permission to offer amnesty. Before we can go forward in a productive direction. In the meantime, I suspect they hoped to transfer the Pittsburgh area Resco districts to Ohio."

Sean Cullen gestured that he go deeper. "Schneider," he prompted.

Emmett shrugged. "Schneider was Tolliver's man. Trust was broken. I reviewed Major Beaufort's emails with Schneider. From this end, the coup didn't appear to change anything. According to Schneider, Taibbi capitulated and Penn was making reparations. No change in policy was communicated." Cullen was frowning harder. "I'm sorry, sir. But, I have to report a break in the Penn chain of command. Beaufort and the other local Rescos were acting independently. Again, I request permission to assure them of amnesty. Governor Taibbi?"

"You're telling me they're guilty of mutiny," Taibbi said. "I have no reason to doubt Schneider."

Emmett sat silent. Cullen sighed, and went to bat for him. "Mutiny would be up to a court martial, Seth. Whether they're guilty of anything. Their suspected ringleader is dead. If I were in their shoes, I'd request a court from outside Penn. Back in my own shoes, Hudson would grant the request. Your Colonel Schneider failed to notice the mutiny for – ten months? Emmett's giving you good advice, Seth. Don't go there. And whatever Schneider's good for, it isn't supervising Rescos."

"I could send Schneider out there right now," Taibbi growled. "Make him clean up his own mess."

To me, this begged the question of why he hadn't done so in the first place, and saved us the trip.

"Governor Taibbi, I request a sidebar," Governor Cullen said mildly. "Please excuse us, Pittsburgh. I'll get back to you." A dark blue background with white 'Stand By' message replaced the governors on the screen. Just to be on the safe side, Emmett also pressed a mute button.

"How nasty are the politics here, Emmett?" Kalnietis asked. "Is there really any chance of western Penn transferring to Ohio?"

Emmett sighed. "Or eastern Penn to Hudson," he suggested. "Taibbi is Air Force. But the border garrisons and Rescos are all Army. If Taibbi is this standoffish with the border garrisons, too, he's not in control. Schneider's a desk jockey, not a Resco. That's not how New England or Hudson does it, that's for sure."

"I don't know," I said. "The ranking Resco in New England is Niedermeyer, and he's Coast Guard."

"Uh-huh. He's Coast Guard," Emmett agreed. "Actively, busily running the Coast Guard. And he coordinates the other Rescos. John knows he's not Army. He's made that an opportunity instead of a problem. Coast Guard, Navy, Merchant Marine, even Air

Force – John brokers those forces for the Rescos in New England and Hudson. Huge advantage."

"Oh," I said. "I never realized you reported to John in New England."

"I didn't," Emmett said. "I reported to Carlos. Carlos reported to John. Carlos has Connecticut. John's got three Army light colonels reporting to him. Plus the Coast Guard. Penn's Colonel Schneider is nowhere near John's league. Or Pete Hoffman's. Colonel Hoffman is my CO, out of New Jersey," he reminded the IBIS agents. "Penn, though... I don't see the Air Force doing Penn much good. Taibbi's forces aren't integrated."

"The scope of your recommendations, Emmett," Kalnietis probed, "does it extend to Penn's martial law government?"

"Uh-huh," Emmett said unhappily.

The screen re-awoke, with only Sean Cullen on it. "Alright, Emmett, Schwabacher's dealing with Taibbi. I'm too busy today. Amnesty approved – he'll send it in writing. Anything else urgent? No? Good. Call me tonight, one on one, Emmett. Thank you all for your good work."

Emmett hadn't even clicked off the mute button before Cullen was gone.

"Did that help us?" Kalnietis asked.

"Helped me," Emmett replied. "Now I've got four other Rescos to draw on. And with the amnesty, they won't need to lie to me."

"Two percent tornado damage," I reported to Emmett in mid-afternoon, astonished. "Maybe more in agricultural land, but we can't tell that from maps."

Emmett nodded. "Perfect, thank you." At my inquiring look, he clarified, "Tornado damage to a field is temporary. Hail is more trouble. That's not a fault in your methodology. I wanted real damage."

"You were right," I said. "That number does put the scary number of tornados into perspective."

"Uh-huh," said Emmett, eyes already back on his computer screen. "Still. Don't get sloppy. Sirens go off, get into a basement. Or best you can find. Oh, hey – do we have Reza on retainer yet? Or do I need to pay her?"

"No retainer," I murmured. He didn't pay *me* anything. I was a managing director on PR News and Amenac, Resco assistant extraordinaire, leading consultant on the meshnet, and more. But without my farm anymore, I didn't earn anything. I just lived off Emmett. As a mistress? No, certainly I was his partner in his work, not just domestically. It still rankled. I needed my own work. But with my location up in the air, pending his next assignment, I was reluctant to start anything in New York. And here I was, in Pennsylvania.

Sourly, I suggested he give her a month's meal ticket. He did so, and made a note to bring our GIS consultant up during Hudson's next budget cycle, to put her on retainer, possibly split with New England.

He seemed more subdued now than he was right after the talk with the governors. "Everything OK, Emmett?" I asked. "Could we take a break? Talk?"

He blew out slowly, but acquiesced, closing his laptop screen. "Uh-huh."

"We didn't finish that discussion the other night," I began ruefully. "I feel like it's still hanging over our heads."

"Uh-huh."

"Emmett, I don't know what I'm doing here," I complained. "Not just Pittsburgh. I used to have a life, a career, a farm. Well, for half a season, I had a farm. You seem to think we've been together long enough. That I should know by now whether to marry you. Emmett, I love you. I don't think it's about you. But I'm not sure who I am, in all this."

"My partner?" he suggested. "Dee, we've been partners for a year and a half. We do good work together. Millions agree."

"But that's your job," I pointed out. "You're a Resco. I'm just an unpaid assistant."

He nodded and reached for his phone. "You should be paid. That's fair."

"Emmett, that's not –"

But he held up a warning finger and tapped out a message. "One topic at a time," he reiterated. He was a stickler for that, when we argued. Besides, numbers and management were his forte, far more comfortable than a domestic argument. "Resolve this, then go on. Just asking Dave what his salary is... Wow. You need a raise, Dave." Dave wasn't really the boss of our Internet empire, but he was more involved than me as a managing director.

More tapping. A snort or two. Then Emmett blanked the phone and put it aside. "Dave gets two meal tickets – and needs a raise – and Amiri Baz gets four as your media star. So for your work on PR and Amenac, I think you should get three full meal tickets salary. Dave should, too. The farm would have netted you what, three more this year? You already got half the proceeds."

"Yeah, about that," I agreed. I frowned in consternation. I hadn't started this conversation to ask for a salary. But disconcertingly, I found it mattered to me quite a lot. My unpaid non-spouse status left me in limbo, and I didn't like it.

"Plus random Resco assistant services," Emmett said. "Invaluable. But part-time. So, one more? Seven total." He paused and thought it over. "Yeah, I could pay you that. Don't know what you're going to do with it, but. Is that fair?"

I felt I ought to tell him that money wasn't important to me. But to hell with it, money was freedom, money was power, security. I gulped. "More than fair. I'm part-time on all of them."

Emmett shrugged. "You're highly effective on all of them." He sighed. "Of course, if I'm paying you, I ought to deduct half of the household expenses." He pursed his lips at me. "Five."

"You pay five meal tickets for the house in Brooklyn?" Wow, that was a lot. But guiltily, I had to concede, he'd taken that palatial brownstone, with all the trimmings, to coax me into living with him in the city. Left to himself, he'd still be in a cruddy one-bedroom somewhere.

"No, I pay ten," Emmett clarified. "Your half, is five. We have the nicest place in the entire city. Second-nicest, maybe." He gazed at me through narrowed eyes. "Dave suggested a spouse gets half of my income. But that doesn't mean anything. I get 75 meal tickets, but that's intended for seed capital, not personal expenses. I'm probably drawing more in salary than any other Resco in Hudson."

I nodded and said quietly, "Two meal tickets in salary would be good. Thank you."

He looked like he was calculating something in his head. "If you leave, you still get two, I think," he said. "You'd have your farm back. I wouldn't contact you for help." He queued up the payments.

"Whoa," I said. "Where did that come from?"

Emmett blew out unhappily. "We're not moving forward, Dee. I'm not OK with living together indefinitely. I don't want to break up with you. I want to marry you. Maybe we should take a break."

"Emmett, what the hell?" I cried, furious. "Take the damned salary back, if you resent it so much!"

"I don't resent the salary."

"Awesome. You resent something!"

"No, I don't," he claimed. "Alright, maybe I do. Dee, I've bent over backwards trying to please you. Apparently that doesn't work. I want to be married. You don't. Or not to me anyway. I'm not OK with this limbo."

"Limbo," I echoed softly. Wasn't that what I was just thinking?

The discomfort and insecurity, not knowing where we were going next? But, "Wait a minute," I said. "We were fine when we left the city. Weren't we? Emmett, this fight started when fundamentalist fruitcakes called me a harlot. And somehow, you agree with them," I accused.

"Fundamentalist fruitcakes," Emmett repeated. "Born-again Christians. Like me."

Oops.

"Please leave now," Emmett said coldly.

"Emmett, I've never –"

He walked to the door and opened it for me. "Now," he repeated. He added to the soldier on guard duty outside the door, "Specialist, I don't want to be disturbed the rest of the day."

I woodenly picked up my gear to decamp. Meeting him at the door on the way out, I attempted, "Emmett, you don't want to do this."

"Uh-huh," he replied. His face was set in lines of rage. He didn't meet my eye as he closed the door on me, just glared over my head.

I was right. It was a very bad sign if Emmett didn't cry when it hurt.

Feeling utterly humiliated and fighting back tears, I asked Andy Wiehl for another room, and moved my stuff out of Emmett's. Wiehl was kind and gentle about the whole thing. But there were no unassigned rooms near Emmett's in the military block. After the tornados last night, Emmett had relented and allowed Brandy and her IndieNews team to stay at the hotel, as far as possible away from him. My new room was right across the hall from hers. I could picture the headlines already. 'PR Lovers Split Over Religion?'

No! I screamed internally at the empty bland hotel room. *You're not allowed to do this, Emmett! You can't break up with me. We do too much good together!*

Problem was, I'd said that before. To Zack. My last lover, until he died. Emmett's best friend. And Zack had told Emmett all about that fight. Another fight with Emmett came to mind. *I think you have me confused with Zack.*

Besides, was that really why I was with Emmett? Did I believe our public mission was more important than our private life? If that was true, he really ought to dump me. Because I believed him. Emmett wanted me as a wife and emotional support, more than as a work partner. No matter how good a partner I was. To be partners in public, and cold in private... Neither of us wanted that. His heart would bleed. Mine?

I tried to cry, I really did. Lying across the bed, I even tried to come up with a list of issues to resolve before I'd be ready to marry Emmett. But it seemed wildly irrelevant, out on this particular limb. If he decided we were incompatible because I wasn't Christian enough, there was nothing I was willing to do about it. He'd never said that, but I worried anyway. I considered calling friends, or other Rescos, or people who were both, to vent and ask their advice. But that was irrelevant, too. And possibly damaging to his work relationships.

Emmett and I just needed to cool off and talk this through.

Instead I got to surfing Amenac, to check on the fallout from the big reveal on the Hudson Constitution. Along the way, it occurred to me to wonder, just who were these crackpot religions, anyway? What did they believe in? On the general principle of live and let live, I'd turned a blind eye to the apocalyptic religions springing up like evil toadstools.

That afternoon I set the blinders aside and started studying the new adversaries with intent.

14

Interesting fact: According to British historian David Bebbington, the four core beliefs of Evangelical Christians are conversionism, the belief that life needs to change via a 'born-again' experience; activism, the expression of the gospel in effort; biblicism, a particular regard for the Bible; and crucicentrism, a stress on the sacrifice of Christ on the cross.

"Missed you at dinner," I began lamely, as Emmett opened his hotel room door to me. I stopped talking because he had his ear to his phone. Scowling, he handed it to me. "Momma," he explained.

"Hey, sweetie!" Emma MacLaren crooned to me. "I hear my son's been an idiot today. I'm sorry, that must be painful."

"Um, thanks, Emma," I said uncertainly. Emmett closed the door and went back to flop to the foot of the bed, head on his arms, glaring at the dresser and mirror a few feet away. I was glad to see that he'd been crying. He mopped his eyes and nose with a handkerchief. No one used tissues anymore.

"Your timing is excellent, Dee," Emma continued. "I just suggested to Emmett that I could help you two work this out. You know I love you, girl. I want you to marry my boy, sooner or later. This just won't do."

"I –" I sputtered. Don't get me wrong, I love Emmett's mother. But she was even pushier than him. Visions of mother-in-law danced in my head, not quite advancing Emmett's cause. The two of them tag-teaming me through the years was a daunting prospect. When we fought, I thought to vent to my friends. OK, our friends. But he talked to his mother?

"Put me on speaker," Emma directed.

I obeyed, and sank to the chair by the dresser, near Emmett but not crowding him.

"Emmett, back up and tell Dee about Marilou Beaufort," Emma directed.

"What?" he complained, nasal and twangy. The Ozark accents came on thick and heavy when these two spoke together. "Alright. Dee, I should have told you. Got news from back in Fort Campbell this afternoon. About an hour before we fought. Marilou and the kids died while Dane was away on his last deployment. Flash flood. The younger kids, Dane's. The older boy, Colin, was away at military school. He'd been acting out. Dane wanted him under some discipline while he was overseas. Haven't found Colin yet."

"I'm sorry to hear that," I said sympathetically. "Did you know Marilou very well?"

"Too well," Emma commented. "Keep going, baby."

Emmett glowered at the cell phone, but continued. "Had kind of a thing about Marilou. We didn't *do* anything, Momma. Just, back at Leavenworth, my first year, we prayed together. Marilou helped me try to sort through my divorce with Susie. Talked."

"Baby, if you had to put a stop to it because you had feelings for her," Emma opined, "then it went too far."

"Uh-huh," Emmett admitted. "Still didn't do anything." He swallowed uncomfortably.

"What was she like?" I asked, more or less at random. *And what does this have to do with me?*

"Sweet," he said. "She used to run around. Sowed her wild oats. Straightened out. Born again. Devoted to her kids, to Dane. It's not that I wanted...her, exactly. Just wanted what they had. Instead of that emotional wasteland I had with Susie."

"Uh-huh," Emma cut in. "And then you're stressed out," she led.

"I'm not comfortable with this assignment," Emmett murmured. He shook his head. "I'm trained to lead soldiers in battle. Lots of paperwork. General Taibbi, the Resco structure of Penn, this religious landscape. The new constitution pushed through in Hudson as soon as I'm out of the way. I'm in over my head. And I shouldn't have brought you with me to Pittsburgh, Dee. Not with murderers running around. No matter what the brass want."

Emma pounced, "Darlin', what do you mean, soon as you're out of the way?"

"I disagreed with licensed religion, Momma," Emmett replied. "Not wild about voter testing, either. 'Channeled' freedom of speech." He sighed. "Not crazy about being on the succession. That's president of a country, Momma. Me? They're all furious at me, too, for getting a headline and upstaging them, even from Pittsburgh. That constitution announcement was supposed to be Cam and Sean's big hurrah. And Ash, Sean's number one. And look who grabbed the headlines again. The Project Reunion lovers."

"Uh-huh," Emma said. "So aside from the guilt for bringing her to Pittsburgh, none of that has anything to do with Dee, right? He's just stressed out, Dee. He really needs you by his side, so instead he pushed you away."

"Been there, done that, Momma?" Emmett suggested sourly. I could suddenly and vividly picture him as a boy, aged 8 to 12, a captive audience to his mother's courtships.

"And how," Emma agreed. "Know where else I been, baby? Surrounded by holier-than-thou yahoos, calling me a harlot.

Judging me for leaving your daddy. Taking you with me while I tended bar to make ends meet. Dating before I re-married. Getting pregnant with you in the first place, out of wedlock. We heard a lot from those people, didn't we? Bet you hated that."

"Yeah," he bit out. "I hated that." He sighed. "You know I don't blame you, Momma."

"Oh, but you did, Emmett," she gainsaid him. "Furious. In tears some days. Clutching your Bible, memorizing your verses to prove you were a good Christian, no matter what they said."

"I didn't... Did I?" said Emmett. "Yeah, I guess I did sometimes. Dang, Momma. You shoulda drowned me."

"Tempting, sometimes," she admitted. "But no, you're a keeper. Even if you are a bit of a robot sometimes. Like today. Point is, Emmett. You want to keep that crap? Or keep Dee?"

"Dee," Emmett agreed promptly. "Darlin', I'm sorry," he breathed to me. "This assignment's pushing some buttons."

"But you're really not OK with us living together?" I asked.

"Ah..." he said. "I'd rather we were engaged," he bit out, lips pursed angrily. "Dee, explain this to me. If we intend to get married – why aren't we engaged?"

"Shut up, baby," Emma broke in. "You're picking a fight again. It's Dee's turn."

"I –" I started, then stopped. "Emmett, would you really rather have someone like Marilou, than me?"

"No," he breathed. "Wouldn't rather have anyone than you." He didn't meet my eye.

"Well...I'm stressed, too," I admitted. "It sounds petty, but the salary helps. Gives me some security, money to fall back on. The world keeps shifting under my feet. Three months, I'd just gotten used to Brooklyn, and now here I am in Pittsburgh. I thought we were going to Long Island, but Cam took your territory there. Here, so far we've been lied to, shot at, dodged tornados. Harangued by religious fruitcakes. They insulted me and you took their side – stop!" I warned, when he moved to respond to that. "I'm venting. You listen.

"You're suddenly in line of succession for head of state," I continued. "And that whole constitution was a real eye-popper. Not at all the simple unarguable stuff I was expecting. No idea how long we're staying here in Pittsburgh. Or where we're going next. So, no home really. I gave up my farm, my home, to be what, your camp follower? In a world reverting to the medieval?

"And you know what really pisses me off?" I concluded decisively. "We don't have a single nice anniversary. Every anniversary we've got commemorates a horrible day. The day HomeSec nearly killed me, and I met you. And I went home with Zack that night, not you. The day Zack died. The day Angel disappeared. If you want me to marry you, Emmett, could you please pick a happy day to ask? Just one anniversary of a nice day. Is that too much to ask? But no! Instead I get an ultimatum because some nut job calls me a harlot!"

Emma laughed. "OK, you kids. I'll get off the phone now. Love you, baby. Love you too, Dee!" She didn't wait for a response, just hung up.

Emmett was still chuckling, flipped over onto his back. "Point taken, darlin'. You done?"

"Well," I admitted reluctantly, "there's practical stuff. Like, we've never talked about having kids."

Emmett said softly, "I trust you on that." Judging from the speed of the response, he'd thought this through. "I'd like kids. Might not be able to take them with me, where I need to go. But we can make sure they're safe. And you with them when they're small, if you want. But if kids don't come, that's OK."

"You're sure you can make me safe, Colonel MacLaren?" I challenged. "Let alone a baby?"

"Safe as anybody," Emmett replied. "Look, Dee, neither of us wants to set out to make a baby right now. But if one comes, I'd want it. And we can handle it. You know that."

A tension released in me, one I didn't know I was holding. "Yeah, I knew that," I admitted. "But some things need to be said, Emmett."

He nodded thoughtfully, and flipped back onto his stomach to face me. "Dee, I feel raw. I cried myself hollow, or half of this would be a fight again. Couldn't make love to you and make up tonight if I tried. And I still need to call Sean Cullen back. Probably get chewed out again, too."

I nodded sadly. "OK, I don't move back in. Tonight, anyway."

"Probably won't be here tomorrow night," he added. "I want to meet the neighboring Rescos on their own turf. Look around. Get to know them, their seconds. Long drives, then take our time talking."

"Why?" I asked, intrigued.

"Best option for a new Resco for Pittsburgh," he replied, "is probably one of them. If he's any good. If his second can step up. Our best backup, too, short of calling out Ohio's border garrisons. Anyway, I leave before dawn. You stay here. Stay safe."

"Doesn't sound so safe," I said.

"Not as safe as I'd like, no," he admitted. "But you'll have most of the guards. Tibbs and the IBIS agents. Don't underestimate Gianetti and Kalnietis, Dee. They look like mild-mannered suits. But FBI agents are more lethal than regular G.I.'s. Better trained, and a whole lot smarter. All else fails, Captain Johnson can button up in the tornado shelter downstairs, and call in the cavalry. I'll try to keep in touch, but comms are sketchy."

"OK," I said softly, picking at my pants leg. "Anything you want me to do while you're gone? Aside from stay safe. I started profiling the local religions this afternoon."

"You be careful doing that," Emmett said sharply. "Some of these outfits don't have a positive outlook on women, darlin'."

"I noticed," I agreed.

"Oh, there's one other thing you could do," he suggested. "Taibbi gave me 90 Penn meal tickets for a budget. See if you can find businesses to seed from a woman's perspective. Woman-owned. Making women's lives better. Whatever. Or farming or tech or any enterprise you feel comfortable with. Don't make promises. Just bring me proposals."

"Ooh! That sounds fun," I agreed, with a smile.

"Good," he said.

The silence stretched between us. "OK, I guess I'll go," I murmured. I rose, and squeezed his hand, unsure of whether to kiss him. He pulled me down for a quick peck.

"You be careful," he said.

"You, too," I agreed. "When you're back, Emmett? Let's try to make a date night. Not out on the town or anything. Just here in the room. You and me."

15

Interesting fact: Some of the trillions of dollars spent in Middle Eastern wars ended up back in U.S. communities as equipment gifts to local law enforcement. Allegheny County, surrounding Pittsburgh, modestly picked up 26 assault rifles, 10 night vision sets, 1 mine-resistant armored personnel vehicle (MRAP), and 2 other armored vehicles. New Haven County, in Connecticut, received 137 assault rifles, 16 night vision rigs, 14 shotguns, 3 grenade launchers, and 4 MRAPs and other armed vehicles. Los Angeles County took 3,408 assault rifles, 1,696 body armor pieces, 827 night vision sets, 7 armored vehicles, 15 helicopters, and a plane. All for use on their own citizens. Naturally, a large number of officers on these police forces were experienced in such equipment from having served overseas. Martial law under the Calm Act came as more of a linear progression than as a shocking change.

There was fighting overnight in the streets, as Paddy Bollai had warned us. Emmett's room was on the safer back side of the hotel, overlooking the scenic Monongahela River and downtown. My new room faced the bulk of Mount Washington off to the right, with lower slopes and mixed commercial and residential neighborhoods in the middle, and another hill rising to the left. The valley between the hills seemed to be contested territory. Gunshot and muzzle flashes broke the night. Plus an occasional bigger flash and vibrating boom from more powerful weapons.

I watched through the window, and on my meshnet map, for a couple hours. The locals were definitely picking up the knack of marking trouble on the map. Though my focus was riveted by the surrounding neighborhoods I could see, the map showed fighting off to the east between the rivers as well, and north of the Ohio River to the west of downtown. North of downtown, across the Allegheny River, seemed relatively quiet. The immediate neighborhood, close to the hotel, was also quiet. If there was fighting in the suburbs and farmlands, no one was reporting it. But meshnet coverage was thin out there, and connections to us broken by distance as people hunkered down for the night.

Cats, Pocs, Jugs, Gels, Baps, and Prots, explained the markers on the map. Catholics, Apocalyptics, Judgment, Evangelists, Baptists, and mainline mixed Protestants, based on my afternoon's research. The nearest conflicts seemed to be the Catholics and Apocalyptics of Mount Washington teamed up against the next hill's allied Evangelists and Baptists, with a smattering of Judgment in the middle.

What they were fighting for was clear as mud.

"MR. WIEHL, WON'T YOU JOIN US FOR A MOMENT?" I WAYLAID THE passing hotel proprietor during breakfast with Gianetti and Kalnietis. Once he was seated, I asked as sweetly as I could, "I wanted to ask you about the fighting last night."

"I'm very sorry about that," he attempted.

I smiled warmly. "I'm sure it's not your fault. But what exactly were they fighting about? Do you know?"

Wiehl shook his head sadly. "It was quiet for a while. But then news of Beaufort's death spread, and they're at it again. Maybe they think they're fighting for control of the city."

"Who are these fighting units?" Kalnietis asked. I'd already briefed him and Gianetti on what I saw and surmised last night. But Kalnietis seemed fond of collecting alternate perspectives without saying anything to prejudice the answers. That seemed wise, to me. He helpfully pushed our tablet toward Wiehl, showing the meshnet map of the disorders.

"Neighborhood militia," Wiehl replied. "They're supposed to keep the peace and stop looters in their areas. But sometimes they get to fighting each other."

"They seem to be labeled by religion," Kalnietis prompted. "Though we don't see any here near the hotel."

"Here we're protected by the Pittsburgh PD," Wiehl quickly assured us. "The militias don't tangle with the police department. Full SWAT teams, Army surplus armed personnel carriers, practically tanks, armor. Very well trained. The regulars, I suppose. The police are controlled by the city council and the chamber of commerce. But the other neighborhoods are policed by the militias. There were too many fights between different religions within mixed militia units, so they separated the units by sect. But sometimes the units fight each other. It's a big mess."

"Was this Major Beaufort's idea?" I asked. If so, it seemed like a bad one.

"I don't think so," Andy Wiehl said. "I think it started, and he couldn't stop it. I don't understand the Resco model, really. All alone, what could he do?"

He could call in fire and brimstone the likes of which the local fruitcake sects could hardly dream of, I thought. But I held my peace. Besides, if the Resco chain of command was as fractured in Penn as Emmett seemed to think, maybe Wiehl was right. Maybe Dane Beaufort was all alone here, with no markers to call in for reinforcements. The nearest garrisons belonged to

Ohio. His CO, Colonel Schneider in Harrisburg, was far away without a clue, to the point that Beaufort pulled the plug on their communications. Emmett, on the other hand, had an intact command chain and friends galore. I wondered what Emmett would do.

So far, Emmett was off to visit the neighbors.

"But what exactly are they fighting for?" Kalnietis followed up. "Are these religion-specific neighborhoods?"

"No," Wiehl said. "They're becoming more so, because of the fighting. But Pittsburgh was a normal American city. Different faiths side by side, except for a few neighborhoods. Like the Muslims. Dane moved them into a suburb for their own protection."

Kalnietis continued, "So the militias fight to win their own sect more land? More resources?"

"Well," Wiehl said reluctantly, "I think they fight to kill each other. Because they think the other religions are wrong, and they're right. About God. I'm sorry, I'm not very religious. I go to church now, of course. But only because they make your life hell if you don't. The Unitarian Universalist church is quiet. My wife gets involved in the church functions. Not much else going on these days. I just nap in the back on Sundays, myself."

"So you're a 'Prot'?" I asked.

Wiehl waved head and hand in vehement denial. "I have nothing to do with the militias."

Good to know. Apparently the Cats-Prots-Jugs labels applied to militia units, not civilian beliefs.

"Did anyone win last night?" Gianetti asked.

"There's nothing to win," Wiehl replied, face wide open. "I imagine a few lost. They died."

TO STUDY GOD, I TEAMED WITH THE DEVIL. OR RATHER TO STUDY

indigenous religion, I hit up Brandy O'Keefe of IndieNews. I slid into her booth at the hotel breakfast buffet and gave her my biggest smile.

"Brandy!" I crooned.

"Dee, darling!" she crooned back. "I'm surprised you're not hiding from me, sweetie. My viewers want to know all about your little troubles in paradise. Separate rooms?"

"Emmett and I are tight," I lied with a double wink and nose scrunch. "Couldn't be better. Split rooms because we're working different schedules at the moment. And professionalism. You know."

"You don't lie well, do you?" Brandy critiqued.

"I know. It's part of my charm," I replied. "I had an idea you might like to collaborate on. Wouldn't that be fun? Girls' day out?"

"I'd prefer an exclusive on your breakup."

"Oh, well, if you're busy," I said. "Catch the fireworks last night? I sure am glad I have armed guards to escort me. Didn't bring my camera woman, though. But I suppose I could find someone local to hire."

Brandy's producer and camera guy raised hungry eyebrows. With martial law governments as our underwriters, PR News paid better than Indie. Well, except for me, until yesterday. The armed guards were also a potent bribe.

"I'm listening," Brandy allowed sourly.

"You'll love it," I assured her. "Pure human interest stories, sure to get past the censors."

"Joint story, Indie and PR?" Brandy clarified, eyes narrowed.

I shrugged. "We share the footage to do with as we want. And the censors have the last laugh. Let's just see what we catch, and then decide how to split the stories, alright?"

She shrugged acquiescence. "So what's the story?"

16

Interesting fact: Vatican Council II, held between 1962 and 1965, decreed a number of revisions to Catholic religious practice. Most visibly, it declared that Mass could be celebrated in 'vernacular' language, such as English, instead of the previous pure Latin. Women were no longer required to cover their heads in church. A number of vestments were simplified, especially the more ornate nun's headgear.

"I have the capacity here to wash 160 full sets of bedding, and six towels per room in a single day," Mrs. Wiehl – Vivian – bragged proudly, showing us the heart of her hospitality empire. "We also provide wash, dry, and fold service for our guests."

Brandy and I widened our eyes, equally horrified at the idea of washing 160 sets of bedding and towels, used by strangers. *Ick-ick ick.* But the banks of industrial-grade laundry machines were indeed impressive.

"Beats hell out of that beer-cooler laundry operation on Long Island, Dee," Brandy pointed out to me. "That was awesome footage," she added wistfully. "Glad you didn't actually get raped for it. That was the best part, though."

I shot Brandy a dirty look, and explained the reference to Vivian Wiehl. About a year ago, I'd been on Long Island interviewing another woman laundry entrepreneur, at a rather different level on the Resco scale of bootstrapped re-civilization. Mary on Long Island was at level 1, living at the mercy of rape gangs, and doing laundry by hand in a beer cooler. I helped.

"So, with just us here at the hotel," I resumed the interview, "you have a lot of excess capacity."

"Yes!" cried Vivian with enthusiasm. "And most women don't have power. So they're doing all this by hand. I don't have any coin-op machines, so I can't let the public in here. But I bet lots of people would like a wash-dry-fold service. Don't you think? And that would bring more traffic into the hotel. They could enjoy our new phone-charging facility, and the dinner buffet. Maybe even the swimming pool and the hot tub!"

"How did I not know of this pool and hot tub," I murmured, entranced.

"And what will you do with the proceeds, Vivian?" Brandy asked.

"Well, I don't know," Vivian replied, taken aback. "Give it to charity, I suppose. I certainly don't need to eat any more."

We all smiled. Indeed, Vivian was well-padded, with the middle-aged thick waist that had all but vanished in Hudson and New England. This woman had never gone hungry. She would attract hostile stares on the gaunt streets of the Apple. A full meal ticket back in Brooklyn was 1600 calories a day, if you could earn it. Vivian would serve us more than that for lunch, and try to ply us with seconds.

"But wouldn't it be fun for everyone?" Vivian continued happily. "There's so little to do these days. Except church." She pursed her lips, clearly not enthused by church socials. "We don't pay any money for the electricity, or the hotel. So it's just a way to throw a party for the community, really." She smiled hopefully.

"Thank you, Vivian," I said with a smile. I jotted down a final note. "So you don't need any capital at all? Just permission, really?" She nodded. "I'll pass your plan to the Resco, and we'll see."

"Vivian, while we've got you," Brandy followed this up, "we're hoping to speak with women from different walks of life. Different religions, too. That seems so important here. Could you tell us how to meet with, say, an Apocalyptic housewife?"

BEATRICE HAD A WOOD-FRAME HOUSE ON MOUNT WASHINGTON, not wildly different from Dane Beaufort's. Although her land was closer to level, and her view correspondingly not as good. A thick candle and a thicker Bible held pride of place on the dining table, a black coal-burning stove the centerpiece of the living room.

It gets cold in Pittsburgh, much colder than the Hudson Atlantic coast. I fervently hoped we wouldn't be here long enough to experience their snowy winter. In Beatrice's house, the brave little pot-bellied stove was the sole source of heat, not only for the rooms, but for wash-water and cooking. A stockpot sat upon it now, to heat water. I didn't see any more candles, either. Apparently after the Bible was read for the night, they went to sleep.

We'd met up with Beatrice as the soup kitchen closed its breakfast service at her Apocalyptic church a few blocks away. She volunteered there six mornings a week. The seventh morning was Sunday. Her church allowed only Apocalyptics to attend on Sundays, and they fasted until after services, when they held a meager pot-luck brunch of penitential foods. Her words, not mine. Last Sunday, her offering was uncooked oats mixed with home-made yogurt.

The other women at the soup kitchen didn't want to speak with us. They hustled away quickly, with furtive backward glances. Beatrice seemed to feel duty-bound to host us, her husband a captain of militia.

Their eldest daughter, a grubby ten-year-old in a plaid dress and braids, kept peeking at us from the stairwell. I wondered how well she remembered life before the borders cut them off from the rest of the world. She'd gone to school once. Her dress looked like a well-worn parochial school uniform of the dull jumper sort, that surely belonged to someone else back then. She'd have outgrown her own school clothes. It was only two years now since the world had changed. But children tend to believe what their parents want them to. She was much put out by the way Brandy and I and our two female soldiers were all wearing pants. Girls were supposed to wear dresses.

"Beatrice, if you could work outside the home now, what would you want to do?" I asked. She used to work in IT at a bank downtown.

"I do the Lord's work," she replied. "I want no other."

I nodded, smiled. "What if the power were turned on again tomorrow?"

"I would turn it off," she said severely. "It was man's grasping and misuse of power that led us to the straits we're in today. That caused the climate to turn against us, and sent the tornados to rend."

I blinked, wondering if Beatrice intentionally conflated electric power with social power, or was just being rather literal about fossil fuel burning.

"You wouldn't want the refrigerator back?" Brandy prompted. "The washing machine?"

"No," she denied. "They are tempting. But I would resist temptation, and bear my penance."

"So you take personal responsibility for climate change?" I asked.

She nodded vehemently. "We are all, each and every one of us, guilty of bringing this calamity down upon us. We pray and do penance for atonement with the Lord."

"We're unfamiliar with Apocalyptic doctrine," Brandy said. "But we're trying to explain this viewpoint to others. What do you see as the goal, Beatrice? Of this praying and atonement and penance. When we have done 'enough' penance," Brandy supplied the quote marks with her fingers, "what happens?"

"Judgment Day is coming," Beatrice said. "It is nigh at hand. Whether we have atoned or not."

"Prayer and penance won't prevent Judgment Day?" I asked.

"Prevent it? We long for Judgment Day," Beatrice said, nodding, looking relieved. "It won't be long now."

"What is this?" a man bellowed from the porch. "What are you shameless women doing, polluting my home?"

"My husband," Beatrice explained to us, rising with alacrity to meet him at the door. She opened it and bowed her head. To speak to him, she spoke to her feet. "Spike, these women asked to interview me, so that they could understand Apocalyptics better. The soldiers are from the new Resco, Colonel MacLaren. This is Dee Baker, the Colonel's woman, and Brandy O'Keefe, a news reporter, and her camera man, Blake Sondheim. My husband, Spike Crowley."

Spike Crowley looked like a Spike. He wore militia camouflage, with single silver bars. That meant he'd once served as a commissioned lieutenant before the militia. Or at least, that's what those bars meant in Hudson and New England. Living with Emmett, I was catching on to these things. Spike wore several piercings in ears and eyebrow. Tattoos spilled from his shirt up his neck and down his forearms onto the backs of his hands, multicolored and covering every inch of skin.

"Are you a Jew, Blake Sondheim?" Spike demanded.

"Yes, I am," Blake replied evenly. He carefully lowered his camera to his waist politely. He was still filming Spike.

"Is that a problem?" I inquired.

Spike scowled as I met his eye. "You will cast your eyes down, woman," he barked at me.

"Excuse me, Mr. Crowley, but we are not Apocalyptics," I said firmly. "We do not follow your ways. We are here trying to understand your ways."

"Then get the fuck out of my house," Spike replied. "All of you. And you!" He yelled, pointing at the 10-year-old. A sound of pelting footsteps receded up the stairs. "Do not get foolish ideas from fallen women!" he called up after her.

Qwanisha, my black female guard, leveled her rifle at him from the porch. "If you could step aside, sir," she said, "so they can leave."

"How dare you, bitch?" Spike made a grab for her gun. Qwanisha yanked it away easily, while her squad-mate Penny fired a warning shot at the porch. Now he had four guns leveled at him.

"Just step outside for a moment, sir," Qwanisha directed. "Over there."

A third squad-mate – the biggest one, Jorge – reached in and grabbed Spike out of the door frame. The angle was bad for me to watch what happened next. The gist was that Spike ended up laid out on the porch with guns trained on him.

"We'd better go," I said faintly. "Thank you so much for your help, Beatrice. It's been very illuminating. I'm sorry we've brought…"

"No trouble," Beatrice denied.

"Can I give you my meshnet number?" I asked in concern. I wondered what the fallout was likely to be on her, when we left.

"I have no use for such things," Beatrice said. She didn't press us to leave faster or anything. She just stood holding the door open, in apparent unconcern. Fatalistic in this as in all things, perhaps.

We walked carefully – sometimes backwards or sideways so as not to turn our backs on Spike – to the waiting news van and troop SUV. Brandy and I quickly agreed to rendezvous at the Catholic church next, and hopped into our respective vehicles. The guards on the porch worked their way out of there without any bloodshed or further shots.

The guards vetoed our instructions and stopped a block away to confer with Sergeant Becque regarding the unwisdom of our plans. It took me some wheedling, and a promise not to invade anyone else's home unless the man of the house invited us in. But we finally got moving again.

"PRE–VATICAN COUNCIL II?" AGENT GIANETTI ECHOED IN surprise. Apparently Sergeant Becque had tattled on me. The IBIS agent joined our expedition at the Catholic church on Mount Washington, along with Tibbs for added muscle and cunning. Based on their names, I was unsurprised to learn that Donna Gianetti and Brandy O'Keefe were better versed on matters Catholic than I.

"There was a general feeling that the reforms of Vatican Council II perhaps went too far," Sharon Wentworth told us, our latest respondent. The younger woman wore knee-length sober brown dress and pumps, hat with veil, and thin gloves. We'd caught her as she exited the church following a noon weekday Mass. The small children she'd walked with had continued on without her. "That returning to a way of life before the social disturbances of the 60's, and climate change acceleration, would help us return to God." She smiled beatifically beneath her lacy veil.

Donna and Brandy both appeared horrified. Not under-standing what that was about, I dove in. "We'd like to understand your goals and problems these days, Sharon," I prompted with a smile.

"I seek a good marriage, of course." Fair enough, I thought. Not something I ever would have said, but most women in their twenties – let alone men – spent the bulk of their leisure time thinking about seeking sex, one way or another. "And to bring more people back into the Catholic Church," she added.

"Back?" I asked.

"All these Protestants," she clarified.

I still didn't get it. "Have many Pittsburgh Catholics converted to Protestants lately?"

"We seek to heal the Reformation," Sharon Wentworth clarified.

Ah, she meant the Protestants who split with Rome centuries ago.

Brandy winced, and wrested control of the conversation back. "On a more mundane level, Sharon. What do you do for a living these days?"

"I teach at the parochial school." She prattled on a bit about her class, apparently first grade. Aside from the usual fundamentals, she also taught them catechism. "We're on break for lunch and Mass. I really ought to get back now, excuse me. Peace be with you." She took hands with each of us in turn with a warm smile, repeating the benediction.

"And also with your spirit," Gianetti and Brandy modeled the ritual response for me, although Sharon's version was, "And also with you." We beamed smiles until the locals were out of earshot again.

"That was disturbing," Brandy said. Seeing my puzzlement, she added, "Dee, they've reverted the Church. Revoked the modernizations."

"Vatican Council II was major," Gianetti confirmed. "Mass in the vernacular. Modernizing the clothes. Women included in more roles."

"I hate the hat," Brandy groused. "My grandmother was always after me to wear a hat and gloves to Mass. 'Nice girls still do.' It's archaic. I wonder if they've brought back the flying nun habits, too."

I pointed mutely behind her to a trio of nuns boarding a minivan. They wore full-length black habits, white wimples and black trailing veils. No flapping seagull hats.

Gianetti was less concerned with the apparel. "Respecting the separation of church and state. No longer blaming Jews for the crucifixion. Vatican II covered a lot of ground. And catechism for six year olds? These days we wait to start children until around nine." She looked up thoughtfully. "Ladies, we want insight into everyday women's lives. Perhaps this is a systematic error, catching them as they emerge from church."

I couldn't argue with that. We walked over to the priest, Father Uccello, who was alone by now, but still lingering at the front steps. We asked him where we might meet women who were employed outside the home and church. The markets, perhaps?

But apparently the churches had cornered the market on markets, as well. There were monthly flea markets, at the churches, but food and other basic goods were also distributed through the all-Christian churches. There wasn't much employment to be found, and most of the jobs outside the church were taken by men. They needed the work more, so that they could support their families. We thanked the priest for his time and went back to consult by our vehicles.

Brandy grumbled, "Over half of all families in America with children to support, are led by women. They deserve to starve?"

"Or remarry," Gianetti replied, playing devil's advocate. "As a high priority."

"What a goal," Brandy complained. "Let's all return to 1950's America. Or more like 1920's, without refrigerators."

"Suburbs?" I suggested brightly. "I'd like to meet an Amish family."

"But they don't want to meet you, Dee," Brandy replied. "Amish are mostly in eastern PA. Lancaster. Even if they were here, they wouldn't talk to us. The Amish would shun a woman for talking to the English."

"English?"

"Us," Brandy clarified. "English speakers. Not Pennsylvania Dutch. Outsiders."

"Oh. Well, if the women are all embedded in churches," I countered, "maybe we are at the right place. We should just... attend services?"

Gianetti looked at me appraisingly. "I don't think that would do you any good, Dee," she said gently. "You don't have the background to understand what you're hearing. Like here. Brandy and I understood, because we're Catholic. You're an outsider to all churches, aren't you."

I sighed. She had a point. This was mostly gibberish to me. Except for the overall take-home message. That was clear as day. Most of the women of Pittsburgh had been swallowed up by the churches. "I respect churches," I said vaguely, in my defense.

Brandy snorted. "Enough for today. Let's go back to the hotel."

Fat raindrops started to splatter the pavement by the time we got there, the day's light overcast fleeing as dark thunderheads chased it eastward. By four, the tornado sirens were warbling again. Emmett prudently stayed the night with the second of the three Rescos he'd traveled to interview.

But the early sirens brought a standing-room-only crowd to the hotel's tornado shelter basement. We didn't need to go hunt natives to interview. They came to us.

17

Interesting fact: Even before the Calm Act, the Catholic Church was the largest non-governmental provider of education and medical services in the world.

"So all we're missing is Judgment," I said, looking over my notes. "From the fighting sects. We have good coverage on non-fighters, too."

"I'll have you know my judgment is excellent," Brandy quipped back.

We were meeting after lunch the next day in the hotel lobby, to take stock of the project so far and decide where to go next with it.

"Oh! And the Pittsburgh PD," I added, making a note. "Could use some interviews from the burbs to round it out. But I haven't heard of any fighting out there, just protection from looters. That's what militia is supposed to do."

"We have more than enough footage, Dee," Brandy countered. "Focus, girlfriend. So do we envision this as a series of short cameos? An in-depth story, maybe 10 minutes?"

I blinked. "You call 10 minutes an in-depth story?"

"On housewives of Pittsburgh?" said Brandy dubiously. "I'd call it rather long. Footage of the militia fighting would be better. But we're not Amiri Baz."

PR's Amiri Baz was a double Pulitzer Prize–winning war correspondent. He and his team provided us stunning footage during Project Reunion, from inside the starving city, food riots and living conditions and shoot-outs with gangs, and from Penn's war-opening attack on West Point. But no, Brandy and I, and earnest young Blake Sondheim on the cameras, were not war correspondents. If I asked the guards for help, they'd threaten to lock me in the basement.

On second thought, I suggested, "We could position Blake on the roof. He could call us if there's anything to film."

"Sucks to be Blake," Brandy agreed. "You paying him?" she inquired with batted lashes.

Without jokes or teasing in return, with pure business manners, I paid her and her team 2 weeks in Hudson dollars, and picked up their hotel tab, including unlimited use of the buffet. Apparently their producer was cheaping out on them. They'd only been eating breakfast in the hotel, then snacks from the van for the rest of the day.

Money transfers completed, Brandy sat back to gaze at me thoughtfully. "What kind of story do you want for PR, Dee?" Her eyes narrowed. "Is this really a story for PR?"

"This is Dee doing research," I evaded. She pursed her lips at me. "Maybe this is Dee assisting Emmett. But he didn't request this. I just don't understand what's going on here in Pittsburgh. People don't do this in Totoket, or Long Island, or the Apple. Fighting between sects? Reverting a hundred years in women's roles? I mean, I understand women's work. Technology is a girl's best friend. But dresses only? And the women – at least in the fighting sects – they seem as militant as the men. And there's no reason. I mean, Emmett thinks with a couple tweaks this town could easily be level 9 –" *Oops.*

Brandy smirked.

I scowled at her. "I'm sure there's a good story about the women, too," I said primly. "If it makes no sense, there has to be a story in there somewhere. Doesn't there?"

Brandy shrugged, with a smile. "With some battle footage from the roof, and that level 9 comment, I could make magic." Before I could forbid her to use that comment, she quickly changed the subject. It's not like I could have unsaid it, anyway. "So did you talk to Emmett's mom about the Evangelists? That is so bizarre, consulting with your boyfriend's mother."

I didn't bother to defend that again. Emma was a sheriff, and a Resco, and an Evangelist. Asking her made sense to me. "She said the same as Donna Gianetti, basically. That I don't know religion well enough to be poking at this. But she said 'Evangelist' is such a broad term, nearly any Protestant could fit under that umbrella."

"No hierarchy," Brandy differed. "Born again implies adult baptism. Jesus Christ as a personal Savior. Active preaching and modeling a righteous life. As they see it. Bible freaks."

"Well, she said 'in practice.'" I sighed. "That's why I need your help. This stuff is gibberish to me. I mean, I understand the words. But the distinctions don't matter to me. And worth dying over? No. So I'm paying you as a research assistant. And you're welcome to use the footage. Help me out, Brandy. What am I missing?"

She shook her head. "Everything?" Brandy wasn't just being mean. I think she truly wanted me to understand. "Dee. You don't get religion. Look, I'm not saying you're not a spiritual or moral person. I'm sure you are. But the whole worldview of God, or Jesus, or the Bible or the clergy or the congregation, or even Emmett and the martial law government – anything outside of you, dictating what is right. That's not you. You don't see the value."

I'm usually a quick study, but it felt like I was struggling to put two plus two together, even counting on my fingers. "What value?"

"The value of bowing your will to a higher authority."

I bowed my will with the utmost difficulty, even to men pointing guns at me. "Are you kidding?"

Brandy groaned and shook her head. "Try to stay with me here, Dee. If it's all up to God anyway, it's not your fault. Right?" I nodded that this logically followed. "You have this part to do, and you know how to do it. And you believe that if you do your part, Jesus or God, or even Emmett, will take care of the rest."

"I think Emmett would really object to that statement," I objected.

"I'm sure he would," Brandy agreed, "if he's an Evangelist." *Oops.* Emmett preferred to keep his religion private. He hadn't even told *me* he was an Evangelist for months.

"But you're missing the point, Dee. Try to stay with me here. If the world has gone insane, turned upside down, and fixing it is entirely beyond your power –"

"You do the next right thing," I supplied.

"No, Dee. *You* do the next right thing," Brandy explained patiently. "But that's not a religious response. That's what I'm trying to tell you."

"I don't get it."

The lobby doors opened, and in walked Emmett with his entourage. "Saved by the bell," Brandy said. I shot her a look. "Who's that, with Emmett?"

That was a very tall woman officer, taller than Emmett and even more upright and perfect in posture and uniform wrinkles than our gay friend Lt. Colonel Cameron. Severely straight dark blond hair was severely parted in the middle and tacked into a bun at the nape of her neck. This was common enough for a lady soldier, but getting the hair to stay so strictly tidy was no mean feat. The guards were constantly poking at their hair. I got the feeling that this woman did not, as a rule, fidget, with her hair or anything else. Her overall presentation screamed out assured command presence.

"Emmett!" I called out, and rose from my armchair with a smile. "Welcome back!"

He smiled and came toward me, directing the woman with a brief touch on the elbow. He paused a half step in puzzlement as he took in the fact that I'd been sitting with Brandy. They stopped to stand rather formally in front of us.

"Major Caroline Drumpeter," Emmett introduced, "may I present my partner, Dee Baker, and her, um, friend, Brandy O'Keefe. Brandy is a reporter with IndieNews. The competition for Dee's Project Reunion News. Ladies, Major Drumpeter."

She gave us a bracing smile. "Pleased to meet you, ladies. Call me Drum."

"Drum is Resco for northwest PA. On Lake Erie." Emmett's voice trailed off. "Dee, what are you wearing?"

I was wearing a modest brown knee-length coat-dress with librarian heels. Brandy had selected a mid-calf beige pleated plaid skirt under beige turtleneck sweater for her ensemble, with her tiny cross on a chain as the sole decoration. Both of us had our hair tied back.

"We got these from the hotel lost and found," I explained. "Lake Erie. Isn't that far from here, Drum?" I'd forgotten that Pennsylvania touched the Great Lakes, but yes, they held a stretch of lake shore between Buffalo and Cleveland.

"I'm based in Meadville," Drum replied. "Ninety miles north of Pittsburgh."

"Why are you dressed like a librarian, darlin'?" Emmett pressed. For Drum's benefit, he explained, "Normally she wears red and maximum cleavage," he pointed to Brandy, who grinned, "and Dee wears steampunk. Or navy chinos and blazer. Or farm coveralls. Anything really, except…that."

I curtsied slightly, and explained, "Drum, we're interviewing women in Pittsburgh. Trying to understand their lifestyle choices." I paused. "And the religious wars."

"Dee doesn't understand religion, though," Brandy said with a sigh.

Drum smiled and nodded, without unbending her perfect posture in the slightest. She even kept her combat boots 6 inches apart and perfectly parallel, hands clasped behind her in habitual parade rest. A model officer. I found her unnerving, and wanted to slouch.

"Uh-huh," Emmett said. He pursed his lips thoughtfully and narrowed his eyes, then seemed to mentally shrug it off. He dismissed me with a peck on the cheek. "See you at dinner, darlin'. Drum, let's get you checked in."

I struggled to get back to work and keep my eyes off Drum and Emmett on their introduction rounds, despite our excellent vantage point in the lobby. Drum had an entourage, militia from her district by the look of them, a couple dozen.

Brandy laughed at me. "Jealous, Dee?"

"Perplexed," I answered in reflex. *Oops.* No, I didn't want to discuss Emmett's Resco decisions with Brandy.

But why on Earth did he bring a woman Resco to Pittsburgh? He wasn't thinking of putting her in charge, was he? They didn't appoint black officers to organize majority white districts. New Haven inherited a black Resco after Emmett, but only after it was organized and doing well. Though in truth, women were the majority in every district. I debated asking him for a moment in private to voice my concerns, but decided against it. Emmett hadn't asked for my opinion. Apparently he thought he knew what he was doing.

"You know what?" I announced. "I'm sick of city. Let's go check out the burbs." I pulled up my layered analysis maps of the district on my computer, that we'd done to figure out the extent of the tornado damage. I swatted Brandy away when she tried to look over my shoulder. There was something... Yes. In Green Tree, the falsely reported suburb of Dane Beaufort's death, we had some curious features marked on the 'unidentified' layer.

"Heya, darlin'," Emmett said, folding me into his arms for a deep kiss. Alas, we were not in either of our bedrooms, but rather the hotel meeting room Emmett had claimed for his office. And Major Drumpeter would be along soon. I'd hoped for some quality time, alone together after dinner. Instead he and Drum would be working into the night.

Still, it felt awfully good to touch him again. I'd been holding a tension in my shoulders ever since our first stupid 'harlot' confrontation, that grew with the militia fighting in the streets, and him leaving for days without our fight fully resolved. Emmett's businesslike greeting when he came back only made it worse. *'Are you mad at me?'* hung over my head like a pall. It took only a single private kiss to evaporate that question. His face was open, boundaries down. He touched without reservation. He was glad to see me.

"Hey, you, too," I said, exploratory. "How you been, stranger?" OK, maybe my boundaries were still a bit prickly.

"Not bad. Got a lot of answers from the neighboring Rescos. Plans coming together, " Emmett reported, somewhat evasively. "Missed you, though."

"Uh-huh," I replied. That was usually his line.

"Uh-huh," he echoed with a smile. "Can't tell you what's going on."

"You're wired," I accused. "Not expecting another night of gunfire in the streets, are we?"

I didn't often get to see Emmett carry out a military operation.

I didn't belong anywhere near one. And even if a camera crew were standing by, he'd typically forbid recording. But the man truly loved his job, and his eyes were alight. I recognized the signs. Mayhem was in the works.

"Couldn't tell you," Emmett replied. "Tonight I'll be in here, working with Drum. If I were planning something, couldn't tell you. Ops details, darlin'. So how's life with Dee?"

He wasn't asking what I was up to. I'd prattled on about that at dinner with IBIS and Drum. Agent Donna Gianetti, at least, had been intrigued to hear that Judgment was the one militant faction I still had no handle on. Emmett, Drum, and Kalnietis seemed more of the persuasion that it didn't matter if Judgment thought the moon was made of goat cheese. The local militia needed to keep their beliefs inside their pointy little heads and stop shooting at each other. An inarguable position.

"Better now that you're back," I said, and settled my body more firmly against his. "About that date night idea," I suggested leadingly.

"Sorry, darlin'," he said. "Not for the next few nights. Gonna be working long hours with Drum."

"Is something going on between you and Drum?" It just blurted out. I didn't mean to say it.

He laughed out loud. "Dee, Drum's a brother officer."

"Sister."

"No difference to me," Emmett assured me. "Dee, you work with a nearly all-male crew at Amenac. I don't see you drooling over Popeye or Dave. Same difference. Drum's a team-mate."

"Why would you pick a female Resco for Pittsburgh?" I asked. "Emmett, have you noticed how far these people have backslid on women's equality?"

"Sure have," he agreed. "They need to get over it. I met with three Rescos, Dee. Drum is the best qualified. I don't want to go into this now. She'll be here any minute."

"But you know what you're doing," I said doubtfully.

"Uh-huh," he said.

"And there will be mayhem."

He gave me a deep kiss instead of answering. "Wanna talk. Wanna have that date," he murmured after, laying his cheek against mine. "But it'll be a few days. I need to do my job now, darlin'. Trust me a little while."

Drum arrived, and I turned to leave.

"Oh, Dee? One more thing," Emmett requested. "Now that people are home for the night, I'd like you to split the meshnet into subnets. Maybe twenty or so for the city, six for the rest of Allegheny County outside the city. Try to break it along any militia boundaries you see on the map. Can you do all that tonight?"

"Sure," I said, intrigued. "Closed subnets?" If I closed them, communications would cease between subnets except for people with override rights. At the moment, everyone with overrides resided in the hotel with me. Closed subnets were one of the control features I balked at when we were specifying the public mesh. How quickly I'd become inured to tyranny once I flipped to the ruling side. In the Apple Core, we could close a single subnet to isolate a mini-city before martial law cleanup operations.

"Not yet," he said. "Just get the subnets assigned and propagated. I'd like to be able to close them later."

"Actually, Dee?" Drum broke in. "If you could sketch your proposed map, and then bring it to me? I might want to adjust." She smiled at me professionally. I returned the smile.

And I left them to it. Whatever it was. It was foolish to feel jealous. Except it wasn't that Drum was a woman that I felt jealous about. I wasn't a partner on Emmett's secrets and schemes this time, and she was. And the militant sects left me deeply uneasy.

At least I had plenty of work to do to keep me busy. It took me over two hours just to figure out where that many subnet boundaries should go. And it was Drum, not Emmett, who reviewed my map decomposition and suggested adjustments. She was cool, competent, and professional. She was appreciative of my work, and asked good questions about my decisions. Then she was not one bit shy about ordering me to shift a border, just as matter-of-factly as Emmett or Cam or Ash would do. Drum seemed a fine officer.

18

Interesting fact: The U.S. as a whole was over 50% deeply religious before the Calm Act. In contrast, its fellow wealthy English-speaking countries – the UK, Canada, Australia, and New Zealand – hovered around 20% religious.

"Wow, Brandy, what great footage!" I praised her. "You too, Blake, well done!"

While I was gerrymandering the meshnet last night, the militia sects resumed their re-enactment of the Thirty Years' War on the streets of Pittsburgh. Brandy and Blake spent the evening on the roof filming. Camera man Blake Sondheim did us proud with steady footage of weapons in the distance, and daytime shots to clarify the same terrain. Brandy did a polished job in the talking head department, making liberal use of our local religion research in an attempt to explain the fighting.

Not surprisingly, they'd slept in until lunch. We were using Blake's bedroom as a workroom, since his equipment was a hassle to move. IndieNews was flatly forbidden access to the meeting room and interrogation corridor where Emmett had claimed an office.

"Hey, Blake," I said thoughtfully. "Could we edit together about a ten-minute segment of this?"

"What are you thinking here, Dee?" Brandy asked.

"Honestly? I'd like to show it to Emmett and Drum and the IBIS investigators," I told them. "Probably our troops as well."

"An audience of what, fifty?" Brandy complained. "Christ, Dee." No doubt she was hoping for a top news story to grab millions of viewers.

"Well, we might get it past the censors," I allowed. "What do you think our chances are of that?" Brandy sighed agreement. Not much chance today. "But once Emmett has such a video, he'd show it to the military governors. Cullen, Schwabacher, Taibbi, Link. You'll play to a small but very select audience," I coaxed. "Besides, I already paid you for it. And some of the footage will get declassified, sooner or later."

After a little more wheedling, they conceded that they didn't have any brighter ideas that could reach today's headlines. We cobbled it together quickly, though Blake and I made time to shoot a short sequence on the Monongahela river walk near the hotel. That was just a quick script – me on screen, saying here we are in Pittsburgh, over there's the deserted downtown damaged by tornados, we've found a city torn by religious conflict. Just enough to preface Brandy's war from the rooftop narrative. Indie-News had collected enough footage for filler, including the wreckage of the famous Monongahela Incline and assorted other tornado damage closeups. At the end, we tacked on the local meshnet map, annotated with factions. That segment could simply drop off anything we tried to publish.

We invited Emmett and company up for a screening after dinner.

Major Drumpeter was enchanted. Closeted with Emmett on their mysterious business, she'd seen less of the nocturnal fireworks than the rest of us. And she'd certainly never worked with a news crew preparing custom briefing materials. Not many officers had, aside from Emmett.

"Why is there no fighting close to the hotel?" Drum pounced. She had her meshnet map out on her phone to follow along. We explained how the well-equipped Pittsburgh PD faction held our turf. Drum eagerly claimed ownership of Blake to poke through his other footage, while the rest of us edged back out into the hall. Sucks to be Blake, as Brandy would say. Though in fairness, Blake seemed flattered by Drum's appreciative attention. Brandy and I were more inclined to treat him as a useful doormat. Some guys just invite that somehow.

"Any chance you'd help us past the censors?" I asked Emmett.

"No," Emmett said flatly.

"But –" Brandy attempted.

"Cross purposes, Brandy," Emmett told her. "You're in Pittsburgh, and want headlines. But I don't want attention on Pittsburgh. Nothing passes the censors for now. Great video, though. Thank you, darlin'. And your team, Brandy," he added grudgingly.

"I was thinking it might make good orientation footage," I said. "For Drum, the governors. Maybe the troops. Put it on a secure server for you." I'd already sent him the link and password.

"Is that wise?" Kalnietis said. "Dee and Brandy have drawn subtle conclusions here, that I'm not sure I'm ready to make. I prefer to keep an open mind."

"Uh-huh," agreed Emmett. He shrugged. "Generals are used to that. Yeah, I'll send it along. And Captain Johnson at least. A few others. Up to them what they do with it." He excused himself and hurried back to work in his office off the lobby. Kalnietis left as well.

Donna Gianetti lingered a moment. "Dee, Brandy. Any clarity yet on the Judgment sect?"

"Sorry, no," I said.

"I was watching the meshnet last night, during the fighting," she continued thoughtfully. "Judgment seems to appear briefly, then vanish."

I nodded. "I think they edit themselves out when someone tags them on the map. The other factions haven't caught on to that yet. The meshnet is new to them."

Gianetti's eyebrows flew up. "You can edit someone else's map marker?"

"Several ways," I said. "If you want a map marker to vanish, the easiest way is to drop another icon square on top of it, saying something else. Then no one notices that there's another marker underneath. Or, you can comment on someone else's marker, but that won't remove their comments. Unless you have overrides. But you're also allowed to add more icons to an existing marker. Only one gets shown. Unfortunately, it's whichever icon is lowest on the list, not the one that was added first."

"Lowest on the list?"

I showed her the full list of icons, about 500 to choose from, though I'd curated a quick-pick list of 25 suggested icons, in a different order, displayed to the user first. The rest were hidden under a 'more' button. Naturally, the majority of markers used on the map were quick picks. The natives had selected smileys in assorted colors and expressions to represent militia force positions, in assorted colors. Judgment's was a little devil. The Catholics' angel, Apocalyptic purple frown, and Evangelist toothy grin were lower on the master list. Icons currently visible were automatically added to the quick-pick list, which had grown to about 40 with other people's selections. Markers expired off the map in a day, unless updated or made 'sticky' by someone with the right permissions.

"The devil is an interesting choice, for a Christian sect," Gianetti murmured.

"Never let your enemy define you," I countered. "Besides, do we even know that Judgment is Christian? I mean, probably. But that's an assumption." I looked up to see that Drum had joined us, and was listening intently.

"What do other groups say about Judgment?" Gianetti continued probing.

"That they don't know any," said Brandy. "Followed by something slanderous. They eat children. They keep slaves. They're mass murderers. They worship Satan. They want to rush us to Judgment Day."

I frowned at her. "When did you hear that? I thought that was the Apocalyptics."

Brandy sighed. "You were probably sitting right next to me. In the tornado shelter the other night. You just don't know what you're hearing." She relented a little and allowed, "Also hard to keep track of who's slandering who."

I scowled in frustration. I knew there was something important here, in what these sects believed, but I just didn't get it. Brandy was probably right.

Drum smiled at me sympathetically. "Dee," she asked, "is there a way to display only icons of a particular type?"

"Sure," I said, and demonstrated. Little devils of Judgment sprang up all over the map. I frowned, and panned around the map a bit. "They're everywhere that fighting erupts," I murmured. "More than I thought."

"That's very helpful," Drum encouraged, with a smile. "Thank you." Her phone chirped and she excused herself.

Before Gianetti left, too, she tapped my screen. "You're onto something, Dee. I know this is hard for you, but please keep me apprised. OK?"

I sighed and nodded agreement.

"What next, PR master?" Brandy asked sourly, after Gianetti was gone. "Your boyfriend just promised to squelch anything we do."

"Temporarily squelched," I corrected. "Doesn't mean it will

never see the light of day, Brandy. Just that we can't go public while it might interfere with his operations."

"Which are?"

"Would I tell you if I knew?" I returned. "And I don't know." Although I thought I could guess. The prime directive of martial law was to enforce public order. Fighting in the streets was not a Resco's idea of order. Ergo, I assumed Emmett and Drum were busy figuring out how to suppress the militias.

But, "Postcards from Pittsburgh," was what I said. "We continue filming and spinning stories. Just can't publish them yet. We'll have great stories when we're done, spun to explain the IBIS conclusions and Emmett's recommendations."

"You publish to back them up," Brandy countered. "I publish to question them."

"Then your stories will be forever censored, while mine play," I said. "Brandy, look. Are you OK with religious factions fighting in the streets? You want to live here like this?"

"No," she admitted sourly. "I know Emmett's just doing his job, Dee. Not so convinced these people deserve it, though."

I shook my head in disapproval. Nobody deserved to live in chaos. "At any rate, our viewers love seeing ex-U.S. stories. How people are coping in other super-states. The human interest stories will get watched. Not every story can make top ten."

My phone chirped with a message from Emmett. I told Brandy, "Gotta go. Talk to you tomorrow." I slipped into my room and locked the door.

"Thank you for joining us, Dee," Hudson Governor Sean Cullen greeted me, when I joined the video conference in progress. I'd been cooling my heels in my bedroom alone for half an hour on standby, at Emmett's messaged request. The other conference attendees had time to watch our video segment and discuss it before bringing me in.

I smiled wanly at the array of people on my screen. In addition to Emmett and Cullen, we had Penn's General Taibbi and Ohio's General Schwabacher. Captain Niedermeyer, top Resco of New England. Emmett's commanding officer Pete Hoffman from New Jersey. And two more brother Hudson Rescos, Tony Nasser from upstate and Ash Margolis from Manhattan-Bronx.

Note to self: before dramatizing my ideas to get attention, ask first, 'Why do I want attention? What will I do with it?' Emmett looked like he might be wondering the same thing.

"Why did you produce this video?" Cullen asked. "Thank you, by the way. It was very illuminating."

"I'm glad," I said. "Eventually, PR News and IndieNews would like to publish this footage. But when I saw it this afternoon, I thought it might make good briefing material for Drum – Major Drumpeter. And we can't publish anything now, so... Just trying to be useful, I guess."

John Niedermeyer and Ash Margolis knew me best. Their eyes seemed to dance with mirth. OK, I had to admit it sounded stupid.

"Ms. Baker," Penn's Seth Taibbi stepped in. "What do you think these people are fighting for?"

"I think that's a crucial question, sir," I replied. "I'm not convinced we've found an answer. The hotel manager seems to think they want to kill each other, over religious disputes. I was just studying the map with Drum. There's one sect we still don't have a handle on, Judgment. On the map, it looks like Judgment might be instigating these fights – I don't know how – then covering their tracks. It isn't clear whether they stick around to participate."

Lt. Colonel Tony Nasser of upstate looked particularly concerned by this. Which was a new look on him. Tony was relaxed and affable the few times we'd met. Sean Cullen invited him to speak candidly.

"Yes, sir," Tony acknowledged. "Dee, we've suppressed the details of this. But we've had serious run-ins with a sect in western New York. Part of their pattern is to run and hide in Penn. They seem to instigate armed conflict between Christian fundamentalists. Emmett, have you run into any mass graves?"

"Probable," Emmett agreed. "Identified by Dee's satellite survey. Don't want to investigate until the area is pacified. Not worth the risk now."

"What?" I couldn't help blurting it out. My survey showed mass graves?

Looking slightly harried, Emmett displayed my layered map on his feed. "Dee, on the 'unknown' layer. Here, in Green Tree, where Paul Dukakis and the original video post claimed that Dane was killed."

I'd noticed that feature before, and already mentioned to the IndieNews crew that our reporting team might go take a look. There was recently disturbed land, that looked something like a dump, but greener and lusher than the surroundings, with no machine debris. My heart sank, especially to think that Emmett and the other Rescos had seen enough mass graves to recognize them on a satellite image.

"There are a half dozen sites like this," Emmett continued, "plus a much larger one outside West Mifflin, east of Allegheny County. Nearly the size of the Staten Island barrow yard. Anyway. Why, Tony?"

Tony looked grim. "When you can get out and look around, you might find some of the mass graves have signs, carved into a tree or something. I've dubbed them the Sixers here, because some signs said '666.' Trying to lighten the tone. But another used an upside-down crooked cross."

Emmett's irate face replaced the map. "What Christian would adopt the number of the beast?"

Tony shook his head. "They aspire to be the beast, Emmett. They want to help destroy the world. Get on the winning side, I guess. They've murdered whole hamlets upstate. No, correction. They wipe out whole hamlets, but we only find about half the bodies. We think the missing bodies are either converts or slaves. They take a lot of younger men and women, probably slaves. Some say their goal is decimation. No more than 35 million should survive, baptized in blood. Just them, having destroyed any rebuilders. That would be us."

"This is not a religion," Sean Cullen broke in. "Emmett, don't treat it as such. If you find that your Judgment group is more of these Sixers, exterminate them." He amended his tone. "Or, that would be my order in Hudson. Seth?"

Seth Taibbi nodded slowly in distaste. "Agreed."

Emmett pressed, "Tony? The size of the *Staten Island* barrow yards? That was hundreds of thousands of bodies. Are you suggesting *that* could be these Sixers?"

I could see Emmett's gruesome point. An isolated hamlet could be wiped out by a large survivalist band. A force capable of killing – and *burying* – as many people as Ebola and starvation in Staten Island – that was a whole different league. A force far beyond the few dozen soldiers we had here to protect us.

Tony shrugged apologetically. "Mostly hundreds in upstate. One mass grave over a thousand. I don't know what anything Staten Island's size could be about. I assume you're not missing that many from Pittsburgh. It's not that big a city."

Ash Margolis volunteered, "I heard over a million were resettled out from Philadelphia. Makes sense some of them would be sent toward Pittsburgh, Emmett. Colonel Schneider ought to have records, where they went."

Emmett asked, "Permission to add Major Drumpeter to this call, sirs?" The governors nodded and Emmett went offline a moment, presumably to brief Drum. He didn't introduce her, so I supposed she'd been introduced on the video call earlier, then gone back to work. Maybe they wanted to discuss her behind her back.

Pete Hoffman, Emmett's CO from New Jersey, offered, "Emmett, here's another clue. We tried to track these Sixers on the Amenac boards. Penn wasn't talking at the time. But our incidents were northeast of your location. I found some others southwest, in West Virginia and Ken-Tenn. Different names. Apocalypse. Reckoning. Armageddon. Couldn't match the sixes, just mass murders and taking slaves."

"If I may," Drum said diffidently, "I've seen nothing like this in the northwest corner, my Resco district. But there are ten counties east of us with no Resco at all. Tony, that would stretch nearly to I-81, south from Binghamton. Just not very many people in there."

"Ten counties!" Sean Cullen said. "Drum, how many counties do you have?"

"My district is four counties, sir," Drum said. "There are ten more counties without Resco running from the center of the state southwest to the West Virginia border. So about twenty contiguous unsupervised counties altogether, cutting across PA. There used to be a Resco with four counties to anchor the middle. But he vanished when General Taibbi took over. So western PA is pretty cut off. Except for the railroad, of course. Neighboring Rescos try to keep an eye on the railroad through the unorganized zones."

"They pay taxes," Taibbi said. "Lot of agriculture in those areas. Seem peaceable, so far as I know."

Sean Cullen and Charles Schwabacher, Taibbi's neighboring peers, pursed their lips in censure. Schwabacher voiced their feedback. "Seth, if you don't have eyes on them, you don't really know what's going on in there. Twenty counties? Emmett, please make note of this for your recommendations."

"Sir," Emmett agreed.

"I could ask the gran caravans," I suggested. "They cross between upstate and Penn all the time."

Taibbi and the other governor-generals looked pained. Their borders were supposed to be impermeable. But how could they be? That stretch of border between Penn and Hudson was a hundred miles of depopulated hills, with trees. The border with West Virginia was the same, plus mountains.

Emmett just smiled sadly. "Thank you, Dee."

"Alright," Sean Cullen said slowly. "Emmett, I approve your plans." Taibbi and Schwabacher nodded. Pete Hoffman shrugged, but he wasn't really Emmett's commanding officer at present. Niedermeyer looked dubious as well, and Ash and Tony concerned. "Thank you, all," Cullen said. And the video conference ended.

I didn't know what plans they were talking about. But I went ahead and emailed my contact Jean-Claude Alarie with the gran caravans, asking for information on Judgment or Sixers, or any other sect they'd run into in Penn that seemed bent on destruction and decimation.

To my surprise, Pete Hoffman called me on the phone. "Hey, Dee? Forgive me if this is out of line, but I hear you and Emmett are having some relationship problems."

"That's kinda personal, Pete," I agreed.

"I'd like to ask a favor, Dee," Pete pressed. "Put it aside. Live in the moment. Emmett can't be worrying about you right now. Deal with your relationship after you're home safe. OK?"

I pursed my lips, unwilling to agree on the principle that he shouldn't be asking. But then again, maybe he should. What was Emmett up to, anyway? "OK," I said grudgingly.

Five minutes later, Emmett appeared at my door. "What's wrong?" he asked. "Pete told me to break off and visit you ASAP."

I laughed. "Your boss ordered you to make a booty call?"

"Uh-huh," he said with a grin, and closed the bedroom door firmly behind him. "Pete's a great CO."

I explained while I drew him toward the bed. "Pete advised we live in the now."

Emmett pulled off his shirts, and warned, "Good, because I don't have much time."

"Use it well," I suggested.

Later, relaxing for a few minutes in bed before getting dressed again and back to work, Emmett said, "Darlin'? Thank you for that video. It really helped frame a negotiation with the governors. But especially, you backed up Drum. That was really nice of you, to make a whole video to brief her. She needs your support. That means a lot to me. Thank you."

"Uh-huh," I said thoughtfully. "So Drum is your pick for new Resco of Pittsburgh? What did you get out of the governors?"

He sighed and sat up. "Gotta go. You'll see."

I draped myself over his back. "I love you, Emmett. I know you'll make good choices out there. I know you can't tell me now. But you will tell me sometime."

He snorted softly. "I love you, too, Dee. You'll be OK with the choices I'm making here. Promise."

"Good to know."

19

Interesting fact: Though undeniably charismatic, storms in the U.S. weren't particularly deadly before climate change turbo-charged them, and the weather service stopped issuing warnings. On average, about 300 people a year died from tornados, thunderstorms, and hurricanes combined. In contrast, about 35,000 died annually in traffic accidents, 16,000 were murdered, and 3,400 drowned.

"How was your nap?" I inquired of Emmett the next afternoon. I'd never known the man to take an afternoon nap before. But that's what he'd done after lunch. He ordered the rest of us to be back at the hotel no later than 3 p.m. I was sitting in the hotel lobby with my computer.

"Great," Emmett replied, stretching. "How's the weather report?"

"Overcast, with continued overcast," I replied. "Not a sunny town, one feels."

"Great," Emmett repeated. "Subnets all propagated?" He plopped down beside me on the couch.

"So far as I can tell," I said.

He nodded and looked at me searchingly. "Want to take part in an operation? I could use you to manage the meshnet." He leaned closer and kissed my ear, before whispering into it, "You could see what's going on."

Pete was right. We'd only spent a half hour playing together last night, but it made a huge difference. Emmett and I felt like partners again. The marriage issue was strictly off-limits.

"Tempting," I allowed. "If I don't?"

"You'll implode from frustrated curiosity," Emmett predicted. "About 36 hours. Give or take. Locked in the basement. Out of the loop. With no answers."

I laughed out loud. "You're right. I'd climb the walls."

"Uh-huh," he agreed happily. Yes, the man was definitely wired for action. "You in?"

"I'm in."

"Then post this ASAP," he mailed me something from his phone, and mine chirped accordingly. "And be in my office in a half hour. Oh, is everyone back yet?"

"Blake's not," I said, concerned. "We sent him to Green Tree to collect footage."

Emmett raised an eyebrow in pained disbelief. "Dee, I said *we* wouldn't go to Green Tree, because it wasn't worth the risk. With armed guards. Why'd you send a camera guy?"

"Because a camera guy is non-threatening?"

Emmett shook his head. "If he's not on the road yet, tell him to shelter in place."

"What does that mean?" I asked.

"He needs to stay put," Emmett said, "and find someplace to lay low. Trying to flee in front of what's about to happen, could be very bad for his health. Dee, you can't explain it any further. Just send him a text, verbatim. 'Shelter in place, do not return to hotel.' See you soon, darlin'." He rose and headed for his office meeting room.

That was worrisome, but I posted Emmett's announcement first.

> **IMPORTANT:** Curfew tonight 5 p.m. Everyone proceed to your own home IMMEDIATELY, including militia personnel. All businesses to close NOW. Sirens to command attention. Please notify neighbors not on meshnet.
>
> No exceptions. If you believe you have a valid exception, and have not received separate instructions, contact @RescoCDrumpeter#NoExceptionsMeansNone. And be home by 5 p.m.
>
> By order, Resco Colonel Emmett MacLaren, on behalf of PA Governor-General Seth Taibbi.

That notice would be received by everyone on the Pittsburgh meshnet, with a rude priority *blatt* for attention. The locals used the tornado siren system to count down the final 15 minutes to curfew, by 5 minute increments, every night. So that was a familiar system to them, and shouldn't send people scurrying to the tornado shelters. Though to be on the safe side, Mrs. Wiehl scrambled past me to deploy a new sign at the hotel entrance. I loved the Wiehls, I really did.

I wondered what on earth Emmett planned to do at 5 p.m., with only a few dozen troops and borrowed militia on hand. Allegheny County, Pittsburgh's over-sized Resco district, still held over a million people. It should have had three Rescos from the start, not one, as I understood the Resco guidelines.

I texted Blake verbatim as per Emmett's instructions, only adding 'where are you?' and copying Brandy. By then, Sergeant Becque was bearing down on me to demand where Blake was, and ask for a photo of him and description of his vehicle, including license plate. In minutes, Brandy and her producer also piled into the hotel lobby to demand what all this was about. I introduced them to each other to supply Becque's needs, and excused myself to clear out the phone charging bank and queue. Facility closed, go home.

I tried to collect some snacks to bring with me into Emmett's meeting room. But Mrs. Wiehl intercepted me, and assured me she'd dispatch her daughter with a snack trolley. So I just ate my own slice of pie, packed up my stuff, and reported for duty. The door was closed. Tibbs, Nguyen, and a couple of Drum's people were already waiting, carrying their computers.

Belatedly, I realized I hadn't tested the contact link. So I sent a 'testing' email. I claimed I was a daycare provider with five children on hand, and couldn't leave until their parents picked them up. True to form, I got a form mail response.

Thank you for contacting the martial law government. We are currently carrying out a police action in your area to insure public order. No one will respond to your email.

We keep a list of public services to consider in the event of police actions, in case they need alternate instructions, such as waterworks, militia units, and power plants. If you have not received such separate instructions TODAY, you are required to obey the general instructions.

In the unlikely event this is in error, you can use the contact link below. If we do not agree that your concern merits our attention, you are **guilty of interfering with a Resco operation**. The maximum penalty is death. The minimum penalty is 24 hours in jail and a black mark on your record.

@RescoCDrumpeter#ImWillingToGoToJail

"Wow, Drum's really polite," I commented, already tapping in my jail bid test email. I didn't have any milk in the house to feed the children, I claimed.

"That's polite?" one of Drum's people asked, with a laugh. Her name was Renata.

"Oh, yeah," I assured her. "Emmett sure doesn't thank people for talking back to him. And with people behaving like this? Militia shooting each other in the streets over religion? Emmett would have promised to fire upon anyone who fails to obey instructions. Sometimes he suggests putting them in stocks, naked, for public display. Cam's actually done that to people, out on Long Island. Apples think it's funny."

Funny, once upon a time I was stunned that my boyfriend would say such a thing. After the past three months in Brooklyn and Queens, putting people in stocks naked sounded rather tame. The shell-shocked apples of New York responded best to a firm hand. Besides, once upon a time I was horrified by martial law. The world had changed since then. Martial law sucked, but armed chaos and starvation were a whole lot worse. And to receive this email, you had to be silly enough to argue with a martial law directive first.

"Deeb," the other of Drum's pair, Christopher, informed me solemnly, "you are hereby sentenced to spend the night locked in this hotel for interfering with a Resco operation. Running out of milk is no excuse."

"You got stuck with that mailbox, eh?" I grinned at him. "My condolences. Don't forget my black mark, now. I'm a known trouble-maker."

"Oh!" Christopher said. "Yeah, how do I do that?"

We bent heads together as I showed him how to forward a contact for arrest and punishment. Maintaining the word 'testing' in the subject line, of course. Sergeant Becque was kind enough to RSVP that I'd been secured and punished, thus pushing my case into its terminal bucket.

Systems test complete. For that subsystem, anyway. The

tornado sirens emitted a brief wail on the quarter hour, to encourage people on to their curfew destinations.

Drum opened the door with a smile, and invited us all in.

"Hey, darlin'," Emmett greeted me with a smile. "Ready for action?"

"Sure!" I said. "Ready to know what the action is, anyway."

"One step at a time," he said. "First step. Tonight we're using subnet slices, instead of closed subnets. I'd like for you – now – to slice the meshnet across the Allegheny, Monongahela, and Ohio Rivers. Also, slice east of Carnegie-Mellon. So the downtown triangle subnets are sliced off together. They can talk to each other, but not across the slices. Got it? Oh, and slice all Internet-to-meshnet traffic. For everybody."

He pointed out the slice lines on a map on the big display, the centerpiece of our little operations center. Naturally I stepped up to the screen and peered at a lot of other interesting things marked on that map.

"Dee?" Emmett prodded gently. "First set up your computer, and do the slices, OK?"

"Oh, right. Sorry." I chose a seat, cabled in the computer, and brought up the meshnet administration console to make the slices that prevented any communication across those meshnet borders. For normal users, that is. Our override messages would cross loud and clear, including back and forth from the Internet. In fact, I noted, they'd be louder and clearer than ever. Emmett must have sent people to deploy repeaters, because there were no gaps remaining in Allegheny County.

"Emmett," I called, "there are a ton of new meshnet users outside the county. There aren't that many people out there."

"That's correct, Dee," he said. He was busy on his computer, and didn't elaborate.

After I made the slices, Tibbs asked my advice on setting up traffic filters. Apparently he and Nguyen and Drum's female militia assistant – Renata – would be our email spying division.

They had several lists of keywords to flag on all communications across the meshnet that weren't from people with override or 'IOI' permission. Apparently IOI was a new type of override group that Emmett had created just for this operation. The crowds outside the county border were chock full of IOI's. So apparently those were the forces Emmett was bringing in for this operation, whatever that was.

I showed Tibbs how to sort flagged messages into buckets automatically based on keyword priority. I gave him another bucket labeled '#Escalate', and suggested Nguyen and Renata divvy up watching all the other buckets. They would forward to #Escalate anything for Tibbs to consider acting on, while Tibbs monitored only that one bucket. More urgent escalations could be red-flagged, or called out verbally.

It was a complicated setup, and these three hadn't done meshnet administration before. The flagged message traffic volume was also way too high for just three of them to monitor effectively. As one of the meshnet architects, I knew every trick there was. The tornado sirens wailed a couple more times while I tutored and tweaked. But at last I had all three with a comfortable stream of messages to skim. They could open and close the spigots a bit by turning on and off assorted buckets into their visual stream. For instance, I could confidently predict that the #guns bucket would remain turned off for hours, if not the duration. 'Guns' was just too common a word in emails, in a situation like this.

I was standing watching them process email when Emmett came up behind me. "They all set here?"

I nodded judiciously. "They could use a couple more people. But they know how to tune down the roar."

"Excellent," he murmured. "Time for another announcement. Ready?" He forwarded it to me.

IMPORTANT: Effective immediately, **all Pittsburgh militia are**

disbanded. At 5 p.m. all militia-issued weapons, munitions, and uniforms must be deposited at curbside in front of your home for collection. No exceptions. **Personal firearms must also be relinquished at curbside.** Tag personal items with owner's contact info, for return at later date. Electronic surveillance and physical home searches will be used. Report location of any munition stashes to @RescoEMacLaren#Stash.

We anticipate this lockdown will last 36-48 hours. Your full cooperation is required.

That was the version for inside the city and suburbs. There was a softer rendition for the outer exurbs. There, personal weapons would be inventoried at curbside, but not confiscated.

"Wow, Emmett," I breathed. "How the –" I looked back up at the big map. Emmett stepped in to block my view and playfully frowned at me. I took the hint and broadcast his announcement before asking anything further. The tornado siren pealed again, to mark 4:30.

"Not everyone's on the meshnet," I pointed out.

"We have loudspeakers, too," Emmett said. "You just worry about the meshnet."

I dutifully sent a test message to @RescoEMacLaren#Stash, advising of weapons, munitions, and pies here at the hotel. Drum's other assistant, Christopher, proved the unlucky winner of that mailbox.

I selected a nice red bomb icon for him, and demonstrated how to position the red bomb on the hotel on the meshnet map, and paste in my email report, all on a layer privileged so only overrides and 101's could see the reported arsenals. Christopher was gratifyingly quick on the uptake. But his assignment took a lot more manual fiddling than the mail spies' job. And he couldn't ignore anything, while the responses started flooding in.

We also needed to set up a nuisance response form letter (no, you don't have second amendment rights – that country no longer exists, and your neighbor's safety trumps your gun collection), plus a one-click system to forward an email for punishment and simultaneously suspend the user's meshnet privileges, because those who emailed us defiance tended to mouth off repeatedly. Soon another special case came in, a report of a neighbor stealing guns at curbside, and we had to invent a pathway to escalate that for follow-through.

For the final quarter hour of the run-up to 5 p.m., the tornado sirens sounded off every 5 minutes instead of 15. There's something about count-downs and warnings that really gets under your skin and sets the adrenalin pumping. Christopher and I could have done without the added excitement.

Emmett was behind me again, hands on my hips, as a longer fog-horn of doom from the tornado sirens announced the onset of curfew enforcement. I froze. "Take your time, get it right, darlin'," Emmett murmured softly to me.

I blew my breath out and watched Christopher work, and leaned back into Emmett. Another question or two came up, and I answered them. After 5 minutes more, Christopher declared himself to be all set, and I didn't see anything more I could contribute to ease his chores.

I turned and planted a kiss on Emmett's nose. "Now do I finally get to ask?"

"No," said Emmett. "Now we eat dinner." He laughed out loud at the expression on my face. "Short dinner break, Drum?" he called over to her. Major Drumpeter was sitting at her computer, frequently talking over a headset. She nodded for us to go ahead.

So Emmett and I got to eat at the buffet before all hell broke loose on Pittsburgh.

20

*Interesting fact: Pittsburgh rebounded from the fall of American steel
with high-tech industries, robotics, pharmaceuticals, and health care.
It was also home to H.J. Heinz ketchup and pickle manufacture.*

"Our steeds have arrived?" Emmett asked Drum, as soon as we were back in the situation room. Maddeningly, eating at the buffet meant that Emmett couldn't tell me anything over dinner about what came next. We didn't linger long, though.

Drum grinned. "Ready to roll, sir. Colonel McNaughton is eager to say hello."

A lazy smile bloomed on Emmett's face. "Old Naughty, huh? Look forward to catching up after the funeral. I'll call him in a minute. First, time we brief our team, Drum. Dee's about to strangle someone."

"Yes, sir," Drum agreed. She took a parade rest sort of stance at the front of the room. "Your attention please. As you've gathered, tonight's operation is to disarm the civilian population of Allegheny County, with especial focus on the militia. Who have been fired."

"Very fired," Emmett confirmed. He perched lazily on a table corner near Drum.

"We believe there are about 1400 active militia in the county," Drum continued. "We know where most of them live. There are also roughly 1.1 million civilians. At the usual rate of private gun ownership in America, we estimate well over a million weapons in private hands. We hope to disarm everyone inside this line around the city proper." She used a laser pointer to draw a ring around the inner suburbs. "And possibly trouble spots outside the line.

"Due to previous attacks on Colonel MacLaren and Major Beaufort," she continued, pointing to the locations of those attacks, plus the mysteriously framed Green Tree, "we will begin by disarming the downtown triangle between the rivers, and our own environs here across the Monongahela. After a delay of a couple hours to assess effectiveness, we will either double down in those areas, or commence disarming this region northwest of downtown, where fighting has also been heavy.

"Obviously, we cannot accomplish this with our few troops here and the 900-member Pittsburgh P.D.," she continued. "Those forces will continue to secure our immediate neighborhood. And contribute armored loudspeaker vehicles to communicate with the populace. The sweep to collect arms will be carried out by Colonel MacLaren's alma mater, the 101st Airborne Division out of Fort Campbell, Kentucky." She beamed at him.

"Part of the 101st, anyway," Emmett agreed. "Ten thousand troops, experienced in counter-insurgency in the sandbox. Supported by truck transport from the Ohio line, and the Penn Air Force."

Ten thousand troops was only part of the 101st Airborne? My mind boggled.

"Question, sir?" Tibbs raised his hand. "The 101st wasn't distributed to border garrison duty?"

"Nope," Emmett confirmed. "Ken-Tenn decided on border

surveillance, plus a centralized mobile force to deploy to handle problems. Suits the thinly settled rough terrain, and the fighting style of the 101st."

"Niedermeyer will want to know if they offer markers," Tibbs said, on behalf of his New England master.

Emmett shook his head. "Not available for Hudson or New England. Or I might have hit them up myself before. But like me, Dane Beaufort was 101st. Otherwise they wouldn't visit Penn, either. It's nearly 600 miles."

Brooklyn to Pittsburgh was under 400 miles. I could relate to the effort required these days. Traveling sucked in our new world. These troops had come a long way out of their way to get shot at. And it seemed very likely indeed that they'd be fired upon. Americans do like their guns.

"Our job," Drum resumed, "is oversight and coordination from the civilian perspective. We're taking input from the populace." I supposed eavesdropping was a form of taking input. "Leads on arsenals, complaints, watching for trouble spots. The PA Air Force is providing aerial surveillance. Operational command lies with the 101st Airborne. But we are in effect the civilian authorities."

No doubt I looked suitably dubious. But the martial law governments did consider Rescos to be the spokespersons for civilian interests. In New England and Hudson, this seemed less problematic, since the Rescos policed each other pretty thoroughly. In Penn, Drum and Beaufort had been on their own, completely free agents. Their government hadn't even noticed when they mutinied.

"Drum is in command here," Emmett added. "I choose to assist and advise. What we tell the world outside this room may differ. This operation is approved by Penn, Ken-Tenn, Ohio, Hudson, and New England. Greater Virginia chose to neither approve nor disapprove. Ontario was informed as a courtesy. None of them will interfere."

"Any more questions?" Drum asked brightly. "No? Then back to your stations!"

I didn't imagine they could find every gun, even with house to house searches and scans. But no doubt they'd lean extra hard on known militia members and hostile households. If a courteous grandpa hid his backup pistol in a vacuum cleaner bag, he'd probably get away with it. We weren't concerned with courteous grandpas.

I didn't have a station or task, particularly. But Emmett snared me, and had me close the mesh subnets for the first three attack areas, plus the wide exurb subnets.

Then he and Drum were both busy on the phone with the 101st forces. I looked over Drum's two computers. She had one set to the meshnet admin interface, and another running the military map showing on the big screen. In effect, the meshnet map was us communicating status to them, and the military map communicated their status to us.

But her view was cluttered with church rants and yesterday's fights. I got on my own computer and sifted and filtered my meshnet map view to convey only the information I might want to keep the 101st apprised of. Reported arsenals. Weapons theft. Outbreaks of violence and other new markers since the first curfew announcement. I added another privileged layer called Misc in case I thought of anything else later. And I packaged that up with a brief introduction and a link to regenerate that map view and legend, and sent it to Drum with a red flag, in case she found it useful.

She read my message within a minute, and switched her mesh map view immediately. She looked it over, and forwarded it on to the 101st. I got a big thumbs up and grateful grin from her. Emmett peered at it and gave me a big smile, too.

At loose ends again, I looked around to see where else I might be useful. I forwarded my '101st view map' to Tibbs. If he was in charge of escalation, that was a good place to put things. I drifted over to him, and we chatted about that for a while. Aside from marking people for later investigation or jail time, he wasn't unduly stretched handling email escalation. Renata and Nguyen were riveted to their screens reviewing keyword-flagged civilian message traffic, but they seemed in the groove.

"Dammit!" said Christopher. I'd just been wondering about him, still bent laboring over his maps. Surely all the civilian arsenal reports would have come in by now. Perhaps we needed to sort them by subnet location to get the information complete for the 101st active areas.

"How can I help?" I offered, sinking into a chair beside him.

"I don't know if it's a bug or what," he complained. "But I could swear I've placed a bomb marker here before. But it's gone. How am I screwing this up?"

There wasn't anything to screw up. If you could see the marker on the map, it was added. Or at least queued to be added. I opened my phone map to the location, and sure enough, his most recent marker appeared. I recognized the neighborhood from previous mysterious clashes where Judgment appeared, then disappeared. Drum and I were looking at the same area just last night.

"You're doing fine, Christopher," I assured him. "I'll look into it. How many messages do you have left to go?"

He rubbed his hair in frustration. "I keep going back, because markers have disappeared."

"OK, don't do that anymore," I said. I created him an escalation route, to send me any message where he needed to add a marker where he thought another had disappeared. "Just go forward at full speed. Are you about half through? More?"

"About a third," he said, dispirited.

I took his remaining queue and sorted them by subnet. Then I selected the subnets where the 101st was already going in for action, and put them at the top of the list. "Let me know as soon as you get through these, OK? These are the priority. Then maybe you can take a breather." He snorted in appreciation, thanked me, and got back to work.

"Dee?" Emmett inquired, as I sank back in front of my own computer. "Problem?"

"Could be, could be," I allowed grimly. "Tell you when I know."

Tibbs told Renata and Nguyen to let him know if they escalated anything urgent – recommending people for jail could wait – and took up a seat next to mine to observe. I gave him a brief smile of welcome, and otherwise ignored him for the moment.

It took me fifteen minutes of hacking about, but I managed to get a log of all edits to bomb markers not done by Christopher, Drum, or myself. That should have been an empty list, but instead there were six other mesh ids editing the bomb markers. Tibbs had tweaked two, Emmett one, and they verbally confirmed this. Which brought us down to four editors, and seventeen affected markers.

Interesting question number one: where were these people? One was in the low spot south of the hotel, between Mount Washington and the next rise, a couple miles away. I was beginning to mentally dub that neighborhood Judgment valley. Christopher's latest missing marker was roughly thataway, too.

The other three bomb marker editors were currently in the hotel. Two of them right on top of each other and looking like one. A little-known feature of the meshnet we found handy, especially in the high-rises of Manhattan, was that markers stored elevation as well as 2-d map location. No budging those two coincident mesh phones. They were on one person. That was interesting. And they seemed to be between the 3rd and 4th floor.

"He's on the lobby doors," Tibbs said, pointing to the third editor's icon. A quiet and careful observer, my pal Tibbs. He'd silently followed everything I'd done, over my shoulder. "I bet the other one's in the stairwell. With double phones. Want me to get eyeball identification of who? In addition to electronic," he offered.

I thought about that. "Or just take them?" I suggested.

He considered that. "I want to know who," he decided. "Before spooking them."

I nodded. Tibbs texted someone to walk down the stairs from the 4th floor, and text him back, then went out for a bathroom break to identify the bodies on guard duty on the hotel entrance.

I looked back to my computer to notice that Drum and Emmett were standing in front of me, arms crossed. "Update?" Emmett inquired mildly.

"We have four mesh phones editing the arsenal map data, who shouldn't be," I reported. "One in Judgment Valley south of the hotel. Three inside the hotel, on two persons. One on guard at entrance, one in the stairwell with two phones. Tibbs is attempting visual ID on which persons. I'm about to look at their data tracks. This marker," I paused to bring up the map again, and snorted a laugh. "This marker that's missing, yet again, is a suspected Judgment arsenal. High priority."

"Or a trap," Emmett murmured. "Alright, thank you." He turned to get on the phone again with 101st command to direct their most ardent attention on that spot.

Drum was still standing over me. "Do we have any idea how much of our communications are compromised?"

A movement caught my eye on the screen. The suspect guard on the door moved, possibly to the other side of the door. "Everything on the meshnet," I answered Drum absently. "Please go away." I didn't take my eye off the suspects on the screen, so I don't know how she took that.

In a few minutes, Tibbs came back. Nguyen immediately greeted him with, "Tibbs, I got a hit on 'Canber.'"

"Hell," said Tibbs. "OK, Nguyen, that has to wait."

"Canber!" said Emmett, alarmed. "Tibbs, why did you keyword Canber?"

"What's 'Canber'?" I attempted.

"I said *wait*," Tibbs insisted, and came to me. "Goff and Sharif are on the entrance. Goff crossed to the other side while I was in the bathroom. Sharif stayed put."

"It's Goff, then," I said, "from Brooklyn."

"Breckenridge from Meadville on the stairs," Tibbs added. "Has he moved?"

"Gone dark. On all three phones, including his official one," I reported. "Goff went dark on the hack phone, and his official one was still alive. Where..." I refreshed the screen. "No. Both gone. Drat."

"Notifying Pittsburgh P.D. and Captain Johnson," Tibbs said, stepping urgently to his keyboard.

"Canber," Emmett repeated forcefully.

"Colonel, please *wait*," Tibbs insisted. "Dee?"

"Emmett," I said, touching his arm, "we were infiltrated via Drum's troops and our own. Sharif's been with us how long? And they're running. Give Tibbs a chance to catch them. They won't be easy. Not if they could do this."

Emmett scowled. "They had overrides to edit the map. We all did. No big deal."

"No, Emmett," I insisted. "They didn't use our access to edit the map. Those phones were on meshnet id 666. Sound familiar?"

"Hell," he said. He raised his voice. "I still need a debrief on Canber," he said forcefully for Tibbs' benefit. Tibbs hunched deeper into his followup. A methodical young man, my friend Tibbs.

"What's Canber?" I repeated doggedly.

"You don't need to know about Canber," Emmett murmured.

A *boom* shook the hotel. I flinched, and glanced up at the wall display map of 101st operations. "It's alright," Drum assured us, though she looked deeply concerned herself. "The 101st called in an air strike on the arsenal in Judgment Valley. Decided it was too wonky to approach with infantry."

"But that was a civilian house!" I objected. From the map, it looked like a close-packed neighborhood, too, like Dane's. Homes were only steps apart, mixed in with blocky apartment buildings.

"Don't judge, Dee," Emmett advised me quietly. "Can't second-guess the commander in the field."

Drum conceded sadly, "There is likely to be collateral damage. We expected some tonight, Dee."

What I expected was firefights with guns, one on one. I didn't expect aerial bombardment. Then again, I expected some incompetent drooling lunatic fringe of a religious sect. Not one that could hack into our our meshnet from their own clandestine copy, and infiltrate our guard detail. Deep cover infiltration, at that. Goff lived in the barracks brownstone next door to me in Brooklyn. He ran in the mornings with Emmett, doing laps around our mini-city town green. Captain Johnson's company was a hand-picked group of trusted soldiers, or so I was told. Lunatic or no, our adversary seemed amazingly competent at hacking and the spy craft. Both Ameni and Canada's best hackers had certified the security on our meshnet from the ground up.

If Judgment were that good, or rather that capable, then maybe a bomb really was the best idea. "OK," I conceded to Drum, and sighed. I looked to Tibbs, still working furiously, and my eye settled on Renata, between me and Tibbs. If forces unknown had slipped in or subverted Goff and Breckenridge, how did we know that everyone in this room was legitimate?

"Renata," I said calmly, "what can you tell us about Breckenridge?"

"Nothing," she said too quickly. She hunched toward her screen, intently following her message stream instead of paying attention to the drama around her. Some might call that being a good soldier. To me, it just looked fishy. No one was that incurious. I frowned at her.

I located the Canber message and forwarded a copy to Emmett for safekeeping, without reading it.

I looked back, and Christopher started to volunteer something, but I shook my head slightly. "So Renata, how long have you worked with Breckenridge?"

Emmett had his phone out, tapping a message. His poker face was excellent. I had no idea if he was following up on Renata or Canber, or something else entirely. Tibbs, beside Renata, had paused in his work to pay attention to my questioning her.

"I don't remember," Renata lied, leaning farther into her computer screen.

Tibbs took her in a head-lock and rolled her chair backward, away from her computer. I noted sadly that she didn't deny anything, or profess her innocence. Another real pro, aside from her weak acting ability. It's not enough to say the right things. It takes believing with the whole mind and body, to generate the right body language.

"We'll talk to you later, Renata," Drum promised softly. "Too busy right now."

Tibbs handed Renata off to Sergeant Becque and another soldier at the door. They closed the door while they processed her. But when Tibbs came back in, he laid a cell phone, a shiv, a pocket-knife, wallet, and boots on a side table, to look over later. No doubt the other guards would strip-search her and put her into pajamas, and deliver the rest of her clothes to Tibbs later.

Or not Tibbs. Apparently Emmett had the same thought. "Dee, could you brief the IBIS agents on this for me? I'd like them to follow up on our staffing problems. I need you and Tibbs here. And a replacement email sifter."

"Two more email sifters," I said. "One to go back over what Renata was supposed to monitor the past few hours." Off the cuff, I suggested, "I like Penny and Qwanisha."

"Captain Johnson's call, but I'll suggest them," Emmett allowed. "How do you feel about Christopher and Nguyen?"

They both looked to me, stricken. I smiled back. "They're the best." Tibbs snorted amusement. "Of course, if Tibbs were an enemy agent, we'd never know it," I teased.

"Ma'am," Tibbs acknowledged wryly. He took the gibe as intended, as a compliment.

"Oh, he's an agent alright," said Emmett. "Niedermeyer's. Friendly." There was a certain sour note on the 'friendly' part.

"Sir," Tibbs acknowledged. "I don't think the police will catch Goff and Breckenridge, but I did my best. I'm free for that other discussion now."

"Just show me your instructions on the subject from Niedermeyer, Tibbs," Emmett directed. He read the email over Tibbs' shoulder. "Thank you, Sergeant. As you were."

"So Emmett, are you going to explain – ?" I hazarded.

"No. Drum, please excuse me. This may take a while. Dee, please brief IBIS."

Drum protested, "Sir, I wish you'd stay –" Another *boom* shook the building. "Here," she completed the sentence lamely, gazing at the map on the wall, as though willing it to tell her what that explosion meant.

"Point taken," Emmett agreed. "Dee. IBIS. Now."

21

Interesting fact: Pittsburgh regularly placed on lists of the best places to live in America, offering many good jobs, a low cost of living, few natural disasters, many universities, rich cultural and leisure opportunities, and the most bars per capita in the nation.

That second explosion was an IED in a school. The enemy baited the trap with a dozen children. Some 101st troopers went in to check that the kids were OK after the arsenal explosion down the block. I don't usually believe in evil, per se. But whoever these people were that we were up against, they were doing a bang-up impression of evil.

But I learned that later, after the disarmament operation was over. That first night was too crazy busy. I brought the IBIS agents up to speed on events, so they could investigate that our remaining troops were trustworthy, and the IndieNews bunch as well. I told them to skip Tibbs and Nguyen, because they were known agents on loan to us by an allied power. Likewise, Emmett and I had dangerous and subversive backgrounds. But the governor-generals already knew about us, and picked us for this assignment accordingly.

I treasured the expression on Kalnietis' face on hearing that. I broke his bland. Gianetti looked wired and eager to play.

Back in the command center, I brought Qwanisha and Jorge up to speed on the message traffic filter assignment. I never learned why or who had overruled my suggestion of Penny, though she was still with us after the dust settled. For such a big guy with thick fingers, Jorge was surprisingly nimble with a keyboard. He was the one going back over the message streams Renata had already reviewed.

Jorge asked what was to keep Renata from simply deleting any messages she didn't want us to see. Good question. So I investigated that. She'd deleted maybe 20, that I restored directly into Tibbs' escalation queue. She'd also modified another 10, that I created another escalation bucket for. But there was no way to know what the flagged messages said before she changed them.

In the meantime, the weapons collection sweep of Pittsburgh was proceeding. The battle of Judgment Valley inspired a new flood of citizen arsenal reports for Christopher to process. Plus another flood of messages reporting theft of weapons left on the street for pickup. In contrast, the weapons pickup around Carnegie-Mellon University seemed relatively civil. There were only tens of casualties, and a couple deaths there. Bremen and Lohan were both collected and held for questioning.

The exurbs were casualty-free. The locals' cooperation or non was inventoried by aerial photograph. By 9 p.m., Emmett had me announce that the rural folk were free to collect up their weapons and bring them back indoors. No troops went door to door confiscating weapons there. Both sides understood that isolated locals needed their weapons and would shoot anyone who tried to take them. No need to argue about it.

By 10 p.m., I was finally free to get back to the galling fact that these loons had broken into my hacker-proofed meshnet. And redundantly, at that. The three infiltrators I knew of had been trusted with valid overrides, and could see and edit anything.

And that's exactly what Renata did. Yet that's not what Goff and Breckenridge did. Instead they'd hacked in from another mesh-net, edited our data using those accounts, and likely transferred information over to their own net.

I characterized what I could, and called in my biggest gun to take it from there. Popeye, the profane and scary biker-looking hacker on the Amenac team back in Connecticut, was our top security and counter-security expert. He led the team that vetted security on the meshnet protocols during software development. Popeye's team included members from Canadian intelligence. We'd set it up as a sort of contest, between the meshnet development team on Long Island trying to build and bullet-proof, while Popeye's team tried to break.

Well, no matter how hard we tried, we knew all along that if it was communications software, it was doomed to be hackable somehow. The viral system for forcing software updates phone-to-phone nearly guaranteed it, in my private opinion. Popeye insisted that was only a problem if the hackers were smarter than him and his team. He had grounds for his arrogance. But his ego really didn't care for what I was telling him.

"Who the fuck are these guys, Dee?" he demanded. "We fucking tested this against mother-fucking Israeli intelligence!" Most further expletives deleted. Popeye swore so badly he made the soldiers surrounding me sound like boy scouts in comparison.

"Popeye, we've already found three inside agents, just tonight," I pointed out. "Any fortress can be breached by someone opening a door from inside. But is that what happened here?"

"Fuck... That's not knowable," Popeye said. "Maybe."

"Maybe," I agreed. "And maybe we could counter-strike? Push a software update into this 666 net and force it to behave?"

"I doubt that," Popeye said darkly. "This won't be quick, Dee. Days, weeks. Never."

"Understood," I said. "I'll need to brief Lieutenant Colonel Cameron."

"*Fuck!*" Popeye roared in my ear, and hung up on me. Cam was the Resco who commissioned the meshnet, not Emmett. Its principal programmers worked for him.

At least Cam didn't swear or scream at me. But he was in central Long Island now, an area still not far along the march back from a destitute and primitive level 1. He didn't have the means to carry out a secure conversation. He passed me off to his husband Dwayne in the relatively posh level 3 environs of eastern Long Island. We had fun visiting for a few minutes – I hadn't spoken to Dwayne since his promotion from Coco to Resco. But he couldn't really do much for me. He promised to chat with the meshnet team daily, and bring Cam up to speed in person when he came home in a couple days.

"Status, darlin'?" Emmett inquired, when I came to a stop.

I shrugged. "The meshnet is compromised, and that won't change any time soon. Followup is launched."

"Uh-huh," he said unhappily.

Emmett brought me along with him into the Internet cafe room, where we provided the governor-generals with an overdue progress report on the disarmament operation. Drum and Tibbs had to stay behind, as Emmett and I were their respective reliefs for the duration. Colonel McNaughton, commanding the 101st troops, joined us on the video screen.

The brass were not happy at the loss of civilian life. They were unhappier at the spies and interference by an unknown enemy. But, they seemed delighted by the sheer volume of munitions already removed from the equation.

"Hell, Emmett," Governor Cullen of Hudson concluded. "You were right. This operation needed doing."

"Thank you, sir."

"Any feel for how the civilians are taking it?" Emmett's CO, Colonel Pete Hoffman, asked.

Emmett deferred to me to answer. I said, "We're only monitoring the angry ones, Pete. At this point, message traffic is evaporating. People went to bed." The thought made me stifle a yawn. It was nearing midnight. "But earlier, more people volunteered information after they heard the explosions. Even informing on their own families. I think people here know that they need this. Something's gotta give. Won't make the medicine go down easy, though."

They dismissed me before delving even deeper into sensitive discussions. I went back to the command room to spell Tibbs so he could grab a few hours' sleep, before I got a chance myself around dawn. Long night.

We exceeded Emmett's estimate of 36-48 hours before the operation to disarm Pittsburgh was complete. Our monitoring work in the operations center was grueling, but mostly because it was boring and we didn't get enough sleep.

Another tornado outbreak suspended operations in the streets for 6 hours. The 101st units took shelter in civilian basements. Emmett and Drum deemed our windowless first floor office safe enough, and we kept working. After the tornado outbreak, a blue norther carrying an unseasonable freeze blew in. We just kept going.

Emmett handed me announcements to post from time to time.

IMPORTANT: Weapons pickup is proceeding well, but there have been pockets of violent resistance. To date there have been 1,216 casualties, 127 of them fatal. **Your full cooperation is required.** We will not back down until this city is disarmed and peaceable. Let's get this done, people.
Reminder: Report location of any munition stashes to

@RescoEMacLaren#Stash for retrieval. Report any planned attacks on police or soldiers to @RescoCDrumpeter#Insurgents

IMPORTANT: Weapons pickup is complete in your area. Lockdown ends effective 6 a.m. tomorrow. Operations continue in other parts of the city, so you cannot leave your neighborhood. Food distribution will resume after the entire city is disarmed. Plan meals accordingly. If any violence resumes in your area, head home and report to @RescoCDrumpeter#Insurgents. Thank you for your cooperation.

IMPORTANT: Weapons pickup is complete across Pittsburgh. Total 1,473 casualties, 185 of them fatal. We collected enough weapons to equip the ex-U.S. Army twice over. For heaven's sake, people! Any remaining lockdowns end effective 6 a.m. tomorrow, and travel may resume between sections of Pittsburgh, but not to rural areas. Food distribution to resume the day after tomorrow. Schools remain closed. If any violence recurs in your area, head home and report to @RescoCDrumpeter#Insurgents.

IMPORTANT: Food distribution will resume tomorrow at schools marked on meshnet map. Experienced volunteers please report to closest school. **No food permitted in churches. No religion permitted in food centers.** Food distribution is a secular government activity. Proselytizing and inter-faith conflict in food distribution centers, or any other public venue, will be punished severely. This is the American way, people. Remember it. Report infractions to @RescoCDrumpeter#SeparateChurchAndState.

IMPORTANT: Food distribution has resumed. All remaining travel restrictions are lifted. Church restrictions are permanent

– food is banned from all churches and places of worship, including pot-luck dinners, throughout Allegheny County. A funeral will be held for Resco Major Dane Beaufort tomorrow. The general public is not invited. Flags to be kept at half-mast until New Year's Day as a reminder.

IMPORTANT: Effective immediately, Major Caroline Drumpeter is promoted to Lieutenant Colonel, and appointed Army Resource Coordinator (Resco) of Pittsburgh and Allegheny County. Lt. Colonel Drumpeter is also appointed lead Resco of Western PA. By order of Governor-General Seth Taibbi. Guard her with your lives, Pittsburgh. If another Resco dies here, nuclear options will be considered.

Drum laughed at that last. I wasn't so sure Emmett was joking. But after days locked in a room with her, I was sure Pittsburgh and Western PA – the locals called it PA, not Penn – were getting a very good lead Resco indeed. By the second day, Emmett told Drum to quit deferring to him and just take over as acting Resco. She passed her audition with flying colors, cool, collected, professional, and surprisingly kind.

She posted her own announcement later in the day of her official promotion, the appointed shepherd addressing her flock by herself for the first time.

IMPORTANT: Please stop asking when you'll get your weapons back. We will revisit next year. In the meantime, enjoy peace in the streets. Sincerely, Resco Lt-Col Caroline Drumpeter.

W e buried Major Dane Beaufort with full military honors. Three of the four Rescos of Western Pennsylvania attended, and most of our investigation expedition. Ohio–West Virginia sent the closest garrison commander, a colonel, to convey their respects.

I invited Paddy Bollai and his family, and asked him to contact any of Dane's real friends in Pittsburgh. There were a few.

And, of course, Emmett and I attended, along with a large contingent from the 101st Airborne Division of Kentucky–Tennessee.

The casket arrived at the burial place by horse-drawn cart. Emmett and other officers who had served with Dane acted as pall-bearers. Dane's casket was draped with both the deep blue flag of the Commonwealth of Pennsylvania, and the stars and stripes of the ex–United States, which Dane had served for most of his adult life.

An Army chaplain from the 101st performed a non-denominational service. There were no personal words. The mourners chose to keep their thoughts to themselves and keep the ceremony polished and professional. Taibbi's Air Force sent fighters to perform a fly-over in the missing man formation. Seven soldiers in an honor guard fired a three-volley salute. A bugler played Taps.

In the absence of any surviving next-of-kin, Caroline Drumpeter received the folded Pennsylvania flag, and Emmett accepted the flag of the ex-U.S.

Walking back to our car, I squeezed Emmett's white-gloved hand. I'd never thought before about what would happen if he died. The mechanics of it, I mean. "Is this the kind of funeral you'd want, Emmett?" I asked softly.

He pulled me under his arm and kissed my head. "Uh-huh. Funerals are for the living, not the dead, darlin'. Military honors are for morale, and respect. If I can serve again after my death, sure. It's not like they'd give you a choice, now."

I laughed softly and hugged him. No, how they buried the Hero of Project Reunion would not be left up to me. Ash Margolis would probably arrange full honors and a burial in Central Park, attended by heads of state. Ash was arranging a major event right now for Halloween in the Apple Core, a memorial for the dead and consecration of the Calm Parks. I hoped we'd be home in time. We'd hate to miss that.

I was glad for Marilou's sake, and the kids, that Dane Beaufort was not buried alone.

The reception back at the hotel was a moment of glory for the Wiehls' hospitality. Liberally fueled by Kentucky bourbon, the reception supplied all the personal reminiscences that the formal ceremony had lacked. Emmett enjoyed catching up with old comrades from the 101st, and introducing me around. His Ozark accent re-bloomed and proved itself seasoned more than a little with western Kentucky. Old friends regaled me with tales of Dane and Emmett's lowest moments and most striking defeats and embarrassments. And then turned to him and demanded when he was coming home to Ken-Tenn and the 101st. He just laughed. "Uh-huh."

I liked the men and women of the 101st Airborne. It was fun seeing Emmett fit in so well. They'd loved him. He belonged with them, once upon a time. "You miss them?" I asked. "Think you'll ever go back?"

"Don't know," Emmett replied. "No regrets. New Haven was the best career move I ever made. Then New York." He squeezed my shoulders with a smile. "But who knows? We might visit Ken–Tenn, someday."

When the reception was over, Emmett pulled me to him. "Come to bed with me, darlin'? I don't want to sleep alone tonight. In fact could we just go get your stuff? Move back in with me. We'll work it out."

"Yeah, we will," I agreed. "We'll fight a little more along the way," I warned, with a grin.

"Uh-huh," he agreed happily.

22

Interesting fact: Pittsburgh is the largest city in Appalachia. Greater Pittsburgh is considered part of the Northeast, and extends into the South, the Midwest, and the Great Lakes. More to the point, Pittsburgh is where these regions meet.

After such a dramatic demonstration to the people of Pittsburgh, and the transfer of power to Drum, it was easy to feel like our work here was wrapping up. But the investigation still had major unanswered questions. And wresting control away from the militant sects and restoring Pittsburgh to secular martial law control was only the most pressing of Emmett's recommendations, pre-requisite for any further actions.

We had Bremen and Lohan in custody, the Baptist leaders from around Carnegie-Mellon University responsible for the attack on our train coming in. So far, they claimed they were merely trying to intercept us, before we fell into Judgment's clutches and the mysterious deaths and dysfunction around Mount Washington. We still hadn't found Paul Dukakis, the man who delivered Dane's body to Paddy Bollai. Emmett and the IBIS agents weren't done yet.

Neither were PR and IndieNews. We had tentative permission to publish stories on the disarming of Pittsburgh and Dane's funeral, provided we could coax them past the censors.

Brandy and I took stock and decided we wanted two more video sequences. One was the footage in the suburb of Green Tree. We still hoped Blake Sondheim and his footage would reappear, but as the days passed with no word from Blake, our hope was fading. For now, Emmett ordered us to steer clear of Green Tree, and stay close to the hotel. He asked the 101st to hunt for Blake. Most of the airborne infantry went home to Fort Campbell after the funeral, but a thousand lingered to solidify Drum's control.

The more important sequence for our special report was in Station Square.

"Ah-g!" I cried, half-gargled, as Brandy mock-dashed my head into the pig-iron furnace beyond the fountain.

"Stop that!" she scolded me. "Dee, we're not re-enacting this, just explaining it. No corny crap."

"Just trying to lighten things up," I said meekly. "It's going to look goofy no matter what we do, Brandy."

"No. I think it will look very professional," Melinda insisted, our second-string camera woman, deeply earnest and sincere. I wondered when I'd grown old enough for a college graduate to look like a kid.

And every time I looked at her, I felt guilty all over again about our missing Blake Sondheim. Blake was a good guy. It wasn't entirely my fault he went out after Green Tree. Brandy sent him. Hell, Paul Dukakis sent him, and whoever posted that video of Dane's death on the Internet, claiming it happened in Green

Tree. But I added the suggestion that Blake look into a possible mass grave site while he was there. And I still thought I should have stopped him from going to Green Tree on a day when Emmett ordered us back in the hotel by 3:00.

Brandy rolled her eyes. With my best attempt at sincerity, I said, "I'm sure you're doing a great job, Melinda. I just feel a bit silly."

"A man died here," Melinda informed me. "Murdered, violently and viciously."

Yeah, kid, I caught that part.

"That's the story we're conveying, yes, Melinda," Brandy snapped at her. "From the top again. Without the giggles, Baker." She pulled me back a couple feet to our starting position. "The murder weapon was this pig-iron furnace," she told the camera. "In a scuffle, Dane Beaufort's head was dashed into this steel protuberance." I managed to keep a straight face this time.

"But the wound wasn't immediately fatal," Brandy continued. "Major Beaufort broke away." She let go of me. I dashed to the fence. She caught me by the shoulders again. "There was another scuffle here, but he broke free again, fleeing toward the docks on the river."

Melinda hopped the fence, and took up position to film at the far edge of the tracks. On her signal, I vaulted the fence and ran to the dying place alone. Then I lay down in the gravel and Brandy took a knee beside me, posed with a fist drawn back as though to pummel my face. "Only a few feet from safety, his attackers beat him here, and left him unconscious, bleeding on the rail bed. The brain injury continued to swell, and killed him within a few hours."

I sat up and dusted myself off, and spoke to the camera. "There are still a lot of unknowns here. We still don't know who killed Major Dane Beaufort. Only that this is how he died."

"And cut," Brandy said. She gave me a hand up to standing.

"Take it from the top again? Or review the video and see if it's good enough?"

I considered our earnest young camera woman. "Melinda? Why don't you go back to the van and have Martin review the footage? Let Martin decide." I beamed at her encouragingly, and she trotted off to Brandy's producer. "It's probably fine, Brandy. You do live coverage all the time."

Brandy considered and pointed. "We could add a sequence trotting onto the dock, showing how close he was to escape and safety. Adds drama."

"Nah," I decided. "We'd just end up cutting it for length. Or Emmett or IBIS would cut it, because we don't know that for sure. Let's just stick to the facts. Oh! I wanted to show you the ThingSpace!"

I dragged her into the dancing corridor, and demonstrated. "Isn't this awesome?" I cried. "Best public Internet and power in all Pittsburgh. Only nobody noticed."

"Internet?" Brandy asked.

"Sure," I said. "Those voice recognition databases are huge. And I haven't asked for a song yet it couldn't play for me. It's getting all that off the cloud, not stored locally. Pick a song!"

Three songs later we were laughing like loons, leaning on each other and taking a breather.

"Dee Baker," a man's voice said behind me.

I whirled toward him in surprise. A vaguely attractive man stood there, hands casually in his pockets, about Emmett's age. His brown hair was cut military short, but his clothes were unusually fresh and clean civilian, a heavy burgundy fatigue sweater over olive cargo pants, bloused into work boots. His expression was blandly pleasant, yielding no clues.

"I'm sorry, do I know you?" I said. I was sure I'd never seen him before in my life, but spoke the polite response on automatic. I wasn't worried. We had four of Drum's guards from Meadville with us, around here somewhere. He probably walked right past them.

He took a few steps to my left and pushed the big button to activate the ThingSpace again. "Alexa, play *American Pie*, by Don McLean," he told the machines. "Louder. Louder."

> Bye, bye Miss American Pie
> Drove my Chevy to the levee but the levee was dry
> And them good ole boys were drinking whiskey
>   and rye
> Singin' this'll be the day that I die
> This'll be the day that I die

He turned back to me and confided, over the now loud song, "I love the old tech, don't you? You don't know me, Dee Baker. But I'm an old friend of Emmett's. From Leavenworth. We took ILE and SAMS training together. I'm Major Canton Bertovich, retired. Call me Canber." The ghost of a smile played in his eyes. "Did Emmett ever mention me?"

I stared at him for a moment. The Calm Act went into effect right after Emmett left Leavenworth. His classmates weren't permitted to retire. Tibbs added 'Canber' to the meshnet traffic filters at Niedermeyer's suggestion. Emmett had seemed alarmed.

"*HELP!*" I screamed and turned to run for it. Someone in 101st Airborne uniform already had a thick gag over Brandy's mouth and was laying her out on the ground. I tore past, trying to make for the river. Running for the street might have made more sense, but I was reacting, not thinking. Dane Beaufort had run for the river. So did I.

I yanked out of my pursuer's grasp twice and tripped forward, my hands and knees scraping on the concrete plaza. With two runners behind me, they corralled me along the building, not letting me break out into the open. But the storefronts would end as soon as I reached the walkway at the pseudo train platform, where the blast furnace sat. Only 60 feet, then 40, then 20.

But Canber got a firm hold on me next to the fountain, and flipped me onto the ground. His partner got a gag over my face. I fought the cloth, thinking it was chloroform or something. But that was simply to muffle me. To incapacitate me, they used a taser.

Damn, that hurts, being electrocuted. Dazed and twitching, unable to speak or control my limbs, I could only watch and listen for a minute or so. The soldier took away the cloth gag and forced me to swallow a pill. Then he stuck duct tape across my mouth, and flipped me over to tape my wrists together thoroughly. He patted me down quickly and removed everything from my pockets, strewing the contents across the sidewalk, except for my phone. That he handed to Canber. My shoes he chucked at the abandoned storefront. Then he cut my hands with a knife, and turned me onto my side, so he could stamp my bloody paw prints around the sidewalk.

Not exactly subtle. They were painting *Dee was attacked here* in big bloody letters, intentionally. *Why?*

In front of me, Canber tapped out a message on my phone. He held it up to show me, a happy light in his eye, mouth partly open in delight. A message to Emmett, from me, a single word:

Canber

Canber artistically used my own bloody finger to send the message, then dropped the phone from waist-height by one of my shoes. *Dee was attacked here, by Canber, Emmett take note.* No, not subtle at all. Why the hell was Canber baiting Emmett? A second soldier walked by, half-supporting and half-dragging Brandy. Sadly, I recognized him as one of my guards from Meadville. The IBIS agents hadn't found them all. My electroshock grogginess was turning into drugged wooziness.

"Did you rufie her first?" Canber asked the second soldier. "Good. Carry them from here. Let's go."

Canber set off across the platform fence and the train tracks, toward the docks. The first soldier carried me after him. I was fighting desperately to remain conscious, and losing the fight. 'Rufie' her indeed. They'd fed us date-rape drugs.

Dane didn't flee across the railroad tracks, I thought muzzily. *They dragged him this way. I wonder if Paul Dukakis spotted them, and cried out. Then they dropped Dane and ran for it.*

But why would they...? Oh. The ThingSpace. Maybe they came here to use the Internet and power. And Dane just ran into them by accident. But Dane would have recognized Canber. Canber would have been a Resco. There's no good excuse for Canber to be here. No good at all. If I'd been thinking clearly, I would have noticed leaps all over the logic here, but at the time, I simply realized this as the truth of what happened to Dane Beaufort.

They dumped me into the wet bottom of a Boston whaler, alongside a bunch of guns and electronics, bait and tackle, and Brandy. She was already out cold, her hair bloody.

There were no whalers out of Boston, I reminded myself, as though this were a momentous clue, my mind going. We learned these things in childhood along the Sound. Boston whaler was a brand name for a simple fiberglass open-hull boat with an outboard engine, around 15 feet long, one of the cheapest motor boats available. I learned to water-ski off the back of a friend's Boston whaler. *Do teenagers water-ski on the Monongahela? I bet the water's cold. Does it get warm in the summer like the Sound?*

They didn't need to start the engine right away. They just kicked off from the dock and let the current take the boat out of view. They threw a tarp over us and the gear. The tarp smelled only of gasoline and mildew. *Nobody went fishing. It's all people bait. No fish bait.*

I'm glad I moved back in with Emmett first. That would hurt him, if I died while he thought I was mad at him. I'm not that mad at him.

He just worries about God too much. God, take good care of Emmett for me. He's a good man. He tries so hard to save the world, but that's Your job. Screw You.

American Pie is a long song, over 8 minutes. It was still playing when I blacked out, still telling God how to do His job so Emmett wouldn't have to do it for Him.

23

Interesting fact: Before the Calm Act, West Virginia was the second-poorest state in the U.S., surpassing only Mississippi. Churches in the rugged Appalachians tended toward local idiosyncratic sects, isolated from the large national congresses. Coal mining and natural gas were major industries.

My eyes drifted open leadenly. I was in a bus seat, head bouncing against the window. Somebody lay heavily against my shoulder. _Morgantown, West Virginia, 30 miles,_ proclaimed a sign flowing past. Next time my eyes opened, I stubbornly held out for a sign to tell me what road I was on. It was an interstate, empty of traffic except for the caravan my bus traveled with. A methane-powered bus, not gas or electric – I could smell that much.

The road wended its way through endless steep hills, the landscape seemingly uninhabited, primordial hardwood forest starting to turn its autumn colors. I lost the fight and closed my eyes twice before spotting the longed-for sign: I-79 South.

Not that I had any clear idea where I-79 South was, or Morgantown, West Virginia. I vaguely recalled that West Virginia wrapped around the southwest of Pennsylvania. Whether Morgantown was south or west or southwest of Pittsburgh, was unclear. Probably more south than west, or else the interstate would have an even number. Interstates out here didn't hug the coastline the way they did in New England, and say 'North' when they actually traveled east. OK, so I was heading south to Morgantown, some city I'd never heard of, yet big enough to be worth mentioning on an interstate sign. Maybe.

This act of passive defiance accomplished, I dared to turn my head to see what warm body was lying against me. Oh, good – Brandy. Someone had bandaged her head, too, though blood still matted her gorgeous red hair.

I was right not to look before. A woman across the aisle noticed, and stared at me. She was gaunt, with matted brown hair, dirt on her face and bare feet and ragged dress. Her crazed eyes bugged out, bloodshot white showing around the irises. She dug into a grubby skirt pocket and brought out another of the rufie capsules in her filthy fingers. She ripped off the duct tape over my mouth – *Ow!* – taking several layers of skin off with it. She forced me to swallow the pill. It was almost a relief when she pinched my nose off, because it cut off her reek. I was glad she didn't put the duct tape back on. My wrists were still duct-taped, but at least in front of me now, instead of behind me.

As my head nodded back to bouncing against the window, I noticed my own clothes had been replaced with a brown rag dress, as well. Not that it was originally brown. I suspect it started out blue. But if cotton cloth is stained badly enough, long enough, it turns brown. The idea of Bug-Eyes stripping me and dressing me again was as revolting as her putting her filthy fingers in my mouth.

Charity, I decided firmly. *I shall call her Charity, not Bug-Eyes.* Charity was rocking in her seat, last I looked. She was muttering, possibly to a demon, but maybe God. *Charity deserves my charity. She must live a very uncomfortable life. If the demons whisper all the time, how scary for her. And her feet must get cold. Yes, if I lived Charity's life, maybe I would act as she acts. There but for the grace of God go I.*

And the rufie fairies carried me away again.

"I'm so sorry, Dee," Blake sobbed, rocking back and forth over me. He hardly looked like Blake anymore, though. Blake was such a tidy young man, with neat hair, usually in a pastel preppy sweater over an Oxford shirt and business-casual chinos and loafers. Now one black eye was swollen nearly shut, a fat split lip curling his mouth into an unintentional sneer. His workman's brownish collar was blue once. "I tried not to say anything," he moaned.

"I forgive you, Blake," I murmured groggily. "Forgive me, Blake. I'm so glad you're alive." That was the main thing. But I was puzzled. "What are you sorry for?"

"About you," he said. "They wanted to know how to hurt Emmett, how to lure him out. I told him about you." He broke down in tears.

I struggled up to a seated position and hugged him to my shoulder, and encouraged him to cry it all out. I needed him to start talking sense, but it probably wasn't urgent. I wasn't tracking too well yet myself. And hugging someone familiar was nice.

I contemplated our surroundings. Brandy was a couple feet away, huddled with her head on her knees. Her wardrobe was as degraded as ours, feet muddy with a broken toenail. We were in a basic one-car attached garage. Rainy day gray light streamed in through high garage door windows.

A typical American garage provides all manner of tools and potential weapons in its piles of stored junk. But this one had been stripped to down to empty shelves. There were still the shelf brackets. Hefty springs running along the garage door track. No life light on the door opener, so probably no power. A bucket in the corner, apparently our excuse for bathroom facilities. Smelly blankets.

Oh, well. Weapons weren't exactly my medium, anyway. Emmett refused to teach me how to fire a gun, on the grounds that I had better options. Tech whispering, for instance, with a lesser talent for mind games and manipulating people. Two minutes with a cell phone and an Internet connection could solve all my problems. I'd just have to play mind games until I got my chance.

"Are you alright, Brandy?" I asked softly.

"You slept forever," she complained faintly. She turned her head to face me, but didn't raise it from her knees. Her body language screamed utter defeat.

"I woke on a bus headed down I-79 toward Morgantown, West Virginia, with you passed out on my shoulder," I informed her. "Then they dosed me another rufie. Do you know any more?"

"Blake and I are hostages for your good behavior," she said. Tears ran down her cheeks, but she didn't sob. Her voice just sounded dead.

"Good information," I encouraged her. "So what am I?"

"Bait, to make Emmett crazy," she supplied. "According to Blake. Keep your voice down, or they'll beat us again."

Extracting information from my team was slowed by their emotional needs. But I persevered, alternately asking questions and bleeding off their fear and hurt. I was an old hand at this, from dealing with the Apple Zone survivors, especially our once prickly housekeeper Gladys. The basic formula was, 'OK, that sucks, but we deal with it. You are strong, capable, and appreciated. Next problem?'

I started with Brandy, and let Blake cling to me until he calmed down. She must have awoken not long after Charity drugged me again on the bus. She couldn't see out the window as well as I did, but we'd turned left off the interstate at some mid-sized town onto an empty country road. Based on eavesdropping, she estimated we'd spent an hour on that road, before turning right onto even less of a road.

Soon after that, we'd arrived in a patchy little Appalachian town of the no-street-light-required variety. The town center was a T-intersection with a gas station and tiny decrepit church, plus a few visible trailer homes and impoverished little houses. The caravan disbanded there and spread into the woods. Our garage was maybe a 10 minute walk from downtown, such as it was. The attached house was the most upscale she'd seen, maybe a 3-bedroom ranch. It was getting dark by the time we arrived here, so maybe net 5 hours since we'd been abducted, unless we were missing a day. After that, I'd slept through until morning.

"So who told you about this hostage and bait concept?" I asked.

Brandy turned her head away. I put a hand out to stroke her back, and crooned, "You're alright, Brandy. We're together. We'll get out of this."

"They raped her," Blake volunteered. "Last night." His tears had subsided by then, but he'd stayed quiet on my shoulder for comfort.

I didn't see any useful follow-up questions to that. "You're OK, Brandy," I insisted. "Their sick actions have nothing to do with you. Ready to talk, Blake?"

According to Blake, when he arrived before the big disarmament operation six days ago, he found Green Tree an ordinary looking, prosperous Pennsylvania suburb. He'd stopped in to chat at a farm market. People seemed excited about the new meshnet communications, but alarmed by the news that Dane Beaufort was dead. They liked Dane. There was plenty of food available. A nice baker fed him lunch in return for stories about life back east, and news about the world. The nice lady rolled her eyes at what was going on in Pittsburgh, and said she avoided the city.

She avoided the mass grave site, too. Some bad people had moved in there. Besides, *suicides*, she said were buried there, with a shudder. Blake got the impression she meant the oxycontin volunteers for depopulation, from the first winter under the Calm Act. Seriously ill? Afraid for the future? Mentally ill, or disabled? The oxycontin suicide kit was a one-size-fits-all final solution, handed out by doctors in the millions all over the U.S. that winter. Like everybody, I kept several bottles of the stuff at home for use as a painkiller or last resort. Oxycontin was easier to obtain than bread.

Blake filmed some footage of the farm market and the helpful baker, then drove over to the graveyard. They were old graves. The barrow mounded as tall as he was, but didn't smell. The encroaching greenery looked like it had grown all summer. He recorded perfectly usable footage of that, too, even clambered on top to show its extent. The mound climbed the middle of a narrow wooded valley like a million others, between steep hillsides. The kind of landscape where effective visibility was maybe 50 feet. From New England, I knew those kind of woods intimately. You could hide almost anything in them. No one would know unless they stumbled across in person.

It's a shame he didn't leave then. But Blake figured he had another half hour before he needed to drive back into Pittsburgh to meet Emmett's deadline. I'd mentioned that the grave might have signs cut into trees. So he nosed around, walking along one edge of the barrow.

The first mark carved into a tree was a simple fish glyph, nose down, with an arrow pointing onward up the sloping valley. The next said '666', with another arrow. The third looked like a Nordic rune. Then he stepped into a clearcut for a high-voltage long-distance power line, perpendicular to the barrow mound, running up the bracketing hill slopes. A corpse hung from one of the power poles.

Now a sensible person would have high-tailed it back to his

car at that point. But I've noticed this about my camera men and women, and wished to strangle them for it. They kind of disappear behind the lens, so intent on the images they're capturing that they don't have the sense God gave kittens. On Long Island, my camera woman Kyla faced off a would-be rapist by turning her lens on him. Not an effective defense.

That corpse was fresh, and Blake wanted a closeup of his face.

His face was Paul Dukakis. One of Emmett's informants had provided a good photo, and Emmett broadcast it across the meshnet asking for leads, so Blake recognized him. Blake got great shots, he told me proudly.

And that's where they nabbed Blake, while he was too intent on his camera to notice the three guys walking up behind him.

They dragged him through the woods and over a little rise into their encampment. Maybe several hundred people camped there. The well-fed, better-dressed sort had tents around a couple cabins. About a hundred more lived in a slave pen, walled in with a chain-link fence topped with barbed wire. They stripped Blake of his stuff, forced him to change into his new rags and bare feet, and threw him into the slave pit for safe-keeping.

Naturally enough for a news professional, Blake grilled his fellow inmates, mostly attractive young women and teenage girls at that hour of the day. They were new converts to Judgment, they told him. It was a choice of that or death, apparently. Once they came into the fold, no one left to carry tales. The guards would come and take a team out to work or service them, then bring them back. No one got fed in the pen. They got picked for work, or they starved.

The goal of Judgment was to carry out Lucifer's work, and rid the land of the human infestation until no more than one in ten survived, and inherited the earth. God had ceded the field to his right hand angel, and left Satan to cleanse the world. And Judgment were his legions. All hail Satan.

As a good little well-educated, well-adjusted non-observant

Jewish boy, Blake had trouble believing anyone could buy into this. But the women seemed sincere. In fact, when he argued, they shunned him, afraid to be seen anywhere near him.

I pointed out that even if the women weren't sure in the beginning, it sounded like sincerity was the price of dinner. And most people wanted to live. In the Apple Zone, we could take it as a given that a woman of a certain age range had performed sexual favors in exchange for food at least once.

Emmett and Drum unleashed the 101st on Pittsburgh that evening, so Blake had a couple days to get mighty hungry before anyone had time to question him. All the slaves got hungry, and the men weren't nearly as kind when they came back from their work details for the night. Blake didn't realize it until later, but the slave pit also suffered from opiate withdrawal. Emmett's police action preempted their chance to work for their fix as well as their food.

Eventually the Judgment community's religious leader, Uriel, took Blake out of the pen and got his story in exchange for a meal. Blake was given oxycontin to make him happy and cooperative.

"That's good stuff, oxycontin," Blake said despondently. "I told him anything he wanted to know. He was my best friend. He's a monster, Dee. He really believes Jesus screwed up and now it's Satan's turn to purify the Earth. The storms and pestilence and climate change are Satan's tools. On the drugs, I happily believed it all and wanted to help him."

Eventually Uriel sent Blake to Canber. "Canber's something else, Dee. Cool and collected. Better informed than anyone else I've met in Penn. Knew about you, and Emmett. What you've accomplished. I told him more."

On the day Brandy and I were captured, the camp was already packed and ready to move out. They just waited for Canber to return.

When Blake's anguished story ran out, we fell into silence for a few minutes. Then the guards came and took Blake away. I couldn't help wondering if that was intentional. Maybe our captors put our friend in with us to teach us the ropes.

"You're alright, Blake!" I called out after him softly. "You're a good man." I almost wished I hadn't said it. His face crumpled, on the brink of tears.

24

Interesting fact: Oxycodone is made by chemically altering one of the natural opiates. The oxycontin pill form is designed to be long-lasting, providing pain relief over 12 hours. For a more intense high, abusers crush it to defeat the time-release feature. The simplest method is to chew it. All opioids are products of the opium poppy. Afghanistan produced more opium than the rest of the world combined. But in the Americas, the opium poppy also thrived in Mexico and Colombia.

I was awfully thirsty by the time the guards came to take me to Camber. It was raining lightly, and I stumbled along with my head back, mouth open to catch every drop I could. *Thank you, clouds. Bless you, rain.* There is nothing so delicious as water when you're truly thirsty, a bite of food when you're truly hungry. And it was a long block, down a hill and around a forested bend, to the house Canber claimed.

Fortunately, the ratty plaid-clad men didn't object. When we entered the house – quite possibly the nicest in town – one of my escorts even fetched me a glass of water. He handed it toward me, then yanked it away.

"Swallow this with it," he said, sticking a white pill in my mouth and leering at me. "Or don't. Spit it out and you'll regret it later when we rape you." Then he handed me the water.

I drank it, every drop, and swallowed the pill as well. Much as I resent obeying orders, I suspected he gave good advice. The water was excellent, my duct-taped wrists little impediment. The pill was probably oxycontin. I gave it a brief chomp before swallowing. No, I had no experience at abusing oxy. But the stuff was so ubiquitous, those days even an 8-year-old would have heard the tricks.

The guards smirked. They delivered me to the home office, and closed the well-hung door genteelly behind me. I gazed around appreciatively, drinking in my surroundings. A corner office, with two walls of cheery windows on the glorious dripping autumn woods, reds and oranges and yellows glowing, vivid color almost pulsating in the grey day. Built-in bookcases and office storage cabinets lined the solid walls, in a beautiful oak veneer to match the generously sized desk. A cheerful print comforter and plump throw pillows lay on the daybed under the windows. Flawless joinery on the oak-stained wood molding and windowsills.

The tech was so lovely, too. Video cameras on tripods for two angles. A matched pair of large computer monitors. LEDs blinking happily to proclaim excellent Internet service and WiFi, ample processing power, best quality gear. I knew the person who bought this equipment was a fellow connoisseur of fine machines.

I loved this office. I remembered not to fixate on the tech, letting my eyes roam right past to appreciate other features. The oak floor. The lovely shade of soft grey wall paint. I didn't need to focus on the hardware. I could feel the Internet surrounding me, the electronic lifeblood that connected me to the rest of the world. I could almost reach out and touch Emmett. No need to even reach. I stood bathed in the same radio signal that touched him.

"Hi, Canber!" I finally greeted the man seated at the desk, with a beatific smile. "I love your office!" He smiled back crookedly, and waved an invitation for me to take a seat on the daybed.

"So you and Emmett are old friends from SAMS!" I burbled on, taking a comfortable seat amidst the puffy pillows. "You must know Cam and John, too." Our friends Cam Cameron, Resco of Long Island, and John Niedermeyer, ranking Resco of New England, were Emmett's room-mates at Leavenworth. According to Canber's introduction back at Station Square, they must have worked together vetting the Calm Act. That was a deep dark secret. But that was OK, since Canber already knew.

"Cam?" Canber inquired.

Oops. "Oh, that's right!" I said. "Cam wasn't in your SAMS class. They just knew each other at Leavenworth. I forgot. Well, anyway! So you said you're retired? How'd you manage that?" Resigning from the Army had been barred for over two years now, for the duration of the climate crisis. That's why the anti-slavery clause in the shiny new Hudson Constitution was such a big deal. Bless Sean Cullen for that. Such a nice man, our governor-general.

"I worked closely with General Tolliver," Canber shared. "It didn't seem wise to stay on after you killed him."

"Me? I didn't kill him," I denied. "Seth did."

He chuckled, surprised. "You're on a first name basis with Seth Taibbi, too? Military governor of PA? My, you have been a busy little girl, haven't you, Dee!"

I waved that away. "They're really Emmett's friends," I confided.

"They?"

"Seth, Charles, Sean, Ivan." Off-hand, just for example, I named the four governor-generals who sent us to Pittsburgh. Lovely men, other than that. "Not really my crew. I mostly hang with other geeks," I confided. "So Canber. What brings us here?"

"So, Dee," he replied in kind, tapping his desk. "You've caused me all sorts of trouble. Amenac. Weather reports, saving lives right and left. Safe trade route reports. Project Reunion. Meshnet communications, no need for infrastructure. Emmett, even. Don't get me wrong, your boyfriend was an adequate field officer. Even bright enough for SAMS. And I'll admit, the Resco concept was rather brilliant. Though I question how much of that was his idea. Cam... Now would that be Major Cameron?"

"Lieutenant Colonel now," I corrected him. "Yeah, Cam got a promotion for his work on the Hudson Constitution! And Long Island. We're so proud of him."

"Ah, yes. That Cam," Canber agreed thoughtfully. "How did they know each other again? Back in Kansas."

"They were room-mates," I supplied. "Cam and John Niedermeyer and Emmett."

"Hm, interesting. I did not know that," Canber said. "Anyway, I was saying. Emmett's adequate. But without you, he wouldn't have branched out and claimed New Jerkzey. He says so in all his hero interviews. He wasn't supposed to be in the Northeast at all." Sounded like sour grapes to me.

"Hudson," I corrected him sunnily. "New York–New Jersey is named Hudson now."

A brief flare of anger crossed Canber's face. He didn't like to be corrected. But he smoothed it over and plowed on. "You cost me several million lives in New York, Dee," he scolded pleasantly. "And who knows how many with the weather alerts and so forth. All of New Jerkzey. That was mine to take for PA, not his. You've been making him way too effective."

"What was your job for Penn?" I asked.

"PA," he corrected. "Our enemy calls us Penn. Well, you obviously know Rescos were put inside the borders to help survivors rebuild, yes?" I nodded. "But surely you understand that wouldn't work, unless the population was culled. They even admitted it publicly, that the minimum necessary culling was to 200 million Americans."

I nodded.

"That's still too many," Canber informed me, shaking his head in disapproval. "And we didn't even get there. We still have 230 million. Far too many. I still think 200 million was a mistake – 30 million is more than enough humans, and more in line with our targets on other continents. People like Emmett have failed to abide by their agreements."

"What agreements?"

"Never mind," Canber said. "The point is that Emmett's been far too effective at saving lives."

"I'm confused," I confessed. "So I'm here to make Emmett less effective?"

"That, too. But mostly I want you to stop helping my opponents. We'll use you ourselves, of course," Canber clarified. "Amazing, isn't it? Hundreds of millions lost their livelihoods. Yet you and I still have skills in hot demand, Dee."

"Use me to do what?" I asked.

"You'll be surprised to hear that I have my own meshnet," he shared. He didn't like to be corrected. So I didn't mention that I already knew that. I just smiled. "You'll make modifications for us."

"Oh, good!" I cried, and reached for his phone.

In a flash, he was sitting with me on the daybed, arms around me, my wrists in his vice grip. "If you try to touch tech again without my permission, Dee, I'll cut your hands off. You wouldn't like that. Would you."

"No. No, I wouldn't like that." That made me cry, just the thought of all the things I enjoy doing, that I wouldn't be able to do without hands. Gardening. Putting my own clothes on. Sewing new clothes. Making love. Playing with tech. Of course, there were voice interfaces. So awkward, but I was sure I could get that to work. I'd need to hire people to supervise for some of the rest –

He pushed my chin up. "Look into the camera, Dee." I looked. One of the video cameras was trained on the daybed. "Now what do you think would drive Emmett crazier. If I tortured you? Or raped you?"

"Torture," I replied instantly. They were both torture.

"Rape it is," he crooned. "Here, swallow this." He rummaged in his uniform breast pocket, and handed me a familiar rufie.

"I already had oxycontin," I objected. I looked sadly straight into the camera, to beg Emmett's understanding.

"Yes, I noticed," Canber replied. "But you don't want to remember being raped, do you?"

"No. I don't," I agreed. I swallowed the rufie with alacrity.

"That's right, darling," Canber encouraged, stroking my ear, my cheek, my neck. "This little video only needs to be between Emmett and me. No need for you to suffer. You're my asset, now. My own pretty little tech wizard. And I take very good care of you."

I couldn't see Canber behind me, with my eyes riveted on the camera. His build wasn't so different from Emmett's. Emmett called me darlin'. Canber couldn't know that, could he? I tried to take it as a sign, tell myself that I wasn't really being raped. Emmett was making love to me, not Canber making hate. It was the only way Emmett could reach me now, and me him. No, it wasn't very convincing.

Canber twisted my nipple, hard, through the fabric of my dress. "Does Emmett ever do this to you?" he asked.

"Not that hard," I replied blearily. It didn't hurt in the slightest. I was feeling no pain.

The two drugs combined with unholy power, and flew me away. It's almost like a bear-in-the-woods joke. If you're raped but can't remember it, were you ever really raped?

Hell, yes.

But I don't remember it.

25

Interesting fact: Stockholm Syndrome arises from a captive's compassion for the situation and goals of her captors. In their fairly benign care, she comes to identify with her captors as being in the right.

I roused slowly to a tuneless and desperate demonic muttering. A blanket was thrown over me. But my back was in agony from the cold concrete floor, my breasts sore, my thighs sticky and – *sore*, I firmly told myself. Just sore. And very cold.

I cracked an eye open to check on my surroundings before committing myself to being awake. Back in the familiar garage. I turned my head ever so slightly. Not demonic muttering. Brandy praying.

Stiff as a board, I rolled to my side, and creakily levered myself up to sitting. Brandy remained focused on her muttering, and didn't acknowledge me. So I set to stretches and bits of yoga until my body regained some flexibility and warmth. Our bathroom facilities had improved. We now had a covered bucket for a toilet, and a second bucket of clean water, with a ladle. I guzzled two cups greedily. One of the patch pockets on my dress was coming unstitched, anyway. I ripped it off and used it as a washcloth.

How was I supposed to feel about being raped? Even thinking the question made me nauseous and woozy. Rape was about power, terrorizing a woman into submission. Well, into submission was a place Dee Baker did not go. Helpless was a state I refused to enter. To hell with that. I might not be big, or strong enough to beat a man off, especially when I was tied up. But I wasn't powerless. I knew that. *Absolutely.*

That realization bought me some emotional breathing room. With that, I realized that Canber's attack didn't even seem directed at me. Of course it wasn't. Emmett was the one Canber spoke to, through the video camera. Canber was using me to punish Emmett. Using my body against my lover.

That thought sent me mentally reeling again. But hang on, forget about Canber for a moment. Could I trust Emmett to deal with this? *Absolutely.* I could trust Emmett. Could I trust me?

Trust me with what? I hadn't done anything wrong. None of this had anything to do with me. Emmett could trust me. I shook my head and focused on washing this whole rape off me, body and soul.

When I was feeling almost human again, I sank beside Brandy, who had never ceased her muttering. "Good morning, Brandy. Afternoon? What are you doing?"

"Rosary," she replied shortly, and resumed her muttering. *Hail Mary full of grace...* Her fingers worked a tiny scrap of grubby yellow. She'd fashioned herself a miniature Catholic rosary out of yarn teased from the woven cotton blanket she sat on.

What a great idea. I yanked my blanket over and folded it for a seat beside her.

Rosaries I didn't know so much about. Our Brooklyn housekeeper, Gladys, had prayer beads. But Gladys was Greek Orthodox, not Catholic. She'd explained to me the differences once.

Orthodox beads simply counted a single prayer, recited a hundred times, while the Catholic rosaries used an elaborate sequence of cross and different beads and contemplations and prayers. Brandy didn't have any beads, so used knots instead, to track her progress in the prayer cycle. She must have known the rosary well, to remember how to construct one.

"Teach me how to do it?" I asked.

She turned her face to glare at me. "Busy, Dee," she said shortly.

I hadn't seen before in the gloom. The far side of her face was grazed and red, her eye socket blackened, the white of her eye bloody. I ignored her tone and touched her face tenderly. "Let me wash it for you," I murmured.

I brought over the water bucket and ladle, and my scrap of wash cloth. I cleaned Brandy's face and hair as best I could, sparingly to eke out our water supply. There was something in the Bible about washing feet, too. I gently but insistently tugged out one of her feet to wash it. Clearly the biblical stuff meant something to her, if not to me. Physically caring for someone else, though, that was universal.

"It's afternoon," Brandy eventually admitted. "You went to see Canber yesterday morning. It's been two days since we were captured. Dee?" She grasped my wrist intently. "I don't want to know. If I forget, don't remind me. About anything."

I nodded slowly. "But we will get out of here, Brandy. You'll see. Emmett knows we were taken captive. Canber is baiting him. He'll find us."

"Dee, if Canber's baiting Emmett," Brandy said reluctantly, "that means it's a trap."

Well, true, and that sucked. That meant we shouldn't struggle to get word of where we were to Emmett or the local authorities. Because that would play right into Canber's hands. *And so we become prisoners of our own devising,* I thought.

"Screw that," I said decisively. "I refuse to help Canber jail us.

Or Uriel. Or whoever's in charge of this madhouse. Emmett's smart, and careful, and has a bazillion allies. If I find a way to contact him without losing my hands, I'll take it."

"Losing your hands?" Brandy asked.

"Never mind." I wouldn't be their accomplice at terrorizing people, either. Let them deliver their own threats. "Teach me the rosary."

"No. Why?"

We argued back and forth, Brandy still convinced that I was tone-deaf to anything religious. But I was adamant that it was high time I learned this stuff. There are no atheists in fox-holes, they say. Millions – billions – agreed, over the centuries. When the chips were down, turn to God, and He'd help. Brandy finally gave in and directed me on how to tie my knots.

I finished the first twenty knots, and told her I'd get to the rest later. "So how does this prayer go?"

She didn't bother trying to teach me me first prayer, The Apostle's Creed. She just recited it for me and crossed herself. The Lord's Prayer I knew, or at least, only needed a reminder of the words. I could certainly relate to the *deliver us from evil* part today.

Next came a few *Hail Mary*'s. Brandy recited it for me whole first, and paused. "Dee, do you earnestly and sincerely believe what I just said?"

"No," I admitted softly. In my experience, a *hail mary* was a pass in football, a hopeless attempt to score, when you didn't 'stand a prayer' of succeeding. *Hail Mary, full of grace.* "What is grace, anyway?"

Brandy nodded. "Good. Grace... The idea is that we yearn for salvation, for God's complete forgiveness and acceptance and divine love. We know we don't deserve it, and couldn't possibly earn it. But by the grace of God, we receive it anyway."

Brandy considered the puzzled frown on my face. "Tell you what, Dee. It won't do you any good to recite prayers that don't mean anything to you. How's this: every tenth knot, the double-knot, either recite the Lord's Prayer, or something else you know is true. Absolutely know, it is absolutely true, and it comforts you. Something you can hold onto like a lifeline." I could relate to that. I'd just done that, thinking over the rape. "Then for each of the next ten knots, contemplate some aspect of that truth, and feel yourself strengthen in it. And just keep going. You don't need any more knots."

She restarted her rosary from the top again, silently.

I tried coaxing apart the *Our Father* again to follow her lead and start from the top, but my mind just nit-picked at it. *Thy will be done on Earth as it is in Heaven.* What did God demand of us, anyway? Wasn't that Dane Beaufort's red herring, that launched me toward my doom?

Why are you asking someone else?

The thought came clear as a bell. *Oh.* That's what Brandy meant. I needed to pray what *I* believed, not anyone else. Christianity left me lukewarm at best. OK. The game of understanding Christians was a task for Pittsburgh. I'd only tried to debug them, after all, like a computer program gone wonky. Not join them. I was done with debugging Christians for now.

I hold these truths to be self-evident. I felt God in beauty, natural beauty. The glowing colors of a flower, or the autumn leaves outside. Gentle waves lapping an orange sand beach, in a sheltered bay of Long Island Sound. The power of gravity below me, the sun above. Brandy was a pain in the ass in our real world. But here, her courage and dogged determination to say her rosary and cleanse herself of the evil done to her body, were so beautiful I had to blink away tears at the thought. *I salute God's grace in Brandy O'Keefe. Bless you, Brandy.*

This isn't new to me. I've been here all along. I was just reminding myself of things I always knew. *Oh!*

And thus my catechism began.

I WAS BLESSED WITH A COLD.

I might have caught cold anyway. I slept on cold damp concrete, in a chilly and thoroughly damp climate, in damp cotton clothes, drugged senseless. But to cinch the deal, that night we had a thunderstorm. We enjoyed no tornado sirens in Nowhere, West Virginia, but the storm was just as ferocious as the lashing supercells that propelled us into the hotel basement back in Pittsburgh.

Judgment didn't celebrate tornado weather quite the same way. Instead, Brandy and I were dragged out into the storm and tied spread-eagled onto the chain link fence around the slave pen. They had one of those here, too. By the looks of it, originally the fence enclosed the exercise yard of an animal shelter. But none of the slaves skulked by the kennel for protection.

Instead, the slaves stood with faces to the sky, sometimes raising their arms to the sky. And they danced, and yelled, cackled and laughed. Rain and gale-force winds slashed at us, heavy wet hair whipping our faces. Hail pelted us with sharp ice. By the one-alligator-two-alligator test, the lightning bolts were right on top of us, part of the time. My bare feet sank an inch into cold liquid mud, oozing between my toes.

The non-slaves were outside enjoying the storm as well, guards dancing around like fools. Occasionally, someone fired a weapon into the sky, hooting. Brandy pointed out Uriel to me, the sect's religious leader, a strongly built, gray-bearded workman dancing past in glee. I didn't see Canber anywhere. Blake, inside the pen, dared to visit us. He squeezed our hands, so the three of us were linked briefly. Then he stole back away, to blend in with the idiocy to our backs.

I had to admire the Judgment group's approach to dealing with the out-of-control devastating storms of climate change. These people didn't cower, or whine, or try to revert to some

1950's sitcom ideal. They ran straight out into the storm, tempting fate. *Wanna kill me, God? Here I am!* Truth to tell, I was more sympathetic to their viewpoint than the cowering. Except that it was damned uncomfortable. Perhaps if I'd been allowed to dance and stay warm.

As the storm died back, guards dragged women out of the slave pit to couple in the mud in wild abandon. Some came to pull us off the fence, but were playfully batted away with gun stocks by other guards. "Canber's!" they laughed. Brandy closed her eyes against the pornographic frenzy. I watched everything, drinking up the sights, the sounds. Not because the rutting mud-pit was erotic. I'd never felt so un-sexy in my life. Through my chattering teeth, the slippery bodies on the ground didn't make much impression. But this was my first chance to really take in our surroundings, not hemmed in by trees.

What I saw during distant lightning flashes was as bad as Blake had described. The tiny town was ringed by tall forested hills, or the shoulders of mountains. The road by the slave pen was a rutted gravel mess. The few little houses and mobile homes looked like they'd been perched haphazardly. Aside from the military vehicles that arrived with us, the native pickup trucks looked old and rusted. I spotted a single satellite dish, mounted on a steel tower, maybe thirty feet up. No one would ever find this place on satellite images. No line of sight to the satellites.

Gradually, the clouds shredded into fast-moving tatters, to unleash moonlight and brilliant stars, by the time the Saturnalia ran its course. The relatively professional uniformed men who watched over Brandy and me finally untied us from the fence. I fell to the ground and curled into a ball, my teeth chattering out of control. My guard finally gave up trying to coax me back onto my feet. He took me back to the garage in a fireman's carry.

In an action movie, Navy SEALs could no doubt get up the next morning and run 10 miles into a rain-drenched forest to accomplish a daring rescue mission. But like ordinary mortals, I just got sick.

I WAS BLESSED WITH A FAREWELL.

The next afternoon I was presented to Canber again, my grubby cotton dress still wet. It was colder today, not freezing, but down around 40 degrees, with a stiff breeze rattling the colorful fresh-fallen leaves along the road. Arriving at Canber's house, the guards debated giving me oxycontin again, but decided I didn't look so good. I couldn't hug myself to keep warm with my hands still taped. I tended to curl down into a ball, shuddering, if they didn't hold me upright.

Canber sat at his desk working. His work accessories, pens and paper, tablet and calculator and folders and computer monitors, were arrayed much the way Emmett would have them. Tidy, methodical, organized. Aside from having similar builds, they didn't look much alike. I didn't like to consider that they might think and work alike.

I didn't wait for an invitation. I just zombie-shuffled straight to his daybed. Once there, I curled my feet up under one pillow, face-dove into another, and huddled shaking. His room was the most warmth I'd experienced all day. It wasn't nearly warm enough.

Canber laid a cool hand on my forehead briefly, then went away to yell at the guards in the hallway. I was sublimely indifferent to what all the yelling was about, but I caught the gist. His soldiers shouldn't have been stupid enough to let Uriel and the Judgment nut-jobs take me out into the storm. "We *use* the lunatics, we don't join them!" was the way Canber put it.

Eventually, he came back. He lay a down blanket around me and levered me up to a seated position. He held out two thick white pills and a glass of orange juice.

I blinked at them blankly. I hadn't seen orange juice in a couple years. Oranges don't grow in New England or Hudson. "Whussat?"

"Extra-strength Tylenol," he replied. "You have a fever."

Damned straight I had a fever. From past experience, I suspected it was well north of 103 degrees. With great solemnity, I took one of the two pills he held out, and washed it down with a gulp of orange juice. "Thank you." I tried to turtle back into the blanket.

"No, take the other one, too," he insisted. "And drink your juice. You need the vitamin C."

"I don't like orange juice," I objected. I was overcome by a huge splattering sneeze, and a coughing fit. I tried to cover my nose and mouth, but the bindings and blanket fought me. In distaste, he moved away and handed me a handkerchief. I mopped up, and he tried to hand me the orange juice again. I shook my head violently, then regretted it because it felt like my brains were sloshing inside my skull. "Starve a fever," I whispered hoarsely. "If I drink that, I'll throw up."

The orange juice was hastily retracted. Canber returned to his desk. "Hell," he said. "I need to go to – I need to leave. I can't take you with us like this."

I slumped into my down cocoon, and let my eyes close. I jolted back awake as my head jerked down. I tried to focus. "You're not the head of Judgment, are you?" I croaked.

"No," he agreed. "Uriel leads them." He shook his head in tired disapproval. "There are a thousand Uriels and Judgments. But they're useful. Until they're not. Just tools." He waved at his desk, so neatly ordered like Emmett's. "I'm just another Resco, Dee. Using what comes to hand."

"Why do you do it?" I asked. "Not just another Resco. They save. You kill."

He scowled at me. "I'm saving the planet. You think you could have your nice little moral life without me? If 22 million survived the Apple Zone, instead of 5? With 8 million people around Philadelphia instead of only 2 million? With all the people who suicided on the drugs I supplied? Or died like lemmings following some religious Pied Piper? I don't think so. Your life wouldn't have been worth living. Your ecosystems would have been destroyed beyond hope of repair. Emmett knows that as well as I do."

I considered that muzzily. Emmett never pretended to have told me everything about his classmates, the men who vetted the Calm Act with him. Of their identities, their assignments and locations, he refused to tell me anything at all.

"Yeah. No," I said in simple fairness. "I hate it. But we needed the culling. But we don't anymore. We're done with that. Can't you stop now?"

"They didn't even meet the target of 200 million," Canber said bitterly. "And there are scenarios. A year out. Five years out. Milestones have to be met. If they're not, more need to die."

"That must really suck for you," I said sympathetically.

Canber's face twisted in rage. "I don't need your pity!"

"No," I agreed. His rage didn't bother me. High fever brought out great objectivity and deep indifference. "But you deserve a thank you for your service." I frowned. "Did the SAMS draw lots and you lost or something?"

"'*Thank you for your service,*'" Canber hissed. "Do you know how many times we heard that? Coming back from I-crap and Crud-istan?"

"What else is there to say?" I croaked back. "Pathetic politicians should never have sent you there. Idiot public with their knee-jerk reactions. Military-industrial complex and their profit margins. Burning oil until there wasn't a drop of profit left, and the planet was doomed. I didn't want you to go. But you were soldiers for my country. And you went. I know I owe you, for what you did. Whether I approved or not. I still owe you thanks."

Canber pursed his lips and glared at me. "We didn't draw lots. I love this planet. People suck."

I nodded sadly. "People suck," I agreed. "Nature is so beautiful. I hope we haven't killed the planet. Emmett seems to think we're fiddling while Rome burns or something, that it's a lost cause. I'd like to see this beautiful world saved. Thank you for your service."

Grudgingly, he acknowledged this with, "Thank you." I could see that he finally believed that I meant it, for whatever that was worth.

I sneezed and mopped my face again. My head really hurt when I moved that violently. "Are you going to rape me again today?"

He looked repulsed. "No. Just fall over and go to sleep."

"OK." I keeled over, back into the pillows.

Canber said softly, "That was about Emmett, not you."

I froze, listening. But he didn't say any more. And I couldn't stay awake.

26

Philippians 4:8 King James Version (KJV): Finally, brethren,
whatsoever things are true, whatsoever things are honest, whatsoever
things are just, whatsoever things are pure, whatsoever things are
lovely, whatsoever things are of good report; if there be any virtue,
and if there be any praise, think on these things.

I was blessed with shelter.

When I woke, Blake and Brandy and I had been moved to a small toasty mobile home all to ourselves. We had two bedrooms, with real beds and sheets and pillows and warm comforters, a whole bed apiece. We had a working bathroom with clean musty towels. A kitchen, complete with propane stove, and a refrigerator stocked with orange juice and fresh milk and eggs. The lights even worked.

We still didn't have shoes. But the previous owners had left clothes behind, including two pairs of slippers. One pair even had enough rubber on the sole to walk to the mailbox if the mud wasn't too deep. Not that we were allowed to walk to the mailbox. None of the clothes were the right size for Brandy or me – Blake got lucky – but they were heavenly compared to the rags we wore before. So we all dressed from the wardrobe that fit Blake.

Dressed for bed, anyway. The first couple days we weren't interested in much besides the Tylenol and vitamins and orange juice left in the kitchen. For clothes, we were grateful for Blake-sized pajamas and sweats and layers of socks. I'm not sure if this Tylenol was the same as the stuff Canber had given me, but its 'extra strength' was codeine. We slept comfortably.

One fairly sane soldier and several of Uriel's freaky devotees visited a couple times a day while we were sick, to make sure we were still alive and bring us more food. We carefully stashed the food to eat when we could keep it down, and to keep it coming in the meantime. I got the impression Canber had left firm instructions that there would be dire consequences for the Judgment sect if any of us died without permission.

My fever broke after a couple days. Brandy and Blake had been more badly mistreated, so they would take longer to mend. Alright, then, we didn't want to be rescued just yet. I selected a personal project in the meantime. I would develop the world's fastest case of Stockholm Syndrome to earn my captors' trust.

I would identify with Canber's crusade, not Uriel's, thank you very much. Canber was safer. He wasn't there.

Besides, I did understand what Canber was doing. Mind-game aficionado or not, it was just too big a stretch to pretend to believe I was Satan's minion and aspired to roll around copulating in the mud. Loving nature, wanting to defend the Earth from an infestation of humans, I could relate to, more than I felt comfortable admitting.

I found a pen and an old composition book in our lovely manufactured home, and tore out the used pages. Someone had built a big deck onto the side of our tiny house, with resin deck furniture of the thrift store variety. I sat out there, wrapped in a blanket, to make myself ostentatious in my contemplation. Yes, I remember that thing where Jesus taught we should pray in the closet. But I wanted rewards on earth, not in heaven. I sought a physical salvation.

The deck was a good place for prayer, for me. Our little scrap of level lot was barely wide enough for the mobile home and a pickup truck. The broken mountainside resumed its forested climb not thirty feet away to the right, brilliant in its autumn colors. Squirrels and chipmunks cavorted there. A heavenly chorus of unseen frogs and toads, insects and bats and birds, and a hidden burbling brook all sang to me. To the left, downslope, perhaps the soil was too shallow for trees. Wildflowers still bloomed among the ripe grasses and herbs, tiny and pale, in white and lavender and yellow.

I wrote about my prayer progress with Brandy, that I was one with God in natural beauty. Within minutes, I'd forgotten that I was ever pretending. I felt the Earth's reassuring pull, the sun on my face, breathed the deep air. I smelled the woods, listened to the wildlife. I felt my way back across the Earth to Long Island Sound and its gentle waves, to Burlington Vermont and its cold lake, to the tides of New York Harbor lapping Brooklyn, the broad Monongahela River flowing through Pittsburgh. As my fever climbed back a little in mid-afternoon, I could soar with the little wisps of cloud in the deep blue sky. I could hold out my hand and feel the waves of WiFi stroking me. Tenuous here, but my body was still connected to my native cyber world, too.

I was as big as the Earth, greater than any captor could possibly be. And I blessed them.

The soldier and Judgment guards returned in the evening with more food. The latter were much put out by my assertive euphoria, and fled as quickly as possible. The soldier, Thomaston, nodded quizzically as I conveyed my epiphany.

The codeine in the Tylenol helped a lot.

I was blessed with a teacher.

Uriel dropped by the next morning, the leader and preacher of Judgment. A gray drizzle had returned, making the brilliant red and orange leaves glow, throbbing bright against the wet-darkened tree trunks and grey skies. We sat at the diminutive dining booth in the kitchenette. Brandy and Blake still huddled in their beds behind closed doors.

And Uriel explained to me the tenets of Judgment.

I played along, honestly admitting that Christianity left me rather flat. I told him about my attempts to understand the fighting sects of Pittsburgh, and my colleagues' efforts to explain to me the differences they fought over. In turn, he admitted those Christian distinctions were minor. It had taken sustained effort on Judgment's part to keep the Pittsburgh militias fighting one another. But they were slaves to fear, addicted to coddled comforts, weak sheep pathetically looking to a celestial shepherd to save them from themselves, instead of watching where they stepped. Judgment in Uriel's metaphor were the wolves that thinned the weak, purified the stock, until only those select who deserved Eden would remain.

"Eden," I pounced. "A wild world. Returned to the garden. Unfettered by asphalt and agriculture. Where people are rare. Small against the majesty of nature."

"Yet always the top predator!" Uriel exulted. "It is the nature of man to rule the Earth, red in tooth and claw!"

"I still have trouble with that," I admitted. "I mean, I love the goal. But I still can't see myself killing people. Maybe I have a different calling? To persuade people over the Internet? Instead of culling overpopulation directly."

Uriel scowled at me for derailing his oratorical climax. But he nodded reluctantly. "You're a woman. Women bear an excess of compassion, in order to tend to men, and nurture children. Killing is man's work. But the world needs no children now. You must struggle against your womanly nature, to find within your-self your murderous true nature, and bring it forth.

"Defense, is the key for a woman. A man can easily grow to embrace offense. But as a female animal, your instincts are to defend. You will bear no children. The world has more than enough people. Instead, claim the wild and feral beauty of the Earth as the fruit of your womb. Feel Earth's head cresting, aborning from your birth canal." *Ouch.* "See yourself defending your baby with your whole heart and soul." He tapped my compo-sition book. "Write on this. And contemplate. We will speak again."

Brandy emerged from our bedroom after Uriel left, and plopped down across the table from me, swaddled in a blanket. Her eyes were still glassy with fever and congestion, but she was on the mend.

"Dee, what in hell are you doing?" she asked.

"Developing my spirituality," I told her in dead earnest. "I think I'm finally getting a handle on religion."

"That man is pure unmitigated evil," she countered. "Dee, all this defense of nature claptrap is a crock. What animal besides man preys on its own species? What predator besides man kills except to meet its needs?"

I frowned at her. "I'm working toward salvation, Brandy. Our emancipation from physical bondage." Further than that I refused to go, to speak that this might be an act. I'm a terrible liar. Therefore to be persuasive, I must believe.

"I pray for your soul," Brandy whispered. Then she grabbed the white bottle of codeine-laced Tylenol. "No more candy for Dee."

"Hey! That's a fever-reducer. We need that!"

"There's good clean old-fashioned aspirin in the medicine cabinet," Brandy countered. On second thought, she reluctantly moderated her stance. "We save the opiates for enduring abuse. Promise me, Dee. No more opiates unless you need them.

Because your brain is turning to cottage cheese. These people don't care about me and Blake. Emmett and Hudson don't, either. Without you, we're dead here."

I had to concede she had a point, though I glared at her until she shut herself and the codeine back into our tiny shared bedroom. I had plenty of practice lately invoking nature-worship euphoria. I could get high on life.

Opiate withdrawal truly sucks. I hadn't abused it long enough for any of the dangerous withdrawal symptoms to appear. But by evening I was blessed with the full body itching, as though fire ants marched under my skin. Even the backs of my eyeballs itched. I scratched deep gouge tracks down my arms, then washed them with soap to avoid infection. Which made all of me itch all the worse.

The moody irritation helped with my homework, though. I easily got in touch with my inner murderous mama. I wrote it out in my composition book, in complete honesty.

I WAS BLESSED WITH A TECHNOPHOBE.

Technophobes bemuse me. I myself was born under a computing planet, innately dancing to the music of the spheres. I naturally perceive the world in the mathematics of pattern, and exult in the power of a remote control. I saw the computer and the computer was good. We understand each other, technology and me. We complete each other in a synergistic whole, where together we are so much more than either of us apart. Technology sitting dormant calls to me a siren song. Come, let us play together!

In contrast, technophobes seem to believe that the innocent friendly tech is out to get them. One of my grandmothers suffered from the affliction. Utterly convinced that she was unequal to helping with simple math homework, preparing a tax return, or mastering a new TV remote.

Of course, I couldn't get too cocky. Bathroom plumbing issues left me feeling like a gibbering idiot. But my prayers and diligence at cultivating Stockholm Syndrome were rewarded. I had established trust.

"The meshnet isn't working," Canber's soldier Thomaston confided to me anxiously. "I can reach Canber on the computer in his office, but everything else says this." He stuck his phone out toward me.

I firmly tucked my hands into my lap, seated in my kitchenette. "I'm not allowed to touch technology without Canber's permission," I reminded him piously. "Though I could talk you through it," I allowed, with a gurgling sniff.

Brandy and Blake were well on the mend, and I was downright well. We'd lost a few pounds during our fevers, but we'd gained weight at Mrs. Wiehl's buffet in Pittsburgh. And we were eating again now, so we came out about even. But we didn't want to look too healthy yet. So I'd chopped an onion, and we rubbed the onion juice on our eyes when we heard boots crunching up the gravel road. Onion-induced tears and general tail-dragging might eke us out another couple days of looking too snively to work.

I gently probed Thomaston's computer savvy on the way to Canber's house, about a mile. But the fact that he'd walk a mile before I even looked at his phone gave me hope. *He cannot think straight if technology is involved. Yes!*

"OK, so first, show me how you know the Internet is working here," I coached Thomaston at Canber's desk. I stood behind him as he showed me Canber's last three emails, opening each one for me to read on the big monitor. As of three hours ago, Canber was in Greensboro North Carolina, and planned to spend the next two nights in Charlotte before heading south to Savannah. Good to know.

"But see, I can't get that email on my phone," Thomaston complained, demonstrating on his phone. Of course he couldn't see the email. The computer was reading Canber's military IMAP email account, and Thomaston had the meshnet up on his phone, logged into his own account.

I prayed I could spin this out for a while before someone texted him over the meshnet. He might get a clue if that happened. "Wow, that's bad," I assured him. "Here, I'm going to give you some commands to type in. Let's use the computer, so I can see. The screen's bigger."

Without ever touching the keyboard, I eventually got Thomaston logged in remotely to meshnet102, the small testing meshnet we ran at Amenac headquarters. Popeye used it to test and attack meshnet101, the software development team on Long Island. My password was unmemorable gibberish – which I failed twice, intentionally, on login – and he didn't write it down. Those login failures would write to the error log. But I feared no one would notice that. Instead, we brought up the meshnet's arcane command line interface.

"OK, sorry, this next command is really long," I warned him.

SEND @POPI DEC10911DEEBEMLSOSCBI79SWV

I worried that I'd laid it on too thick with that one. Surely Thomaston would notice something fishy in it. Dec 10 was the date that Penn went dark, scribbled all over the walls by Station Square. The 911 was simply a 911 emergency call. Deeb for me, EML for Emmett MacLaren, SOS, CB for Canber, I-79 south to West Virginia.

But Thomaston was too focused on his laborious hunt-and-peck typing. He didn't blink at the gibberish content. I'd already cured him of asking for explanations. "It didn't do anything," he complained. "God, I hate computers."

"I understand completely," I commiserated. "I feel the same

way about plumbing. All the gibberish they spew in the instructions, you know? Allen wrenches, O-rings, washers." I shuddered melodramatically. The soldier sighed and nodded sadly. Apparently Thomaston was an equal-opportunity technophobe.

"Next step," I encouraged. "Could you bring up maps on the phone? Yeah, that one." I had him look up our current GPS coordinates, and carefully transcribe them into the next command.

SEND @POPI LOC39.5914264,-79.8309698QT

I could only hope Popeye would take the hint of the QT part to be quiet about this. "Now we're getting somewhere!" I assured my victim. "Uh, what's your meshnet address? Like, I'm 'at-Deeb', you're...? OK!"

SEND @POPI &MESH666@KTHOMASTON TESTDEEB

"Drat, that was dumb of me. I'm sorry," I said. "I meant..."

SEND &MESH666@KTHOMASTON TESTDEEB

"Oh, I got a text!" Thomaston said, astonished. "'Test Deeb.' Oh, did we just send that? And another one. 'POPI911 RCVD.'"

I grinned and traded high-fives with the soldier. "OK, type control-Z three times, that's right! And close that window! You're all set!" Yes, by all means, close that window quickly. Thomaston was starting to think, and I couldn't have that.

"But I still don't have my email from Canber," Thomaston protested.

"Well, I can't fix what happened before I got here," I reasoned. "So that's just gone. Good thing you have it here on the computer."

Thomaston looked very frustrated. So I offered, "Well, we could set up an email forwarder bouncing system, so every email duplicates and echoes to your phone. Using an IMAP Internet pipe. That would take a lot more typing." Actually it would take two minutes, and likely get him killed for stupidity when Canber came back. Of course, Thomaston might not live to see Canber again anyway. The real risk was that email forwarding was so straightforward that Thomaston might understand it.

"No!" Thomaston quickly assured me. "No, this is good enough. No more typing." He was all too eager to walk me back to our single-wide mobile home, and wash his hands of me for the rest of the day.

Our deck sported a flagpole. With a ballpoint pen, I drew a faint tree on a white pillowcase and affixed it to the top of the pole. To proclaim my allegiance to the natural world, as I explained to Uriel later when he dropped by for my catechism lesson. He was pleased with me.

Brandy and Blake didn't need to ask. Anyone who'd followed Project Reunion would recognize the point of a white flag. The day Emmett landed on Staten Island a year ago, without any other communications available, the starving city survivors used white flags to send a welcome to the relief forces, to promise they wouldn't fight. Emmett's forces sent in drones to peek in on Staten Island before landing, and spotted the white flags. I imagined Emmett would send in a drone here, too, to snoop around before coming in.

As much as possible, all three of us sat on the deck the rest of the day, under the flag. Brandy's hair was such a brilliant red, and Blake's so beautifully dark. As a threesome, we were readily identifiable.

I could hardly have said it any clearer: *Hey Emmett! Rescue us here!*

27

Interesting fact: A study attempted to prove that it was the culling of the American people that led to increased religiosity after the Calm Act – that the devout were more likely to survive. But although fewer religious people committed suicide, most of the change was from people becoming more religious as a result of their experiences.

Brandy and Blake and I woke to the sound of rotors overhead in the small hours before dawn. As we scrambled to pull some clothes on, most of the choppers passed us, headed toward the center of Nowhere. I never learned the real name of that town. Guns started chattering thataway. It sounded like one copter remained hovering right over our heads, the noise and wind rattling the poor little trailer home.

We were debating whether it was smart to peek out the door, when someone started pounding on it. "Ohio Army! Open up!"

Blake opened the door. We all grinned welcome. "So good to see you!" I cried. "Would you happen to be looking for –"

"Dee Baker, Blake Sondheim, Brandy O'Keefe?" he demanded right over me, checking to identify our faces. "Come with me! Nowhere to land, we'll need to pull you up."

It wasn't my imagination. The huge attack helicopter was hovering just feet above the mobile home. Rope ladders hung down both sides. Blake ran for the other side. I pushed Brandy ahead of me to go first. She didn't wait for them to pull up the ladder, just scrambled up as fast as she could go. Once she was secured inside the chopper, an arm from above waved for me to come next. The Ohio soldier stayed behind, anchoring the rope ladder. The climb wasn't too bad, only about 25 feet, though there was a disconcerting jerk halfway up.

The arm that waved me up also grasped my arm at the top and yanked me in, pulling me to fall onto his body. In the dark and crowded copter cabin, I tried to pull away apologetically, but he held me tight against his chest.

"Thank God, darlin'!" he yelled in my ear over the noise, and kissed me hard. "You alright?"

"Emmett!" I cried. I might not have recognized him even if the lights were on, or even recognized the feel of his body against mine. He was in full combat gear with infrared goggles on. But the kiss and the voice were pure Emmett. "We're good!"

He nodded, kissed me again, held me close. But his attention quickly veered back to the operation. As soon as my anchor soldier made it into the chopper, Emmett yelled into his mike, "Mission accomplished! Let's go, let's go!"

I didn't joggle his elbow while he was focused on the retreat. I did wriggle around to sit on his lap, but he kept one arm locked around me. Apparently the other choppers bugged out as soon as he gave the all-clear. Then we were all speeding away. There was one surface-to-air missile explosion to add a touch of terror, but fortunately it missed.

When Emmett started to relax a little, I yelled over the noise, "Did you take out the Judgment camp?" He seemed to think the action was over by then. Airborne Infantry, after all. He must have done this dozens of times. I'd never expected to see him in action, though.

Emmett shook his head. "Only objective was you."

"Canber wasn't there," I told him. "He's in Charlotte, North Carolina." Emmett nodded, gave me a squeeze, looked away. My eyes had adjusted to the slightly LED-lit gloom. Emmett's jaw was set. But this was no place to talk. "Where are we going?"

"Border garrison, north of Morgantown," he replied. "Van from there to Pittsburgh. Then home."

"How much longer in Pittsburgh?" I asked. I desperately wanted to go home to my own bed, in Brooklyn.

"We're done, darlin'," Emmett said. "Just needed you."

Yelling over the rotors was exhausting. We left it at that.

"You want a bath?" Emmett asked awkwardly. Finally we were alone in our room together, back at the hotel. Brief bits of information were conveyed along the early-morning drive back from the Ohio–West Virginia border garrison. Brandy and Blake and I sketched our story for Emmett, accounted for our days away. But he'd seemed reserved and strangely incurious.

I leaned against one side of the short entry hall by the hotel room bathroom, him propped against the opposite wall.

"Not really," I replied. "Just had a shower last night. Emmett?"

He half-smiled sadly. "Not sure how to treat you now. Do you want to see a counselor or something? That's what they tell us to do next in officer training. For one of our troops."

"God, no," I said, heartfelt. "I hate shrinks." Women who play mind games should not play with psychologists.

Tentatively, I reached for his hand. "Emmett, I'm alright. Really." He gazed uneasily at our lightly linked hands, not even squeezing back. "My knight in shining armor came through for me again. Thank you, for getting me out of there. I knew you would."

Suddenly, violently, he yanked me into his arms, hard. I *eeked* a little, and he pushed me away again. "I'm sorry!" he said in panic.

"For what?" I asked. "You just surprised me." I stepped back to him and clutched him tightly to me around the waist. "I want you to hold me!" He'd been holding me all the way back from Nowhere, on the chopper and van. I didn't understand what his problem was now.

Reluctantly, tenderly, he enfolded me in his arms and stood holding me, cheek to cheek. He started crying. "I was so afraid I'd lost you." I just held him, letting him cry. "Canton sent me a video, Dee, of him..."

"Raping me," I completed the sentence. "I don't remember it, Emmett. Only the first part, before he gave me a rufie. I was already sky-high on oxycontin. I mean, being raped, that's repulsive. But, I'm not hurt."

"That wasn't directed at you," Emmett whispered.

I stilled in his arms. So Canber had said, and I had concluded. But *Canton,* Emmett had said, not Canber. And no, that rape scene was directed at a video camera, not me at all. Canber drugged me to keep me out of it. "How well do you know Canton Bertovich, Emmett?"

"Well," he reluctantly supplied. "We were friends once."

I drew Emmett to the bed and sat cross-legged beside him, while I drew the story out of him.

They weren't just slightly friends. During their first year at ILE school in Leavenworth, before they'd ever heard of the Calm Act, Canton and Emmett had apartments in the same building. They carpooled to classes together. Ate together most days, at least one meal. Studied together. ILE was a course full of happily married men and women, like Dane and Marilou Beaufort. Their classmates eagerly seized the opportunity of being stably state-side for the year to bond with their families. The social scene was replete with family barbecues and kids' ball games. Meanwhile, Canton was enduring the last death throes of a vicious divorce, and Emmett was recently and miserably divorced as well. Both ardent environmentalists. Both brilliant and analytical officers. Doing outdoor sports and weekend trips together to escape the happy families. Both roped into planning and vetting the Calm Act the following year.

At one point, Emmett even considered Canton as a replacement best friend for Zack Harkonnen, the man who'd brought Emmett and me together. Zack had left the Army behind, and never really enjoyed it. At the time, Emmett thought maybe he should let Zack go, let that friendship fade. He and Canton had more in common, it seemed.

"That was then, this is now," I murmured. "He's a mass murderer now, Emmett. Did you see the signs?"

Emmett plucked at the bedspread. "Uh-huh," he finally settled on. "I don't think they'll ever catch him, Dee." He wouldn't look up.

My eyes narrowed. "Never catch him? Or never look?"

"Uh-huh," Emmett breathed.

The Ohio Army attack force hadn't even gone after the Judgment camp in West Virginia. Just kept them occupied while Emmett's team extracted us. Then we left. No one was going after Judgment, or Canber.

"Why did he kill Dane, Emmett?" I hazarded. Judging from Emmett's flinch, my guess was right.

"Dane had gone rogue," he whispered. "Moral crusader. No other leverage to keep him quiet. And Canton didn't kill Dane. Just beat him up. Didn't know the head injury was serious."

"What leverage does Canber have against you?" I demanded. Emmett just shook his head. "Emmett, I think I deserve an answer. It's one thing to honor a promise to your secret SAMS club. But Canber dragged me into his secrets, not you."

Emmett didn't want to answer the question, but I waited him out. "You," he eventually said. "Among other things. Other people. For leverage."

It felt like a sucker-punch. Based on what Canber had said, this shouldn't have come as a surprise. Canber was certainly angry with Emmett. I was so caught up in my own thoughts, it was a few minutes before I glanced up at Emmett again. He looked scared.

"It's not your fault, Emmett," I said, giving his hand a squeeze.

"Uh-huh," he breathed.

"Canber is responsible for what Canber did," I insisted. "Not you."

"Uh-huh." He grasped my hand back, hard. His mouth worked in several false starts. "Maybe I should get another room this time?"

"No." I sighed. "Emmett, you say you want to marry me. If you really mean that, we need to face things together. No matter how –" I hesitated. "Life sucks sometimes. I thought we were good at facing that together."

"Uh-huh."

EMMETT LEFT WITH DRUM THE NEXT MORNING, TO SERVE UP A final harangue to the Pittsburgh community leaders, church leaders, and ex-militia, at a large auditorium at Carnegie-Mellon University. I followed along separately with the IndieNews team. Blake Sondheim recorded the event.

The address was a command performance – the audience was required to attend. No-shows were to be rounded up, stripped naked, and locked into public stocks for display. A Puritan-era punishment for resurrecting the wars of the Reformation. Attendance was good. Only a dozen or so individuals volunteered for the stocks to help Drum make her point. They were all religious dissenters, so later Drum displayed them on the front lawns of their respective churches.

The Resco manual, which constituted the written orders for

Emmett and Drum and other Rescos, advised that a Resco must first, last, and always establish himself as the biggest bad-ass in the neighborhood, the authority that cannot be thwarted. And simultaneously, he must establish himself as the community's best asset and opportunity for help from outside the local district. What a Resco declares is law, and the citizens' best hope for a good life is to cooperate and implement the Resco's plans.

And there were ample rewards. Drum laid out a one-year plan for Pittsburgh's Allegheny County. Based on local agricultural output, everyone could earn a full meal ticket – a 2500 calorie per day Pennsylvania meal ticket at that – if they were willing to work full time. Power would be rationed, but free, and restored throughout the city within a few months. Every household could have enough power to run a refrigerator and freezer, and a few lights. The details were complex, but homes could be heated to at least 55 degrees in winter, and might have hot water, depending on their equipment. Jobs would be available accomplishing all this. God knows, if it took steel and machinery, Pittsburgh had the means.

The churches were to remain shuttered and barred except during religious services. No food was allowed in church. No discussion of religious views would be tolerated outside church or the home. There would be no single-sect work crews. Punishments for infractions would remain harsh.

The city's primary and middle schools would reopen after New Year's. Religious groups were forbidden to operate a school, and mention of religious ideas at a public school would be punished.

The re-industrialization joint venture with Ohio was off the table, pending proof of restored order in Pittsburgh. General Schwabacher of Ohio–West Virginia wouldn't invest until he was convinced that Drum was in firm control, not only in Pittsburgh but all of western Penn.

Based on personal interviews and Dane Beaufort's records,

Drum found most of the rural and outer suburban militias to be perfectly sound, and re-authorized them. Inside the city and certain suburbs, the militia units were permanently disbanded in favor of expanding the Pittsburgh police department. Ex-militia were invited to apply for the new jobs. If hired, they would be isolated from previous team-mates and co-religionists for a fresh start, and receive training.

I rather thought Paddy Bollai, Dane's handyman, would make a good cop. Also the Apocalyptic militiaman who asked if Emmett could stay on as Resco during Q&A that night in the tornado shelter, despite glares from his fellow militia. There were good people to be freed from the old dysfunctional militia structure.

Drum's speech to her new flock comprised most of the lecture, but Emmett took a turn. He recounted the investigation's official findings, that a terrorist organization called Judgment had waylaid and badly beaten Dane Beaufort and his second, Dwight Davison, and that both men had later died of their wounds. Judgment was not to be mistaken for a religion. They were a sophisticated and highly dangerous terrorist group. Any suspected Judgment activity should be reported to the police immediately.

Emmett also hammered home that Drum had the complete trust and authority of the Commonwealth of Pennsylvania behind her, and the backing of Hudson and Ohio–West Virginia as well. He said that anyone who dared to call a Lieutenant Colonel a 'whore' or 'harlot' deserved every minute they spent naked in the stocks as a result. Verbally abusing a woman for her clothing, or non-conformity to someone's idea of her proper role, constituted a violation of the rule prohibiting the mention of religion in secular life. Treating women with respect and courtesy, at all times, was required.

Drum happily added that women were encouraged to apply for jobs in the Pittsburgh P.D., and any other job funded by the Resco government. Pittsburgh would be an equal opportunity employer, with equal pay for equal work. *Absolutely.* Day care would be subject to the same religious prohibitions as public schools.

No religion in public. Period.

Brandy O'Keefe of IndieNews sat next to me and took copious notes. At the end, outside the auditorium building, she handed me a distilled bulleted list, and made me introduce, then summarize the meeting on camera. To do that required looking directly into the camera, but one side of her face was still too battered for that. Her face wouldn't make it past the censors, because we couldn't explain the injuries.

Brandy did carry out exit interviews with attendees, getting reactions of the locals to their new Resco and her plans. For that, she could turn the unmarred side of her face to the camera. Her interviewees ended up looking mighty shifty on video, embarrassed by the obvious signs of abuse written across Brandy's face, which our Internet viewers never saw.

I LEFT MOST OF MY EMAIL TO CATCH UP ON DURING THE LONG TRAIN ride back to Hudson. But one item leapt out at me. Jean-Charles Alarie of the gran caravans wrote back about their experiences with 'sixers' and the huge swath of Pennsylvania not controlled by any Resco.

Heavily encrypted, Jean-Charles' email told me what the gran caravans knew and suspected about Canton Bertovich and his far-flung operation. That the culling of the American people was by no means left to chance and rogues, but was carefully orchestrated. The sixers and other doomsday cults were fronts for systematic extermination. And their East Coast operations found their best sanctuary in central Pennsylvania.

Jean-Charles strongly recommended that I not mention this to Emmett or any other Resco. At some level, they already knew.

But civilians like myself tended to disappear if they knew such things. The end of the U.S. hadn't changed that.

Good warnings. Sadly, his email had arrived in my inbox a couple hours after Canber abducted us.

I HAD A LATE FAREWELL LUNCH WITH BRANDY AND BLAKE BEFORE we went our separate ways back to Hudson. IBIS agent Donna Gianetti joined us. Mrs. Wiehl's buffet was as magnificent as ever. But we'd eaten our fill. None of us were very hungry.

"I don't see how that speech solved much," I admitted. "It's like Drum and Emmett just played good cop bad cop." I didn't care for my hero playing bad cop. I'd worked too long on his PR campaign painting him a hero, perhaps.

"I think it was good for Pittsburgh," Brandy surprised me by saying. "They need a public act of contrition, to work their way back from this mess. Strong punishments and firm rules will make them feel better. Not that I'd support this high-handedness on IndieNews, of course. Not allowed to say anything about this on IndieNews." Her voice trailed off, haunted, on the last.

We had both been informed by our censors that our abduction had never happened. And specifically that Canber did not exist and would not be mentioned. Our original explanation of Dane's death, that we filmed just before our kidnapping, as edited by Brandy's producer in our absence, was approved for publication. Modifications or corrections would not be approved.

"You can always talk to me," I offered. "If you need to talk, Brandy. Any time. You too, Blake. I owe you. And I care about you." Blake, sitting next to me, engulfed me in a hug.

Brandy nodded. "Same here." She sighed. "Although you're still going to know more than us about what's going on. And you're still not going to tell me."

"One day in the garage," I reminded her, "you told me you didn't want to know. You were right. You don't want to know."

Gianetti backed me up. "Dee's right. I know more. Maybe not everything, but... It wouldn't make you happy and you can't change it. You know, the long range weather forecast was updated while you were gone. The pattern looks like a repeat of two years ago. Hundreds of tornados for Pittsburgh. Strong thunderstorms, Alberta Clippers, hurricanes, blizzards, freaky ball lightning, the works."

"And that's what it's all about," I said. "Martial law and the Resco Raj. Just a way to maintain order while the weather goes to hell and the whole social structure unravels."

"The semblance of order, anyway," Gianetti quibbled.

"I'm damned glad the Rescos are in control," Blake argued. "I've never seen something as beautiful as those Army helicopters when they came to fly us away from Judgment."

We could all agree on that.

"Oh, hey, Donna," Blake added, "did you ever figure out Paul Dukakis and Matt1034?" I was glad he asked. That had bothered me, what the original poster of the death video, Matt1034, was trying to accomplish. And why Paul Dukakis tried to save Dane, failed, and delivered the body, yet claimed it all happened in Green Tree.

Donna Gianetti nodded. "Paul Dukakis was a militia informant Dane planted with the Judgment sect. Paul led Dane Beaufort and Dwight Davison back to Station Square later that day, after the rally, to surprise a Judgment operation. Judgment got the drop on them, but Paul managed to escape. He snuck back later and found Dane beaten and unconscious. He didn't find Dwight. We think Dwight went into the river during the fight with Judgment. Anyway, Paul loaded Dane into his truck and tried to get him to a doctor. But Dane died on the way.

"Matt1034 was Paul's girlfriend. She recorded the rally on her cell phone. Paul edited together her footage with his own snapshot of Dane and posted it on Amenac using her account. The Green Tree encampment was Judgment's headquarters here in Pittsburgh, so he tried to direct interest there."

"Judgment caught and killed him," Blake offered. "I found him hanging from a high-voltage power line pole in Green Tree."

Donna nodded. IBIS had already found the body of Paul Dukakis. "With Dane and Dwight both dead or missing, Paul didn't know who else to turn to. He figured posting that video on Amenac would get high-powered attention from other Rescos outside Pittsburgh. He succeeded."

"Why didn't he flee Pittsburgh?" I asked.

"According to his girlfriend, they planned to," Donna said. "But he left her to pick up some things from his apartment first, and never came back. She escaped. We found her hiding with a cousin in West Mifflin. Anyway, Paul Dukakis was one of the good guys here."

With many hugs Gianetti and I saw Blake and Brandy off to the IndieNews van and waved them good-bye. I tried to be just as fulsome in my farewells with the Wiehls and Caroline Drumpeter at the train station. But I was happy to wash my hands of Pittsburgh. Pretty nice town, really. But as fellow Americans, we'd drifted apart.

And Pittsburgh was less than 400 miles from Brooklyn, still a northeastern city. The ex-US spanned over 3000 miles in just the contiguous states. How much further had the rest of America drifted apart from us? Or we from them.

28

Matthew 5:38-46, Good News Translation (GNT): You have heard that it was said, 'An eye for an eye, and a tooth for a tooth.' But now I tell you: do not take revenge on someone who wrongs you. If anyone slaps you on the right cheek, let him slap your left cheek too. And if someone takes you to court to sue you for your shirt, let him have your coat as well. And if one of the occupation troops forces you to carry his pack one mile, carry it two miles. When someone asks you for something, give it to him; when someone wants to borrow something, lend it to him. You have heard that it was said, 'Love your friends, hate your enemies.' But now I tell you: love your enemies and pray for those who persecute you, so that you may become the children of your Father in heaven. For he makes his sun to shine on bad and good people alike, and gives rain to those who do good and to those who do evil. Why should God reward you if you love only the people who love you?

Homecoming was strange. It gave me a whole new appreciation for how alien it must have felt for Emmett to visit me in Connecticut after months in the city during the evacuation.

We'd been gone not quite a month. But with the summer heat fled, and plenty of rain, Brooklyn had greened. The warehouse district by the ferry terminal was orderly these days. No more broken glass on the streets, no more endless conveyor belt of trash dumpsters and debris. The engineers had frowned on the ziggurats of salvaged bricks past the warehouses. A good hurricane wind could turn the loose masonry into so many airborne projectiles. So the step pyramids were now smoothed with a concrete exterior. A team of artists were busy painting a mural on the second tier wall.

But the biggest change was in the Calm Park past the pyramids. This green belt, and fifty like it around the Apple, was burial ground and memorial, the very soil built of demolished buildings and the city's millions of dead bodies. The grass and forage plants, still tender and threadlike when we left, had grown in well, for a vivid carpet of deep emerald green, glowing in the overcast daylight. The long-awaited young trees had been installed, and brick walkways and picnic table pavilions. Workers were hammering together the stage for the local Halloween dedication event. The dust and the stench were gone. The Calm Park was becoming beautiful.

Like many, I hopped atop the knee-height brickwork wall edging the greenbelt to walk, holding Emmett's hand while he walked along below me. I smiled. He didn't. Halloween would soon be upon us, the day Ash Margolis had selected to finally hold a memorial service for the dead of New York, and consecrate the Calm Parks. A colossal ceremony was in the works. We wouldn't have missed it for the world.

Inside our mini-city, Prospect, with its huge town green, things hadn't changed so much. The municipal water-park had closed for winter. The green was tough enough by now for grazing livestock and rowdy football games. No street-corner preachers were in evidence. But then, Emmett and his model town of Prospect never had much patience with those.

At long last, we peeled off our omnipresent guards, and stepped into the chill gloom of our brownstone entryway. "It's good to be home," I told Emmett with a smile. He squeezed my hand and sighed, and attempted a smile in return. His didn't quite work.

I left the luggage for later, and continued on to say hello to our back garden. It was too cool to swim anymore. Our lonely full-grown maple tree was bare, the leaves neatly raked away for compost out in the square. But Gladys, our housekeeper, had installed a new toy behind the kitchen, in our absence.

"Emmett!" I squealed in delight. "Gladys got us a hot tub! Come on, let's try it out!"

He stepped out of our office to look, shaking his head in dismay. "Dee, that is all kinds of not-OK. Do you know how much power it'll take to run that?"

"I'm paying for it!" Gladys called up from her lair downstairs.

"It's not a matter of paying for it!" Emmett objected. "It's a waste of power!"

"I'll join you in the hot tub, Dee," Gladys yelled. "Just getting on my bathing suit."

"Meet you there!" I agreed in glee. My luggage turned light as feathers as I trotted up the stairs to our bedroom to change.

Emmett sat down in the office and resumed catching up on his mountains of email. I had mountains of work to do, too, of course. But right after a grueling overnight train trip wasn't the time to do it.

In the hot tub, Gladys caught me up on all the latest gossip and events at home. The preacher sweep was a non-event in Brooklyn and Queens, Emmett's boroughs, though there were some ugly riots in Manhattan and the Bronx. Staten Island and Jersey-borough were somewhere in between, with orderly demonstrations against the new rules, just as orderly dispersed after a couple hours, without violence.

Voter registration was a big hit. Gladys, a public school

science teacher in her past life, had volunteered to serve as a voter tester. She told me about her training, and cheerfully criticized the idiots she flunked and tutored.

I was happy for her, getting out of the house on a more professional level. She'd spent most of the starving time alone atop a twenty-story building, hiding from everyone. Her lingering agoraphobia was intense, disabling some days. It had taken persistent effort on Emmett and my part to break her out of her porcupine hostility to become friendly with us. Alternately attending Orthodox church services, and tripping our delivery men into bed, provided weird and limited social interaction outside the three of us at home. I was glad to see her branching out.

"Do you know if you're staying yet?" Gladys asked guardedly.

I shook my head, and sank deeper into the luxurious hot swirling jets of water. "No news. We just got in the door." That thought was a downer. I'd just gotten home, but didn't know how long it would be home anymore. Until his final report was complete, Emmett was still a Colonel of Pennsylvania, his newly confirmed Rescos of Brooklyn and Queens reporting to Ash Margolis. We were in limbo.

The brownstone had only been home a few months, anyway. But it felt like home. Mostly, it felt like Emmett must really love me, to go so far trying to please me with this outrageous house.

"Emmett seems cold," Gladys observed. "Rough trip. Popeye told me you were raped." My eyebrows flew up. I had no idea Popeye knew, nor that he talked to my housekeeper. She'd lured him into bed when he visited, of course. But she did that to almost anyone unsuitable who happened along.

"I'm sorry," she continued. "It sucks. But you get past it."

"Do you?" I asked. "I'm different. Emmett's weird." I didn't mention it, but I rather doubted the Brooklyn schoolteacher had been in the habit of yanking handymen and plumbers and hostile tattooed hackers into her bedroom for rough games before the Calm Act. Not that I judged, exactly. But Gladys still had some baggage to work out.

"Everything you go through changes you," she said philosophically. "But life goes on. Right now, I'm safe and warm, in an awesome hot tub, with a friend. Great house, great job, great food. Chickens." She eyed one of those in disfavor, and flicked some water at it to discourage it from coming closer. "Emmett loves you. Whatever his problem is, he'll get over it," she said confidently. "I just hope you'll stay here. Because I'm selfish. I love my bosses. I love this job. I love this hot tub." She sank into the bubbles, up over her ears.

I grinned back at her. Thoroughly overheated, I braved the chilly lap pool for ten lengths, then gratefully splashed back into the hot tub. Yes, the changes in Brooklyn were good.

THE CHANGES IN EMMETT WERE LESS GOOD. WE HADN'T MADE love since he retrieved me from West Virginia. Not because I didn't want to, but because he couldn't. That had never happened for us before. Or failed to happen. He owed me a date night, a romantic evening together, a talk about religion. Maybe even a marriage proposal if we managed a really nice day. We were headed in the wrong direction for that.

I refused to believe the problem was distaste for me because I'd been soiled by Canber's rape or something. Emmett couldn't be that unfair. He cried plenty, alone if I didn't catch him, but in my arms when I did. But unlike his usual pattern, crying didn't seem to get him past whatever was bothering him.

"Emmett, talk to me," I begged him one night, as he lay beside me in bed, wrung out from crying and still miserable. "What's wrong? Are you mad at me? Even if it's unreasonable, just *say* it. Out with it."

"I can't talk about this with you, Dee," he insisted. "Too much classified caught up in it."

"Then talk to Cam. Or John Niedermeyer," I suggested. They'd been Emmett's room-mates and partners during that Calm Act vetting year at Leavenworth. Niedermeyer already knew about Canber.

"No!" he barked. "Sorry. No, darlin', John wouldn't understand. And you can't breathe a word of any of this to Cam. He wasn't in on...this. I don't remember if Cam even met Canton. When they handed Cam his death angel markers, he would have filed them under NFW – no effing way."

"Cam can kill," I said thoughtfully. "I watched him order men executed."

"Uh-huh, I saw the video," Emmett said. "Of course he can kill, Dee. He's a soldier. He also showed you his authorization afterward, didn't he? I love Cam like a brother, but he's a boy scout."

"Why not Niedermeyer?"

"Can't tell you that." He dropped a limp hand on my head and twirled a strand of my hair. "Let it go, Dee."

I considered him for a few minutes, propped on my elbow. "What exactly is a death angel marker?"

"Resco top secret. Dammit, Dee! I never said it. You never heard it."

"Emmett, you have to talk because it's tearing you apart. It's tearing *us* apart. Canber and his goons kidnapped me, drugged me, raped me, tied me to a fence in tornado weather. Canber can't steal you from me, too. I won't let him!"

"Uh-huh," he breathed, defeated.

I sat up, cross-legged. "I know. We need to forgive him. Both of us. An act of forgiveness, to put this behind us."

"Huh." He rubbed his face tiredly.

"Contact him," I encouraged. "Arrange a video conference."

"*What?!*"

"DEE INSISTED," EMMETT TOLD CANBER RELUCTANTLY. MY RECENT abductor was on our huge display in the office in Brooklyn. Emmett and I each sat at our own computers, our separate desks, for this video conference. Seeing Canber's face again didn't bother me as much as I'd feared. I'd escaped, outsmarted him, and Emmett had rescued me. I was safe at home now. That was triumph enough to leave me feeling I was on equal standing with him.

There was no way of knowing where Canber spoke to us from. His cyber-security was at least as good as mine. He sat in another beautiful office, but not the one I visited in West Virginia. The Internet route trace said he spoke to us from nearby in Brooklyn. The pine forest visible outside the windows behind him spoke otherwise.

"And why would Dee do that?" Canber asked, eyes narrowed. One of the limitations of video conferencing is a disconnect on who someone is really looking at. But I fancied his eyes were glued to Emmett, not me.

I responded anyway. "Canber, I think you attacked me as a way to punish Emmett. You succeeded. He's haunted. I'm haunted. I'm terrified that we can't get past this. Maybe, if we could all forgive each other ― "

"Forgive me!" Canber interrupted incredulously. "Fuck. You. Oh, that's right – I already did."

"Dee," Emmett bit out, a hand held up to beg that I hold my peace. "Canton, I hate what you did to Dee. But I understand it. And I know it was partly my fault. And I hate what you've had to do." He paused, started tearing up. "I'm sorry."

Canber replied, "As I already told Dee. I don't need your pity."

"Uh-huh. Not pity, exactly," Emmett said. "Just pain. Regret. We were friends once. I know why you had to become a death angel. You were good at it. If you can call that 'good.' And I made that worse for you. I wish... I wish there were some way for us to go back, chuck all this. Just you and me. Go camping in the Adirondacks or something. Be who we used to be again, before the Calm Act. For Dee and I to go back, when she didn't know you existed, and I could be the hero of New York City. There is no going back."

"No," Canber agreed. "So what's the point?"

Emmett sighed, and wiped his eyes. "If you want to stop, Canton. This life, for you, must truly suck. If you want to lay it down, come in from the cold. We could figure out a way to make that happen."

That enraged Canber again. "You think what I do doesn't *matter?* That this is all *optional?* That it's *over?* You know damned well it's not over! I should have culled New Jersey already. But it's your fucking problem, Emmett. I won't quietly solve it for you and let you pretend your hands are clean. You need to ask for it. Take responsibility."

Emmett swallowed, nodded microscopically. "It matters," he whispered. "I'm not ready to ask today. But you're probably right. Soon."

Ready to ask what? I wondered uneasily. Culling New Jersey sounded horrific.

"That's why, Emmett," Canber replied bitterly. "That's why we set it up this way. If your goal is to care and build and help, it's too hard to turn around and destroy. So you get to play hero while I play demon. Both whole-heartedly."

"My heart feels pretty broken right now," Emmett admitted. "And I can't believe yours is all that whole either, Canton."

"People suck," Canton breathed. "It's not so bad."

Emmett nodded ever so slightly. "They suck. They can be petty and obnoxious and cruel. And then I meet someone like Dee. Or you, once. Like Ty Jefferson and the others here in New York. People who held communities together through the epidemic and the starvation. They take my breath away. They're the heroes. I'm not. I know that. What you do... I don't get to do what I do, without you doing what you do. I know that. And I'm sorry for that."

The men stared at each other, out of words for the moment. I waded in again. "Maybe I don't know what's at stake. How hard it would be. But Canber, I thought we needed to make the offer. Two years of...doing what you do. Maybe it's not enough, maybe it's not over. But you've done enough. If you want to retire, we can make that happen. That's what we wanted to say today."

"She's better than you deserve, Emmett," Canber observed.

"Uh-huh."

"There is no way back," Canber said.

"Maybe a cottage in the Catskills," I suggested. "A cabin in Vermont. Live off the land where no one knows you. I know you love natural beauty, Canber. Just like I do. Sure, people suck. But most don't suck as bad as Uriel and Judgment."

"The offer's open. Old friend," Emmett said with finality. "I won't take over your job. I couldn't do it. I don't think anyone else will, either. But if you want to lay it down, we could make that happen."

"Strangely, I believe you," Canber replied. "The answer is no. But thank you for offering. It's a pretty fantasy. Apology accepted. For what it's worth, Emmett, I forgive you, too. Don't contact me again, except on business."

Emmett crumpled into sobs. I held him a long time, crying too. We were alright after that. Not great, still in limbo on all fronts, but at least we were facing limbo together again, as lovers.

29

Interesting fact: The Apple Zone's death count was millions lower than in southern California.

For the most solemn Halloween party ever, we'd never had so many people in our house in Brooklyn. Since the Governor-General and top Rescos of Hudson presided over the ceremonies earlier, naturally they were staying in town for a planning conference afterwards. And naturally we hosted at our palatial brownstone, which could sleep all eight guests comfortably.

But then PR and IndieNews decided to broadcast same-night special coverage of the big event. Naturally my office was the local production facility due to the time crunch. Between Emmett's, mine, and ours, we had twenty-four people in the house, mine working feverishly against a deadline, his drifting in all day as their Halloween assignments ended. My guests tended to put a damper on conversation for his guests, but at least his could retire to the bedrooms for privacy.

I stuck my head out of the office French doors into the living

room and waved. "Hi, everybody! Welcome! Sorry I suck as a hostess!"

"Uh-huh," Emmett agreed from mid–living room. "But I don't." This was true. Emmett was an accomplished host. I suppose being an Army officer was good training. His guests were warm and dry and fed and enjoying each other. "Broadcasting on time, darlin'?"

"Of course we are! Might still be editing when the first segment goes live. Hey, Emmett, could we all watch out here in the living room? Amiri needs to broadcast live from the office."

"Ah, will do." Emmett checked the time. "We'll start setting up now."

By the time most of my team were chased out of the office, I feared we'd be stuck standing in the back. But Emmett prepared for that. Brandy and Blake, Melinda and Martin of IndieNews got a whole small couch to themselves. Our censor, the lead Resco of Connecticut, Lt. Colonel Carlos Mora, took his daughter Maisie's seat on our couch, and hugged her back onto his lap. Popeye likewise slipped in under Gladys, next to our fosterling Alex, then me on top of Emmett.

"I have the remote!" Shimon Margolis proclaimed proudly, Ash's 13-year-old son. Now lead Resco of all six Apple boroughs, and master of ceremonies for the day, Ash bent over my old tablet with his son, figuring out how to tune into the Internet broadcast and dim the living room lights. They looked so adorable together, heads bowed in matching yarmulkes. Emmett and I didn't have the heart to interrupt. We could have voice-operated any electronics in the room.

The PR News team in Totoket composed the opening sequence from footage we sent them. Halloween dawned dark, and provided a drenching rain over the city and all its mourners. Rain poured down on dark green empty Calm Parks throughout the city, in the early morning gloom. Sheets of grey shrouded big orange ferries and Navy destroyers as they lumbered through the slowly waking harbor. As with all funerals, there was no rain date for this memorial, no indoor venue. Gradually, the screen showed a few people walking in the rain, hunched in raincoats. The few coalesced into streams, the streams fed into crowds, the crowds into a tile-work of close-packed umbrellas.

Over this played the slow Pachelbel's Canon. Elegant script faded in and out, a line at a time, recounting the story of New York City and its dead.

HALLOWEEN MEMORIAL FOR NEW YORK CITY
OVER 9 MILLION PEOPLE ONCE LIVED HERE
LESS THAN A MILLION REMAIN
EBOLA BROKE OUT ON DECEMBER 3RD, ACROSS THE CITY
CALM ACT BORDERS CLOSED TO CONTAIN THE CONTAGION
NEW YORK CITY WAS LEFT TO STARVE
THEY STARVED FOR NEARLY A YEAR
THIS YEAR, WHEN IT CAME TIME TO REBUILD
THE DEAD WERE MOVED TO NEW GREENBELTS
THE CALM PARKS
TODAY WE CONSECRATE THE CALM PARKS
AND REMEMBER THE FALLEN

"Wow," Amiri Baz said, wiping his eyes. I was already crying along with him, just from the intro sequence. Amiri was our premium anchor for PR News. He chuckled at himself for crying. "And I've already watched that sequence twice today." He went on to soberly recap the basic facts of why we were here today, and the purpose of the special.

Video of Governor-General Sean Cullen in the rain, arm around his wife Mary Grace: "The people of the Apple have been through so much, and accomplished so much this year rebuilding. When my Rescos showed me their initial plans for rebuilding the city, with these new greenbelts called the Calm Parks, I was overcome with emotion. They proposed a sort of pilgrimage. Walking the Calm Parks as a way of mourning the world we once knew. Not just the dead of the Apple, but of the whole world."

"Governor, is the city actually named the Apple now?" Brandy O'Keefe asked.

"Oh, I think so," said Sean. Mary Grace nodded beside him. "That's not an official Hudson pronouncement. But it isn't the same city. We have six boroughs now, instead of five. This is a new city, fifty new cities, emerging from the old one."

Brandy followed up with, "Governor, there's been some concern that consecrating the Calm Parks with a public funeral is a violation of the new constitution."

"Not at all," Sean Cullen denied, looking faintly offended. "I can't imagine a more appropriate occasion for religion. No one's forcing their views on someone else here."

Cut to the Cullens bowing their heads at the front of a huge crowd, while the new archbishop of the Apple consecrated the New York Calm Park, an extension to Central Park. Beside him stood a mullah, a rabbi, and a half dozen other clerics, who would each consecrate the cemetery in turn, and say a few words.

The program continued with Lt. Colonel Ash Margolis, hugging his son Shimon: "I grew up on Manhattan, Lower East Side. My mom, grandmother, sister, her kids. I don't know how many friends from school. Yeah. But also, my wife and I are Israeli-American. I mean, we chose American citizenship. But my wife served in the Israeli Army first. And we had family all over. We all have dead. A third of all Americans are dead, right? Pretty much all of Israel. And I've never been to a funeral for them before, a memorial. I'm hoping that this ceremony today, inviting the world in, that we can give everyone a chance to mourn."

Jennifer Alvarez of PR News prompted, "You choreographed all of today's services, is that right, Colonel Margolis?"

Ash shrugged. "Supervised. But arranging the memorial was nothing compared to building the Calm Parks. Nearly a million people in the Apple, and it took just about all of us. We're still rebuilding. But we've come a long way. And we want to say thank you, to all the people outside the city, who helped us. And show off to the world what we've done with your help."

Ash and Shimon, his wife Deborah and daughter Shira, prayed with a rabbi and the crowd in what was once the Lower East Side.

Ash Margolis lost 11 family members in New York City

Emmett, standing with Ty Jefferson, leader of Staten Island: "I didn't have family or friends in the city. I mourn the people we couldn't reach in time. I'm from Missouri. I never really got to mourn them, you know? I wanted to save Kansas City, Joplin. I failed. They're gone now, those towns. Vanished. The refugees from the Dust Bowl. Everything I've done for the Apple was inspired by the dead of the Dust Bowl. I couldn't save them. But maybe I could do something here."

Ty Jefferson beside Emmett, shaking his head: "Too many to count. The survivor guilt. We all of us suffer from that crippling survivor guilt. With these memorials, let us lay that guilt down. And live."

Emmett and I shared an umbrella between Ty Jefferson and Adam Lacey's family, Alex and the Niedermeyers, listening to a sermon.

Emmett MacLaren led the Project Reunion evacuation

Ty Jefferson led Staten Island while over 400,000 died

The special report went on and on. Some segments didn't have an interview, just Amiri and Jennifer speaking over the footage. Our friends Cam and Dwayne were among the chief mourners in Hoboken, Dwayne sagging on Cam's shoulder, Cam looking grim. Carlos and his daughter Maisie stone-faced in Queens, the closest service they could find to where Carlos' wife and older daughter died of Ebola, trying to flee to Long Island and then home to Connecticut. Other sequences had only interviews, mostly of ordinary apples, and what the day meant to them.

The ceremony ended with bugles playing taps at each Calm Park, followed by a slow 21-gun salute fired in unison from the destroyers off-shore throughout the city.

"Thank you for joining us to remember our dead," Amiri finished solemnly. "On behalf of all of us at PR News, and Indie-News, on this All Hallows' Eve, God bless you and those you have lost. May this memorial bring you peace. Good night."

The credits rolled over the opening sequence of rain scenes again, to Pachelbel's Canon. After the brief credits, the confirmed death toll was given for each borough of the city, followed by every county in Hudson.

"That was like devastating," Alex commented, snuggled under Emmett's other arm, next to me.

"Too much, you think?" I asked him.

"No, you done good, Dee," he assured me.

"Very good," Emmett concurred, kissing the crown of my head. "Perfect." He raised his voice only slightly to Gladys, on the other side of Alex. "What do you think, Gladys? I think you're the only apple in the room."

Gladys nodded wordlessly, all cried out. She rose and held out a hand to Popeye, and drew him down to her apartment. Several of the guests looked puzzled at this, but Emmett and I took it in stride.

"I'm an apple, too," Maisie Mora piped up. "A Lawn Guyland apple. Bet Daddy won't let me celebrate like Gladys." She *oomphed* and grinned as her daddy Carlos squeezed her around the middle, reminding her to behave. The girl was fourteen now, a real dark-haired Hispanic beauty with flashing mischievous eyes. She was too mature and out of reach for young Shimon Margolis, but she'd already caught our Alex's nervous attention. She'd left prostitution behind when she escaped the Apple Zone back to her family in Connecticut last spring. But that chick was hatched.

"That's right," Cam pounced, lead Resco of Long Island. "What do you think, Maisie – should we hold a Long Island memorial too?"

"Nah. This one was ours, too," she replied. "Like they said on the news, this was for everybody, not just the Apple Core. We didn't have like whole mountains of dead bodies like here. And we had green land already. The Lawns of Lawn Guyland."

Cam nodded his amused thanks. I jumped in. "So Maisie, do you think this was a good ceremony? And the video coverage?"

"Yeah," she allowed. "You know the best part, though, for me. Daddy and I hunted for where Mom and Jessie died. It was hard to find, you know? Because everything has changed so much. Buildings and roads are gone. It's pretty now. But we traced the whole way, from Manhattan to Queens. I showed Daddy. I never told him all that stuff before."

"Felt like it was safe to talk about," Carlos suggested. "I thought it was an outstanding memorial. Gave closure. My congratulations to everyone. Thank you."

"Yes!" I agreed, standing. "To the Rescos who staged today's event!" I led a round of applause, and waved the last of the PR News team out into the living room. "And yay team, PR News! Great job, gang!" More applause. "And to IndieNews! Our esteemed competition! May we have many more successful collaborations!" Along with the applause, we shared high-fives, handshakes, and hugs between PR News and IndieNews.

I clung extra long to Brandy and Blake. Searching gazes met minute nods. We weren't over our shared ordeal. But we were getting better. IndieNews and PR News would continue to pursue different editorial focus, as we must. But it was a warm and friendly competition. We'd collaborate again. With more cameras and reporters and assets, both news teams could do more with less, report more widely on the events of the Northeast.

The party broke up after another half hour or so. Curfew was extended for the big Halloween event, with last trains pulling out of the city around 11 p.m. IndieNews maintained an apartment in Harlem near the Hudson River and New Haven train lines. But most of my news guests would head home on those last trains, and needed to get moving. Alex chose to leave with Carlos and Maisie Mora. He was in good hands, as always, more young friend and farming partner to us than fosterling, since I left Totoket.

Soon we were left with just Emmett's guests. But the Rescos of Hudson were my friends, too.

∾

"BEST WAY TO OBSERVE A FUNERAL," I MURMURED, SATED, BESIDE Emmett in bed. "Affirm life."

"Uh-huh," he agreed happily. He'd cooled off enough, and dragged me back onto his shoulder to cuddle. "So, Dee. Was this a good day? I think it was a good day."

"Very good," I agreed. "That vision you had, or Will had, of the pilgrimage of the Calm Parks. That was cool. We accomplished that today." Will was the artist who drew the original Calm Park concept sketch.

"Good enough for an anniversary?" Emmett pressed. "Or would you get all prickly about me proposing to you the day of a funeral?"

"Hm. What are you proposing?"

He laughed, groaned, and rolled out of bed. He fished around in his nightstand, and brought out a small velvet box. He knelt to present it to me, to do it right, box snapped open to display the ring he'd chosen. "Dee Baker, will you marry me?"

I picked up the ring, entranced. "Bedroom, soft lights," I said, and the lights warmed on minimum so I could see the ring better, plucked out of its navy silk nest. In a city with literally millions of cast-off gold and diamond rings on offer, Emmett had selected simple stainless steel, set with a gorgeous emerald, with matching emerald-and-steel stud earrings. "It's beautiful, Emmett," I assured him, and tried it on. "And it fits."

"Is that a yes?" he breathed.

"That is a yes," I agreed, grinning. I pulled myself up to rub noses and kiss him.

"I have a further request," he said, and held out Dane Beaufort's gold wedding band, the one engraved with 'God For Me Provided Thee.' "I've wanted to wear this ring ever since you handed it to me in Pittsburgh. It fits." He demonstrated. "We can figure out what kind of wedding later. But could we just act married, starting now? Monogamous. Forever. I love you. I need you. Partners."

"You know," I warned him, "if you call me your wife in public, wearing these rings, it probably makes us common law married. Eventually, anyway."

"Uh-huh," he agreed happily.

"You're not worried that I'm not a good Christian?" I prodded. "Because I'm not, you know. I spent a lot of time thinking in West Virginia. I meet God in nature, in math, in tech. I think that makes me some kind of pagan, Emmett. You're sure that's not a problem for you?"

"I know who you are, darlin'," Emmett assured me. "If God speaks to you through tech and trees, I know you're listening. I trust your heart." He placed his hand on my breast to illustrate.

I nodded thoughtfully. "Why steel and emerald? Instead of gold and diamond."

He brushed hair out of my face and traced my jaw. "Strength of steel, eyes of green." He shrugged. "The others all looked the same. Frail and girly. This one made me think of you. Not a porcelain doll. Beautiful, but tough enough to face life with. Practical. High tech. If you don't like it, we can trade it in on another. Need to return the presentation box anyway. They're short on those. Whatever you choose, I'd like to get it engraved to match."

"It's perfect," I assured him. "Thank you. Happy zeroeth anniversary, love."

He laughed. "Leave it to a programmer to count from zero."

"Of course," I agreed, drawing him back into bed. "Bedroom, off lights."

30

Interesting fact: One of the key arguments for keeping the University of Connecticut open was that continuing research in renewable energy had never been more important. Northeastern super-states encouraged physicists and technologists in the field to congregate at UConn to pursue their work. A similar energy research center flourished in the Virginia naval yards.

"Let's get started," Sean Cullen announced, Governor-General of Hudson and commander in chief of the Rescos assembled around our dining table the next morning. Everyone had already congratulated us on our engagement over breakfast.

"First of all, a promotion," Sean continued. "Tony Nasser, effective immediately, you are a full Colonel in the Hudson Army Resco service. Congratulations!"

Sean pinned a Colonel's eagle on Tony's lapel. Heart-felt hugs and handshakes proceeded around the room. No mixed feelings among this group – 'Chandy Anthony' had more than earned his promotion. He had only four years in service as a lieutenant colonel, but Sean had already established four years as Hudson's minimum time in grade when he promoted Cam to Lt. Colonel. Aside from supervising the Rescos of the far-flung New York upstate, Tony coordinated and secured power and fuel supplies for all of Hudson and New England, and Internet besides. Many millions had reason to thank God for Tony Nasser the power czar.

Once we all settled back into our seats, Sean quipped, "I believe the Hudson Resco service does not require more than two full bird colonels at present. Emmett." The joking left his eyes. "Your eagle belongs to Penn, not Hudson. Taibbi could use a decent O-6. He'd let you keep that rank. I won't. You've done well. You've performed miracles. But you have only a single year in grade as a light colonel. You're not ready."

Emmett shook his head. "I agree, sir." He detached Penn's colonel insignia and placed it on the table. "I understood the rank bump as a tool for the job. Not a permanent promotion."

Sean nodded slightly, but narrowed his eyes. "New England, Penn, Ohio, Virginia-Del-Mar, they all want you. They'll make bids for you. Hell, probably Ken-Tenn, and whatever Missouri is these days, too. You can write your own ticket. But Emmett, I need a team player. We did not appreciate the constitution getting upstaged by you again. If you can't get back into the chorus as a light colonel, maybe you should entertain one of those other job offers."

Emmett shook his head minutely. "No sir. And I apologize to the team." He looked around at each of them. "I didn't intend to get famous. I needed public support for Project Reunion. It was for the good of the operation, not my ego. Dee and I will try to douse the media, much as we can. But I'd like to stay with this team, in Hudson. In fact, I'd like to stay right here, if I could. New Jersey has waited long enough. I'd like to work for Pete. Organize North Jersey. Keep the house here for Dee to stay nearby." He swallowed nervously.

Sean grinned. "Good. I wanted that settled before our final recommendations meeting this evening."

"Sir," Emmett interrupted. "If I may, I'd like to speak to Pete privately first."

Puzzled, Sean waved permission. Emmett led his commanding officer upstairs to our bedroom to confer. They were gone for a long while, while the Rescos attended to other business in the dining room. Cam would report to Tony now, to take some workload off of Pete Hoffman in Jersey. Emmett and Ash would continue with Pete. Cam used the time to report his progress so far in bringing central Long Island under Resco organization.

When Pete and Emmett returned, Pete stopped at the sideboard and poured himself a two-finger drink. Emmett simply sat down, subdued. His colonel's eagle had been stashed away, normal lieutenant colonel insignia back on his uniform.

"Is that scotch, Colonel?" Sean inquired sourly. "It's 10 a.m."

Pete Hoffman sat with his drink. "No, sir. It's good Kentucky bourbon. I just need the one."

"What exactly were you talking about up there?" Sean asked, perturbed.

Pete shook his head. "Plans for north Jersey." He took a pull on his drink. "They're coming along. It's under control, sir." He looked haunted. So did Emmett. Sean continued staring at them. "You don't want to know, sir."

"I rather think I do," Sean said dangerously.

"If I may, sir," Emmett cut in. "I think we have good plans for north Jersey. It'll work. One of the key components is building settlements for retiring service members. People who want to muster out. They'll strengthen the militia backbone. Meanwhile organize civilian work details. Restore wetlands. Raze substandard housing, decrepit communities, disrupt the inner city ghettos. Especially around Newark and Trenton."

Pete finished off his bourbon, and slid the heavy tumbler away in finality. He nodded. "It'll work. Not all that different from what we've done in the Apple Core."

I stared at the glass and thought of 'death angel markers,' and Canber's insistence that Emmett needed to ask, to solve Jersey. Canber wouldn't do it for him, unless he asked. No, that wouldn't go over well with Pete Hoffman. Sean Cullen wouldn't approve at all. Of all the Calm Act military governors, Sean was the most eager to declare the population culling over, forever, good riddance and never to return. Standing by while New York City died had been more 'culling' than the man could take.

Pete sighed. "We'll get started on that right away. I believe Emmett has preliminary drawings. Shall we adjourn to the office?"

"After a fifteen minute break," Sean agreed. He drew Pete away into our drippy garden for a tongue-lashing. I doubt Sean learned much. Pete just stood mute and took it. I hoped the bourbon fortified him. The other Rescos shot uneasy glances outside through the French doors, and at Emmett, but didn't comment.

Emmett slipped his arms around my waist at the kitchen sink-island. I was filling some water pitchers to bring into the office. "You alright with this plan, darlin'? I'd try to come home most weekends – home here – and talk to you every day. Like Project Reunion again. I'll start with Newark." Newark was the next town west from Jersey-borough, across Newark Bay. Before the epidemic, Newark was the largest city in Jersey, almost entirely poor non-white inner city. "Could come home during the week some nights. But North Jersey's a hell-hole now. You don't belong there."

I knew that. Alone of the Rescos here, Pete Hoffman was still bogged down in a shooting war, fighting gangs and insurrection in south Jersey. North Jersey, still barricaded in by the epidemic borders to north and south, and barred from the Apple Core, was a war zone, too. With some rural land to produce food, and charity shipments, their situation had never been as dire as in the Apple Core, the now-six boroughs of New York City. But the locals were shooting each other over food and everything else. Not much order had been re-established yet. Emmett had been studying the situation since we returned from Penn, and visited a couple times.

"I understand," I said. I looked Emmett in the eye. "Really." I tapped one of his silver oak leaves, that had replaced his temporary eagle. "I'll see what I can do about suppressing the press. Until Jersey looks prettier."

"Thank you, darlin'," he said sadly. "Maybe in spring we could find a nice place with a garden out there. If things calm down."

I shrugged. "Maybe. I'm good here." The ghosts of New York lay quietly now. I wondered how long it would take before Jersey stopped feeling haunted to me.

ONE OF THE THINGS THAT CAME UP DURING THE CONFERENCE WAS salary for me and mine. PR News. Amenac. The meshnet programming team on Long Island. My friend Reza on satellite intelligence. My latest project for an online distributor clearinghouse for the city's warehouses full of salvage. The gleam in my eye for a match-making service to place retiring soldiers in communities. Governor Sean Cullen was shocked that all these projects were bankrolled by Emmett and Cam, and told Pete Hoffman to deal with it.

My projects weren't entirely bankrolled by them. We had other sponsors. Like Canadian Intelligence, and whoever funded Homeland Security, and possibly others Emmett didn't tell me about. But we didn't complicate the discussion with that.

Emmett's point was that his princely salary, and Cam's and Ash's, were intended for seed capital for bootstrapping new private industries. And they'd done well with those companies. But in practice they'd funded arguably public enterprises as well. The private startups either failed or succeeded, but didn't

continue drawing salaries. The successful quasi-public operations kept sucking down more and more of their salaries.

Tony shook his head. "I never used my discretionary funds on
the power grid. Couldn't if I tried – it cost too much. Obviously a
public good all along. So we bankrolled it on the state from the
start. Charge New England, too."

Pete nodded. "Yeah, same in Jersey. And with feeding the
Apple Zone, and all the specialized skills we hired. We pay the
engineers out of public funds. Dee's got a mixed bag here,
though. The meshnet is clear, at least. Hudson should assume
that expense.

"Amenac and PR News are more complicated. If New England
isn't one of your sponsors, Dee, it should be. PR News is in New
England. Hudson is home to IndieNews. For better or worse. If
we fund PR News, we ought to fund both, or give even more to
Indie." He looked at me apologetically.

"So you think I should wean off Amenac and PR News?"
Emmett said unhappily. "Make them seek other sponsors to
replace my funding?"

"Not a chance," Cam said. "We get huge benefits from them.
Amenac powers the meshnet, our weather reports, Resco coordination. No question that they do other things besides supporting
Hudson. But they also have other sponsors. I say we continue
funding them, even expand their funding. Giving Indie some
funds couldn't hurt. Might sweeten them up a little." He looked
doubtful on that point.

"This past month," I put in, "we've collaborated with Indie-
News for the first time. And the results have been excellent. On a
personal level, I owe them my life. And we did fund them in Pittsburgh, and for the Halloween special yesterday. I like Pete's
suggestion of funding IndieNews, too."

"Owe them your life?" Cam inquired.

"Let's not go there," Emmett interrupted. "But I agree with
Cam. I don't want to cut off funding, unless I've secured alternate

funding. That's what I'm hoping to do here. I can just keep paying Dee and her teams for all this –"

"You only just started paying Dee," I growled. Cam already looked mutinous on the lack of explanation on owing Indie my life. His glower deepened at the news that Emmett hadn't been paying me.

"Uh-huh," said Emmett. "So, fine. Cam, Ash, would you be willing to split salary for Dee and Reza? We're the ones who use them most."

"Whoa," Pete interrupted. "I hadn't got there yet, Emmett. I think there may be a class of...pseudo-Resco. Resco staff positions, maybe. I mean, Dee doesn't lead a community or coordinate Army resources. But she serves other Resco-like functions. She's usually included in our meetings, and I'm glad she is. I wouldn't mind if Tony and I felt we could call on her services, too."

I probably looked worried at that. Pete smiled. "Sometimes, Dee. You could beg off if you're too busy. What I'm thinking, is maybe pay Dee a Resco's discretionary fund and let her figure it out. A small pile, maybe 25 meal tickets? I don't know what Emmett was paying you."

"Two," I said shortly.

"Dump the cad, and I'll pay you ten," Cam pounced immediately. "Emmett, what the hell were you thinking?"

"I'd take that action," Ash volunteered with a grin. "But you're here in the city, Dee," he wheedled. "You want to focus your projects here, not way out on the Island. Too inconvenient. Work for me, not Cam."

"Can it, guys," Pete quashed the ribbing. "I'll pay her. Out of Hudson funds, not mine. And being paid by her fiancé – no. Not a good idea. Dee, is 25 meal tickets enough for now? That's in addition to the meshnet team and PR News and Indie. Those get public funding too, but not out of your budget. Or Emmett's."

I could feel my eyes glow. "Yes! Thank you, Pete!"

"Uh-huh," growled Emmett. "So all I get is 'cad' for negotiating this, huh?"

"How much do you pay the housekeeper, Emmett?" Cam inquired dryly.

"Gladys gets one and a half," I supplied. "Plus room and board. Cad."

"Cad," Cam agreed, with a grin at Emmett. "How you get such good results from women is beyond me, Emmett."

"Dee, you'll report to me for book-keeping purposes." The ranking Resco Pete Hoffman doggedly continued his lonely path on the high road. "And referee as needed." He glanced around the other Rescos to suggest they not attract his attention as referee. "Monthly and quarterly budget forecasts and actuals, separate salaries and hardware, the usual. I'll supply you the paperwork when you need to complete it. You've managed a good-sized budget and staff before, yes?"

I nodded assurance. "I managed up to twelve million at UNC."

Emmett appeared to be having a d'oh moment. *Yes, Emmett, of course I've managed a serious budget before.* A pittance compared to the ruinous sucking pit of an Army brigade, but still. Responsible people trusted me with money.

"Uh-huh," Emmett said contritely. "Congratulations on your raise, darlin'. I thought you were OK with the two meal tickets."

"Not so much," I said. "I lied."

31

Interesting fact: Pittsburgh lay in the Marcellus Shale fields,
producing natural gas by fracking. This natural gas was crucial to
supplying power and heat to Hudson and New England while they
continued conversion to renewable energy. Pennsylvania and West
Virginia also supplied coal, but the Hudson Rescos refused to use coal.

"Emmett, your written recommendations were silent on
the super-structure of Penn's Resco forces," General
Schwabacher of Ohio pointed out from the big
screen. "Let's start there."

We took time out of the Hudson Resco conference to hold the
final video post mortem on the Pittsburgh assignment. Emmett
had asked for time to write up his final report, and for Lt. Colonel
Drumpeter to settle in and begin implementing the plans they'd
brainstormed while he was in Pittsburgh. Emmett's commander
Colonel Pete Hoffman, Hudson's Governor-General Sean Cullen,
and new Colonel Tony Nasser joined Emmett and me in our
office for the video conference. General Link of New England
again elected to delegate to his ranking Resco, Coast Guard
Captain John Niedermeyer, a peer to Hudson's full Colonels.

Penn's military governor Seth Taibbi and the new Resco of Pittsburgh, Caroline Drumpeter, joined us by video, as did the IBIS agents Kalnietis and Gianetti.

The putative top Resco of Pennsylvania, Colonel Schneider, was again conspicuously absent. Schneider hadn't been invited to one of these meetings yet.

"Yes, sir," Emmett agreed to Schwabacher. "I felt PA's Resco structure was best handled verbally." Emmett had drafted Penn-level recommendations several times, then edited them out of his official report. "By the way, sir, apparently Pennsylvanians consider 'Penn' a pejorative from the war. I'm trying to say 'PA' now."

"'Penn' is a pejorative from the war," Schwabacher agreed. "Which they lost. Do you believe Penn should continue as a state, Colonel MacLaren, or be divided between Ohio and Hudson, is the question."

Emmett took a drink of water to stall for time. Perhaps he hoped Penn's General Taibbi, or even his own Governor-General Cullen, to step in and say that call was above Emmett's pay grade. Alas, they waited.

Emmett sighed, and proceeded. "I do have recommendations. PA is three separate regions at this point, without much common feeling or shared identity. The western tier, Pittsburgh and the three Resco districts to its north, is cohesive. And will grow more cohesive under the leadership of Colonel Drumpeter, as we agreed. There is a problem Resco in the southwest corner. Let's get back to that.

"The eastern tier, dominated by Philadelphia, with Harrisburg and Scranton to the west, is fairly well-run and coherent. Between these two organized areas is a big swath of lightly populated counties in the middle, with no remaining Resco. They're not really under martial law."

"They pay taxes," General Taibbi suggested.

Emmett wobbled his head yes and no. "They bring produce to

market. My read is more of a detente with the border garrisons along the edges – feed the soldiers and don't get attacked. In the middle, people trade produce for electric power."

"You said 'no remaining Resco', Emmett?" Governor Cullen prompted.

"Major Canton Bertovich was the assigned Resco in the middle of this unorganized area, sir," Emmett replied. "Had four counties assigned to him, around State College."

"Oh," Hudson's Cullen acknowledged. "Him."

Emmett had reported that Canber and the Judgment sect were Dane Beaufort's killers during a meeting while I was in West Virginia. Today they didn't reopen that topic.

"My recommendation at this time," Emmett continued, "is to leave all that be, and leave it as PA. General Taibbi has been cooperative and open to suggestion. I don't believe PA poses any current threat to Hudson, Ohio, or Virginia–Del–Mar."

"Thank you," General Taibbi said forcefully.

"But I do have suggestions, sir," Emmett said. "First, I believe Colonel Schneider is not suited to head PA's Rescos."

"Amen," agreed the three attending O-6 level Rescos – Pete Hoffman, John Niedermeyer, and Tony Nasser – Schneider's peers.

Colonel Pete Hoffman expanded on that. "Sir, Emmett asked me to vet his suggested replacement, Lieutenant Colonel Sandoval in Philadelphia. I've worked with Diego Sandoval extensively since the war. I highly recommend him. A bit young in grade for promotion to O-6, but that can wait. Good leader, fine mentor. Creative. Philly was a hell of an assignment. The other Rescos there look to him, like him, trust him. I believe their results in Philly were as good or better than could be hoped."

"Philly is a hell-hole," Taibbi noted sadly.

"Yes, sir," Pete agreed. "But it's under control and improving. For a city that size, that's a miracle."

"Thank you, sir," Emmett said to Pete. "So my suggestion is to have Sandoval head the PA Rescos. Our detailed recommendations would be better addressed with Sandoval, if you agree to appoint him, General Taibbi. But the key is that we suggest both he, and you, meet with your lead Rescos in person, several times a year. This may be a cultural difference between Army and Air Force, sir. But it's unnatural for a mid-level Army officer to be left alone, holding the bag."

Caroline Drumpeter nodded vehemently. The O-6's nodded in solidarity.

"Colonel Drumpeter will do the job for you, sir," Emmett continued to Taibbi. "I have every confidence. But she'll do better – PA will do better – with regular skin-to-skin contact. She needs your personal support. I hope that you and Colonel Sandoval visit Pittsburgh. See the people. Spend a night in the tornado shelters. Feel the tornado sirens thrumming in your bones. It's a gut-level thing. Please, sir. You can't delegate leadership. You need to model it in person. And embrace the Army as your own."

"Good suggestions," Taibbi said humbly. "I thought it was better to let the Army lead its own. But if it's *my* Army, then, you're right. I need to get more hands-on. I'm not sure I can spare Sandoval from Philly, though."

Pete Hoffman shook his head. "With respect, sir. Sandoval is where he needs to be. Less than fifty miles from me, for the same reasons. He'll tell you when he needs to be somewhere else. He has to be a hands-on Resco himself. Head Resco just adds organizational duties. And most important, mentoring. No Resco in Hudson is without someone to call on for advice, a higher authority, or just a second opinion. No bad Resco falls through the cracks. There is a plan, and we help each other. That's my job as head Resco. Sandoval knows the score. And he's welcome to call me or Tony Nasser any time. Just like we call John Niedermeyer."

No one brought up the possibility of Emmett taking the head Resco role in Penn. From which I surmised that Cullen had already informed the other generals that Emmett's decision was made. He was staying with Hudson.

"Cooperation is life or death to the Resco model," Ohio's Charles Schwabacher concurred. He pursed his lips in consideration. "What say you, Sean? Are you buying this from your Rescos?"

Governor Sean Cullen shrugged. "My Rescos are the best. I trust them. As for splitting Penn, hell, Charles. I need Philly like I need a hole in the head. And then an unorganized border to the west? No thanks. You think you can do better than Emmett's scheme for Pittsburgh?"

"No," Schwabacher agreed promptly. "I would like followup, however. What say you, Seth? Are you willing to implement these suggestions? And review progress in one year?"

Seth Taibbi appeared to consider this high-handed. With ill grace, he nodded. "Agreed. Sandoval top Resco. Visit Pittsburgh in person at least twice, both of us." Sourly, he added, "And review progress in one year."

"Thank you, sir," Emmett said gracefully. "I think you'll be pleased with the results. And General Schwabacher? One year from now, I think Colonel Drumpeter may be ready to revisit the Ohio-Pittsburgh re-industrialization plans. Drum?"

Drum nodded with enthusiasm. "Looking forward to that, sir," she assured Schwabacher. "Civilian morale is already improving. In a year, I think we'll be ready to make real commitments." Schwabacher pursed his lips, but nodded agreement.

"Civilian morale is improving," Sean Cullen echoed skeptically. "Because you confiscated their guns and inflicted penance? Punished all the churches?"

"Yes, sir," Drum assured him. "Penance is good for the soul. It's necessary, I think, to formally regret prior actions. Leaves people free to follow a new path."

"That may be more of a Midwestern outlook, sir," Emmett suggested. "Might need a different approach in Hudson or New

England. But our little round of good cop, bad cop should be plenty to get Pittsburgh back in line."

"I'd hate to see your idea of a big round of bad cop, Emmett," Cullen replied, but conceded the point. "Leaving theology out of it, do you think this disarmament would work in Hudson? Like Jersey."

"Sorry, sir," Emmett replied, "but Ken–Tenn's not willing. The 101st went out on a limb for me and Dane because we were family. Hudson's too far. We can talk about it. But Pete and I plan a different approach in Jersey."

"Not many generic guidelines falling out of this," Cullen observed. "For the edification of other Rescos."

"No, sir," Emmett agreed. "Except, it was a unique situation. I expect unique situations will be the norm. The Resco model was designed to embrace that uniqueness. Every community is a bit different. The ex-U.S. is falling apart. The bits and pieces are going their separate ways. We expected that.

"Oh!" Emmett interrupted himself. "And the religion thing. I think that's a crucial guideline anywhere in America, sir. Americans are unusually religious. The country was founded by and for religious extremists. That's who we are. But we cannot, must not, ever allow religion to get the upper hand. The price of religious freedom was separation of church and state. The Rescos in my muster, south central, discussed that from the start. In the Northeast muster, they assumed religion was a non-problem. But religion is bigger than ever. The U.S. Constitution may be gone, but that fundamental compact has to stay. No forcing your religious views on others, and that includes moral views."

"Agreed," Cullen sighed. "Seth, Charles, John for Ivan, I'm sure Hudson will continue tweaking our version of controlled freedom of religion. But if you learn anything from us going first with our Constitution, please understand. Your version needs something there. Maybe our version isn't right for you. But something."

Charles Schwabacher and Seth Taibbi nodded thoughtfully. John Niedermeyer nodded and made a note to discuss it with General Ivan Link, his commander-in-chief in New England.

"Write it up for the Resco boards, Emmett," John Niedermeyer suggested. "I know we didn't back you last time. We will this time."

Emmett made a note of it. "Thank you, John. That's all I intended to cover at this meeting, sirs," Emmett said. "Anything else?"

Schwabacher raised a finger, and asked, "Emmett, I realize Dane Beaufort was a friend. But I still need to ask. What mistakes did he make in Pittsburgh?"

Emmett responded slowly, "Sir. Leading to his death, Beaufort underestimated the Judgment sect. As we discussed in a smaller meeting, Beaufort was not apprised of culling operations in his district. A sound relationship with his head Resco could have prevented that. Or not."

"Understood, Emmett," Schwabacher agreed. "Other than that?"

"Sir, I think there were some weak choices," Emmett allowed. "Stone-walling his superior was a tactical error. He didn't have any stake in the Penn-Hudson war, so it was pointless to object on principle. That left him with no viable markers for escalation or backup. He couldn't appeal to the Ohio garrisons nearby, or eastern PA. But if he expected no help from eastern PA anyway, that was moot."

"If I may?" Drum hesitantly offered. Emmett nodded for her to continue. "Emmett is correct, sirs. The western Rescos never received help from eastern PA. No one honored our markers."

Emmett nodded acknowledgment and continued. "So within that structure, cut off from advice or any real hope of help. First, I think cutting power and communications for the civilians, as a way to control them – I don't believe that works. In practice, it encouraged balkanization and a devolving social structure. Talking is better.

"Second, I understand there were inter-religious conflicts within the militia, that led Beaufort to authorize single-sect units. That led to a religious instead of military chain of command. There, I think he should have fired any militia who engaged in religious conflict, and disbanded whole units if need be. Ceding military control is not an option.

"Lastly, I think it was a mistake to pursue the Ohio deal in advance of developing morale in the district, appreciation for what they already had. Bribing people to instill morale, doesn't work. They need to earn it. In practice, I believe a Resco needs to be equally willing to punish or reward, and make people work for it, to develop morale. And morale is a crucial pre-requisite. That may be a style argument, though."

"Not a style argument," Pete Hoffman said. "I agree. Morale and control have to precede rewards like the Ohio deal. Beaufort didn't have the civilian foundation to carry off that joint venture." The other Rescos at the meeting concurred.

"Those points probably also merit discussion on the Resco boards, Emmett," Hudson's Sean Cullen directed him. Schwabacher nodded.

Emmett made a note, then prompted, "I believe IBIS has completed its investigation into the burial ground in West Mifflin?"

"Yes," Agent Kalnietis replied. "We estimate a third of a million people in that burial complex. Our samples identified missing persons from all over the Northeast, not just Philadelphia. It seems to have been another religious movement, following a Pied Piper. A charismatic leader, leading to essentially a mass suicide."

"My God," said Taibbi, shocked. He frowned. "Wait, was this another 'culling operation'?"

Kalnietis shrugged. "The leader and followers are dead.

Outside of the people in this meeting, I don't know how to inquire about...culling operations."

"Probably," John Niedermeyer offered. "Probably a naturally occurring movement, nurtured by a culling operation."

Taibbi scowled. "How do I coordinate with this 'culling operation'?"

"Through your head Resco, sir," Niedermeyer replied. "But the lines of communication are weak."

"And the lines of command and control?" Taibbi demanded.

"Weaker," Niedermeyer supplied laconically.

"You need to leave it be, Seth," Schwabacher told Taibbi. "It is what it is. We don't have oversight."

"Dee," Cullen said, changing the subject. "Any closing thoughts on Pittsburgh? From a civilian perspective."

"I agree with Emmett's recommendations," I said tentatively. Emmett and Cullen nodded for me to go on. "I think the key is to get these people back on the Internet ASAP. There's a normative effect from seeing other people handle problems similar to your own. Drum, you weren't there yet, when we watched the Hudson Constitution special with random locals. That was a real eye-opener for both sides. They were entranced. 'Hey, that sounds good. Why can't we have that?' We made a real impression."

"There's a dark side to that normative influence," Cullen mused. "If PR and IndicNews start accepting commercials."

I nodded vigorously. "We've discussed that. Commercials selling nonsense to keep up with the Joneses. Making people feel bad about their lives. So we would only allow commercials saying, 'FYI, we have a product that solves X.' And commercials would be a match, level-wise, to the community we show it to. Right? Showing a home washing machine ad to level 2, is just cruel. But getting the word out, 'Hey, we offer biodegradable trash bags,' or 'Visit the Apple for free voter testing every day, with an optional tour of the Calm Parks.' Those commercials are a valuable public service. We don't need a profit, so we can limit commercials to one minute every ten, or something. And no forced commercials – you can always skip them."

"I like it," Emmett encouraged. "But we digress. Pittsburgh." He smiled at me.

"Yes, sorry," I agreed with a grin. "Um, women. And children, especially girls. I was delighted to hear Drum's equal rights policies on women. I encourage her to hold firm there. You know, at the lower levels, there's rape, and killing rapists. But at Pittsburgh's level, the abuse and ways of subjugating women are more subtle. Women can't take jobs from men. They either have to marry, or do women's work, or prostitution. It's like a level 9 version of rape gangs. In fact, if there aren't equal rights for women and minorities, it shouldn't qualify as level 9. I was worried when Emmett brought in a woman as Resco. That she just would not be able to get their respect. No offense, Drum. After I got to know you, I realized Emmett was right. You were perfect for slapping some sense into them."

Drum smiled. "Thank you, Dee. Would you like to write that up for the Resco boards? Or shall I?"

"Dee isn't a Resco," Taibbi pointed out.

"Actually, sir, Dee is now a civilian Resco, of sorts," Pete Hoffman interjected. "But she hasn't been introduced on the boards yet. I will correct that oversight after the meeting. Drum, how about you start a thread. And Dee can back you up." We nodded agreement.

"Anything else?" Emmett prompted.

Taibbi sighed. "There was the southwest corner? You decided not to go in there, Emmett?"

"I considered going in with a thousand friends from the 101st, sir," Emmett said. "But then Dee was abducted, and the 101st had to leave before we got to it."

Cullen asked, "A thousand friends?"

"The Resco, Major Wiggins, is not responsive, sir," Emmett said. "To anybody. Tried phone, email, video. He's alive, and active on Amenac social forums. Not the Resco boards. Schneider couldn't get him to answer, either. Dee did a land-use analysis by satellite photos. Looks like Connecticut's Litchfield County in there. Bunch of ark kingdoms, armed to the gills. What role Wiggins plays – not a clue."

Drum volunteered, "Sir, the other Rescos near Pittsburgh don't know any more, either. Wiggins is just rogue."

"Establishing some kind of communications would be nice, I suppose," Emmett suggested. "I'm not sure it would do any good. The border garrisons report food tax payments have ceased. The locals are too well-defended to argue about it." He shrugged.

"Just leave ark kingdoms alone," John Niedermeyer advised. "They're Plan D. Who knows, maybe Plan D will save humanity after we're all dead." Pete Hoffman nodded resignedly. Tony Nasser, the newly minted second O-6 Resco in Hudson, looked like he was puzzling out what Plans A through C were. "As for Wiggins, I suggest dishonorable discharge."

"Agreed," Taibbi said, and made a note of it.

"Emmett, I'm confused," Tony Nasser hazarded. "You recommend we also leave these unorganized counties in the middle as-is? The ones that produced Judgment and Bertovich and killed Dane Beaufort? All these rogue regions – just leave them be?"

"Um," Emmett said.

"We're dealing with that at a different level, Tony," Captain Niedermeyer put in.

"Sidebar after the meeting, Tony," Pete directed. "Leave it for now." Tony acquiesced.

"If I appoint Sandoval head Resco," Taibbi groused, "do I finally get to know what they're talking about?"

"Not in my experience," Sean Cullen said sourly.

"Oh, General Taibbi," Emmett redirected lightly, "I still have forty PA meal tickets. Would you mind if I invest them in Pittsburgh?"

"Not at all," Taibbi said. "Invest in what?"

"Biodegradable trash bags," said Emmett. "Drum, Hudson is a huge market. Philly, too. You've already got the local industry. Just scale up."

"Thank you, sir!" Drum said, sitting forward with an eager grin. "I'll get right on that!"

We closed the video-conference, to expressions of mutual esteem, followed by fervent wishes that we not need to meet like this again. I wished sometimes that I knew more about the hushed-up Penn war. Because Taibbi sure kowtowed to Cullen and Schwabacher. Though perhaps it wasn't surprising, if he had this little control over Penn and its Army, and he knew it.

"So we're Plan A?" Tony asked, as the screen went dark and Sean Cullen rose from his swivel chair to stretch.

"I'm Plan A, with the armed borders," Governor Cullen corrected him. "Beaufort's killers work for Plan B. Rescos like you are Plan C. Arks are Plan D. Beyond that, I defer to Pete. I don't even know how many letters there are. Excuse me, gentlemen. Thank you for your contributions in the meeting. Dee, let's leave them to it."

32

Interesting fact: Before the culling of the Calm Act, New Jersey was the most densely populated state in the U.S., followed by Rhode Island, Massachusetts, and Connecticut. New York and Pennsylvania ranked 7th and 9th.

The Rescos handled a lot more business at our house before they adjourned, but I missed it. They planned our petition responses for the first annual state of Hudson address in November, and the first revisions to the new constitution. How to embark on enforcing the new civilian limited weapon rules, and how to allow soldiers to muster out. Top priorities for upstate, Long Island, the city, and Jersey.

They even got experience first-hand in directing the Brooklyn defense network against a serious coordinated attack. The governor-general and top Rescos all clumped together at our house proved too tempting a target. Hudson's insurgents weren't all bottled up in Jersey. I've seen Emmett's living room command center in action before. Even to civilian eyes, it was pretty slick. No doubt the Resco team had a blast, literally. Boys and their toys. Those placid Calm Parks turned into death traps at the flick of a switch, and the mini-cities were designed with roof-top defensive batteries.

I even missed the group outing for Chinese food in the new Chinatown mini-city. I was really looking forward to that, too. And Gladys threatened Ash Margolis with a meat cleaver one morning at breakfast. Ash was teasing her that with Emmett reassigned to North Jersey, maybe he should take over the Brooklyn Mansion. Like most apples, Gladys suffered some PTSD days.

Gladys redeemed herself with Ash later by suggesting a new Apple Core tourist industry. Since the Hudson voter test was the same nation-wide, we could offer special tour packages that combined expedited voter testing at the train station, visiting a few Calm Parks and mini-cities for Chinese food and knishes, and a ferry ride around the boroughs. That proved a popular tour, especially with Hudson parents for a sixteenth birthday present, to celebrate their child becoming an adult Hudson citizen and voter.

On Sunday morning, most of the gang trooped off to church. Sean Cullen was devout Catholic, and Pete at least nominally Catholic, so Emmett took them off to Mass, and Dwayne tagged along. Emmett's own taste was a raise-the-rafters rowdy evangelical service, but he was playing host. Tony Nasser would have joined them, until he realized Gladys was off to a Greek Orthodox service, his own faith, and he happily escorted her instead.

Apparently they had a lovely time at church. The Orthodox priest gave Tony the star treatment. The sect was proud and delighted to have Tony, one of their own, listed second on the constitutional succession. Emmett and Sean's group were mobbed with admirers, too. Roman Catholics in Hudson were accustomed to ruling the roost, but the memorial service and especially the religious licensing workshop were big wins with the parish priest. Hudson's move to licensed religion was warmly received by the venerable established churches, and less so with the raw upstarts.

Meanwhile, Cam and Ash and I opted for some spiritual quality time in the hot tub. Ash was an orthodox Jew, with nothing to attend on Sunday. Cam simply smiled politely and declined the Catholic offer. Unlike his husband, Cam wouldn't darken the doorstep of a church that disbelieved in homosexuals. And he couldn't be bothered to hunt for a mini-city with his own denomination, Presbyterian, which didn't have a branch near Brooklyn Prospect.

The hot tub in the garden was beautiful. That Sunday was dark and grey, only slightly above freezing. A bit of snow fell in big slushy clumps through our bare maple tree, encouraging us to keep our shoulders drawn down among the bubbles. A moody kind of November stark beauty.

"So Dee, engaged, huh?" Cam crooned sweetly. "I'm so happy for you! What are you two doing about religion? I mean, is Emmett still...?"

"Born-again Christian, yeah," I replied, happily letting a water jet dissolve tension from my neck. "And I'm pagan. Yeah, I never really thought too deeply about religion before Pittsburgh. I thought the Pittsburgh sects were completely insane, when I dug into them. But after I was captured, I kind of found God. I bless them for that."

Cam, bless his heart, never skipped a beat. I'd seen his composure under fire before. Ash was on my other side, so I couldn't see his expression. Cam said, "Oh, yeah, your capture! So you prayed a lot?"

"Yeah! Brandy taught me the Catholic rosary," I shared. "That doesn't mean much to me. But I started really seeing the possibilities when I claimed my own God. In natural beauty and the sky and sun. Because Canber and Judgment – you know, my captors – were nature worshipers, too. I mean, aside from the evil. Deep down, the rape and mass murder, the doctored drugs, and keeping slaves, torture, they were all just tools. Their real aim was to defend Gaia from the human infestation. Free Earth from its torturers."

Cam nodded, in perfect nonchalance. "So you came to understand their viewpoint and found it uplifting. They didn't rape you, did they?"

"Only the once," I agreed. "I was sky-high on oxycontin, and then he added the rufies. But I don't remember it. I've made my peace with that, mostly."

"That's some serious praying," Cam observed, a thoughtful frown just starting to disturb his brow. "That's a hard thing to forgive. Of course, he's dead now, right?"

"No," I replied. "No, we've talked to Canber and forgiven him together. Emmett and me." Cam nodded encouragingly. He's a phenomenal actor, Cam. "And the praying, I mean, I set out to give myself a case of Stockholm Syndrome. You know, so they'd trust me, so I could get at some comms and tell Emmett where we were, to come get us."

"Of course," Cam agreed smoothly. "So you convinced yourself that you agreed with them and their aims."

"Exactly."

"And you told Emmett this?" Cam inquired. "About the Stockholm Syndrome scheme?"

"I guess that never came up," I said. "I kept the notebook. I wrote all this down in a notebook, you know, convincing myself they were right. I didn't want to leave it behind, when the helicopters came to get us."

"That'll be helpful," Ash murmured behind me. Unlike Cam and Emmett, who commanded fighting infantry, Ash Margolis served in military intelligence before the Calm Act.

"Is that up in your room, Dee?" Cam asked. "The notebook."

"Yeah," I agreed, before misgivings set in. "Well, I'm not going to show it to you, Cam! That's like a diary. A spiritual journey is personal."

Yeah, they wheedled the notebook out of me. And then they

insisted that I needed deprogramming, to clear out whatever I'd implanted in myself to support Canber.

"I do not!" I objected. "I'm perfectly OK!"

"You don't know whether you're perfectly OK or not, Dee," Cam insisted. "Deprogramming will just make you look through it again and clean it up. And in your position, we need to know we can trust you. Think of it as debriefing."

I might have objected harder, but Cam was leafing through the notebook pages where I'd convinced myself I was a natural murderer. OK, so that part could stand some revisiting and cleanup. Though I still felt I should be allowed to work it out in privacy.

Ash shook his head sympathetically. "Dee, it's harder to dislodge these things than you think. You have to re-assume the mindset where you made the decisions, and decide otherwise. Very hard to do that alone. Because you're not willing to go back there."

Ash was unwilling to deprogram me himself, because he and Emmett had finally started to get along really well. He didn't want to jeopardize our relationships. So Cam called on HomeSec, who promised to send someone to fetch me. The church-goers returned. The shouting match was in full swing when the door-bell rang.

HomeSec dispatched my old friend Marine Sergeant Tibbs and the IBIS agents Kalnietis and Gianetti to deprogram me. They'd all come for the big Halloween memorial, and stuck around to sightsee and walk the Calm Parks for the weekend. I knew that. We were just too busy to get together with them. My screeching objections quieted to snuffling unhappiness.

Donna Gianetti took me in a hug. "Oh, Dee! You should have told me! We'll take good care of you. Nothing to worry about."

"She'll be fine," Kalnietis assured Emmett, who was currently restrained by Tony and Pete. Emmett had already swung on Ash and Cam.

"But – Dammit!" Emmett yelled. "She *cannot* be debriefed!"

"I have that clearance," Tibbs assured him calmly. "So do they." He nodded at the IBIS agents. "It seemed best, after Pittsburgh."

Clearance, indeed. I learned later in the day that the IBIS assignment in Pittsburgh had included investigating charges of Resco abuse of power from Ohio to New England. Bet they learned more than they bargained for. I could relate to that.

Closely chaperoned, Tibbs and the IBIS agents let me kiss Emmett good-bye. "The part where you agreed to marry me. Tell me that's real, Dee," Emmett whispered in my ear in anguish. I nodded, hoping that was true, but a little worried on that point. Gianetti kindly removed my engagement ring and handed it to Emmett for safekeeping.

The HomeSec safe-house apartment wasn't bad, located in a mini-city between Central Park and the Harlem train station. Central Park had become the mother of all Calm Parks, dedicated to the late great state of New York. The view was lovely. The food was good. My deprogrammers were trusted friends, and kind. And they tanked me up on opiates and walked me step by step through the notebook, through everything I'd convinced myself of, making me argue other points of view, to relax my earlier decisions.

That wasn't so bad. I mostly returned to my native mental state, not exactly lacking religious convictions, but more like no conclusions regarding God. God and I coexisted amicably in the world, and I happily perceived Him in pretty things and math and cool tech. I haven't heard of other adherents to my faith, but that's OK. We wouldn't get together and hold church services anyway.

The part where my handlers wanted me to reverse my forgiveness of Canber got pretty ugly. We eventually had to call that one a draw. They wouldn't compromise on accepting mass murder as a means of serving God and saving the Earth. Opiate withdrawal sucks. I agreed to the terms. Mass murder is wrong. Mass murder is not what God demands of us.

Or at least mass murder was none of my business. In self-defense, I kept my private opinion of Rescos using death angel markers to myself. But the deprogrammers succeeded to the extent that I never wanted to accidentally discuss Canber, my abduction, Pittsburgh, death angels, or the dark side of Emmett's Resco work ever again. Or take an opiate.

Yeah, I'd rather have stayed home, helped plan the near-term fate of Hudson, and gone out for Chinese with the guests.

"How about this one?" Emmett suggested, holding up a man's simple stainless steel ring. His choice closely matched the engagement ring he'd picked out for me, only wider. We'd already selected a no-gem plain band for me to go with the engagement ring. We were rummaging in the wedding ring department of a huge pre-owned jewelry emporium in Midtown Manhattan, where Emmett found the ring he proposed to me with.

"I like it," I assured him. "But do you? You can still have gold if you want, Emmett. They don't have to match."

"Uh-huh," he said, and kissed me. "I want them to match."

I'd admitted I didn't really like him wearing Dane Beaufort's wedding ring, inscribed for Marilou. A wedding ring should make him think of me, not Pittsburgh or the Beauforts, or Evangelism. And though the sentiment was kind of cool, the words 'God For Me Provided Thee' sounded stilted. I preferred a simple 'Partners' as an engraving for contemplation. We were partners in so many areas, and it meant something. You told a partner what they needed to know. You made the big decisions together, because the results had to be good for both of you. In life, in marriage, working on projects, partners are in it together. What

God did or didn't intend, or demand of us, didn't seem to me to inform domestic compromise. The principles of fairness and partnership did.

Engraving the rings would take an hour, so we dawdled and window-shopped through the vast central recycled goods hub. I felt wealthy beyond measure. So much stuff, and I could buy anything I pleased. But I didn't need anything. I laughed to realize that even the battery and electronics stores didn't tempt me anymore. I did buy some massage oils and rocks, though, in a spa store, for later.

Emmett drew me along to the nearest Calm Park, with its fleet of food trucks. He picked falafels, me teriyaki chicken on a stick, and we shared and laughed and talked. The local goats came after us, so we climbed onto on a brick wall to fend them off while we finished eating. Those were some fat and pushy goats, by the food trucks. No pigeons anymore. It might take years for the pigeon population to recover from the starving time. Pigeons were good eating.

The engravings came out perfect. We put on our rings, and headed south. Our guards closed in tight through some rough neighborhoods, but mostly gave us space. We couldn't walk through the Apple Core without them. But nobody tested their patience. Manhattan still held thousands of tall buildings, mostly empty, and probably would for years yet. It's not easy to demolish a skyscraper.

In the shorter-building Lower East Side, on the way to the Brooklyn Bridge, we dropped by Ash Margolis' apartment to show off our rings. Ash and Deborah insisted on celebrating with a meal, and took us to their favorite deli. Ash introduced us to Reuben omelets with potato pancakes and applesauce. Their son Shimon shared his ponderous choices about his impending bar mitzvah. The younger Shira bragged about her violin playing. On the way out, we dawdled to listen to a street symphony playing by their mini-city green. Joining them someday was Shira's shining ambition, for now.

By then it was well after dark, so we took the nearest ferry back to Brooklyn Prospect.

We followed the instructions that came with my massage rocks and set Emmett up on the massage table in our room, each sipping a glass of warm hard cider. Definitely one of the better luxury toys we'd bought, that massage table. We'd learned that one or the other of us got a massage, not both in the same night. I pummeled him down and experimented with warmed rock placement until he was fairly dripping off the table in relaxation.

"You OK now, Emmett?" I asked, draping a towel over him. He wasn't, neither of us were alright, when I came back from deprogramming. We clung to each other, anxious if out of each other's sight and touch. He tried to leave for work in New Jersey the next morning, and came back five minutes later in a panic attack. We called Pete Hoffman and asked for a few days alone together to catch our breath. Pete was easy. He told us Newark wasn't going anywhere. Emmett could take whatever time he needed.

"Uh-huh," Emmett murmured contentedly. "Good day."

"Oh, wow!" I agreed. "Two good days, in the same week! Maybe we're getting better at this. We even got a good day on a day off."

"Uh-huh," said Emmett. Well, OK, we wouldn't have goofed off all day if things weren't going well in our world.

"Are we going to talk about what you're doing in New Jersey, Emmett?" I asked softly. "You know, if you dread doing it, maybe you shouldn't."

That roused him. He sat up and wrapped the towel around himself. He thoughtfully took and held my ringed hand to his, so the rings touched. "What exactly do you think I'm doing in New Jersey, Dee?" His eye met mine searchingly.

"Calling in a death angel marker," I said reluctantly.

"Several," he agreed softly. "Just drugs, Dee. We offer good

work, a good plan to follow. Neighbors tear down decrepit housing. Build themselves a good new place to live. People can choose
that work, that new life. Or they can stay home in their shrinking
ghettos, and take the drugs. Easy to get. Flooding the inner cities
and delinquent hangouts and gangs."

"Their choice," I echoed sadly. "Do they get any food if they
don't do the work?"

"Nope. No one does." He scratched his jaw. "Dee, there are
guidelines to all this. Ones we should have followed all along.
There's no quota, you know. Not any more. As many people who
want to take the high road, can have it. My part is to make sure
that better option is as good as I can make it. Really tempting.
Free of drugs and weapons and violence. A life worth living,
doing work worth doing."

"But a lot of people will choose the oxycontin," I said.

I knew how many of the pills were doctored. Judgment forced
Blake to do that, during his slave time. In a bottle of 50 pills, he'd
take out 10 and dope them with something – he didn't know
what. Then he'd close the bottle cap and mark it. It drove him
crazy while we were in the mobile home in West Virginia, to
think of how many of the slaves would forget to mark the bottle
cap. Not just oxycontin, either. All kinds of opiates, even the
codeine-laced Tylenol. I was glad Blake didn't tell Brandy and me
until after our fevers had broken. I was pretty sure our drugs
came from Canber's private stock. But the man didn't seem averse
to a game of Russian roulette.

"People always pick the drugs," Emmett confirmed. "People
don't like to change, Dee. These people have had a raw deal all
their lives. They're in their rut. But the rest of Hudson won't
support them for doing nothing. Not here in the Apple Core, not
in Newark, not anywhere. And it's no secret. They see people
around them die from the drugs. We tell them the truth. But
they'll choose the drugs anyway." His fingers slipped between
mine to grasp my hand, still ring to ring. "Forgive me?"

I shook my head slightly. "Nothing to forgive. I understand."

He leaned his forehead against mine. "Thank you for making me say it. I should get back to work tomorrow."

I nodded, kissed his nose. "If you can't tell me, Emmett? Don't do it."

"Uh-huh." He didn't belabor the point, but that was a promise he couldn't make.

33

Interesting fact: The word 'kill' in Hudson place names – the Catskills, Little Bunnykill, etc. – originated with the Dutch settlers of New Amsterdam. 'Kill' in Dutch means 'stream' or 'channel.' The narrow tidal waters separating Staten Island from New Jersey are the Kill Van Kull to the north and the Arthur Kill to the west. These sound dire in English, but in the original Dutch meant 'the channel from the ridge' and 'the back channel.'

I traveled to the Jersey Meadowlands with John Niedermeyer and another quiet Resco. I'd seen him before at a conference in Connecticut. He was a major, assigned somewhere in upstate Hudson. We didn't discuss it, though, or use names. They joked that for today's purposes, we were A, B, and D.

I met them at the Staten Island ferry terminal. John led us down the back stairs, and out a minor pier. We claimed a Boston whaler, already supplied with a gas tank, and headed off around the north side of Staten Island along the Kill Van Kull, a skull-name if ever there was one. Flowing between the rusty industrial shores of Staten Island and Bayonne in Jersey-borough, the Kill was not a beautiful river.

John confidently turned right and steered us north through Newark Bay, a once lively port now nearly deserted in the November chill and thin slanting light. Choked in dead industry and concrete, Elizabeth and Newark flowed past us on the left. Their unimproved state gave stark contrast to Jersey-borough on the right, which was already advancing in urban deconstruction and Calm Parks. Both shores were low-lying in the flood plains. The plans called for them to return to marsh and salt meadows again, someday.

We didn't talk much in the boat. John – or 'A' – made clear the rules. He agreed that Emmett needed me to join them, but the other guests didn't want to know me. Emmett had already warned me that Cam wasn't invited, and to avoid mentioning him.

At the top of Newark Bay, we took the Hackensack River onward, snaking north. This was a familiar kind of river from home on the Connecticut shore. Built up at parts, but with pretty bits of salt marsh interspersed, and wide shallow places, a quiet tidal river compared to the mighty Hudson. The whipping wind quieted as we passed farther from the ocean. There wasn't much sound, other than seagulls screeching and our outboard engine. Whatever people did on shore, whatever people remained here, wasn't clear from mid-channel in late autumn. The highway I-95 ran alongside us for a while, with a smattering of traffic, mostly trucks bearing food.

Both of my companions were in civilian woodsy attire, with rubber-foot boots, like me. Unlike me, they were both armed. I saw no evidence of Hackensack River pirates, though.

Another bend in the river, and I-95 retreated. We came to a wilder space, with salt marsh to either side.

"Should be a channel coming up on the left," A reported, "after the cell tower." He found it easily, and steered us into the marsh.

"Need any help navigating?" I offered.

John, A, pursed his lips and shook his head 'no.' We zigged, we zagged, we outraged waterfowl. And we spotted Emmett and some other men standing on a roadway mere yards from the channel. "B, pull up the engine as soon as I kill it," A directed. While B did that, saving the propeller from rocks and muck below, A expertly threw a rope, like a lasso, to a stranger on shore, who drew us in and beached the whaler.

"I'm A, he's B, she's Dee," John announced to the dry-land group, as Emmett lifted me off the boat.

Emmett snorted. "I'm E. Welcome, Dee." He held me close and hard for a moment, before he turned to exchange handshake and hug with A, and a more reserved hand-shake with B. For reasons not immediately obvious, the men with Emmett identified themselves as C, K, O, and V. They didn't have much to say. They, and Emmett, wore civilian outdoor clothes as well, with handguns.

The others had arrived via a road here through the marsh. Their cars were parked in a circular wide grassy area bisected by the road.

Emmett hung onto me, and led the procession across the salt meadow toward a wooded rise. There were water channels to right and left, but it wasn't too marshy where we walked. Emmett stopped just before the trees and turned back to admire the view, while the others caught up.

"Did you dig the grave all alone, Emmett?" I asked sadly.

He shook his head. "Canton did that. Before he emailed me. Then he took the overdose." He pointed to a tree. "He sat down there and looked out over the view."

While he died. It was a pretty view. I've always loved the stark beauty of salt marshes, even died back for winter.

"He was from here?" C asked. "Not Penn?"

"Yeah," Emmett breathed. "As a kid. Moved to Long Island for high school."

"Shit, his family died in the Apple Zone?" K asked.

Emmett shook his head minutely. "Don't know. They weren't close." He sighed and turned to the grave. We all ringed it.

Someone – probably Emmett, hopefully not alone – had already lowered the body into the hole, and arranged it neatly, facing upwards, eyes closed, hands crossed over his heart. There was no casket, no flags. A few shovels stood waiting, stabbed into the mound of earth.

Nobody said anything. After a few moments, I started with, "Thank you for your service, Canton Bertovich." Six servicemen turned their eyes to glower at me.

I continued, "You hated those words when I said them to you, Canber. And I told you what I meant. That even though I didn't care for what you did. I don't agree with what my country ordered you to do. Still, you served my country, and followed orders. Whatever you've done, I share in that. I don't have to like it. But I know I benefited from it. We meant it when we offered you a way back, you know? Maybe that's what drove you here. If you found peace, I'm glad."

Emmett nodded, and hugged me close.

Slowly, C offered, "I can't imagine – no, I don't want to imagine, how you could do this job, Cant. But she's right. We all share in it. God, if you're listening, I know the blame is not all his. May God have mercy on our souls."

C for Carolina, I thought, hearing his accent. *V for Virginia, K for Kentucky, O for Ohio.* Not that it mattered. But they'd traveled far to attend this funeral.

Like an open-air Quaker meeting, there between the browned marsh grass and the bare trees, under a pale blue sky, we fell into contemplative silence until the spirit moved another to speak, K. "I used your markers, Canton. My district needed them. And they worked. That's all it needs to be, I guess. Thank you."

Emmett took a turn next. "You were my friend, Canton Bertovich. Maybe I was your only friend here. You pulled away from me our second year at Leavenworth. I understand why.

But you were more than a death angel. Canton was born here in the Meadowlands, to cold and crappy parents. He was brilliant, and sad. He became a doctor to do bio-research, and went with the Army to pay for his schooling. He wanted to save endangered species." Emmett's voice cracked. "He never got back to that. I know you hated this phrase, too, Canton, but I hate the sin and love the sinner. God bless, and rest in peace, friend."

I squeezed him from one side, along with John Niedermeyer, A, from the other side. A shared, "I didn't agree with Canton. No bones about it. I'm here to support Emmett. But if it's any solace, he was the best of the death angels. The others just did mass murder. Crude. Somehow Canber came up with schemes for volunteers. Selective deaths. Not just wholesale slaughter."

Eventually B, O, and V found their words as well, and offered them.

The men took up the shovels and turned the good earth back down onto Canton Bertovich. All the men except Emmett stood off, and fired three rounds into the sky. Emmett walked a couple hundred feet away and played a recorded taps from his phone, while they stared out at the view, each with hand to brow, offering a final formal salute to the salt marsh.

We walked back to the SUV's in silence, Emmett and I joined at the hip, arms around each other's waists.

At the cars, Emmett let go, and pulled an envelope out of his shirt. "Any volunteer to take over Canton's responsibilities?" There wasn't one, but Emmett didn't pause to see if there was. "Thought not. So we'll share the load. I made accounts for each of the super-states." He handed out a double-folded wad of paper to each of them except B, and still had a few left over.

I balked in silence. *Can't you just let this die with Canber?* But they probably would, if they believed they could. My part here was to support Emmett. I had no say. Even Cam had no voice with this group, let alone me.

"I can deliver to Florida," A volunteered, and accepted a second wad.

C looked relieved, and put his hand out. "Georgia." K and O accepted an extra apiece.

"E, give me yours," said B. "Penn and Hudson."

"I do outrank you, you know," Emmett pointed out.

"Not in this," B insisted. "E, you'd suck at it. And you're in the public eye. You can't move quietly and get the job done. I can. Hell, I can even transfer to Elmira or something, if you back me up with Colonel Nasser." Elmira was a Hudson town near the middle of the long upstate border with Penn.

"He's right, E," A said slowly. "You're only taking this on because you think you're responsible for Canber's death. You're not. A suicide kills himself." Emmett looked mulish. "A vote then," A said peaceably, holding up his hand. "Who thinks B should take Penn and Hudson, instead of E?"

The vote was unanimous against Emmett. He relented and handed over Penn's death angel access packet to B. He scribbled Hudson's codes on an envelope, and handed those over, too. I was relieved. Emmett just looked guilty, for handing off a duty he loathed but thought rightfully fell to him.

You didn't kill Canber, Emmett, I wailed inside. *We offered him a way out. And he found he wanted one. Just not the one we meant.*

"Alright, maintain the capacity that falls in your turf," A directed them. "Log your reasons. Honor any markers that fall your way." Reluctantly he added, "Call me if you need to."

They all sighed, nodded, and shook hands again in parting. The ones with cars dispersed. B left with one of them. Old friends, perhaps, wanting to visit a little longer.

"Come home with Dee, Emmett," John urged. The letter names departed with the other SAMS Rescos, the old colleagues of Canton and Emmett and John's, from vetting the Calm Act. "Bad night to spend alone in Jersey."

Emmett shook his head. "No, I've spent too much time on this already. I need to get back to work." He paused and added, "I need my work." He looked to me apologetically, asking for understanding. I nodded and squeezed his ring hand.

John nodded thoughtfully. "Show us, then. I'll bring Dee home, after. But show us Newark. I'd like to see."

"Breathe this in, then hold your breath as long as you can," Emmett explained, holding an asthma inhaler up. He sat on a building's concrete step, a black boy seated on the step below him, between his knees. The kid looked about 10, painfully emaciated and wearing rags. From experience with apples, I suspected he was 13. "Ready?" The boy nodded and got his dose.

"Alright, Caleb, relax for a couple minutes, and we'll do it again. It's always two inhales, Sergeant," Emmett explained, to a stout black sergeant who hovered nearby to learn how to deal with the asthma attack. "Two minutes apart. You time it for me, alright, Caleb?" Emmett showed the child the time on his phone, and received a breathless nod. "If the asthma doesn't respond to two doses, you need a breathing treatment machine. Usually have them in ambulances, fire engines. Need to set the dose by weight, not age. If you're not sure what you're doing, there are experienced EMT's and fire fighters around. Find them and get them into your contact list." Caleb got his second dose.

"Got it, sir," Sergeant Janika replied. "I shouldn't have bothered you sir, sorry." She'd waylaid us in a panic as Emmett and John Niedermeyer and I drove into this dismal neighborhood.

"Uh huh," Emmett said. "No worries, Janks."

Funny, I'd forgotten how good Emmett was with kids. I liked Emmett from nearly the day I met him. But I think I fell for him when I had a lost little girl for a couple weeks. Emmett would come for dinner and stay afterwards to read to her in bed. She never spoke. He called her Angel. Emmett was great with our fosterling Alex, too, but teenagers are different. Man to man, not man to child. Kids spook easily around a grown man, he'd told me. Especially kids who'd been abused, or not raised with a man in the house. The trick was to talk soft, move slow, be predictable and relaxed.

"Breathing well enough to talk now, Caleb?" he asked the boy, in the same calm unhurried tone he'd used all along. Caleb nodded, still tense. "Asthma's triggered by different things. Smoke, pollen, mold," Caleb shook his head jerkily to deny each of these, "but sometimes just anxiety." Caleb froze.

"Now, the first thing about being anxious, Caleb," Emmett explained, "is to stop and get safe. Like right here. Nothing going on. Just sitting on a stoop, with safe people. Right?" Emmett continued to gently talk Caleb down, massaging his neck, until the boy's rigid shoulders started to unwind and drop. Then just as gently, Emmett got the child to explain the emergency that set off his anxiety attack.

His mom was pregnant with another baby. The baby's dad died, and the mom wasn't doing anything anymore, just lying around depressed. And then this afternoon he saw his mom doing oxy with the losers, and –

"Shh, Caleb," Emmett crooned, rubbing the boy's neck. "Right here and now, remember? Where are your hands? Just focus on that, keeping track of where your hands are. You're alright."

"People dying of the oxy," Caleb argued. But he let Emmett kneed his neck muscles, and bowed his head. "Can't stop her."

"Not a kid's job, Caleb, taking care of the mom," Emmett said. "Supposed to go the other way around, you know? Just take it easy for a bit. Let the world spin itself."

He continued gentling Caleb, but turned back to John and me. "Sorry our tour got interrupted. What we're doing around here is salvage and demolition. These buildings are...moldy."

Moldy was an understatement for the vile surroundings, though no doubt there was plenty of mold. We were in a block of

4-story brick slum tenements, probably a quarter boarded up even before the Calm Act. Now half the remaining windows were broken. The streets reeked of waste. I'd seen four rats just in the few minutes we stood here. A stream of people rotated through the buildings, bringing out salvage, mostly pipes, to load into trucks, then going back for more.

"Pipes?" John asked.

"Copper's valuable," Emmett said. "Trade it upstate for the power lines. There's not much else here to salvage. Some decent electronics. Excuse me. Lady Tiff!" he called out to an older black woman, sort of limping and drifting across the street aimlessly. We were the only whites I'd seen here, even among the Army vets of the militia. Even before the Calm Act, Newark was only 10% white, and most of them were gone. Emmett claimed it was a relief not to have race issues, with everyone brown except him.

"Colonel Sanders!" Lady Tiff replied in a floaty tone. "What can I do for you?"

"Is there an Alateen around here?" Emmett asked.

"Just AA," Tiff said. "But if this young man needs friends, I can take him to Peter Pan."

"You know the Lost Boys, right, Caleb?" Emmett asked. "Tell Peter I sent you, OK? I'm Colonel MacLaren, actually, not Colonel Sanders," he added with a wry grin. Caleb took a deep breath, blew it out, and nodded bravely. He walked away, perforce slowly, with Tiff.

"You live in this neighborhood, Emmett?" John inquired. He tried to sound open-minded, and failed.

"God, no," Emmett said. "The troops and I took a dorm in University Heights. Workers there, too, or wherever for now. No, we're just stripping these buildings, then blowing them up. The copper brings in a lot of food. This neighborhood's too low. Flood plain. All needs to turn back to greenbelt."

He got up from the stoop and brushed his pants off. "I don't know what else there is to see, John," he said apologetically.

"Early stages right now. Working out methods, building teams."
He looked to me. "I got a message. We've got action incoming
tonight. Think you should go, darlin'."

I nodded understanding, as did John, and took another look
around.

"Colonel Sanders," John quipped. "Bet you get that a lot."

"Uh-huh," Emmett said wryly. "About a year now." Ever since
the man half from Kentucky got promoted to Colonel, of course.
If oil and lard weren't so expensive, no doubt Gladys would serve
us fried chicken.

"You ever think of adopting one of them?" I asked, now that
Caleb was far enough away.

Emmett shook his head slowly. "There's one, Peter Pan. I
really like that kid. But the Lost Boys need him. Taking care of
them is his life. I'd rather sponsor him, you know? Like we do
with Alex. Be there for them when they need us. Lots of people
want to adopt little kids. Not so many can handle the half-grown
ones, half-feral. And there are a thousand Peter Pans."

There are a thousand Uriels, Canber had said. Maybe they
canceled out, in some cosmic sense. But what Emmett said
sounded right, for us. "Is his name really Peter?" I asked.

Emmett snorted. "Doubt it. Hindu kid. Who knows what his
real name is. He takes good care of his flock."

I smiled. "You've got that in common."

"Thank you," he breathed.

Sergeant Janika – I never learned her last name – hadn't
wandered far. Emmett waved her over, and asked her to drive us
back to our boat and bring home the car.

He and John shared a hand-shake and hug at the car door.
"Sorry to drag you out here for nothing, John."

"No," John denied, sincerely. "Glad I came. Glad I saw. No way
I'd miss the funeral. And took care of business. Care about
you, man."

"Same," Emmett agreed. "Family. Always." He switched to

hugging me, and held me cheek to cheek for a moment, breathing in my ear. "Love you. Call you later."

"You'd better," I agreed. "You can tell me about Peter Pan and the Lost Boys. I love you, Emmett. Stay safe."

Driving away, we caught sight of the orphan gang a couple blocks away, playing in the street. A grinning older boy held court in Never-Neverland, a small oasis of make-believe surrounded by the wreckage of Newark. I waved enthusiastically. Peter Pan led the kids to wave back.

I was glad to get home, when I eventually got there hours later. The ghosts of New York City lay quiet. Dane Beaufort's death was avenged, for whatever that was worth. I was glad Canber was free of his task, and Emmett released of it as well.

That freed our souls for the next new normal.

ALSO BY GINGER BOOTH

Calm Act, Books 1-4 : Dee Baker

End Game

Project Reunion

Martial Lawless

Tsunami Wake

The Calm Act Books 1-3 (box set)

Short Prequels

Civilly Disobedient (Dee) *

Dust of Kansas (Emmett) *

Ebola Day (Ava & Cade)

* *free for reader group*

Calm Act Feral America: Ava Panic

Feral Recruit

Feral Agent

Feral Courier

Feral Carolina

Nonfiction:

Indoor Salad: How to Grow Vegetables Indoors

www.ingramcontent.com/pod-product-compliance
Lightning Source LLC
Chambersburg PA
CBHW060322180325
23652CB00036B/255

*9 7 8 1 5 3 3 4 9 7 7 7 2 *